THE DEFLƎCTOR

NICOLE LIANG

Grosvenor House
Publishing Limited

This book is published by
Grosvenor House Publishing Ltd
Link House
140 The Broadway, Tolworth, Surrey, KT6 7HT.
www.grosvenorhousepublishing.co.uk

This book is a work of fiction. Any resemblance to
people or events, past or present, is purely coincidental.

A CIP record for this book
is available from the British Library

ISBN 978-1-80381-525-1
eBook ISBN 978-1-80381-526-8

Dedicated to my mother—for everything
I have been and will ever be, I owe it all to her.

Mummy, thank you for showing me
the true meaning of compassion.

Contents

Prologue   vii

1. New Beginnings   1

2. Best and Only Friend   21

3. Return   40

4. Fortune Teller   61

5. Traitor   84

6. Fate   104

7. Presents   124

8. Andelovians   138

9. Childhood Playmates   158

10. Room Search   183

11. Intruder   204

12. Revelations   223

13. Repayment   244

14. Confrontations   264

15. Doom   280

16. Capture   292

17. Betrayals 309

18. Solitude 324

19. Memories 343

20. Reunions 362

21. Distractions 380

22. Kill or Be Killed 408

23. Repercussions 435

24. Family 448

25. Destiny 466

26. Reminders 484

27. Double-Crosser 505

28. Secrets 519

29. Sacrifice 538

30. Intervention 561

31. Home 583

About the Author 605

Prologue

Mari Miyahara clutched onto Akari and tried to maintain their balance on Zephy, their zephanerix, as the gigantic double-horned eagle whirled desperately through the night sky. Mari tore her gaze from her six-year-old daughter and looked anxiously behind. *The Harvesters have given up pursuit—*

A bolt of violet lightning shot toward them from the uninhabited Moira Island, cutting short her sigh of relief. Mari immediately realized why the Harvesters weren't chasing. They were shepherding her and Akari to where Zatori and the remaining Harvesters were waiting.

Tugging brusquely on the reins, Mari navigated Zephy into a sharp swerve, narrowly avoiding the attack. They were not so lucky the second time. A quick successive bolt of violet lightning struck his left wing. Unleashing an unbridled cry of distress, Zephy spiraled toward the ground.

While little Akari clamped her eyes shut and hollered at the top of her lungs, Mari instinctively wrapped her arms around her daughter, bracing them both for the fall. Despite his incapacitated wing, Zephy tried to land as steadily as he could, but to no avail. He lost his balance, twisted his right leg, and crashed into the ground chest-first. The force flung Mari and Akari into a clearing.

A dense encroaching forest, long untouched and forgotten by humans, surrounded them. Plunged into darkness, the brooding full moon was their only light.

Mari scrambled toward Akari, who was sprawled out on the grass beside Zephy. "Akari, my baby! Are you alright?" she whispered anxiously as she sat her daughter upright.

Akari seemed too shocked for words, her eyes wide with fear, her body shaking. Mari touched her daughter's face and hands before she could respond. As a soft white glow suffused Mari's hand, the cuts and bruises on Akari's forehead, cheeks, and palms healed instantly, leaving no trace that she'd been injured just moments before. Yet, despite Mari's gift of healing, it still worried her incessantly to see her daughter hurt even in the slightest.

Mari set Akari on her feet and hastily dusted off her daughter's mangled, elaborate red robe. In an urgent whisper, she instructed, "Akari, go hide yourself and stay quiet. Hurry!"

"Yes, Mama." Akari scampered away obediently. She disappeared behind Zephy's massive body, seeking refuge under his injured wing. For a moment, all Akari could hear were his strained breaths before approaching footsteps overshadowed them.

Dusting off her own dusky pink robe, Mari was about to turn her attention to Zephy's wounds when thirty-odd Harvesters, with their signature iron dragon masks and sweeping black cloaks, emerged from the trees and stepped into the clearing.

The entire surface of their masks was plated with rugged scales and framed by jagged spikes that converged at the crown, while two rows of curved fangs lined their elongated muzzles. Perforations formed upturned eye slits, flared nose holes, and gaping mouth openings, reminiscent of the fire-breathing beasts.

As she surveyed the Harvesters, Mari healed the cuts on her chin and arms with a touch of her hand. A cold lifeless laughter, accompanied by a patronizing round of applause, pierced the frigid air. *Zatori!*

Two Harvesters grabbed Mari and dragged her before Zatori Valakhan, who stood at the center of his pack. The only one without a mask, he was easily recognizable. His pale gaunt face gleamed under the moonlight. While rumor had it that Zatori was at least in his early three hundreds, his smooth skin barely betrayed a hint of wrinkles, like that of a man in his early thirties. Zatori's protruding cheekbones, pointed nose, and chiseled jawline were handsome yet haunting. His black shoulder-length hair with stark white streaks was slicked back with artificial uniformity. Yet, the most unnerving aspect of his appearance was his sinister, sunken eyes—the left was entirely black while the right was entirely white.

Everything about Zatori sent a chill down Mari's spine. But the most terrifying of all was his gift—the ability to harvest the gifts of others. That was exactly what he wanted from her, but Mari had no intention of complying.

"We've already had a long night, Lady Mari. Let's hurry, shall we? Do everyone a favor and give us what we want—quickly," Zatori said with a monotonous drawl.

"I'll never let you harvest my gift. I'll never see it turned against innocents," Mari declared.

Zatori laughed. "You don't quite realize you have no choice, do you, my lady? I know you have company. Philippe, bring me the little one!"

Horror coursed through Mari. "No!" she pleaded. "Leave her alone!" Her desperate flailing was futile against the vice-like grips of the Harvesters holding her in place.

"Yes, Sire Zatori." Philippe Sulech, the unusually short, bald man on Zatori's left, immediately got to work. Armed with a deadly spear, he stalked toward Akari and Zephy with a stiffly straight back—a telltale sign that he was trying too hard to command the presence of a man bigger than himself.

Philippe swiped Zephy's injured wing out of the way with the shaft of his spear. An anguished caw escaped the zephanerix. With her hiding place exposed, Akari stumbled backward to avoid the Harvester's advances, but he lunged forward and lifted her by the collar, choking her. Amidst the screaming and struggling, Akari reflexively placed one hand on Philippe and the other on Zephy to steady herself. An unprecedented surge of energy welled inside her.

Philippe's left arm convulsed and his right ankle snapped. He growled in pain. Dropping both his spear and Akari, he fell to his knees, clasping his chest as though he had been winded. She hit the ground, confused but otherwise unscathed, as a soft red glow emanated from beneath her clothes. An equally bewildered Zephy got to his feet, flexed his chest, and spread his pristine wings.

This wasn't Mari's doing—she was a healer. Akari had, albeit unwittingly, *deflected* Zephy's wounds onto Philippe. Like her mother, she was gifted.

Everyone stared at Akari with a mix of shock and awe. Not even Mari had seen her daughter display her gift. After all, not only were they incredibly rare, but they showed sight only during adolescence. Akari just had a premature first-sighting—a phenomenon rarer than gifts themselves.

Zatori was the first to regain his composure. "Well, well, well... Look what we have here. A little deflector! With her first-sighting at age six... the youngest I've seen in all my years! An early bloomer with a special gift, taking after her talented mother—even surpassing her. This little one's gift of deflection is exceptionally unique, and *far* more useful..." He gave a half-smirk, and ice filled Mari's veins. Akari was now on his list of harvestees.

Celestine Lithezyne, a ruthless, deranged woman with spiky, mousy brown hair, stepped forward from Zatori's right. As if she were preparing to work on some back-breaking chores, Celestine rolled up her sleeves to reveal ten metallic talons extending from her fingertips, tapering to razor-sharp points. Under the moonlight, they reflected an eerie, dark silver glint.

"Let *me* get her for you, my sire. I've mentioned countless times that we can't count on this giftless midget," Celestine scoffed at Philippe as she passed him, making a beeline for Akari. With gleaming eyes and a sadistic smirk peeking through her mask, she made no effort to hide her twisted desire to lay her hands on the child. Celestine wrapped her metallic talons around Akari's arm, forcefully dragging her before Zatori.

"Hurry, Lady Mari. If not, our little deflector will pay for it," Zatori stated.

"You know very well that her gift hasn't developed fully. It isn't ready to be harvested." The tremble in Mari's voice betrayed the cold dread running through her.

"She will die if you don't comply. Now, quickly, my lady." Zatori casually glanced over at Celestine, who had her metallic talons pressed against the soft skin of Akari's neck.

When Celestine flexed her fingers, her gift manifested as a bolt of violet lightning that erupted from her talons and shot through Akari. A pitiful shriek tore from Akari's throat as her body writhed uncontrollably in pain.

Celestine released a shrill giggle. "This is just my warm-up. I could scorch her if you let me, Sire Zatori!"

Zatori shook his head curtly.

"But I'm just starting to have fun..." she protested, indignant.

When he cast her a hard glance, Celestine immediately grew silent, reluctantly loosening her strangling grip on Akari to a firm hold.

Zatori sauntered to Akari and bent over to examine her. His blood-drained face was mere inches from her radiant one, such that she was able to pick up his peculiar ancient scent—a musky mix of frost and dust—that made her nose wrinkle. As his black left eye and white right eye bore piercingly into her, he placed his icy hand on her warm cheek.

Akari's face burned cold, as though she was being branded, but by a searing, frigid object. At the mercy of intolerable pain, she let out a blood-curdling scream that sounded like her life was being sucked out of her.

"Stop it! Get away from her!" Mari cried. "If you let my daughter go, I'll give you what you want."

Zatori raised his eyebrows but didn't budge. With a smirk creeping up his thin lips, he continued cradling Akari's cheek for an excruciatingly long moment, as though he wanted Mari to remember the sound of her daughter in pain.

When he eventually removed his hand, it took moments before Akari's screaming was replaced by breathless heaving. But Zatori didn't so much as give her a second glance before twisting toward her mother.

"You monster!" Mari spat as they locked eyes.

He flashed a chilling smile. "Now hurry, my lady. I'm afraid the little deflector won't survive if I touch her again."

"Alright," she said stiffly.

But when Zatori reached for her face, Mari closed her eyes and began mustering energy from within.

"Stop! Stop the healer! She's using her gift!" Philippe shouted in warning. But it was too late.

When Mari's eyes flew open, she sidestepped Zatori and directed the ball of energy toward her daughter. As it struck her, a blinding circle of white light flooded Moira Island, with Akari at the center of it all.

Zatori and the Harvesters shielded their eyes and staggered backward. Celestine recoiled from Akari as though she were burning white-hot. In stark contrast, Akari stood her ground unaffected, seemingly experiencing none of their discomfort.

The ground beneath them broke into tremors. Seizing the opportunity amidst the chaos, Mari grabbed her daughter and leaped onto Zephy's back. As Zatori and the Harvesters recovered from the shock, the zephanerix— now rid of any injuries—had already taken flight.

From high up in the sky, Mari and Akari witnessed what became known as the White Blaze dilating rapidly until it seemed to reach its limit. For a moment, it quivered with a violent intensity, leaving Mari in breathless suspense, before erupting into an astronomical explosion, destroying everything in its way. Exactly where Akari had been standing just moments ago, the island crumbled and sank into a deep hollow, engulfing Zatori and the Harvesters.

Moira Island was no more.

1. New Beginnings

Ten years later...

Although it's still dark outside, Mari gently nudges Akari to wake her. "Akari, my baby, it's time to get up. We have a long day ahead."

Akari doesn't budge. Since getting home late last night after a tiring day of work, sleeping in is all she really wants. *It's far too early to get up...*

Requiring no gift to read Akari's thoughts, Mari tugs on the quilt, exposing her daughter's side to the frosty air.

Unperturbed by the cold but disturbed by the interference, Akari doesn't bother adjusting herself. "Mama... just a while more, please..." she groans groggily.

"Akari Miyahara! You've said that three times already." Mari's voice is firm now. "It's time to get up."

Akari rubs her sleepy eyes begrudgingly and stares at the aged wooden beams of her bedroom. With some effort, she sits up on her stiff bed.

Her room is bare but clean, and more than decent by the outskirts' standards. Mari's bedroom next door is similar to hers, albeit slightly larger. Outside, they have a basic living area and a simple kitchen. Downstairs, on the lower level of the two-story wood and stone shophouse they occupy in West Cheyvelenia, is Moonstone Apothecary, which Mari runs with occasional help from Akari.

The counter is covered with numerous neatly arranged jars of commonly used dried herbs, several bottles and vials containing a range of concoctions and brews, a weighty mortar and pestle, and a trusty brass weighing balance. Different fresh herbs hang by their stems to dry, evenly spaced out on pieces of twine. The back and left walls are lined from floor to ceiling with drawers that hold a generous variety of medicinal herbs, and a sturdy ladder is kept within reach to access the topmost drawers. A door on the far right of the back wall leads to a small consultation room, and beyond it is a little herb garden.

Their apothecary is a shadow of the ostentatious ones in Andelovia, Xylon's southern capital where they had fled from. It's still amply stocked and provides more than what most can afford in the impoverished outskirts. In Cheyvelenia, the northernmost outskie town where they've settled for the past ten years, Mari has continued her trade as a healer—only secretly using her gift as a last resort—and has managed to make a decent living.

Even so, she knew full well that their lives in Cheyvelenia would never compare to the riches of Andelovia. But Mari was willing to trade all that for Akari's safety. Her daughter mattered more than anything in the world.

Today marks yet another monthly trek to gather wild herbs to replenish the supplies in Moonstone Apothecary An early riser, Mari has long been ready. She wears a belt with a few burlap sacks and a dagger hanging from it, and she's slung a satchel containing more sacks and some food over her shoulder. A brown hooded cloak is draped over her hempen garments to keep her warm.

Akari quickly gets ready in a similar fashion, throwing on a faded maroon cloak over a pilling woolen tunic and pants. Because she's often late for these early morning treks, Akari doesn't get the luxury of breakfast, not that she has much of an appetite at this time anyway. Once she's dressed and equipped, they head out.

A crescent moon and a myriad of stars pepper the inky sky. The early morning chill envelops them. With a plain white paper lantern in hand, Mari walks ahead. Akari trails along quietly, still not fully awake.

Having grown up in the northernmost outskie town, Akari has long become accustomed to its freezing climate. But Mari is still used to the warmer southern weather. She remains scared of the cold, even after all this time.

When her nose twitches in the frigid air, Mari rubs it to warm it up—a habit she developed after coming to Cheyvelenia. She pulls her hood up and tries to do the same for her daughter, but Akari pushes hers back down, embracing the crisp winter morning.

Although Akari spent the first six years of her life in the capital, her early childhood has since become a vague, distant memory. She doesn't remember much of Andelovia, except that it was more intricate, more lavish, more excessive in every sense.

To steer clear of unwanted attention and potential danger, Mari ingrained in Akari never to mention that they hail from the capital, instead letting others believe that they moved to Cheyvelenia from another outskie town. They also never speak of their face-off with Zatori and the Harvesters on the night of the White Blaze—more crucially, of Mari being the cause of it. Akari once asked how she'd created the White Blaze, but her mother shrugged it off and made it clear never to ask again.

Pivoting into single motherhood, Mari has become fiercely protective of Akari. Determined never to let her daughter come in harm's way again, she has sheltered her in every way possible. When Akari was younger, she was neither allowed to venture to the slums nor be out after dark unless accompanied. It had been drilled into her to stay safe, lie low, and keep out of trouble.

Although Akari grew to share her mother's thoughtful nature, she still views the world with a dash of hopeful naivety, a stark contrast to the shroud of watchful guardedness Mari casts.

♦

Ten years ago...

Zatori Valakhan, the most powerful and dangerous gifted in all of Xylon, threatened to depose King Alvaro Ashgenov if he refused to hand over the *Register of the Gifteds*. The king surrendered the official records in a bid to keep the crown on his head, making Zatori privy to the identities and powers of every gifted in Xylon.

Hard-pressed to protect the capital of Xylon, King Alvaro withdrew all military aid provided by the Andelovian Army to the People's Protector, the army of the outskirts. Since the People's Protector was significantly weaker than the Andelovian Army, the outskirts—the expansive northern region peppered with a hundred-odd towns—soon bore the brunt of Zatori's harvestings. The gifted outskies were abandoned by King Alvaro and made the sacrificial lambs of Xylon.

Although the bloodthirsty and power-hungry Zatori had harvested gifts since the dawn of the Ashgenov Empire more than three hundred years ago, the early harvestings had been sporadic and disorganized. They became bigger and more overt as he amassed both gifts and followers—the Harvesters—whose infamy and cruelty became second only to his.

The worst happened after Zatori gained possession of the *Register of the Gifteds*—a ready-made list of harvestees. The hellish Great Harvest ensued, where Zatori systematically hunted down scores of gifteds—largely outskies, who made easier targets—and harvested their gifts. Gifted as they might be, they were no match for Zatori and the Harvesters—many of whom were gifted themselves—and their rare abilities became even more uncommon.

The more a gifted resisted harvesting, the lower its likelihood of success. As such, Zatori and the Harvesters often brutally tortured their targets—and their loved ones—into submission. Many still refused to yield, but their defiance only exacerbated the suffering, culminating in a massive bloodbath.

Whenever a gift is harvested, a sin akin to murder, so are the gifted's soul and life. They will end up insane if their soul is first sapped, or dead if their life is first expended. Historically, most gifteds who crossed paths with Zatori perished and the rare few who lived were never the same again.

This continued until the mysterious White Blaze abruptly ended the Great Harvest. Zatori and the Harvesters were known to be on Moira Island, situated north of the mainland of the Kingdom of Xylon, when it happened. Most were convinced they had no way to survive when the very land they stood on disintegrated beneath their feet that fateful night. While the entire kingdom took comfort in their demise, Mari refused to believe that Zatori was indeed gone forever.

After the Great Harvest, the aggrieved outskies, with the support of the People's Protector, staged the Great Rebellion in an attempt to overthrow the king. Inferior in both strength and weapons, they were crushed by the Andelovian Army.

To prevent another uprising, the king erected the Great Divide, a towering stone wall hundreds of feet high, which cut off the outskirts from the capital. Since then, no one has crossed the impenetrable barrier. Left to fend for themselves, the outskirts have regressed deeper into poverty with every passing year.

Since the Three Greats—the Great Harvest, the Great Rebellion, and the Great Divide—gone are the days when the Kingdom of Xylon flourished, and the capital and outskirts were as one.

♦

Under the moonlight, their silhouettes would easily allow them to pass for twins. Akari bears a strong resemblance to her mother in her slender figure, middling height, and long straight hair. They also share lightly arched eyebrows that frame their almond-shaped eyes and oval faces.

Over the past decade, Mari has largely retained the same graceful countenance, save for a few fine lines that skim her forehead from her constant worrying over Akari. Her black hair, which contrasts starkly against her milky porcelain skin, is always held back by the same white ribbon. Although Mari's dark eyes veer downward nervously if they catch someone looking at her, these same eyes burn with an ardent focus whenever she tends to her patients. Quiet and cautious, she keeps to herself for the most part, letting her walls down only when she's with her daughter.

Having been brought up single-handedly by Mari for most of her life, Akari takes after her mother in many respects—most notably, her inextinguishable compassion. But built into Akari are permanent physical reminders of her father.

As Akari treads along with a light-footed gait, her ash-brown hair sways rhythmically from side to side. Her light bronze skin doesn't turn pink in the cold. And Akari's most stunning feature—her inquisitive honey-colored eyes that people have said can look into souls—are identical to her father's.

Akari had been told by Mari that her father died in the Great Harvest while helping them to escape. A nullus—someone without a gift—he must have just been a distraction to deal with in the Harvesters' eyes. Aside from this, Akari knows very little about him. After settling in the outskirts, Mari made her daughter take her last name as a mark of their new beginnings. Akari has long forgotten her father's name, and her mother has let it stay this way.

Mari said she once loved Akari's father so much that it would be less painful to let him go rather than keep him in her heart. This is why she speaks so seldom of him. And when she does, her eyes are seared with sadness. Afraid to hurt her mother, Akari quickly learned not to mention her father, much less probe about him.

Despite Mari wishing otherwise, Akari often thinks long and hard to recall anything of him. She holds on dearly to any memory, however vague. Although she can't quite picture his face after all these years, there are still snippets she clearly remembers about him.

In one of Akari's last and favorite memories of her father, he'd come home with a present for her on the evening of her sixth birthday...

♦

Ten years ago...

Kneeling down so their eyes were level, Akari's father smiled at her with those honey-colored eyes as he handed her a golden box carved with an intricate mandala pattern. His bronze skin was a shade darker than hers, his wavy ash-blond hair styled smartly above his broad shoulders and tall frame. He was perfect in Akari's eyes.

She reached for the golden box excitedly, her heart skipping with anticipation as she opened it. Inside was a dark gold necklace with a deep red, teardrop-shaped jewel. The jewel, which reflected a million facets of light in every shade of red, was the most beautiful thing little Akari had ever laid her eyes on.

Transfixed, she reached for it gingerly with her tiny fingers. Even at that age, Akari knew this was something precious—something to be careful and gentle with. When she touched the jewel, it seemed to form an inexplicable connection with her, glowing a soft red in response.

Mari froze in surprise, struggling to find the right words to protest. "This is too... too extravagant. It's... inappropriate for a child."

Akari's father gazed at her mother with a light-hearted smile, retorting, "Anything for my little princess." He took the necklace from the box and fastened it around Akari's neck, whispering something into her ear she no longer remembers.

Akari stared blankly at him, not quite understanding his words.

Her father smiled adoringly, proclaiming, "No matter what happens, Papa will always love you, Akari. We'll always be family."

"I will always love you too, Papa!"

He scooped her up with one arm, embraced Mari with the other, and planted warm kisses on both their cheeks. Completely disarmed by his charm, Mari quickly relented, the three of them cozying up against one another. Akari let out a jovial laugh, and her parents followed in unison. Her family had once been whole and happy.

But not long after, Mari informed Akari that, regrettably, the necklace was lost while they fled the White Blaze. There is nothing else left to remind Akari of her father, or her life before the outskirts.

◆

Akari brushes away her thoughts as they walk out of town, heading toward the forested foothills. The

Miyaharas disappear amidst the trees, embarking on a dirt path that's barely noticeable between tangled, overgrown branches. Despite the poor visibility, they continue down the winding path sure-footed, knowing this route by heart.

When the boughs thin out, Mari and Akari step into a meadow, referred to as Havenswill by the Cheyvelenians acquainted with it. The frosted dewdrops coating the blades of knee-length grass have just begun to sparkle as they catch the very first rays of the day.

Dawn is brilliant. The waking sun casts a soft glow over the mountaintops and the glistening snow. The morning light dances with the shrouding mist. Feeling better now that the sun is warming the earth, Mari throws her hood back, blows out the lantern, and tucks it in her satchel.

Gazing at the mesmerizing sunrise, she cups her hands around her mouth and begins kulning. If the jeweled necklace is the most beautiful object Akari has ever seen, Mari's kulning is the most beautiful sound she's ever heard. Her mother's voice forms an ethereal, euphonious melody that echoes around the mountains and drifts to the sky. This familiar tune is what Mari calls the 'Summoning Song'.

With a decade of practice, Akari knows exactly when to join in. Looking up at the sky, she starts kulning the second verse as Mari's echoes fade out. Over the years, Akari's voice has grown astoundingly similar to her mother's, though less tempered with age. When Mari first taught her to kuln shortly after they moved to the outskirts, little Akari had a voice of pure lightness. Back then, she took to it quickly—almost as quickly as she took to flying.

Far in the distance, a coo is faintly audible. Mari and Akari turn toward its source but see nothing except fluffy white clouds. As Akari finishes up the verse, the cooing draws closer. Excitement pulses through her veins.

Eventually, Mari and Akari kuln the last verse, their voices blending to produce an otherworldly, mellifluous harmony. Their smiling eyes meet as they savor this moment that belongs to only them.

A loud caw greets them as the silhouette of a zephanerix appears overhead. Both of them look up in joy. *Zephy!* Their beloved zephanerix circles Havenswill, flaunting his impressive twelve-foot wingspan, before making a smooth landing.

The champagne-gold feathers on his back glint gloriously under the rising sun. Mari and Akari take turns to greet the majestic beast, touching their foreheads to his cool beak and stroking his silky feathers. Zephy nuzzles them fondly, cooing affectionately in response.

After retrieving the zephanerix tack they keep hidden inside an obscured burrow, Mari fastens the bridle with well-practiced hands, while Akari deftly straps on the saddle. Then, they climb onto his back.

Just like ten years ago, Akari sits in front of Mari, although the nearly sixteen-year-old now blocks her mother's view almost entirely. While Mari used to control the reins from behind, Akari has taken charge of steering ever since she learned to fly eight years ago.

She picks up the worn leather reins and kicks her legs eagerly. "Come on, Zephy. Let's go!"

With a flap of his magnificent wings, the zephanerix takes off toward the splendid sunrise. He climbs swiftly but steadily—a testament to Akari's flying skills. Her keen bond with him seems innate, having flown him from such a young age. With her unique ability to read Zephy's thoughts through his every breath and movement, Akari soon established herself as a flyer superior even to Mari.

Zephy continues gaining height until they are among the clouds. Far above the rest of the world is the only place Akari feels absolute freedom—from the burden of her gift, the loss of her father, the worries of her mother... It's only at seven thousand feet in the air that Akari feels completely herself. This gives her a thrill which even Mari can't rein in.

"Here we go!" Akari announces triumphantly with another kick of her legs.

Zephy makes a vertiginous plunge beak-first for the bare winter trees below. As the cold wind rushes relentlessly against their faces, Akari's heart races while Mari's nose twitches incessantly.

"Akari! What did I say about safety?" Instead of rubbing her nose to warm it up, Mari wraps her arms even more tightly around her daughter's waist despite absolute confidence in her flying skills.

Undeterred, Akari flashes a playful smile. "Mama, we had this conversation before. I need to practice flying Zephy regularly to ensure our bond remains strong. We don't get many chances." She tugs on the reins right before Zephy crashes into the trees. He executes a sleek hairpin turn, cutting it dangerously close, his feathery tail grazing the topmost branches before soaring toward the sky.

"I'm sure both of you already have an exceptionally strong—"

"It's the same as having to regularly walk my dog—if I had one—to build a strong bond with it," Akari states plainly. She's been trying to get a dog for years now, but Mari has never agreed. Still, she never misses any opportunity to remind her mother, subtly or not so subtly.

"This," Mari gestures to the flying before reattaching her hand to Akari's waist, "is why you're not getting one. I mean, why do you even need a dog when you have a zephanerix?"

"Well, Mama, I can't exactly bring Zephy home or walk him down the streets, can I? Didn't you say he has to remain a secret?" Zephy is another thing Akari has to keep quiet about. With feathers of varying shades of gold and wingspans ranging from eight to fourteen feet, zephanerixes, originally only found in Andelovia, are incredibly rare and inconveniently conspicuous.

Mari sighs in resignation. Akari can almost feel her mother's eyes rolling behind her back.

She decides to give her peace of mind and navigates steadily for the rest of their ride. As Zephy cruises along, a snowy mountain range, expansive rolling hills, a winding river, large plots of farmland, and the neighboring town of Chlovaesia pass under them.

Beyond the clouds and mist, Akari wonders what Andelovia and the Great Divide look like. It would take at least a week of intensive flying to get there. Before Akari's mind can wander further, she realizes that Zephy is hovering above their destination, patiently awaiting her direction.

She guides him to a smooth landing on a plateau, allowing her mother to dismount first before nimbly following suit. Leaving Zephy to graze in the vicinity, Mari and Akari hike to a nameless glade nearby.

Known to only a few, the snow-flecked glade is a vibrant tapestry of plants, each unique in shape, size, and color. While the touch or taste of some of these could prove fatal, among them are herbs that possess valuable medicinal properties.

When Mari first brought Akari to the glade, she warned her daughter to only collect the herbs she was absolutely sure about. "Some of these can kill you before you know it. If you're unsure, I'd rather you leave it," she'd instructed. Fortunately, Akari quickly learned to distinguish the useful herbs by sight or smell and soon proved to be extremely competent.

Now that the invigorating flight has dispelled her early morning grogginess, Akari, alongside Mari, spends the rest of the morning scouring the glade for herbs, filling her burlap sacks as she goes along.

A soft whimper reaches Akari's ears. Spotting a trembling ball of red fur beneath a cluster of shrubs, she inches forward and discovers an adorable baby wolf curled up on the ground. Her breath catches when she sees one of its front paws twisted in an unnatural angle, jutting awkwardly from its tiny body. With great care, Akari scoops up the little wolf and hurries over to Mari.

"Mama, this baby wolf is hurt. Can you heal it, please?" she asks anxiously. Growing up, she's never been able to bear seeing anyone—human or otherwise—suffering.

Mari nods and places a hand on its deformed paw. With a soft click, the bone snaps back into place, as though it has never been injured.

Realizing it's no longer in pain, the little wolf moves its paw slowly to check if it has indeed been healed. Then it gives its tiny body the mightiest wriggle and tries to lick their faces. While Akari bursts into laughter, letting the pup do as it pleases, Mari skillfully avoids it.

"Can we keep it, please?" Akari begs as she caresses its soft baby fur.

"No, Akari. This is a wolf, not a dog."

"It's not like you were going to let me have a dog either," Akari points out dejectedly, knowing full well she isn't going to be able to convince Mari on this one.

Akari gives the little wolf a reluctant glance before setting it down on the ground. "Go, little one. Go back to your mama. Stay safe this time."

With its round endearing eyes, the baby wolf takes one last look at them before scurrying away.

As soon as it disappears behind the shrubs, Mari grabs Akari's wrist abruptly and pulls her down to the ground.

"Mama, what's wrong—" Akari starts, but her mother shoots a hand over her mouth. She takes in Mari's panicked expression and tense body, her attention focused on something—or rather, someone—in the distance.

When Akari traces her mother's line of sight, she spots two people loitering at the far end of the glade, by the forested area. She's surprised to see anyone around here, much less people who look conspicuously out of place in the outskirts.

A raven-haired boy is tending to his jet-black nequilous—a winged horse used by those who can afford it. A midnight blue cloak, made of a luxurious material with a subtle sheen, hangs sharply from his broad shoulders. A formidable-looking sword and a few daggers rest at his trim waist. He's tall and well built, an indication that, unlike many in the outskirts, he hasn't had to go hungry a day in his life. Even his nequilous, with its sleek mane and tail, looks more well groomed than the average outskie.

A dainty girl stands a fair distance behind him, accompanied by her ginger-brown nequilous. Her fiery red hair, twisted elaborately behind her head and cascading down her back, is complemented by her emerald green cloak. In stark contrast to both her hair and cloak is her pale marble skin, which accentuates her elfin features. Like the boy, this girl is well armed, with an intimidating spear and an array of daggers.

Only one conclusion can be drawn from all of this— these people hail from the capital. Except there haven't been any Andelovians in the outskirts since the Three Greats.

The Miyaharas watch them from behind the shrubs. Although Mari's eyes are fixed on the arresting pair, her thoughts are elsewhere. Likewise, Akari is occupied with endless questions.

"Are they really from the capital? From Andelovia, where we—"

Mari hastily presses her hand over Akari's mouth again. After anxiously checking if the Andelovians have noticed them, she heaves a sigh of relief when it seems that neither of them has.

Despite the gagging, Akari can't help but ask, her voice muffled but curious, "How did they get across the Great Divide? Why are they here? Where do you think they're headed to?" Her mother shoots her a death stare and gives her cloak a sharp tug, urgently motioning for them to leave.

Placing one hand in front of the other, they crawl in the opposite direction of the Andelovians, toward the sloped path leading back down to the plateau. They have only covered several yards when Akari's hand suddenly slips from under her.

Her face crashes into the dirt. A few jagged rocks break the skin on her chin, and blood oozes from the fresh wounds. Before she can help herself, Akari lets out a yelp.

Mari throws her a horrified look. While carefully avoiding her mother's eyes, Akari props herself up as stealthily as she can manage, rising to dust off her hands and robe. She turns her head toward the Andelovians, checking if they have heard her.

Although Akari is certain the far end of the glade is beyond any human's earshot, she finds the boy looking straight in her direction. Her heart lurches.

Neither carefully nor carelessly, he makes his way toward her. When the Andelovian boy steps fully into the sun, his dark, crescent-moon eyes lock with Akari's honey-colored, almond ones. A strange sensation washes over her.

He isn't what she expected. The boy seems nothing like the picture Mari has always painted of Andelovians —conniving, unscrupulous, dangerous. Rather, in his gaze, Akari is surprised to find familiarity within the foreignness, and warmth within the coldness.

This Andelovian boy doesn't look like an enemy... Perhaps he could be... a comrade at least? Or possibly even... a friend? While Akari attempts to figure him out, he seems to be doing the same.

With a quick jerk, Mari pulls Akari back into a crouch. "Did they see you?" she whispers anxiously.

"No... no..." Akari splutters, not wanting her mother to worry.

Mari heaves a sigh of relief. "Akari, my baby, I told you to be careful... time and again... I just want you to be safe..." With a touch of her hand, she heals the cuts on her daughter's chin.

Without any more accidents, the Miyaharas head back to the plateau where they left Zephy. They fly him back to Havenswill, calling it a day much earlier than usual.

◆

That night, Mari sips on her favorite telmezia tea, made from the rare, powder-pink, Andelovian flowers of its namesake. The tea is Mari's sole indulgence, typically saved for unusually exhausting or difficult days like this one—and possibly the only remaining reminder that she's from the capital.

As the pink tea cools in the teacup, Akari senses her mother's thoughts drifting far away, although she can't pinpoint where exactly. However, she's certain her mother is worrying—again—and she doesn't struggle to guess why.

Akari has tried telmezia tea exactly once in her entire life. Inquisitive and naive, she must have been around eight years old then. When she first drank the tea, she tasted a mild sweetness dancing on her tongue, which she didn't mind at all.

It was only when the bitter aftertaste kicked in that Akari scrunched her face in a miserable effort to stop herself from spitting it all out. But she did, and the bitterness still clung stubbornly to her tongue. While Mari laughed in amusement, Akari vowed never to have the vile drink again.

"Mama, why would you drink something like that?" Akari had cried with a dour frown. "Telmezia tea is so bitter! It tastes so horrible!"

The laughter didn't subside as Mari looked lovingly at Akari's shriveled face. "Are you really tasting if you only taste sweetness?" There was a slight pause before she added, "Are you really living if you only feel happiness?"

This was one of the rare times Akari thought she saw a different person in her mother—a more carefree, spirited soul before she was weighed down by all the worrying. Now, Mari's concern was not living, it was staying alive—and staying safe.

After a few glasses of water did nothing to wash away the grimace on her daughter's face, Mari gently said, "Akari, my baby, it isn't so bad, is it? It's an acquired taste. Maybe you'll like it when you're older."

"It's one I'll never acquire!" Akari snapped in conclusion. She'd been too young and too sure.

Akari has always wondered why Mari relishes telmezia tea so much. *Is it more than just the tea itself? Is it everything else Mama loved about the capital, and everything else she's had to give up from Andelovia? Does the bitterness of telmezia tea drown out her fears?*

Mari worries often—about her daughter, mostly. Although Akari wishes her mother would stop, she understands Mari does it out of love, and she, too, loves her mother back with all her heart. This is the reason she tries her best to stay safe, lie low, and keep out of trouble—for the most part. This is also the reason that, despite all she does to be a good daughter, there's one thing she lies to Mari about.

No, Akari isn't working as an assistant at Tinkler's Oddities and Antiquities, an antiques store in East Cheyvelenia. In fact, her work is of a completely different nature—one she knows her mother won't approve of.

Akari Miyahara is part of the People's Protector.

2. Best and Only Friend

"Why do you think those Andelovians were in the outskirts?" Akari asks Tyler Kane, her only and thus best friend. The duo, dressed in frayed garbs of varying raggedness, engages in their usual endless banter as they make their way to the headquarters of the People's Protector.

Ty shrugs, scratching his head cluelessly. "Maybe because they've finally realized what a dreadful place the capital is." He speaks of Andelovia with distaste despite never having set foot there. Then, with a goofy grin, he adds, "Surely the Andelovian boy didn't travel all the way up north just to gawk at you from across the glade."

Akari rolls her eyes. "Seriously, Tyler Kane! Do you think it has anything to do with the rumors... the rumors that Zatori has returned from the dead?" Fear seizes her as memories of her encounter with Zatori and the Harvesters on Moira Island flash through her mind. Ty is the only person Akari has entrusted her secrets and shared her past with.

"You don't actually believe those rumors, do you? Zatori's gone. Long gone! We'll never again have to live in fear of being hunted down like we did in the Great Harvest!" He's aghast, evidently unable to stomach the alternative.

Since Ty joined the People's Protector, his life has begun to take a turn for the better, and the prospect of reliving the trauma of his parents' harvestings and the hardships that ensued terrifies him. "You know how the rumors are in town. They are and will only ever be rumors!"

"I know you want to believe he's really gone, and I do too. But surely, you don't actually believe the White Blaze really killed the almighty Zatori, do you?" Akari asks, scrunching her lightly arched eyebrows. "He'd been around for over three hundred years, and the gifts and powers he'd amassed were unthinkable."

Her expression has Ty breaking into a slight smile. "You look just like your mother when you do that," he jests cheekily, an attempt to annoy her despite holding Mari in high regard.

As expected, Akari returns a scowl.

Ty lowers his voice although no one else is close by. "Forgive me for saying this again, but I can't believe Madam Mari was the one who conjured the White Blaze." He knows full well how protective the Miyaharas, particularly Mari, are about their past. "How did she do it?" Ty asks for the umpteenth time, his curiosity inextinguishable.

"I've told you, my mother says she doesn't know either," Akari replies, her tone just as hushed. "I wish I knew too..."

"Well, it doesn't matter now because she banished Zatori to the depths of hell!" he concludes optimistically. "Zatori is history!"

"If you really think so, why did you join the People's Protector?" Akari challenges. "I mean, it has less purpose than before if Zatori's really gone forever."

"Why else, do you think?" Ty asks, his ocean blue eyes twinkling in amusement. He pats his stomach with one hand and rubs his fingers together with the other.

For the food and money, obviously. Akari rolls her eyes again.

Ty was born into a typically large Cheyvelenian family consisting of his father, mother, and seven older sisters. Growing up, there was simply never enough to go around. Like many children in the outskirts, he knows all too well what it's like going to bed hungry for days on end, and wearing scraps pieced together from his siblings' hand-me-downs.

Joining the People's Protector provided a quick escape from poverty. It put food on the table and money in his pockets—a generous remuneration by the outskirts' standards. In return, Ty has had to, quite literally, put his neck on the line, enduring the People's Protector's arduous training and deadly missions. Even following Zatori's fall a decade ago, the People's Protector has continued to face treacherous adversaries, bandits and pirates alike. There's still a constant threat to the outskirts.

Even so, Akari knows food and money aren't the most defining reasons Ty enlisted. The truth is that, like her, he also suffered losses during the Great Harvest—in a different but perhaps even crueler way. Both of them have since realized that they can't depend on anyone else to protect the people they love.

The names of both of Ty's parents were on the *Register of the Gifteds*. During the Great Harvest, seven-year-old Ty witnessed, from the slit between cupboard doors,

Zatori harvesting Peter Kane's gift of commanding metal, followed by Natalia Kane's gift of commanding plants, after both had put up a fierce fight. Ty had been warned never to step out from the cupboard. However, after watching his father stranded on the brink of death despite surviving the harvesting, he disobeyed his parents and interrupted the harvesting of his mother's gift, only to cause her to be lost to insanity.

Furious that the second harvesting was halted and rendered unsuccessful, Zatori lunged at Ty with a sword. With his last ounce of strength, Peter threw himself in Zatori's way, losing his left arm in the process. Believing death was the easier option compared to the hopelessness life had in store for them, Zatori left the Kanes wallowing in misery. Burning with resentment, Peter participated in the Great Rebellion, thereby losing his remaining arm to the Andelovian Army. As such, Peter and Natalia, a blacksmith and a gardener, both lost their ability to support the family.

Like his seven older sisters who began working from an early age, Ty assumed his father's trade as a blacksmith when he turned ten, starting off as an apprentice. But even then, he wouldn't have been able to feed himself or his family without Mari's help.

When Mari came to know about Ty's tragic past, she always left the door open for him, keeping a spot for him at the dinner table. Often, even after Ty had eaten his fill, she'd send him home with leftovers for the rest of the Kanes. As Ty vowed to repay Mari someday, Akari learned from her mother the true meaning of compassion.

After quite a walk, they step onto a familiar pewter precipice leading to one of the gateways of the headquarters. It is perched at the apex of the highest snowy cliff, extending several thousand feet vertically from where they stand.

A majestic fortress built largely from dark brown stone and dark tinted glass, the headquarters is often referred to as the Quartz. Not only is it a sight to behold—though a pity it's invisible to most—but the Quartz is also virtually impenetrable, impassable by land or water, accessible only via air or its gateways.

Beneath them, stretches of snow blanket the earth, interspersed with bare branches of the forest. A narrow river, now partially frozen, meanders through the trees and the white expanse.

Ty steps to the edge of the precipice and extends a hand toward Akari. She strides up to him, taking it firmly. When they link hands—something they've done countless times—his heart stirs in a way it hasn't before. He fights to brush away this feeling, nudging her in mock reassurance. But Akari doesn't notice anything amiss.

As they lock eyes and share a fleeting smile, Akari and Ty leap off the precipice, free-falling into the snowy nothingness below.

◆

Nine years ago...

Akari and Ty first crossed paths when she was seven years old, and he was eight. Their similar ways—keeping their heads down and trying to stay invisible—almost prevented them from meeting.

Little Akari was sitting on a tall stool at the counter of Moonstone Apothecary sorting herbs while Mari was out running an errand. When she happened to look up, she saw three adolescents cornering a scrawny Ty in the alley across the street.

Although Akari couldn't hear the bullies' words, she knew right away from their scornful expressions and his terrified face that something was wrong. Remembering her mother's words to stay safe, lie low, and keep out of trouble, she tried to resist the impulse to jump to his rescue.

However, Hanwell Weilcox, the trio's leader and son of the mayor of Cheyvelenia, caught her staring. When she hastily buried her head in the herbs, the greasy-faced boy smirked and turned his attention back to Ty. From the corner of her eye, Akari saw the taunting escalate to shoving. It was the last straw when Hanwell flung him to the ground.

While Mari's words lingered at the back of her mind, she also recalled how her mother had never once failed to lend a helping hand to the weak. *Surely it won't be so bad if I do the same...* Little Akari flew out of Moonstone Apothecary, planting herself firmly between Ty and his bullies.

The unfortunate-looking Ty was so bony that his ribcage protruded from under his lacey, threadbare shirt. His unkempt blond hair stuck out in every direction, as though he had narrowly escaped the White Blaze. When Ty made an incoherent attempt to speak, Akari noticed he was missing more than a few teeth. He struggled to stand, and the crotch of his ripped pants started turning wet.

"What happened over here?" Hanwell mocked in a slimy voice, pointing a taunting finger at the splotch on

Ty's pants. His two cronies, Prisci Kennigan, who resembled an underfed mole rat, and Aloy Tentacles, who took after an overfed blobfish, snickered in amusement.

"Haven't you grown out of wetting your pants?" Aloy sneered.

Ty flushed brick-red as he stepped awkwardly behind Akari.

Hanwell's eyes alighted on her. "Aren't you the healer's daughter? My father speaks well of your mother," he said. "Surely you wouldn't want to be caught taking sides with a boy in girls' clothes, with an armless father and a crazy mother."

Akari simply stood her ground, a blank expression plastered on her face.

"Why aren't you going on your way? You're going to get yourself hurt, you foolish girl! Leave while you can!" Looking down at little Akari with his beady, wide-set eyes, Hanwell scoffed at her seemingly futile attempt to come between a fight. She must have been at least two heads shorter than him, even though he was far from tall. His flat, oil-slicked hair did nothing for his height.

"I know this shriveled creature does look like some of your dried herbs, little girl, but I'm sure you want nothing to do with him," Prisci squawked. "He smells like he might've gone bad."

"And wet," Aloy butted in. "Let's not waste our time with her. If she doesn't disappear by the time I count to three, she's going on the ground with him. One..."

Ignoring the bullies, Akari slung Ty's arm around her shoulders and began leading him away. "Let's go," she said softly. But barely a few stumbles in, she realized they were going nowhere with his limp. Ty had snapped his left ankle when he fell over, and his incessant wincing wasn't helping.

"Where do you think you're going?" Hanwell roared as he grabbed her wrist, crushing it with his grip.

As Akari let out a piercing cry, Hanwell's left ankle buckled under his stocky body. He released her wrist and stumbled backward, landing on the ground where he'd flung Ty moments earlier. Hanwell screamed in agony, unused to being on the receiving end of abuse.

Ty gasped, realizing he was no longer in pain. He glanced at Hanwell with a mix of surprise and mild amusement before turning to Akari, his gaze brimming with newfound admiration. "How in the world did you do that?" He seemed half scared and half excited.

Although her eyes grew wide at the turn of events, she wasn't completely taken aback. Akari knew she had unintentionally used her gift again, deflecting Ty's wounds back onto Hanwell. Shame and frustration scuttled through her chest. He'd deserved it, but she'd once again lost control of her own gift.

I should have listened to Mama and stayed out of trouble. Akari stared intently at her faded red boots, keeping silent. She felt even more unsure of herself than when she was standing up for Ty.

"What... How..." Hanwell couldn't find the right words to express his shock, his fearful eyes hovering between them. "Forget it... Let's go! Now!" He frantically reached toward his cronies for support, the three of them leaving as quickly—or slowly—as he could hobble with his new limp.

As soon as they'd disappeared from the alley, Akari looked up at Ty.

To check his limp was really gone, he removed his arm from her shoulders and took a few careful steps. He was prepared to wince again, but quickly realized it wasn't necessary.

"I think I'm all good now," Ty concluded sheepishly. "I guess... I don't have to ask if you're alright?"

Akari gave a faint shake of her head before heading back to Moonstone Apothecary with the biggest strides her tiny body could manage.

"Hey! Wait up! How is it that your gift has already shown sight? Aren't you a little too young?" Ty's long legs allowed him to catch up easily with her.

Stopping at the entrance of the shop, little Akari glanced quietly at him before staring at her boots again.

"It must be nice, being gifted like that... and never worrying about being picked on or getting hurt... I bet that trio is scared of you," he said enviously. "My parents are... were gifted too, and I'm waiting for my first-sighting."

Were. Akari caught the sadness in his voice and wondered if he'd experienced something similar—or worse. She felt an inexplicable bond with the spindly boy before her.

"If you ever need anything..." Ty said, giving her a once-over before continuing, "Actually, I don't think you will... Well, thank you for saving me."

Akari lifted her gaze toward him. For the past year, she'd been told by her mother that her gift was something to be kept under wraps. No one else had admired it the way Ty had—not that anyone even knew about it. Feeling a little better about herself, and perhaps even the slightest bit proud, she gave a small smile.

Finally finding success in eliciting a positive response, he broke into a toothless grin. "I'm Tyler Kane. You can call me Ty. And your name is?"

"Akari Miyahara," she replied softly before heading back into Moonstone Apothecary.

Ty followed Akari in, and then everywhere else for the next few weeks, worshiping the ground she trod on. The duo has been inseparable since.

♦

Their unlikely friendship drew them both out of their shells. Ty's wicked sense of humor has been entertaining for the most part, though at times inappropriate and annoying, which Akari has learned to embrace—if not, tolerate. While she gave him newfound confidence to stand up for himself, he brought out her spritely nature, once hidden to all but her mother. In his company, she's been allowed to venture out of Mari's sight more frequently, occasionally getting up to mischief. All this time, however, Akari has always remained the more sensible of the two—although not markedly so in her mother's eyes.

The years have been a great help to Ty. Besides gaining several inches and outgrowing some of his awkwardness, his adult teeth came through to give him a bright, goofy smile, his disheveled blond hair lending him an air of charm. He shed his effeminate hand-me-downs for the usual raggedy garments of the outskies, no longer sticking out like a sore thumb. Over the past nine years, he'd slowly but surely transformed from a gawky child into a lanky young man.

However, Ty never experienced the first-sighting he'd been waiting for. To his utmost disappointment, he turned out to be a nullus. Although he knew there was nothing wrong with being one, it still took much convincing from Akari before he came to terms with it. He'd wanted so badly to be just a little more like her. But gifted or not, Ty wound up joining the People's Protector three years ago.

Established in parallel with the Andelovian Army at the dawn of the Ashgenov Empire, the People's Protector originally guarded the outskirts from bandits and pirates, as well as Zatori and the Harvesters. The influence of the capital-based Andelovian Army wore thin in the outskie towns, even before the king pulled his troops back to protect the capital.

Prior to the Great Harvest, the Andelovian Army and the People's Protector stood together against threats to the Kingdom of Xylon. However, the Great Rebellion marked the end of that.

Once viewed as an ally, the People's Protector has since been seen as a foe that the Great Divide has helped to keep at bay. Weak in numbers and depleted in resources, the People's Protector found themselves on the brink of ruin until a prodigious donation helped turn things around.

After hearing Ty's stories of his missions, of which he often shared more than was allowed, Akari badgered him to let her join. She didn't actually *need* his permission to enlist in the People's Protector, but he'd threatened to tell her mother if she did. Ty's unwillingness to put Akari in danger—in addition to his fear of incurring Mari's wrath—had prevented him from relenting.

"Ty... you know what I want for my birthday this year. I want to join the People's Protector," Akari declared on her fifteenth birthday. "Alternatively, a dog would be good too."

"I know, I know, Akari... You've said so too many times," Ty said cautiously, not wanting to be caught in the middle again. "But we both know neither is going to sit well with your mother."

"My mother... she doesn't have to know... I'm fifteen now. I'm old enough to decide for myself," Akari protested.

"Madam Mari would still think you're too young. In fact, she'd never think you're old enough for the People's Protector," Ty pointed out. "She has a point though. Enlisting is too dangerous. I wouldn't have put my life on the line if my family wasn't starving. But you, Akari, you don't have to turn to this."

"It's the one thing I want to do. I want to be useful— to protect the people I love with my own hands," Akari insisted. "You, of all people, should know how I feel."

Ty stilled. Akari had a point too. This was the very reason he'd joined the People's Protector—in addition to the food and money, obviously. But aside from the risk of Mari's wrath, Ty knew he could never afford to lose Akari, or even bear the thought of her being hurt.

He looked around carefully, lowering his voice. "You know sometime in the future, *if* it turns out that you and Madam Mari are right and Zatori isn't dead, you'd essentially be serving yourself to him for harvesting. Zatori has seen your face and knows of your gift. He'll want to harvest it if he's back."

"If Zatori returns, I'll make sure he's gone—just like my mother did—except it'll be forever this time!" Akari's honey-colored eyes were ablaze with stubborn determination.

"Fine! I'll bring you!" Ty relented, scowling. "I'll fight alongside you against all our enemies—even Zatori—but you're dealing with your mother on your own!" As he stomped away, Ty vowed to himself that he'd protect Akari at all costs—even at his own expense.

When she enlisted, Akari informed Mari she'd found work as an assistant at Tinkler's, conveniently set in a part of town her mother rarely ventured to. Dread pooled in Akari's stomach—she'd hardly ever lied. However, Mari was surprised but not suspicious, and everything went as smoothly as she'd planned.

With Mari accounted for, Ty kept his promise and brought Akari to the People's Protector. They ventured out of town and into the foothills. In the dead of winter, they trudged uphill through the slippery snow, sliding backward with every step. Although Akari began bubbling with excitement, her patience eventually wore thin and restlessness took hold, especially without knowing where they were going.

"Ty, are you sure we're going the right way? Where exactly is the headquarters of the People's Protector?" Akari asked, heaving. She was familiar with the area and was certain there was nothing out there.

"Yes, I'm sure. It isn't anywhere you'd expect. It's up there," Ty said, pointing toward the mammoth, snow-draped cliffs far above.

Akari's jaw dropped. "And how exactly are we getting there? That'd take days by foot—weeks even."

"Don't worry, there's a gateway," Ty replied.

Akari scrunched her eyebrows in confusion and peered at the distant cliffs. "What's a gateway?"

"It's a portal that can transport us from one place to another. Come, I'll show you," he said. "I thought you wanted to join the People's Protector so badly. Are you having second thoughts now?"

"No, it's not that. It's just that it's impossible to get there on foot." Akari scuffed her boot on the ground, wishing she was on Zephy. "Besides, I've flown over those cliffs. There's nothing there but snow and rocks." *And knowing you, you could easily have gotten the directions wrong again.*

Except Ty was right this time. "Of course, you can't see our headquarters now," he said, grinning. "But you will once you're one of us."

"Right..." Akari replied, with no clue what he meant.

Eventually, he led her onto a pewter rocky precipice she'd never noticed before. He walked to the edge and beckoned her over.

Akari tottered apprehensively toward him. "What are we doing here?" She glanced down to see how big the drop was. Far above the snow-capped trees, they were high enough that a fall would mean certain death.

"We're jumping," he said matter-of-factly. "This gateway is known rather fondly as the Leap of Faith."

Akari's jaw dropped again. "Tyler Kane, are you out of your mind?"

He registered her incredulous expression. "I know it sounds crazy. But look!" Ty kicked a small rock down the precipice. It fell about half the way before vanishing midair, a faint glow shimmering in its stead.

"Gifteds?" Akari whispered, half amazed and half scared.

"Yes, Akari. It's people like you," he said in a soft voice. "You know, sometimes, when you jump down, it can take you to a higher, better place. Now, will you take the Leap of Faith with me?"

"No." She was still unconvinced to jump to what seemed like her death.

Disregarding her refusal, Ty did the unthinkable. He grabbed Akari's hand and leaped off the precipice, taking her with him.

Although flying Zephy has her accustomed to heights, Akari had never fallen before. Her mind went blank, and her deafening scream ripped the brisk air. Somewhere around her, she heard Ty chortling uncontrollably. She wasn't sure how long they'd been free-falling when they passed through a glimmering halo.

The snow-capped trees no longer hurtled toward them. Instead, they were hovering several inches above some tiled floor.

Ty stepped onto the ground with ease while she rolled clumsily onto it. A stifled laugh escaped him as he offered a hand. "Are you alright?"

"Tyler Kane!" Akari spluttered breathlessly. She grabbed his hand, allowing him to pull her back to her feet.

"You did much better than me when I took my first Leap of Faith," he reassured with his best attempt at a straight face, not wanting to incur her wrath. "I may or may not have puked and had to rest in bed for three days."

"How could you just take me with you? You should have at least warned me!" she heaved, her breath uneven.

"I've learned from past experience that the best way to do this is to leave as little time as possible for second thoughts..." he explained innocently.

Akari no longer paid him any attention as she began taking in her surroundings. The bizarreness of the Quartz intrigued her. Whatever she'd been expecting the headquarters to look like, it wasn't *this*.

The Goethite Hall, the massive main hall with its jagged high ceiling, gave the impression that they were encased within a behemoth brown smoky quartz. The floor they had rolled onto was covered in dark quartzite tiles that gleamed faintly when the light hit.

A platform at one end of the hall lay before a rough-hewn wall donning the emblem of the People's Protector—a two-headed lynx. It once represented their complementary role alongside the Andelovian Army in protecting Xylon. Carved into the wall beneath the emblem was the motto of the People's Protector—*Better to die with honor than to live with shame.*

At the opposite end of the Goethite Hall was a vast window several stories high, a construct of tinted glass shards held in place by aged palladium muntins twisted into a peculiar pattern.

Looking out of the window, Akari realized she was indeed at a much higher altitude than before. The Quartz, situated in the northern parts of the outskirts—although not as far north as Cheyvelenia—overlooked the precipice she and Ty had jumped off moments before. She suspected she'd even be able to see Cheyvelenia and its neighboring towns of Chlovaesia and Maynerall, had it not been so foggy.

"How's this possible?" Akari asked, bewildered. They'd fallen from the precipice to a place *higher* than they were before—or rather, a different place altogether.

"We have gatekeepers—Protectors gifted in illusion, invisibility, and telekinesis—responsible for maintaining the gateways and concealing the Quartz from the outside eye," Ty explained. "There are a few gateways spread across the outskirts to access the Quartz from different locations."

"Is it really necessary for the entrance to be so dramatic?" she said breathlessly.

He laughed. "It's to prevent anyone else from stumbling upon the Quartz by accident."

"The People's Protector must have a lot of money," Akari remarked, not quite believing her eyes as she surveyed the raw quartz chandelier hanging from the center of the hall.

"Lord Xavier Vykroux, the former grand advisor to King Alvaro who lost his wife and daughter during the Great Harvest, made a handsome donation in memory of them. This has helped rebuild the People's Protector and kept us alive to this day. Lord Vykroux seems like the only decent person in the capital," Ty said. "And if you think the People's Protector is rich, just imagine how rich the Vykrouxes must be, being second only to the royal family—"

"That's a great introduction, Kane. I'll take it from here."

Akari and Ty wheeled around to face the owner of the slimy voice. *Hanwell.*

Having joined the People's Protector even before Ty did, Hanwell turned out to be the marshal in charge of new recruits. Akari hadn't seen him around

Cheyvelenia since their first and only encounter—probably a conscious effort on his part.

While she'd grown considerably, Hanwell hadn't changed much—his flat, oil-slicked hair included. Even so, recognition—alongside something else—flickered in his beady, wide-set eyes.

"Why didn't you tell me Hanwell is part of the People's Protector?" Akari later asked her best friend privately.

"I couldn't... We're not allowed to discuss the identities of the Protectors," Ty explained.

"Oh..." Akari saw the sense of this and supposed she shouldn't have been surprised, even though she was unfamiliar with the code of honor of the People's Protector back then. "Does he still bother you?"

A grin lifted the corners of Ty's lips. "Although Weilcox is still very much the bully he used to be, he has steered clear of me." His voice had more than a hint of amusement as he recalled his first meeting with Akari. "You know, I think you tamed him."

Although Hanwell tried not to let it show, he always seemed to watch her during training—and made sure to put some distance between them for safety's sake.

Not wanting to stand out, Akari kept her head down and trained hard. She had a quiet grit about her and proved to be an exceptionally quick learner.

Given her years of experience flying Zephy, she took to riding horses and nequilouses rather effortlessly. Her rare ability to read their every breath and movement made her an excellent rider and flyer.

As it turned out, Akari made a competent fighter as well. In no time, she wielded a kris Ty personally smelted for her with a natural deftness, despite having had a choice of superior weapons distributed by the People's Protector. Although brute strength was not her strong suit, she fought with intelligence and dexterity, posing quite a challenge for her comrades during their training. On the infrequent occasion they landed a blow, she'd unintentionally deflect the wounds right back onto them.

Controlling her gift—or specifically, preventing its accidental use—was the one aspect Akari saw no improvement in. There was a mix of reactions to her unique ability—fear, intrigue, admiration—and Hanwell tracked every one of them.

Time has flown by since she immersed herself in training. Just days ago, almost a year after her enlistment, Akari has been marked combat-ready and assigned to Unit Eleven of the People's Protector.

While this will bring more food and money, it also means she could be put on her first mission any time now.

3. Return

Akari and Ty take the Leap of Faith for the umpteenth time, making an easy landing in the Goethite Hall. Barely moments after they've donned their dirt-brown People's Protector uniforms, they are jolted by a deafening beating of drums that leaves the Quartz quaking.

Although this is the first time Akari has heard the drums since she's been marked combat-ready, she knows it means only one thing—an emergency calls for their immediate assembly.

The duo exchanges worried glances and strides toward the platform, joining the throng of Protectors streaming into the main hall. As the last of them gather with their units, the thunderous sound finally draws to a stop.

The Protectors stand at attention, anxiously awaiting their leaders. Akari's heart pounds furiously against her ribs. The tension in the air is so thick that her kris could easily cut it.

As part of Unit Eleven, she is in the middle of the Protectors from all twenty-one units, with One to the far left and Twenty-One at the opposite end. To her right, she sees Ty with his comrades from Unit Twelve.

"I heard that Madam Salam will be leading this mission," Ethan Cook, one of the ten-odd Protectors in Akari's unit who is friendly with Ty, says with admiration. The doe-eyed, floppy-haired boy is the kind of person who's friends with everyone—almost.

Akari has only caught a few glimpses of Salam Esquenald, second-in-command of the People's Protector and head gatekeeper at the Quartz, during the past year.

"They say she used to be part of the Royal Regiment, right?" she asks. The most elite troop within the Andelovian Army, it serves the royal family exclusively. Salam's affiliation is testament to her exceptional prowess as one of the best fighters in Xylon.

"Yes. Madam Salam fights like a beast," Ethan gushes. "She single-handedly took down some of the most feared Harvesters before the White Blaze."

"That woman *is* a beast!" Aloy, a part of Ty's unit, spits in disgust, causing his droopy features and rotund body to jiggle. "Salam Esquenald has bear blood in her! She's a filthy hybreed!" Hybreeds are characterized by the presence of non-human blood, which typically manifests in their physical appearance.

"What does that matter!" Ethan snaps back, indignant. "We all know she'd be first-in-command if she weren't a hybreed!" Akari agrees, but she also knows it isn't that simple. Hybreeds have long been treated as second-class subjects and shunned by the masses.

"Are you dying to be one of her little cubs, Cook?" Prisci, also Unit Twelve, jeers as she flashes her long, yellowed buckteeth, the sole overgrown part of her shrunken body. "Salam should have stayed in the capital, if you ask me. No one wants a hybreed here, much less one from the Royal Regiment! Besides, you know as well as the rest of us that she'd never rise above Sir Maximus."

Unlike Salam, who mostly works in the shadows, Maximus Fontan, who usually addresses the People's Protector, is often the center of attention. Maximus has navigated them through some of its most arduous ordeals with his extraordinarily keen perception since he was promoted to first-in-command ten years ago, after his predecessor was executed for supporting the Great Rebellion.

Shortly after rising to this position, Maximus secured a donation from Lord Vykroux and recruited Salam to rebuild the People's Protector. Since she began to lead the People's Protector alongside him, there's been talk that its emblem, the two-headed lynx, has taken on a new meaning.

"It's funny how the two of you are so against hybreeds when you could pass for a mole rat and a blobfish," Ty quips, offering a seemingly objective evaluation.

Fuming, Prisci and Aloy look like they're about to jump on Ty when Ethan says, a little too loudly, "Better a hybreed than a treasonous rat! Didn't Maximus participate in the Great Rebellion? He's probably biding his time for another opportunity to overthrow King Alvaro." By now, quite a few people have turned their heads toward them. "For the past decade, it's been firmly established that this isn't the purpose of the People's Protector. Our purpose is to *protect*, not to rebel, and never to kill."

"Our purpose can and has changed with time. Sir Maximus has the guts to do what has to be done for the greater good," Aloy hisses. "Without a new king on the throne, do you think Xylon will ever flourish again?"

"But overthrowing the king—" Ethan is quickly cut off.

"Would you rather Xylon stagnate and rot away?" Aloy challenges.

RETURN

"Besides, the People's Protector has attempted it before, and we can attempt it again," Prisci hisses.

"Hasn't it occurred to you that Maximus is eyeing up the throne—" Ethan tries to interject.

But Maximus and Salam walk onto the platform, followed by Hanwell, and the hall instantly falls silent.

Standing at the center of the platform, the silver-haired and silver-eyed Maximus Fontan, clad in a robe of deep bister, sweeps the People's Protector with a somber look. His chiseled but weathered face hints that he must have been quite good-looking back in the day.

After taking a deep breath, Maximus addresses the People's Protector. "We have received intelligence regarding the rogue bandits' hideout."

Gasps and whispers ripple through the Goethite Hall.

"Silence... silence, Protectors!" Hanwell commands, and the Protectors quieten.

"The outskirts have been plagued by bandit raids for a very long time," Maximus continues. "Now we know where they're hiding, we can take them by surprise and root them out once and for all. We'll not live at their mercy again!"

While the rest of the Protectors break into cheers, Akari finds herself shaking with anticipation.

"Tonight, led by our very best Protector, Salam Esquenald, we'll rid the outskirts of these rogue bandits. I'll now leave her to instruct you on the mission." Maximus steps back and Salam takes his place, the two barely looking at each other as they pass.

As Salam takes center stage, Akari studies her with childlike curiosity. She's one of the few hybreeds Akari has seen. At nearly seven feet tall, Salam dwarfs Maximus, who's of well-above-average height. Her extraordinarily prominent presence is made even more commanding by bulky muscles cording every part of her body. However, it isn't Salam's build that sets her apart the most, but her pronounced bear-like features.

Deep brown fur coats most of Salam's dark skin. Her ursine face, topped with small round ears, elongates into a muzzle with a moist black nose. In place of nails, Salam sports claws at the tips of her stumpy fingers and toes. Her oversized paws are incompatible with any gloves or footwear—not that she needs either for protection.

When Salam scans the crowd, she notices Akari scrutinizing her. Abashed at being caught, Akari immediately drops her gaze. Although she's too intimidated to look up, Akari senses her superior's eyes lingering on her. All around, the hall stills before the second-in-command addresses the People's Protector.

"We're going on a mission tonight," Salam growls, revealing four ferocious-looking canine teeth. "Units Six to Ten—Eleven—will be deployed. The rest of you may take your leave."

Realizing she's been put on her very first mission, Akari's heart thumps wildly. Nervousness and excitement make her insides throb. All the incessant pestering and grueling training have culminated in this moment. *I'll finally get to protect the outskirts with my own hands.* A tingle slithers down her spine.

But Akari's heart also sinks when she realizes Ty won't be with her for her first mission. She'd always assumed he would be by her side, just as he'd always been. The thought of facing the rogue bandits without him terrifies her.

As the dormant units march out of the Goethite Hall, Akari catches Ty wearing a worried look, mouthing to her to stay safe, before he's swept along with the rest of the Protectors and pushed out of sight.

As soon as they're gone, Salam launches into the briefing. "The rogue bandits are hiding out in an abandoned farmhouse on the fringes of Casserica..."

The remainder of Salam's instruction passes in a blur. Once it concludes, she dismisses them, and Akari—along with the other Protectors—begin filing out of the hall.

"Akari!" A gruff voice calls after her. When she wheels around, Akari finds Salam prowling toward her.

Although surprised that the second-in-command knows her by name, she's more preoccupied with the fact that she could be in trouble for gawking at her. Akari hesitates slightly before walking over, meeting Salam before the massive patchwork of glass panes.

Although there's no hint of displeasure on her face, the sheer presence of the bear warrior is staggeringly imposing.

"Yes, Madam Salam?" Akari says meekly, pondering the reason she would want to speak with her.

Concern weaves into Salam's furry features. "Are you ready for your first mission?" she asks.

"Yes, Madam Salam!" Akari salutes rigidly in true military style.

Her superior erupts in rambunctious laughter. "Just Salam, please. You can drop the formalities when it's just us."

"Yes, Madam... I mean, Salam!" Akari replies, shifting around awkwardly. Despite being baffled by the reason

Salam Esquenald, the mighty second-in-command of the People's Protector, has granted her this exception, Akari doesn't question her.

After Salam contains her laughter, she raises a paw, pointing her index claw to Akari's heart. "By ready, I mean *here...*"

Akari looks at her blankly.

"You can train the hardest and longest, or be the strongest and fastest, but you can never really prepare your heart for battle," Salam cautions with a low rumble. "Akari, you have to be hard-hearted at times. There's a saying in Andelovia—*Kill or be killed.* Do you think you can do that?"

Akari purses her lips as she contemplates Salam's advice. Looking out from the window, she notices how even the precipice she'd leaped from seems insignificant compared to the cliff the Quartz is perched on. Akari wonders where in this white, wintry mess the rogue bandits could be, and the reality that she'll likely have to take lives—and hopefully not the other way round—starts sinking in.

She brushes away her thoughts, eventually finding her words. "I'll try my best," Akari promises, this time catching her superior surveying *her* instead.

"Has ten years flown by already?" Salam asks. "Has it been that long since you left Andelovia?"

"How... how do you know?" Akari is surprised—shocked, even.

"Though I haven't seen you in a while, I've known your mother for a long time," Salam explains. "Don't you remember me?"

Akari thinks hard but nothing comes to mind. She shakes her head, her brow furrowed.

"Quite a while back, your mother saved my life. She healed me when it otherwise wouldn't have been possible," Salam continues with a knowing wink.

Akari's hit by surprise once again. She wonders if Salam's knowledge of Mari's gift implies her trust. After all, her mother has always been extremely careful about her gift, only using it on others with utmost discretion. *If Salam's aware that Mama is gifted, the two of them must have been close... But why haven't I heard her mention—*

"I owe her a debt I can never repay." Salam's impassioned growl interrupts Akari's thoughts. She looks up to see her superior holding apart her fur, revealing a long, puckered scar running from her chin down her throat and chest, extending beneath her tan linen tunic.

Akari stiffens at the sight, unable to imagine the brutality that had been inflicted to leave such a scar. "What happened?" she gasps.

"Don't look at me like that. At least I have some fur to hide it. Lucky me!" Salam jests, ruffling her fur to conceal the scar. "This was from one of my many battles. Your mother found me on the brink of death and healed me."

Akari shudders, but quickly reminds herself that she may see similar wounds tonight.

"So, how's your mother doing these days?" Salam continues casually.

"She's doing well enough." Akari replies. "She's kept busy with the apothecary... collecting and selling herbs... healing the sick and injured..."

"Good to hear. It's been a while since I've seen her," Salam says before breaking into an amused smile.

"Speaking of which, I'm guessing that she doesn't know you're here?"

Akari's heart skips a beat. Realizing she's been exposed, she hangs her head guiltily, the sight drawing a deep laugh from her superior. "Like mother, like daughter! She'd probably wish she'd never healed me if she knew you're here now."

"Will you please help me keep this a secret?" Akari implores.

Salam's laughter fades, her face quickly growing serious. "Only if you promise that self-preservation will always be your priority. Your mother has tried very hard to keep you alive, and I can't be the one to let her down."

Akari nods fervently. Relieved that Salam is a jolly old soul instead of the scary bear warrior she'd expected her to be, she finally relaxes a little.

"So, is it true you're from the capital too? Like me and my mother?" Akari probes.

"Yes," Salam confirms with a nod.

Warmth wells in Akari's chest. "I've never met anyone else from there. You're the first..." As the words leave her lips, her thoughts stray to the Andelovians she'd seen in the glade, but she quickly pushes the memory aside.

"Andelovia wasn't a bad place..." Salam recalls.

"I've always wanted to know more about the place I come from, but my mother doesn't like talking about the capital very much," Akari says sadly.

"What's it you're curious about?" Salam asks, her voice steeped in caution.

"My past... my early childhood... everything..." she confesses. "If the Great Divide didn't separate us, I'd have loved for a chance to visit the capital..."

Salam's features twist into a horrified expression. "That is *not* a good idea, for goodness gracious sake!"

"I know..." Akari says softly. "Do you think the outskirts will forever be separated from the capital? And will Xylon never be one like it was before the Three Greats?"

"It won't be possible unless the three royal regalia are reunited," Salam replies. "But they've been missing for years..."

"The three royal regalia?" Akari blinks.

"Don't you know what they are?" Salam asks, surprise woven through her tone.

Akari shakes her head. "What are they?"

"It's been said that the one who unites the three royal regalia—the Jewel of Compassion, the Mirror of Wisdom, and the Sword of Courage—will have a legitimate claim to the throne."

Now that Salam has explained the royal regalia, they sound familiar, somewhat. But Akari has no clue where she's heard of them before.

"Over a thousand years ago, the archivians were the first to do so," Salam continues. "With the three royal regalia in their hands, they established the Zo Empire."

Akari's jaw drops in disbelief. "Archivians? Aren't they just creatures that exist in children's stories?" She's been surprised plenty today, but learning of the existence of a special type of hybreed who carry dragon blood takes her a step past that—into incredulity. Supposedly, unlike the usual hybreed, archivians are able to forge between their human and dragon forms.

In human form, although indistinguishable by physical appearance, archivians are said to exhibit sharper senses, quicker reflexes, and greater strength than even the best of humans. In dragon form, they are outwardly identical to those beasts, but breathe frost instead of fire. While gifts are exceedingly rare among humans and most hybreeds, the reverse is true among archivians. Magnificent but deadly, the archivians in the tales Akari's mother told her are both staunchly worshiped and terribly feared.

"There's some truth in every story..." Salam points out with a hearty laugh. "And yes, the kings of the previous empire weren't your typical humans. I'm not all human either, am I?"

"But you... you're... you don't form-forge!" Akari splutters awkwardly. "Wouldn't form-forging allow archivians to live among us without our knowledge?"

"Yes, except they're already extinct," Salam replies. "When the first king of the Ashgenov Empire reunited the three royal regalia, he took over the throne and exterminated the archivians. This was how the Ashgenov Empire was born. Unfortunately, during King Alvaro's reign, the royal regalia have gone missing and our kingdom has degenerated into a state of turmoil. It hasn't helped that Queen Jocelin has not borne an heir. As King Alvaro is sat upon a rocky throne, there have been speculations that history could repeat itself."

"Where are the three royal regalia? And who has them?" Akari's curiosity is piqued.

"I can't say for sure. No one has seen them for years," Salam says, her voice turning solemn. "But I do know many have killed to have them, and many more will— Zatori included."

"And so will Sir Maximus?" Akari blurts. The squabble between Ethan, Prisci, and Aloy has filled her with doubt.

"You know you could be punished for saying that about the leader of the People's Protector, right?" Salam grunts in disapproval, though Akari senses it may just be for show.

"But it's true, isn't it?" she presses, throwing caution to wind. Although Akari recalls Ty recounting a public flogging for theft, she's yet to witness a punishment during her time at the People's Protector.

Salam takes a good look at Akari but doesn't answer her question. "So, tell me," she continues after a moment of silence, "why did you join the People's Protector?"

"To protect the outskirts with my own hands," Akari says from the bottom of her heart.

"Then that should be what you're focusing on," Salam concludes. "Remember what Ethan said about our purpose being to protect, not to rebel, and never to kill? He couldn't have been more right."

Akari, thoroughly taken aback, wonders how it was possible for Salam to have overheard their conversation.

As though she can read Akari's mind, Salam explains, a cheeky smile hanging from her snout, "Bears have good ears, and noses for that matter."

Just as Akari's about to return a smile, she realizes Salam must inevitably have heard the degrading way Prisci and Aloy spoke of her.

"There are times I hear more than I want to, but I've grown used to it," Salam adds. "It doesn't bother me anymore. Coming from the Royal Regiment or the capital doesn't help the fact that I'm a hybreed. There'll always be people who'll never accept my leadership."

"Aren't the Andelovian Army and the People's Protector enemies now?" Akari asks.

"We didn't start out as enemies, and we don't have to be. That was the agreement I had with Maximus when I joined to help rebuild the People's Protector. We came to a consensus that we'd protect the outskirts like we always have, and never again participate in another rebellion or waste innocent lives."

Akari ponders Salam's words quietly.

"You may already have noticed that there are two schools of thought within the People's Protector." Salam's gruff voice recaptures Akari's attention. "The first and original intention of the People's Protector is to help with what King Alvaro has been incapable of—to protect the outskirts. And the second is to entirely replace the king with one capable of doing this."

A moment of silence settles as their eyes meet, before Salam turns toward the emblem and the motto of the People's Protector. "For a two-headed lynx, it may only be a matter of time before one of the heads bites off the other. The question is, which head do you belong to? And more importantly, which head will bite off the other?" she asks. "Which head will die with honor while the other lives with shame?"

Akari remains hushed, clueless as to the answers.

There's a slight hesitation before Salam adds, "Or possibly, which head will live with honor while the other dies with shame?"

◆

As the night draws near, the pit of Akari's stomach twist in knots. She starts preparing, polishing her kris and armor, as though going through the motions can help distract her. When she's done, Akari finds herself tugging at her uniform, rudimentarily embroidered with a two-headed lynx. Although she's worn it countless times in training, doing so for a mission gives it an unusual weight.

Akari doesn't have a chance to see Ty again before embarking on her first mission. When the time comes, alongside Units Six to Eleven, she exits one of the other gateways—nothing nearly as exciting as the Leap of Faith—and heads to the fringes of Casserica for the very first time.

Everything about Casserica, a town nestled near the midpoint between Cheyvelenia and Andelovia, is unfamiliar. Its interpretation of a wintry mess isn't what Akari was expecting—very mild and certainly not very white at all, with snowfall so light it barely leaves speckles. Strange flora lining the landscape bears thick, twisted trunks tinged with hues of deep indigo and dull gray, spiny sharp-edged leaves that shimmer faintly under the moonlight, and the occasional cluster of dark waxy flowers, their petals stiff and angular. The air smells odd, wafting around them with an unsettling, musky scent that has her nose wrinkling.

Under Salam's directions, the Protectors hide themselves along the edges of the woodland overlooking the abandoned farmhouse. The dilapidated two-story structure consisting largely of wood, wattle, and daub barely has half a thatched roof sitting atop it. An extensive portion of the walls on the upper floor no longer exists, and the remains are severely damaged. What's left of the farmhouse is wildly overgrown with creeping vines and strewn with rubble. Although it appears to have been uninhabited for a long time, the eerie light flickering from its first-floor windows suggests that it may house guests.

An uneasiness creeps over Akari. Recalling Salam's advice, she tries to harden her heart and ready it for battle. Despite Akari's efforts, her hands grow clammy, droplets of cold sweat rolling down her back as she crouches in the shrubs. The longer she waits, the more anxiety eats into her.

Just as Akari begins to fidget, Salam raises her spiked mace, a silent signal for the Protectors to launch the ambush. They charge across the yard, barging into the farmhouse through both its front and back doors.

To their bewilderment, the abandoned building stands empty, with no sign of the rogue bandits. Salam's ursine face contorts with surprise, and the other Protectors throw baffled glances at each other. Before them, the fire crackles ominously in the fireplace, casting their shadows on the defaced walls.

Akari surveys the decrepit farmhouse. Moth-eaten drapes hang from the windows and wrecked furniture is scattered across the ground, every forgotten surface coated with dust or mildew. Given the state of it, she can't fathom how even the rogue bandits could occupy this place. Except, it seems they never have.

As she looks to Salam for a cue, her superior's nose twitches as though she's detected something. At first, Akari thinks the foul smell is just stale air. But a few whiffs later, she realizes there's something else she can't quite place.

"Get out! Get out of here!" Salam's feral growl sends tremors rippling through the farmhouse. "It's a trap!"

Before anyone can react, a rapid succession of violet lightning strikes the farmhouse, igniting it with violet flames. The People's Protector is thrown into complete chaos as they make a desperate dash to escape, only to find the doors locked dead. Without a shred of doubt, Akari recognizes the familiar yet petrifying shade of violet, which triggers the most dreaded memories of her childhood to replay in her mind.

Celestine! She wants to burn us alive! Akari screams in her mind. *If Celestine has returned, does this mean that... that Zatori has returned as well?* Paralyzed by her worst fear, she stays rooted to the spot while the Protectors and the violet flames meld into a blur before her eyes.

"What are you doing?" Ethan tugs sharply on Akari's arm, snapping her back to reality. "Ty told me to look out for you! We need to get out of here!"

The view outside the nearest window confirms Akari's dreaded suspicions. Close to a hundred Harvesters, with their iron dragon masks and long black cloaks, have the farmhouse surrounded, waiting to cull any Protectors who successfully escape. But heading out to face them is their only option. Every moment they linger in the furnace of the farmhouse will only spell death. In the suffocating heat, the Protectors scramble to flee from the narrow windows.

Akari shoves the memories of her last encounter with the Harvesters aside. "Get out! Quickly!" she yells. One by one, she hoists her comrades up, their boots digging into her bare hands, so they can climb through a broken, flaming window.

"Akari! *You* need to get out of here!" Ethan hauls her through the window, away from the inferno.

As soon as she touches the ground, a Harvester lunges at her with a war hammer. But he's quickly silenced by Ethan, who has hopped out of the window after her.

"Akari! Promise me you'll stay alive longer than me!" Ethan demands, consecutively taking down two more oncoming Harvesters.

"Thank you—"

"Promise me, now!" Ethan insists, his usually friendly demeanor eroding with each Harvester he finishes off.

"I promise," Akari answers in a daze, and draws her kris. The idea that she'll actually have to *use* it is surreal. Salam's words come back to her. *Kill or be killed.* She tightens her grip and shakes herself.

In the parching heat, a ruthless battle ensues. Both sides attack mercilessly, every blow struck to kill. Although the People's Protector boasts exceptional fighters, the trap laid by the Harvesters has thoroughly rattled them and thinned their ranks.

All around Akari, bodies, heads, and limbs litter the ground, most of them the remains of the Protectors, now drastically outnumbered. Scores are trapped in the blazing farmhouse and will never make it out alive. As the flames cast a sinister violet sheen on the iron dragon masks, the Harvesters seem even more terrifying and inhuman, somehow. Yet, amidst the gruesome bloodbath, Zatori is nowhere to be seen.

"Take down all the Harvesters!" Salam unleashes a guttural roar.

When she spots Celestine, Salam pounces on her, knocking her to the ground with a thundering force. Although Salam's massive frame overshadows her slender figure, Celestine isn't one to be easily intimidated. She fires a barrage of violet lightning bolts, each one crackling with energy as it shoots through the air. Salam barely flinches, her thick, bushy fur absorbing the impact despite being singed. Their fight escalates quickly, claws and talons sinking into each other.

Several Harvesters rush to Celestine's aid, knocking Salam off her. But Salam is a force to be reckoned with. Even when faced with multiple enemies, she shows no fear. Salam swings her gigantic, spiked mace powerfully at the skull of one Harvester before swiftly slashing the chest of another with her claws, finishing off both of them easily.

Celestine's eyes lock onto Akari, recognition flickering within them, bright as daylight. "That's Mari Miyahara's child! It's the deflector!"

Akari stills, her breath hitching. *How is it possible she can still recognize me after all these years?*

"Sire Zatori will be so pleased!" Celestine shrieks in delight. "Get the girl, you giftless midget! Can't you see my hands are full?"

"I'm already on it," a quiet voice replies from behind Akari.

She wheels around to find Philippe stalking toward her, armed with a spear that's already dripping with blood. Akari frantically retreats, tripping over the body of a comrade. A cold smile creeps onto Philippe's face. She scrambles backward, desperately slashing the air in front of her to keep him at bay. But he continues closing in on her as he fends off her feeble moves.

Akari backs up until she hits a huge tree. Philippe reaches out a short scraggy arm to wring the kris from her hand, flinging it to the ground. He pins her against the tree trunk and raises his spear for a blow.

A sharp tug on her clothes frees Akari from his grasp. Ethan pulls her out of the way, twisting around deftly to slash Philippe's legs. To Akari's horror, Ethan lets out a hair-raising cry as he falls to his knees, blood pouring from his own legs.

"No!" Akari screeches, her voice scraping the back of her throat. She knows she has used her gift once again—but this time, in a grotesquely wrong way. Ethan put his life on the line to save her, and she's as good as killed him.

Her screams are drowned out by the mayhem. All the other Protectors have their hands full with the Harvesters, and no one is looking her way.

"Kill him, Akari!" Ethan yells, his features wrought with horror.

Barely recovering from her state of shock, Akari scampers doggedly in search of her kris. Before she can find it, Philippe—freshly healed—kicks Ethan in the head, knocking him unconscious. When he turns his gaze back to her, Akari registers the glee in his eyes.

"Yes, you're indeed Lady Mari's child." Philippe pauses, as if to recollect. "You're the deflector."

Akari shudders. She is six years old again, cowering beneath Zephy's wing. Philippe was the first Harvester she saw up close, and now he's stepped from her nightmares to finish what he started.

"I see you remember me too," Philippe comments quietly. "You've grown up so much and even joined the People's Protector. Your mother must be proud."

Akari is too petrified to form a response.

"We weren't expecting to see you today. What a perfect gift sent right to our doorstep to welcome Sire Zatori's return! He'll be delighted to see you!" Philippe paces toward Akari, evidently finding pleasure in taking his time, toying with her.

"Stay away from me!" she screams desperately, but he continues advancing.

"The White Blaze that your mother caused killed so many of us. I'm sure Sire Zatori will be happy to make your harvesting exceptionally slow and painful," Philippe says. "And when he's done, you'll be left a mad, empty shell—or if you're lucky, dead."

He reaches Akari, his iron dragon mask looming squarely before her. A sickening smile peeks through it as he lifts her up by her collar—just as he did ten years ago—and prepares to plunge his spear into her body.

That's when Akari sees *him*. On the second floor of the farmhouse with broken walls and a missing roof, Zatori stands amidst the raging violet flames, alive and well—possibly never better. Even after a decade, he has barely aged, except his black hair with white streaks has now transformed into white hair with black streaks.

Basking in a haunting violet glow, Zatori overlooks the fight in the yard, smiling in sadistic delight as the Harvesters overpower the Protectors, their bodies burning below him. He raises his arms and hovers, rising from the ashes. *Zatori Valakhan has returned!*

"All hail Sire Zatori!" An eerie wave of greetings echoes throughout the yard as the Harvesters salute him.

"It took me ten whole years to come out of hiding, but I've finally come back stronger than ever. Now is the historic moment of my return! This time, nothing—and no one—can stop me from taking over Xylon!"

Incapacitated by the chilling reverberations of Zatori's drawling voice, Akari squeezes her eyes shut, bracing herself for a slow death. The motto of the People's Protector comes to mind. *Better to die with honor than to live with shame.*

But tonight, I'm about to die with shame.

4. Fortune Teller

Akari has thought about death before—her own, even. When she was younger, she believed she would live a long life and die naturally from old age. Later, when she started helping out at Moonstone Apothecary, Akari thought that she would, like many of her mother's patients, succumb to some sort of illness. Eventually, when she joined the People's Protector, she entertained the possibility of falling in combat. Given how the events of the night have unfolded, it seems regrettably true that Akari might make a better fortune teller than a fighter.

In the face of death, thoughts of her mother flood her mind, bringing tears to her eyes. *I'm sorry, Mama. I truly am. I'm sorry I didn't get to say goodbye. I'm sorry I didn't stay safe, lie low, and keep out of trouble, especially after you tried so hard to protect me all this time. Mama, I heart you with all my love...* She'd picked up this expression as a child and it had stuck since—something special that belonged to only her and her mother.

More than her own death, Akari is terribly afraid that Zatori and the Harvesters will hunt Mari down. *I can't let them get to Mama! But Ty will warn her. We promised to look out for each other's families, and I'm sure he'll remember. He always remembers everything about us. Ty... I only wish I'd had a chance to say goodbye to you as well...*

Just as a teardrop trickles down her bloodied cheek, a figure slams against Philippe and the three of them crash to the ground.

The sinewy newcomer is already back up on his feet before Akari can react. Evidently a skilled fighter, he tackles Philippe with his sword, fending off his every move as though he can predict them, and counterattacking with ferocity and an unexpected elegance.

Never in her life has Akari seen anyone fight this naturally—effortlessly, even. While Salam is undoubtedly a phenomenal fighter, she attacks with massive power and unprecedented strength. However, this newcomer is so light on his feet that it seems as though he's dancing, exuding grace—and a certain softness.

"Don't you dare touch her. Ever again," the newcomer warns in a deadly voice.

"And if I do, what are you going to do about it, young lad?" Philippe taunts.

"There's nothing I won't do." Without warning, the newcomer charges at Philippe with such fluidity that it seems as though he were running on water. The accompanying swordplay is beautiful but lethal, every blow unforgiving and relentless. With a wave of his blade, which moves as a blur to Akari, he slits Philippe's arm.

Although a veteran on the battlefield, Philippe quickly realizes he isn't nearly a match for this new threat. He flees, weaving through the chaos. The newcomer doesn't give chase, turning his attention to Akari instead.

When she takes him in properly, she feels a flicker of recognition. While she's taken aback to see the raven-haired Andelovian boy from the glade, there's no trace of surprise on his face.

Instead, he stares into Akari's honey-colored, almond eyes with an unfathomable intensity, as though he's searching for an answer, but to no avail. In his dark, crescent-moon eyes, she thinks she sees anger—and... concern. *But why? We don't even know each other...*

However, the words of the Andelovian boy don't reflect the grave concern in his eyes. There seems to be only inexplicable anger when he raises his voice. "Haven't you heard? Kill or be killed! Don't do this if you can't kill." His harsh cadence is a stark contrast to his graceful swordplay. "You'll get yourself killed!"

"I don't care about being killed. I care about him!" Akari cries tearfully. She drops to her knees beside Ethan, frantically shaking his motionless body. "I just want him to be alright. He needs to be alright!"

Refusing to budge, Akari attracts an onslaught of attacks from the surrounding Harvesters. The Andelovian boy fends them off in her stead, slaying every one with ease.

"Are you out of your mind? Are you really trying to get killed? There's a bloodbath out here. I need *you* to be alright!" he yells furiously.

"I don't deserve to be. Not when I caused this..." Akari whispers as she attempts, but fails, to lift Ethan's limp, heavy body. "My so-called gift... I'd rather it be gone!"

The Andelovian boy furrows his brow and softens his tone. "You didn't mean to hurt him. You shouldn't blame yourself."

Akari blinks through her tears. "What do *you* know?"

He looks at Akari with a pained expression. "Trust me, I do," he says, and firmly but gently removes her hands from Ethan's body. His touch sends a comforting warmth rippling through her.

A moment of silence lingers between them before the Andelovian boy breaks it. "I also know you're making my job very difficult. So, will you please get up and promise not to put yourself in peril again?" He offers his hand, but Akari doesn't take it. With no time to waste, he lifts her back to her feet, the move effortless.

Before she can respond, Akari spots the fiery red hair of the Andelovian girl as she runs toward them, her petite frame undeterred by her massive armor.

"What are you doing? Why did you save her?" she demands of the Andelovian boy, casting a cold glance at Akari. "You could've exposed us!"

"I just did what I had to," he says with a shrug. "Where were you when I was fighting Philippe?"

"I... I was fighting the other Harvesters," she replies breathlessly, jerking her chin toward her bloody spear. "Why did you have to risk us—yourself—for her?"

"I'm your vice commander, remember? It means you have to answer all my questions, and I don't have to answer any of yours," he says.

"This isn't part of our mission," the Andelovian girl mutters under her breath. "I followed you here tonight despite—"

The boy casts her a pointed look that has her holding her tongue.

"Let's get out of here," he says. He takes one last glance at Akari before disappearing into the woodland, as swiftly as he appeared. The Andelovian girl trails behind him wordlessly.

Somewhere in the distance, Akari hears Salam calling for a retreat.

◆

Despite being back in the safety of her home, Akari has trouble sleeping. When she wakes up yet again and realizes that her mother is finally back after an uncharacteristic night out, she crawls into bed with her, not wanting to sleep alone. Even then, Akari's sleep is interspersed with a series of dreams—nightmares included—that blend into each other.

At first, she sees Ethan, his usual friendly self, running toward her. But before he reaches her, he collapses to his knees, thick blood gushing from deep wounds on his legs. With immense difficulty, he crawls toward her, eyes wild with terror.

"Kill me, Akari!" Ethan's desperate plea is a death knell resounding in her mind.

Akari tries to call out to him, but the words are stuck in her throat. She can neither bend over to help him nor turn to flee. Her body has been rendered incapable of movement.

Ethan wraps his hands around her ankles, shaking them with such tremendous force that it rocks her entire body. His haunting voice continues belting her name until he slowly melts away. Tears stain Akari's face.

The colors in Ethan's hazel, doe-like eyes blend into one another before his left eye becomes entirely black and his right eye entirely white. When they come back into focus, they've become Zatori's eyes. As Akari is pulled toward them, an unbearably excruciating cold overcomes her entire being, just as when Zatori touched her cheek ten years ago. It penetrates her to her core, until it licks her bones and begins eating away at her soul. Akari squeezes her eyes shut and howls in pain.

The very next moment, the blistering cold seems a lifetime ago. When Akari opens her eyes, she's no longer looking into Zatori's lifeless gaze, but into the dark, crescent-moon eyes of the Andelovian boy. Except he is now only eight years old.

Aside from him, there's another child whose name she doesn't remember. This blonde-haired, blue-eyed girl, who stands half a head taller than Akari, has beige and cream feathers covering most of her skin and all of her wings. Her nose and mouth protrude into a white hooked beak. She is a hybreed with owl blood.

This is the day of Akari's sixth birthday. The three children are playing a game of hide-and-seek.

"I'll count to a hundred before I start seeking," the Andelovian boy says. "Whoever stays hidden longer will be the winner." With that, he places his hands over his eyes and begins counting away. "One... two... three..."

The owl girl takes Akari's hand, leading her as they bound through gardens, courtyards, and hallways. Eventually, they come to a stop at the bottom of a stair turret.

"You can hide there," she says, pointing upward.

When Akari lifts her chin, she sees a narrow wooden staircase that spirals up the turret, seemingly without end. Its hollow center is not bound by any banister. A single misstep could spell death.

"Am I allowed there?" she asks.

"Not exactly," the owl girl answers plainly.

Akari blinks at her with wide, innocent eyes.

"But this is precisely why he'll never find you," the owl girl explains.

Akari nods naively in agreement, peering up the turret. *No one will ever find me there!*

When she looks back at the owl girl, she's already vanished in search of her own hiding place. For the sake of the game, Akari begins making her way up the spiral stairs.

Eventually, she reaches the very top, coming before a wooden door. Without giving much thought, she turns the brass doorknob and steps into a circular room spanning the entire cross-section of the turret.

Eight windows with thick brass frames are evenly spaced around the room. The tall curved walls, which taper upward to form a high domed ceiling, are lined with endless shelves containing books, vases, crystals, and all sorts of other ornaments.

Voile curtains drape from the ceiling, obscuring a segment of the room on the opposite side from Akari's view. *This is the perfect hiding place!* Just as she starts making a beeline for it, she hears a thud coming from behind the curtains.

Akari stops dead. "Is anyone there?" she calls out softly before approaching with cautious steps.

"Well... yes, yes..." a girl answers from behind the curtain. Her voice sounds older than a child's, though not quite that of a grown woman.

"Who are you?" Akari asks, not knowing who to expect.

"I'm... I'm a fortune teller."

Brimming with curiosity, Akari reaches to pull back the curtains. But before she glimpses anything, the fortune teller promptly grasps her hand from the slit between the curtains, stopping her.

"You don't get to see me," she says, gently releasing her hand.

"Why?" Akari wonders out loud.

"Because neither of us should be here," the fortune teller replies.

"Are you hiding too?"

"Not exactly."

"Then can you read my fortune, please?"

"I could... for you... just this once."

Akari hears a shuffling of papers coming from behind the curtains.

"Give me your hand," the fortune teller instructs.

Akari extends her small hand between the curtains and the fortune teller takes it in hers, the two of them sharing the same lightly bronzed skin.

The fortune teller clears her throat before reciting,

"Compassion rises from the north,
Wisdom hails from across the Great Divide,
And from beyond the end of land
Comes courage—forgotten but not lost.
Only their treacherous reunion
Shall bring peace of a new realm."

There's a small pause before Akari asks, "What does that mean?"

"Well... that's something you'll have to mull over," the fortune teller says, her voice warm and kind. "And remember, this is an inextricable part of your destiny."

"How do you know?" Akari presses.

"Well, Akari, I'm older than you are, so naturally, I know more than you do."

"How do you know my name?" Akari asks in surprise.

"As I said... I'm a fortune teller," she states simply. "There's one more thing, Akari..." There's a trace of penitence in her words. "Promise me you'll tell your mama that you heart her with all your love?"

This is the first time Akari has heard the expression. "You said it wrong," she points out, not knowing better. "It should be 'I love you with all my heart.'"

The fortune teller laughs dolefully before insisting, "No, it's meant to be said this way... Promise me you'll say it like this?"

"Alright—"

The door swings open and a younger version of Mari strides in. The room grows quiet.

"Akari! Where have you been, my baby?" Mari exclaims, relieved but exasperated. "I've been looking all over for you! Thankfully, Sage told me you went this way."

Sage... So, that's the name of the owl girl.

"Does this mean I managed to stay hidden longer than Sage? Does this mean I've won?" Akari asks triumphantly. "I've been hiding here the whole time, Mama. The fortune teller just gave me a reading."

"A fortune teller?" Young Mari raises her eyebrows before recalling her reason for being there. "Alright, enough playing around. Your papa will be back any moment now and we have your birthday to celebrate." She turns to the partitioned segment, where the fortune teller is still mostly concealed. "We're sorry for disturbing you," she says before ushering Akari toward the door.

Before they reach it, the fortune teller calls out to Mari, "May I read your fortune as well?" Her tone is tinged with wistfulness.

"I guess you could... Thank you for offering..." Mari says politely, although the hesitation in her voice is unmistakable. "Akari, will you wait for me right outside? I'll be with you in a moment." She heads back toward the voile curtains.

Little Akari nods and hops out of the room obediently. As she closes the door behind her, she hears the fortune teller speaking with urgency, "During the Lantern Festival ten years from now—"

Akari wakes with a start. Her head is pounding, her body is sore, and her back is drenched in perspiration.

Although she isn't sure how much of her dream stems from reality, her encounter with the fortune teller feels uncannily familiar, as though it was indeed a part of her childhood. She has an inexplicably compelling hunch that the same holds for the Andelovian boy and the owl girl.

Outside the window, the sky has just been lit by the earliest morning rays. In the warmth and safety of her mother's embrace, Akari remembers that she owes her life to the Andelovian boy. She relishes a brief respite before it all comes crashing down on her.

Ethan's hurt—because of me. The last time she saw him, Ethan had been completely unresponsive, his arms hanging limply as he was carried away by some Protectors. None of them knew if he was going to make it. Akari was terrified that he might lose his life at any moment. Even now, the thought leaves her shaking.

Awakened by Akari's stirring, Mari bends over, concerned. "Are you alright, Akari, my baby? Did you have a nightmare?"

Akari nods weakly. "I... I dreamed that I hurt somebody with my gift."

"It's just a dream, Akari." Mari takes her daughter's hands, squeezing them lightly.

"What if it wasn't?" Akari asks, her hands tightening around her mother's. "What if I actually did hurt someone? Someone who isn't my enemy... Someone who's on my side..."

"Then I'll heal him for you, my baby," Mari says reassuringly. "But you'll learn how to control your gift with time."

Akari nods hesitantly, loosening her grip. "I wish I weren't gifted. I can't bear the guilt of hurting someone every time I use my gift, be it friend or foe." She speaks as though she's in physical pain.

Mari casts her an empathetic look. "There were times I wished I weren't gifted too," she confesses.

"Why?" Akari asks. "Your gift of healing has helped so many people."

"During the Great Harvest, when Zatori and the Harvesters were hunting us down so he could harvest my gift, I was terrified that it would put you in danger and place a target on your back for the rest of your life. Sometimes, I blamed it for the way our lives turned out," Mari explains. Before Akari figures if her mother is referring to their move to Cheyvelenia or the loss of her father, she adds, "But considering how often I've had to use my gift to save you, I don't know what I'd have done without it."

Akari smiles a little before letting out a sigh, lamenting, "But Mama, your gift saves lives, while mine hurts people. Yours is a gift, while mine... mine's a curse!"

"No, Akari. Never say that! My gift may save lives, but yours protects them. It might come at a price, but the same goes for everything that's worthwhile," Mari says, her tone solemn. "There may come a time when I'll have to pay the price for my gift as well... and I'm afraid the time is near..." Remnants of fear from the Great Harvest still shadow her eyes.

"No! I won't let that happen!" Akari shakes her head vehemently, wrapping her arms around her mother. "I heart you with all my love, Mama!" As soon as the words are out, Akari wonders how the fortune teller had also come to know this expression.

"I heart you with all my love too, Akari, my baby," Mari says, caressing her daughter's cheeks. But her mind is far away, her thoughts distracted.

Akari notices but says nothing.

"Akari, my baby, there's something I need to tell you," Mari says when she's finally present again. She takes a deep breath, as if to calm herself down, before unleashing her next words. "Zatori has returned."

Akari gasps, not at the news itself, but at how quickly her mother has heard of it. She has been so overwhelmed since her mission that she hasn't considered how to inform Mari of it. But at least now she won't have to.

"And so have Celestine and Philippe, along with some of the other Harvesters," Mari continues, her voice recapturing Akari's attention. "Together with the new

Harvesters Zatori amassed, they caused a huge fire at an abandoned farmhouse that killed many of the Protectors." Her dark, almond eyes are laced with terror. "This is why I'd never hear of you joining the People's Protector. It's too dangerous. I'm so relieved Ty wasn't sent on that mission!"

"How... how do *you* know?" Akari splutters.

"I heard it from a friend."

"A friend?" This is actual news to Akari, since her reserved mother usually keeps to herself. "But you don't have any—" She stops mid-sentence, realizing she has a good guess who Mari's friend may be. Despite this, Akari asks, cautiously, "Who is it?"

"It's Salam, the bear lady," her mother says.

Of course, Salam is Mama's friend. Just as I guessed...

"Do you remember her?" Mari asks. "She is one of the leaders of the People's Protector, and she saw Zatori return."

Akari shakes her head as convincingly as she can manage. Now certain her mother remains unaware of her involvement with the People's Protector, she relaxes a little and heaves a quiet sigh of relief, silently thanking Salam for honoring her promise to help her keep this secret.

"Is that who you were with last night?" she finally asks.

"Yes, but that isn't important," Mari continues urgently. "What's important is that Zatori has returned— much stronger than before. And we need to be very, very vigilant. Once Zatori or the Harvesters find us, we won't be able to escape so easily this time. Although they were last seen in Casserica, we must be prepared to flee if we hear of them approaching any of the northern towns closer to us."

"But Mama, what if we didn't run this time? What if we fight them instead? We can't hide all our lives," Akari suggests bravely despite being terrified at the thought of facing Zatori and the Harvesters again. But she knows all too well that her mother won't like what she's said.

"No! We're not fighting!" Mari's face turns white with fear, then red with anger. "I thought I'd made this clear ages ago. We need to stay safe, lie low, and keep out of trouble. This is the only way we can survive."

"But Mama, the People's Protector will fight alongside us—" Akari tries to protest.

"There's no room for negotiation on this one, Akari!" Mari snaps, cutting her daughter a warning look before marching downstairs.

Akari sighs softly as her thoughts inundate her. Almost as much as facing Zatori and the Harvesters, she's terrified at the prospect of fleeing Cheyvelenia, especially after having done the same from Andelovia a decade ago. Uprooting her life all over again is the last thing she wants.

Although it hasn't been easy settling in Cheyvelenia, she has grown accustomed to her new, simple life. Cheyvelenia is the place Akari has come to call home.

♦

As soon as Akari and Ty meet at Cheyvelenia's town square, she bursts into an urgent flurry of questions. "How is Ethan? Is he still alive? Did he make it?"

"I'm not sure... I heard that Ethan's life was hanging by a thread..." Ty says heavily. "What happened, exactly?"

As they walk through the cobbled square—past the rows of faded stores, huddles of emaciated homeless, and a defaced stone statue of King Alvaro—Akari recounts every detail of her first mission, the appearance of the Andelovian boy included. After being on the brink of death the night before, she finds the ordinariness of this morning surreal.

Ty listens intently. His willingness to let Akari unload makes her feel the slightest bit better.

"Come on, let's get you something to eat," he suggests as they pass Heavenly Bakery. Despite its worn-down facade, it flaunts trays of breads, cakes, pastries, and cookies of various shapes and sizes prepared every morning by its baker, Madam Celine.

When Ty was young, he'd often linger at the storefront of the bakery, beneath its rickety sign, drooling over the baked goods on display. How he'd longed for just a single bite! But he couldn't come close to affording even a crumb.

Too many times, after imagining the taste of one of those treats, Ty would swallow his spit, lick his lips, and walk away, never once setting foot inside. Whenever Madam Celine caught him, she'd shoot him a disdainful glare and shoo him away.

Akari, however, had the fortune to try these baked goods on special occasions—birthdays and festivals. Once, Mari had even brought Ty along and let him pick out a treat.

After much deliberation, he chose a scorched sea-salt cookie. When he finally sank his teeth into it, Ty had been so moved that he teared up, claiming, "This is the best thing I've ever tasted in my entire life! I'll never have to eat anything else again after this." Needless to say, the latter wasn't true.

Akari has never craved these treats the way Ty has. "That's alright, I'm not hungry..." she says with a shake of her head. "I don't get why you always want to come here. You don't even like Madam Celine."

"It doesn't matter whose bakery it is. You need something in your stomach," Ty insists as he drags Akari inside. Not only is he a firm believer that food is the solution to every problem, there's also a part of him that aches to prove to Madam Celine that he's now worthy of being a patron at her store.

True to its name, the bakery greets them with a warm, heavenly aroma of freshly baked goods. An impressive array of confections covers every corner of the cozy shop, neatly lined and tightly packed. All of Madam Celine's creations carry a distinct scorched flavor, a trademark of her secret recipe. Her signature scorched sea-salt cookies—Ty's favorite—boast a lightly burnt crust while remaining dense in the middle, leaving the children in town constantly begging for more.

The baker, dressed in a blend of mauve and prune, is perched behind the counter as usual. Her brown hair is tucked neatly behind her ears, her lean figure suggesting that she doesn't indulge too much in the treats she bakes. Unmarried and without children, Madam Celine seems to have dedicated her life to running Heavenly Bakery.

"Welcome! It's been a while since I've seen the two of you," she chirps, beaming brightly at them. "What would you like today?"

"Good morning, Madam Celine," Akari says. "I'm alright, thank you."

"But they have those cookies today," Ty announces excitedly before turning to the baker. Pointing at the scorched sea-salt cookies, he places his order without hesitation. "We'll have one of those, please."

"Would you like it toasted golden or scorched brown?" Madam Celine asks.

"Scorched brown, please," Ty answers confidently.

Madam Celine nods before picking out a brown, well-scorched cookie, placing it in a paper bag, and handing the bag to Ty. As she does, Akari notices the baker's right hand shaking feebly, her right forearm shoddily bandaged.

"Are you alright, Madam Celine?" Akari asks. "What happened to your arm?"

"Just another casualty from the oven," she says casually.

"My mother could look at it," Akari offers, but Madam Celine gives a small shake of her head.

"Don't worry, my dear. It'll happen again. It's the nature of my work."

"If you're sure," Akari says. "I hope it gets better."

"I hope it doesn't leave a scar. You wouldn't want to mar your devastating beauty," Ty adds sarcastically, grinning, as he pays for the cookie.

Madam Celine grabs the money with a scowl as Akari makes a hurried attempt to drag Ty out of the bakery.

"You better go before I scorch you like my cookies!" the baker calls after them.

"Stop that, Ty!" Akari warns with a small laugh as they start making their way to the Quartz. "You've annoyed Madam Celine enough over the years!"

Ty has vehemently denied that her treatment of him when he was younger is the sole reason he doesn't like her. "That woman gives me the creeps... There's just something nasty about the way she is!" he claims once again. Nevertheless, his reservations about Madam Celine have by far been overshadowed by his love for her baked goods—and an itch to prove that he's made his mark by becoming a Protector.

Akari gives him a patronizing smile that melts into a wistful sigh. "I miss the old times," she laments as she reminisces about their childhood frolicking all around Cheyvelenia before they joined the People's Protector. Now Zatori has returned, she is certain dark times lie ahead.

Ty takes a sniff of the cookie before reluctantly holding it out to her. "Have something to eat. It's still warm."

Akari, still brooding over Ethan, doesn't have much of an appetite. "Thanks, Ty, but I'm really not hungry." She shakes her head and pushes his hand back toward him. "You should have it. You like it way more than I do."

Startled by Akari's touch, Ty's face flushes red. Although they were always together growing up, he has been especially aware of her presence of late. His heart lurches a little before he quickly pulls himself together.

"Alright, alright... I'll start on it first and I'll save half for you," he relents, trying to act indifferent. But Akari is too preoccupied to notice.

As they trudge on quietly, Ty sinks his teeth into the cookie. Soon, they leave town and begin heading toward the forested foothills.

After a while, Akari breaks the silence. "Ty..." she whispers.

"Yes?" he mumbles, still munching on the cookie distractedly.

"How... how can you even stand being around me? After what I did on the mission..." she asks, her words barely audible.

Akari has Ty's full attention now. He puts what's left of the cookie back into the paper bag and, still chewing, declares, "Our friendship is never going to change, Akari. Not for me at least."

"But I hurt someone... Not even Zatori or Philippe or any of the other Harvesters. Ethan's your friend and our comrade..." Akari's voice starts to crack. "It's my fault he got injured."

"Akari!" Ty's face is dead serious. "It's not your fault. If anyone's to blame, it's me! *I* asked Ethan to look out for you. That's why he came between you and Philippe."

Akari shakes her head stubbornly, fighting back tears. "That's no excuse for what I've done."

"Look at me!" Ty says. She blinks several times before she can make her eyes veer up to meet his. "You can't blame yourself for any of this. It was an accident!"

Akari nods hesitantly, not fully convinced. Even though Ty's response touches her, her heart is still heavy.

"Cookie?" Ty offers again, an attempt to lighten the mood. In the paper bag that he holds up is a morsel of the scorched sea-salt cookie.

"Didn't you say you'd save half of it for me? There's only half a bite left," Akari complains.

"I'm sorry, I was hungry," he admits sheepishly.

Akari's face melts into a smile, both out of amusement and gratitude. "You're always hungry, Ty. Just finish that last bit. I don't feel like it anyway," she insists, and her best friend ceremoniously puts the rest of the cookie into his mouth. Both of them burst into laughter as they embark on the path uphill, heading toward the precipice.

Akari's mind quickly reverts to the mission. "Celestine and Philippe recognized me," she recalls worriedly. "They know who I am. Do you think I've put my mother in danger?"

"You were in Casserica. They won't know that you and Madam Mari live in Cheyvelenia," Ty assures her.

"But now Zatori's back, he and the Harvesters will scour all the towns in the outskirts looking for harvestees. If they find us, they won't let us live." Akari shudders at the thought of this. "Not after what my mother did with the White Blaze."

"Either way, it's never been Zatori's plan to let both of you go," Ty says tightly. "But this is precisely why we joined the People's Protector. This time, we'll get them before they get to you."

"Do you think we're strong enough? And fast enough?" Akari asks shakily. "After how things were the night before..."

"We'll have to be," he answers simply. "Or we'll die trying."

As a momentary silence stills the air, Akari's mind begins wandering.

"You know the dreams I get sometimes about my childhood playmates in the capital?" she begins softly. "I never used to be able to see their faces until last night... And the Andelovian boy was one of them."

8 0

Ty raises an eyebrow. "Are you sure it wasn't just a dream?"

"I have a feeling that there's some reality in it," Akari claims, although she can't be certain.

"Even if it were true, that's history," Ty maintains. "Now, the Andelovians are our enemies, just as the Harvesters are."

"But the Andelovian boy saved my life!" she points out, feeling the need to defend him. "He stopped Philippe from killing me!"

"It's not that simple!" Ty retorts. "You said that those Andelovians were the same ones you and your mother saw in the glade that day. It can't be coincidence you saw them again when Zatori returned. They must have been there for a reason!"

Akari is still hopeful, though. "What if the Andelovians are on our side this time? What if they're helping us fight Zatori and the Harvesters?"

"Most definitely not," Ty claims stubbornly. "The Andelovians won't help us. We can't trust anyone from the capital. The king abandoned us when he was faced with Zatori and stomped on us when we tried to stand up for ourselves. The outskirts and the People's Protector have to fight our fight by ourselves."

"But Ty, I'm from Andelovia too," Akari reminds him.

"You're different! You're one of us now! You have nothing to do with the capital!" Ty insists, his heated voice in stark contrast to the awkward silence that ensues.

Despite their squabble, Akari fully understands why Ty detests the Andelovians almost as much as he does the

Harvesters. The tragedy that befell his family was brought about by King Alvaro and the Andelovian Army almost as much as by Zatori and the Harvesters. This cost him his father's arms, his mother's sanity, and his family's livelihood.

Despite having known him for more than half her life, Akari hasn't gotten used to this side of him—one strikingly different from his usually goofy self. She stays quiet, allowing Ty some time to himself. They walk onto the precipice and make their way to the edge.

Ty senses her unease. "I'm sorry. I was thinking about—"

"Your parents. I know..." Akari finishes for him softly. "I was thinking about them as well... I'm sorry, too."

"Akari, you of all people shouldn't have to be sorry." Ty manages a weak smile.

"Well then, thank you," she says, smiling too, "for the cookie I didn't get to eat."

He scowls, and everything between them is back to normal—almost.

Ty has never had to spell anything out to Akari. Since they have grown up together, she's able to read him exceedingly well. But there's one thing about him she's yet to uncover—something he himself has barely begun to realize.

Standing at the edge of the precipice, Ty extends his hand toward Akari, just as he has done many times. When she takes it this time, a tingling sensation creeps through every inch of his being. Ty's heart begins pounding rapidly.

With a strange nervousness he has never felt before, he turns around so that his back faces the edge of the precipice. "Now, will you take the Leap of Faith with me?"

Afraid that Akari's answer will be "no" again, he doesn't give her a chance to reply. He leans backward and drops into the precipice, pulling her after him. Taken by surprise, she lunges forward, falling on top of him. Despite the shockwaves coursing through Ty when their bodies meet, he wraps his arm protectively around Akari's waist, holding her close.

As they free-fall through the gateway, the cool air rushes against his face, freshening him, and vanquishing all the confusion and ambiguity he's been feeling of late.

Suddenly, everything becomes crystal clear to Ty—he has fallen for his best friend.

5. Traitor

"Here comes the traitor," Hanwell, flanked by Prisci and Aloy, announces unnecessarily loudly as Akari and Ty land in the Quartz. His voice reverberates throughout the Goethite Hall, immediately capturing everyone's attention.

Hanwell, with his bullying streak, is by no means popular in the People's Protector. Some are afraid of him, but most only put up with him because he's the mayor's son. But this time, the Protectors, many suffering from fresh wounds and grieving the recent loss of comrades from this botched mission, stand with him.

Icy glances are shot in Akari's direction and harsh muffled whispers ripple through the hall. A debilitating tension hangs in the air.

How does everyone know what I did to Ethan? Shock and shame batter Akari. She freezes in place, trying to make herself appear as small as possible—or better still, invisible. But by now, the commotion has attracted a large crowd of irate onlookers.

"I didn't mean to..." Akari murmurs as she stares at her boots, too terrified to look into the glowering eyes of the Protectors surrounding her. Hanwell, Prisci, and Aloy take a step toward them.

TRAITOR

"Back off," Ty warns the trio, placing a reassuring hand on Akari's shoulder.

"How does it feel to hurt your comrade?" Prisci taunts.

"Ignore them," Ty says firmly. He tries to break through the crowd to usher Akari away, but Aloy gets in their way.

"Where do you think you're going after injuring one of our own?" he challenges.

"It was an accident..." Akari's voice is so small that she can barely convince herself, not to mention the hostile Protectors.

"Even if it was, you can't just get away with it," Hanwell growls, stalking closer. "The People's Protector will protect the outskirts and our gifteds, but we won't tolerate those who hurt us! Those who do will have to pay the price!"

"Back off, Weilcox!" Ty warns again, his voice raised this time. "Philippe should be the one to pay the price, not Akari!" He adjusts his position, planting himself firmly between Akari and Hanwell.

"Maybe you should think twice about jumping to her defense, Kane. She's going to endanger you at some point, just like she did to Cook that night," Hanwell suggests, his tone mocking. "I mean, aren't you afraid of constantly being around someone like that? You never know what will set off her so-called gift she has absolutely no control over."

"Not at all," Ty says without a shred of doubt. "In fact, being around her gives me a great sense of security. She's proved that to us before, hasn't she?" He grins, cutting Hanwell a pointed stare to remind him of the first time he saw Akari's gift in action.

Hanwell's face flushes red from a mix of embarrassment and anger, but he doesn't back down. Turning to the crowd, he proclaims, with a finger pointed at Akari, "Miyahara and her gift are dangerous—a threat to us all! She'll have to pay for hurting a Protector and should never be allowed to fight alongside us again!"

Amidst roars of agreement from the crowd, Hanwell sidesteps Ty to reach Akari. But Ty swiftly blocks his path, a hand pressed to his chest. "Leave her alone—"

Before Ty finishes, Hanwell grabs his wrist and flings him onto the ground. Although Hanwell's fear of Akari has meant keeping his distance from Ty, his bravado is swollen at the thought of having the rest of the Protectors behind him.

Not giving Ty the opportunity to react, Hanwell twists his arm and pins him to the ground. As Ty lets out an ear-piercing yelp, he whispers in his ear, "I've been waiting a long time to do this. Isn't this just like it was all those years ago, before *she* came to your rescue?"

Hanwell turns to Akari, his eyes taunting.

Akari quickly realizes that he's daring her to demonstrate her gift before the crowd, so even those who are wavering will turn against her. "Let Ty go now!" she warns, trying to maintain her composure.

But Hanwell doesn't say a word, twisting Ty's arm further, causing him to wince in pain. Impatient for Akari to prove his words, Hanwell hurls a punch across Ty's face. A splotchy purple bruise immediately surfaces.

Infuriated that her best friend is paying the price for her misdeed, Akari touches both of their arms, deflecting the wound Hanwell inflicted on Ty back onto him. Hanwell immediately releases him, clutches his newly forming black eye, and releases a howl. Ty, whose face appears as good as new, scrambles to get back on his feet.

The onlooking Protectors gasp at the effect of Akari's gift. A wave of frightened murmurs and accusing cries ripples through the Goethite Hall. Hanwell has achieved what he set out to do. The rest of the Protectors—even the ones who admired her gift—have now taken his side.

Before anyone catches Hanwell's smug smile, he jumps on Akari, knocking her to the dark brown, quartzite floor, while Prisci and Aloy grab hold of Ty to prevent him from intervening. Hanwell swiftly draws his dagger, holding it dangerously close to Akari's throat, an act that seems to be more a personal vendetta than one of justice. Ethan, whom Hanwell doesn't even care for, has simply provided him with the perfect excuse to get back at Akari—an opportunity he's been waiting nine long years for.

"Isn't this how you do things, Miyahara? An eye for an eye? A wound for a wound?" Hanwell yells as he knocks Akari over, pinning her to the ground. "So, shouldn't you have to pay for hurting Cook?"

Akari silently consents. She doesn't resist, staring blankly at the jagged high ceiling and the raw quartz chandelier hanging from it.

Hanwell presses the cold blade to Akari's throat, whispering into her ear, "After I make you pay, I'll make Kane do the same. He's nothing without you or the People's Protector anyway."

Fury boils inside Akari. She won't allow Ty to be hurt in any way—especially because of her. "Don't you dare touch him—"

A guttural growl punctuates the air. The entire hall falls silent, everyone turning toward its source. Salam stands on the top of the stairway, her bear ears tilted back, her bulky shoulders tense.

"The two of you!" Salam barks. "With me. *Now!*" Without waiting for a response, she turns her back and prowls down the hallway.

Hanwell releases Akari with utmost reluctance and sheathes his dagger. Amidst a stifling tension, they get to their feet and dust off their clothes. The crowd quietly parts to let them through, allowing them to follow Salam.

Salam pads up more stairs and through several hallways before finally opening a massive door, one likely made to accommodate her height. She lets Akari and Hanwell pass through and swings it shut behind them. The door slams into its frame with a loud bang, and they both jump.

Before them stretches a long dim office that resembles a bear's den, its low ceiling not much higher than the oversized door. At the very end of the room, behind a gigantic wooden desk, is the sole source of light—a single window overlooking the precipice and the forest beyond.

Akari hangs her head in guilt when she sees Salam studying her, and stares nervously at her boots. Beside her, Hanwell stands as tall as his height allows, arms crossed in defiance, as if he's done no wrong.

After what feels like an age, Salam breaks the hush. "The People's Protector will not tolerate any fighting among ourselves. We've already lost enough Protectors, and we don't need any new casualties." Her gruff voice is intimidating but not threatening.

"Yes, Madam Salam!" Akari promptly replies in true military style.

"*They* started the fight!" Hanwell claims. "Kane laid his hand on me, and I had to defend myself. Miyahara then deflected his injuries onto me!"

"Hanwell, the fight downstairs is inconsequential compared to the one we had with Zatori and the Harvesters," Salam reminds him, seeing through him right away. "As a marshal, you should have known better."

"And what do we do about Miyahara hurting Cook?" Hanwell challenges her, his lack of respect blatant. It puts Akari off, but she isn't surprised. As Maximus's minion, he has never come to accept Salam's authority.

"*You* will do nothing about it," Salam simply says.

"Won't Miyahara have to pay for hurting Cook?" Hanwell presses. "She should be expelled from the People's Protector!"

Akari would be horrified at the thought if she weren't inundated with an overwhelming numbness. *All my efforts to be part of the People's Protector have come to naught, unraveling after just one mission...*

"Didn't Tyler already tell you? Philippe should be the one to pay the price, not Akari," Salam replies with a snarl. "Expelling her won't make Ethan any better, and we won't be short of another Protector without a valid reason."

Akari knows she ought to be thankful for being allowed to remain in the People's Protector. Instead, she feels nothing. All she can think about is what she's done.

"Besides, Ethan is alive and well," Salam informs them brightly, as if reading her thoughts.

At the news, Akari heaves a long, deep sigh of relief, a load finally taken off her mind. In exchange for his wellbeing, she'd have been willing to do anything—even face expulsion.

"Miyahara is too dangerous," Hanwell retorts, completely disregarding the good news. "No one else in the People's Protector trusts her. They're afraid of her! Having her fighting alongside us will affect our safety and morale. We can't allow that to happen."

"That isn't for you to decide. Akari stays. I have the last word on this, and I will deal with her accordingly," Salam says with finality. "Besides, we have more pressing issues at hand."

"Isn't dealing with her the most pressing issue?" Hanwell challenges.

"That couldn't be further from the truth." Salam's tone is tinged with a certain graveness.

"Then what is?" he presses.

"Ten years have clearly given Zatori time to grow his following by multiple folds." Salam speaks slowly to let the words sink in. "And judging by the way our last mission unfolded, it's reasonable for us to conclude Zatori has a spy within the People's Protector." There's a brief pause before she says, "We have a traitor among us."

Akari reels in shock, the pit of her stomach twisting and tightening. *Who's hoping for the downfall of the People's Protector? Who among us is working toward our deaths?*

"So, the farmhouse on the fringes of Casserica really was a trap, wasn't it?" Akari asks, despite knowing the answer and wishing it weren't the truth. "Zatori already knew we were coming..." Her voice is barely a whisper scraping the back of her throat.

"Yes," Salam confirms. "Zatori was waiting for us—an old tactic, it seems. The Harvesters doused the farmhouse in oil beforehand and set it on fire after we barged in, intending for us to die without a fight."

So, that's what the foul smell must have been... Akari realizes, horrified.

"That's not possible!" Hanwell exclaims. "No one in the People's Protector would do something like that!"

"How can you be sure all the Protectors wholeheartedly swear allegiance to the People's Protector?" Salam asks, her deep voice slow and sad. "And that all of us are devoted to the same cause? Don't you see that divisions already exist within us?"

Hanwell, dumbfounded, fumbles for words. "Maybe it's... It has to be Miyahara! She did Zatori a service by deflecting the injuries from a Harvester onto one of us. The traitors have to be Miyahara and her lackey, Kane."

Even before Akari tries to defend herself, Salam gives Hanwell a pointed glare, fixing him.

After a moment, he dares to ask, "If it isn't them, who's the traitor?"

"That's what we need to find out," Salam says. "I'm going to hand over this mission to you, Hanwell. I need you to investigate the identity of the traitor and report back to me. Get Prisci and Aloy to help you as well."

"Yes, Madam Salam," Hanwell responds in military style despite his blatant unwillingness.

"We also need to look into the Andelovians from the night before," Salam continues. "I need to find out if they're with Zatori."

"Those Andelovians weren't with Zatori. They were on our side—our comrades! The boy saved me from Philippe." Akari is surprised by how important the Andelovian boy—a stranger despite her dreams—feels to her, but she's certain he's there to help.

"Not many people can beat Philippe in a fight. This boy must be exceptionally skilled in combat," Salam says, tapping the claws of one paw together as she considers Akari's words. "There seems to be more to the Andelovians than meets the eye. We need to find out what brought them to the outskirts. Akari, I'm entrusting you and Tyler with this mission."

"Yes, Madam Salam!" Akari answers, excitement bubbling within her. Investigating will undoubtedly help feed her own nagging curiosity about the Andelovians—particularly the boy.

"And before I dismiss you," Salam adds, "I'd like to remind both of you again that fighting is not tolerated within the People's Protector. You'll not be let off without a punishment the next time! Do you hear me?" She punctuates her warning with a thunderous growl to make sure they—Hanwell, in particular—do not forget.

"Yes, Madam Salam!" Akari and Hanwell chime in unison.

"Good." Salam nods. "Now, Hanwell, you're dismissed," she orders. "Akari, please stay behind."

"I thought you said you'd be dealing with her accordingly..." Hanwell lingers in his spot, waiting expectantly for Akari's punishment to be meted out in his presence.

"Yes, I will. And *you* will have no part in this." Salam speaks with finality. "Now, you're dismissed."

Hanwell stomps out, and Akari allows herself a sliver of a smile at his disappointment.

As soon as the door closes behind him, Salam turns her attention to Akari, eyeing her carefully, as if deciding on an appropriate punishment.

Any trace of smile disappears as Akari anxiously awaits her sentence. Recalling Ty's account about the public flogging for theft, she shudders at how much worse a punishment her crime might warrant.

Salam's face creases in mild amusement.

"So, what will my punishment be?" Akari asks eventually.

"I never said I would punish you," Salam says with a wink.

Akari furrows her brow. "Didn't you say that you'll deal with me accordingly?"

"Yes, I intend to do that, but not by inflicting bodily harm on you." Salam puts a reassuring paw on her shoulder, before withdrawing it and straightening slightly. "You *will* be suspended from combat missions until I deem fit, though."

Akari blinks in disbelief. "You're not going to have me flogged publicly? Or have my arm or leg cut off?" she checks meekly.

Salam roars with laughter. "No! Of course not!"

While Akari brims with immense gratitude toward Salam for allowing her to escape a painful punishment, the guilt for having been let off too easily also hits her.

She casts her gaze downward, unsure how to respond. Some form of reprimand would almost have been easier to bear than none at all.

"Punishments are for crimes, not mistakes," Salam says gently. "Besides, I have to be responsible for this incident—at least partially. I misjudged your abilities before sending you on a mission."

It's not your fault, it's mine. Akari hangs her head in silence and continues to stare down in shame.

"Don't get me wrong," Salam continues. "I'm not implying that you lack abilities. On the contrary, you possess great potential, Akari. But you aren't ready for battle *here*." She points her index claw to Akari's heart.

Do I have potential? Or am I really lacking the abilities to be a Protector? As she considers Salam's words, her doubt grows further.

"Seeing Philippe brought back your fears and didn't help with controlling your gift." Salam's voice is soft, reassuring. "Has it been ten years since your encounter with Zatori and the Harvesters? You were so little back then."

"How... how do you know?" Akari stutters.

"I told you, your mother and I go a long way back."

Perhaps longer than I'd thought... Akari realizes, her tongue grazing her teeth as she processes the new information.

"Regardless, we need to make sure you hone your gift before you're put on another mission," Salam continues. "Since it seems rather difficult for you to be hard-hearted, we need to train the mind to rule over the heart during battle. First, you'll need to control your fear. Only then will you be able to control your gift. You'll need to practice both."

"How do I... You can't possibly mean..." Akari's baffled, unable to wrap her head around Salam's instructions. *Practice? My gift? Deflecting wounds? Hurting people?* "I wouldn't even do that to animals!" she blurts before realizing the slip of her tongue might have offended Salam. "I'm sorry, I didn't mean it that way..."

"Don't mind me!" Salam waves her furry paw and bursts into her usual rambunctious laughter. "We're not going to hurt anyone, any animal, or anything for that matter!"

Akari squeezes her eyes shut as she wrestles with the impossible question of how to practice her gift without harming anyone. When she opens them again, Salam's office is gone. They've been plunged into a realm of darkness.

"Have you heard how the Quartz maintains its obscurity?" Salam asks.

"Ty mentioned that the People's Protector has gatekeepers who are gifted in illusion, invisibility, and telekinesis... And you're the head gatekeeper..." It finally dawns on Akari that their second-in-command is gifted as well. "Is your gift... that of illusion?"

Salam laughs and nods her large ursine head. "Yes. You'll be practicing your gift within an illusion. No one, yourself included, can get hurt here. This is where you'll learn to hone your gift. Thereafter, fighting in an actual battle will be no different from an illusion," she explains before adding, "Just with the physical pain."

Akari nods nervously.

"In an illusion, good things can happen." Akari is suddenly soaring through the sky on Zephy's back, far above the snow-capped mountains and snow-laden forests. Feeling the lightness of liberation, she relaxes a little, but it doesn't last for long.

"And so can bad things," Salam says. In an instant, the illusion of flying is replaced by the violet inferno of the abandoned farmhouse on the fringes of Casserica. Akari staggers back, the fear from the night Zatori returned battering her once again.

Salam quickly moves on, and the burning farmhouse disappears. "You can also see the people you love," she continues. Back in the realm of darkness, Mari materializes before Akari, an empathetic smile hanging from her face. Beside her, Ty flashes his usual goofy grin. Akari's lips curve upward subconsciously.

"And the people who annoy you." Hanwell, Prisci, and Aloy simultaneously appear next to Mari and Ty. The grimace on Akari's face draws a guffaw from Salam.

"And, of course, the people you're afraid of," Salam finishes. When Akari sees Zatori, Celestine, and Philippe standing opposite her, dread sluices through her veins. She backs away again.

"They look so real," Akari whispers, sure she'd turn tail and run if not for her legs feeling like they've spread roots into the ground.

"Celestine and Philippe recognized you that night," Salam says. "This means that, by now, Zatori and the Harvesters must be hunting high and low for you and your mother. Both your gifts are very valuable to him."

"What should we do?" Akari doesn't need an illusion to imagine those mismatched eyes above a chilling smile as Zatori strides toward them.

"First, you'll need to know your enemies in order to defeat them," Salam advises. "Zatori Valakhan, with his gift of harvesting, is the cause of all this. Zatori has led many lives before the one we now know, although his origins are a mystery. For most of his life, he's been harvesting gifts and thereby the harvestees' lives, which has allowed him to live for so long."

Salam paces around Zatori as she speaks, adding a sense of surrealism to Akari's fear rather than dispelling it. "The worst of it was during the Great Harvest. All hell broke loose until the White Blaze destroyed him, or so most people thought. But now, Zatori has returned and wants to prove to the world that he's more powerful than before—and even more worthy of the throne."

"If that's so, why isn't Zatori in the capital overthrowing the king?" Akari asks.

"He's still in the outskirts harvesting gifts to build his strength. When he decides he's powerful enough, there's no doubt that he'll head to Andelovia to seize the throne."

Next to Zatori, violet lightning surges from Celestine's hands, giving her mask an eerie purple glint. Salam towers over her and continues her descriptions in front of Akari's worst fears.

"Celestine Lithezyne is a wild one, a ruthless madwoman—one of the few female Harvesters around. Like Zatori, she has no known family either," Salam says. "Celestine's best known for her gift of wielding her signature violet lightning, a skill she perfected after sticking metallic talons onto her fingers."

The lightning strikes Salam, but she shrugs. "The real Celestine's gift would have little more effect on me than this illusion. Luckily, my fur can buffer an electric shock, and even hide a scar. But it couldn't shield me from her talons themselves." Salam holds apart her fur to reveal the long scar she'd shown Akari previously. "Celestine was the one who did this to me a long time ago."

Akari stiffens even though it isn't her first time seeing it. "Was that the wound that left you on the brink of death?" she asks tightly.

"Yes. Thankfully, your mother found and healed me," Salam says with more blitheness than Akari expected. "I did Celestine some damage too after befuddling her with my illusions. But regrettably, I didn't manage to finish her off once and for all."

Akari nods in agreement.

"Rumor has it that Celestine's face was terribly disfigured in battle," Salam shares. "But the iron mask hides it all."

Akari stares at the dragon mask and asks, "Is the dragon the emblem of Zatori and the Harvesters?"

Salam shakes her head. "Contrary to popular belief, it's actually an archivian," she corrects.

"An archivian?" Akari asks, surprised.

"Yes," Salam confirms. "It could be because archivians became extinct over three hundred years ago and Zatori might be the only person alive who's seen one. Or perhaps it's because they were supposedly superior to both dragons and humans regardless of the form they chose to forge into."

She bares her teeth in distaste and continues, "Because of the nature of his gift, Zatori has always perceived himself to be superior and likely thought the archivian made a fitting emblem for the Harvesters. If I have my way, those who wear it will meet the same fate as the archivians they exalt."

Akari nods as she eyes the Harvesters' masks, realizing each one is distinct, from the size of the scales and the pattern of the spikes, to the tilt of the eye slits and the flare of the nose holes.

"Last but not least is Philippe Sulech," Salam says. "Although he's one of the few Harvesters who is a nullus, it doesn't make him any less dangerous. Don't let his unimposing stature fool you into underestimating him either. Philippe is one of the most skilled fighters around. But what makes him stand out is his extensive knowledge of gifts—to the point of obsession." She pauses slightly before adding, "Apparently, he had a wife who died giving birth to their daughter."

"Philippe has a daughter?" Akari struggles to picture him as a father. "Is she part of the Harvesters too?"

"Not that I know of. No one seems to have seen her or knows if she's even still alive. But if she is, she'd be around your age."

Just as Akari wonders if she is going to materialize, Salam says, "Shall we have a go at it?"

"At what?" Akari asks cautiously.

"Practicing your gift!" Salam announces with a wink.

"Now?" Akari is hesitant, barely having had the chance to process everything she's just learned about her enemies. But Salam doesn't seem to think it's necessary.

"Yes," she replies. "There's no better time than now."

Before Akari can respond, everyone around her, Salam included, vanishes. All alone in the realm of darkness, her heart pounds with trepidation.

Philippe materializes and charges toward Akari, his deadly spear raised. She buckles at the sight of him.

"Focus!" Salam's gruff voice echoes throughout the illusion although she's nowhere in sight.

When Akari does, she sees that Philippe is no longer advancing. Instead, he stands across from her, with one arm around Ethan's throat and the other hand pressing the spear to his neck.

"Show me your gift, little deflector," he says quietly, driving the spearhead into Ethan's skin.

Blood flows from the fresh wound, and Ethan screams the exact same words as before. "Kill him, Akari!"

Thoroughly paralyzed by fear, Akari is unable to use her gift.

"Remember, fear is only a state of mind!" Salam's voice reverberates all around her. "You need to learn to control your emotions."

"I can't!" Akari shakes her head helplessly, her breathing labored. As blood streams endlessly down Ethan's neck, she sinks to the ground, pressing her hands over her eyes in desperation, as though this will shield her from the monstrosity of Philippe. "Madam Salam, make it stop, please!" she screams. "Make it stop!"

In a flash, everything falls silent. When Akari removes her hands, Philippe and Ethan have disappeared. But she remains in the realm of darkness, Salam reappearing opposite her.

"Akari..." Salam looks at her, concerned.

Akari drops her head down, unable to meet Salam's worried gaze, her body still shaking.

"Akari—" Salam starts again, but Akari's quiet voice cuts her off.

"Maybe Hanwell is right," she begins tightly. "I caused Ethan to be hurt, and I shouldn't endanger the rest of the Protectors. My being here isn't going to do anyone any good. Maybe I *should* be expelled from the People's Protector."

Salam shakes her head profusely. "No, Akari. You need to stay here to hone your gift. Only then will you be able to fight alongside the rest of the People's Protector, and Ethan won't have been hurt in vain. Now, look at me."

Akari gingerly lifts her chin until her eyes meet Salam's.

"I know you have a kind heart and being hard-hearted isn't easy for you, but don't let this become your weakness in battle," Salam advises, her tone grave.

Akari nods wordlessly, though she can't see how she'll manage to follow the advice.

"You must be exhausted. Let's call it a day," Salam concludes as the darkness around them dissipates. Back in the den-like office, Akari finds Salam holding out a loaf of bread and a pouch of money.

Akari shakes her head. "I don't deserve these."

"You do, Akari. All of these are hard-earned," Salam insists, placing the bread and money firmly in her hands. "Now, you should get back, but not before seeing someone who's waiting outside for you."

With that, Salam opens the door to reveal Ethan, perfectly well and unscathed. "Good to see my trusted aide back on his—"

"Ethan! You're alive! You made it!" Akari rushes up and wraps him in a tight embrace, while Salam pats his shoulder and disappears back into her den. When Akari finally releases Ethan, she scrutinizes every inch of him. "You've recovered!"

"Yes, I have. Akari, I wanted to let you know I'm alright, and that you don't have to worry," Ethan reassures her despite the hurt she caused him.

"How... how is this possible? It couldn't possibly have been my... my..." Akari struggles to accept her own hunch.

"Yes, your mother healed me," Ethan says, gesturing to his healthy legs. "Madam Salam made sure she saw to me promptly, alongside plenty of others. Madam Mari's been treating the wounds of the Protectors for quite some time now, even using her gift to heal those inflicted with otherwise fatal wounds. Didn't you know about it?"

Akari shakes her head, reeling in disbelief. "*My* mother?" *How could Mama, who's always disapproved of me joining the People's Protector, be healing them in secret? Why did she hide this from me? And what does she know about my involvement?* "Surely, she doesn't know I'm... I'm part of..."

"No, she doesn't know you're one of us." Ethan's words calm her nerves slightly. "Don't worry. Madam Mari's aware we aren't supposed to discuss the identities of the Protectors. She doesn't ask any questions besides the ones necessary to treat her patients."

Well able to picture her mother that way, Akari heaves sigh of relief. She holds out the bread and money toward him as compensation.

Ethan smiles but doesn't reach for them. "That was your first mission, wasn't it?"

"Yes," Akari replies, embarrassed.

"What luck you witnessed Zatori's return on your first mission. Well, this must be the first time you've been given this much food and money. Eat it and use it well. You earned it with your blood, sweat, and tears," Ethan says, waving at himself as he adds, "And a little bit of mine."

Akari breaks into nervous laughter, glancing at him with worried eyes.

"I'm kidding! You're a good friend of Ty's, so you're mine too. I'll take some bread if it makes you feel better." Ethan playfully tears off a corner of the bread and pops it into his mouth.

"That won't do! That's hardly anything!" Akari protests. "How else can I make up for what I did?"

"You can make sure Zatori's really gone forever this time." Ethan flashes a cheeky smile and chortles at his own joke. When the laughter subsides, he adds, this time in all seriousness, "And don't forget your promise to stay alive longer than me."

Before Akari can respond, he has already sauntered down the hallway without looking back.

6. Fate

After munching on some bread, Akari opens the money pouch and pours twenty hard-earned bronze nuggets into her palm. Her fingers shakily brush their smooth but uneven surface. This is the most money she has ever made. Very carefully, she puts away ten bronzes and takes the remainder to Tinkler's Oddities and Antiquities, where Mari thinks she works.

During her childhood, when Akari used to wander the streets of Cheyvelenia with Ty, she remembers stopping at the storefront of Tinkler's to admire the intricate ornaments that didn't quite seem to belong in the outskirts. In fact, it was precisely these delicate pieces, which reminded Akari of her past in the capital and the jewelry her mother used to wear, that drew her to the store.

However, since they moved to Cheyvelenia, besides not wanting to stand out, Mari also never seemed to have the occasion or money for such luxuries—or barely anything beyond necessity. Every nugget she's scrimped and saved has always been set aside for her daughter. Now that Akari has finally started earning her keep, she wants to give her mother something special. For the very first time in her life, she has the means to purchase something from Tinkler's.

When Akari steps into the cavernous store, she is momentarily swept into an entirely different world. The air is thick with the scent of aged wood and leather. Every corner is crammed with antiques—from ornate furniture and intricate paintings, to gleaming weapons and shiny treasures. The sheer abundance leaves little room to maneuver, with many of the pieces seeming far beyond her means, likely priced in silver or even gold nuggets. After a quick scan of the shop, Akari narrows her focus and sifts through some lacquered jewelry trays, each brimming with delicate trinkets.

A modest ring, nestled among the vibrant, elaborate brooches, hairpieces, and jewelry, catches her eye. Akari picks it up and holds it up to the light. The silver ring has an adularescent, oval moonstone framed with tiny white crystals. It's simple and elegant, reminding her exactly of her mother. Bubbling with excitement, Akari slips it onto her finger. As a vivid image of the ring sitting splendidly on Mari's hand comes to mind, a comforting familiarity sweeps over her. *This is the perfect present for Mama!*

She takes the ring to the counter, where a sloth-like, middle-aged man with fluffy gray hair and thick horn-rimmed glasses dozes in his seat.

"Mr. Tinkler," Akari says, holding out the moonstone ring toward the storekeeper. "Where is this from?"

Struggling to open his eyes, Mr. Tinkler squints at the ring. "I can't tell if it was Cheyvelenia or Andelovia…"

Akari sighs softly, giving up on any small talk. "How much does it cost?"

"It's twenty-two," he replies with a yawn.

Akari's heart sinks, and she realizes it was exceedingly naive of her to assume that prices in Tinkler's are proportional to size. She takes one last longing look at the ring before turning to return it.

Just as she walks away, Akari hears Mr. Tinkler's drowsy voice. "You're Akari Miyahara, the healer's daughter, aren't you?"

"Yes," Akari answers tentatively, swiveling around.

"Is that for your birthday?" he asks. "It's coming up, isn't it? I remember it's around this time of the year."

"How did you know that?" With everything going on recently, she has almost forgotten her own birthday. It surprises her that a man who's practically a stranger remembers it better than she does.

"When I first met you and your mother shortly after you came to Cheyvelenia, I remember her saying it had just been weeks after your birthday," Mr. Tinkler explains.

Even though Akari has no recollection of the event, she says, "Yes, my birthday is coming up. But this isn't for me. It's for my mother."

"Well then, take it," Mr. Tinkler offers with a casual, lazy shrug.

"I can't accept your kindness." Akari just about wheels around to go, but his soft yet firm voice stops her in her tracks.

"Yes, you can. I insist you take it."

"No, I can't..." Akari shakes her head adamantly, pouring the entire contents of the money pouch onto the counter. "But will you please accept ten bronzes?" She thinks her conscience can bear that, even though she knows full well she's still getting the better deal.

"Well, of course. If you insist." Mr. Tinkler gives a slow smile, sleepily waving her away. "I know your mother will like the ring. And happy birthday in advance, Akari."

"Thank you." She beams with satisfaction and turns to leave. Still captivated by the silver moonstone ring, she meanders distractedly toward the entrance of Tinkler's, until she collides into something—or rather, someone.

As Akari's head crashes into his chest, she picks up the smell of crisp mountain air, much like the scent she breathes while flying Zephy. She stumbles, and the ring flies from her grip. But before she can respond, he steadies her with one hand and catches it with the other. As he holds the silver moonstone ring toward Akari, she stares up at the pair of crescent-moon eyes gazing back at her.

"Akari... Miyahara..." the Andelovian boy enunciates under his breath. "That's a beautiful name."

"What are *you* doing here?" she blurts, almost impolitely, taking the ring from him. *And how long has he been here? Long enough to see me try to buy something I can't afford?* The thought has her flushing with embarrassment.

However, this doesn't seem to be on his mind at all. With smiling eyes, he asks, "Is this how you're going to repay me for saving your life?" He exudes a light-hearted playfulness, with no hint of the anger he possessed when they last met.

"I was going to thank you properly when I next saw you," Akari replies, wondering how he expects her to repay him. "I just never thought I would..."

"Is that for your mother?" the Andelovian boy asks.

Akari nods as she dips her eyes to the silver moonstone ring.

He takes a quick but careful look at the ring before pivoting back to her. "It's beautiful. Well, she must be an amazing lady. The two of you must be very close."

"She is. And we are." Akari wonders if it's envy she senses in his voice. She glances at him and finds his penetrating eyes staring into hers, as though he's trying to figure her out. She shifts nervously under the intensity of his gaze.

The Andelovian boy turns his attention to the antiques surrounding them, likely sensing her unease. Akari uses his distraction as a chance to study him instead. The previous times they met, it had either been too distant, too dark, or too dangerous.

The Andelovian boy is devastatingly dashing, his dark, magnetic eyes set above gently protruding cheekbones and a seductively angular jawline. Tall and sinewy, his fine physique alludes to his exceptional combat skills. His wavy raven hair is braided from both sides of his head down the back, and a few strands of loose fringe sweep across his forehead and cheeks, framing his handsome face. This hairdo, one too elaborate for the outskirts, hints at his Andelovian origins.

But even if his hair doesn't give him away, his clothes definitely do. His elegant, snow-speckled, midnight blue cloak—the same one he wore in the glade—cascades from his shoulders. Beneath it, his smart navy robe, a shade lighter than his cloak, is cinched in with a black leather belt holding his sword. Even as he stands casually, the well-groomed and well-dressed Andelovian boy is conspicuously out of place in Cheyvelenia.

Although everything about him looks strangely foreign, much to her chagrin, Akari finds herself drawn to his alluring presence. Just as she's least expecting it, he catches her looking. Her eyes instantly veer down to find her battered boots, and she self-consciously wishes they were a little less abused, as with the rest of her clothes.

In hope of diffusing the awkwardness, Akari lifts her chin, quickly saying, "Well... thank you for saving my life that day in Casserica."

"You'll just have to owe me one then," he replies facetiously.

"I..." Akari opens her mouth to protest but falters, giving up almost immediately when she meets his gaze. She is reminded of the eight-year-old Andelovian boy in her dreams from a few nights ago.

"Forgive me, I never got to introduce myself the previous times we met. I'm Yong Lee," he says with a charming smile and holds out his hand. "And as you probably already know, I'm from the capital."

Yong... Have I heard this name before? "Have we met?" Akari blurts as she shakes his rough, dependable hand with her small, supple one, his touch erupting fireworks inside her. Yong's eyes are so familiar, so strangely comforting. Recalling her dream, she can't help but wonder if she knew him during her early childhood. *But what are the odds? Andelovia is sprawling, massive. It was probably just a dream—*

"In my dreams, perhaps?" Yong suggests with a straight face.

Akari's eyes widen in surprise—shock, even—as she wonders if his dreams are anything like hers. *Could we really have been childhood playmates back in Andelovia?* He chuckles softly to himself, eyes flickering with amusement. Realizing what he must be thinking, Akari purses her lips.

Yong quickly straightens up. "I'm sorry," he says sincerely, though a hint of a smile lingers on his lips. "I didn't mean it like that. To answer your question, this is our third time seeing each other in the outskirts, with the meeting in the glade being the first, and the fight when Zatori returned being the second."

Although Akari is surprised to hear that Yong recognizes and remembers her from their distant encounter in the glade, she doesn't let it show. "You know what they say—*Once is happenstance. Twice is coincidence. Thrice is enemy action.*" She eyes him suspiciously.

"Really? The one I've heard is—*Once is happenstance. Twice is coincidence. Thrice is fate,*" Yong muses with a lopsided smile.

Akari finds her lips curving upward slightly and quickly straightens them. Recalling the mission Salam entrusted her with—and out of her own curiosity—she asks, "So, what's brought you to the outskirts?"

"I'm a trader who serves Andelovian patrons, sourcing merchandise from all over, even the outskirts," he answers smoothly, evidently well practiced, as though he knows people will ask.

"Merchandise? What kind of merchandise?" Akari is unable to imagine that the outskirts would hold anything of value to the Andelovians, given their lavish tastes.

"Whatever their hearts desire." His reply is deliberately ambiguous.

"Have you found what you're looking for?" Akari presses.

Yong looks directly at her as he says, "Some of it."

Akari finds herself lost in his dark eyes. Yong's startlingly good looks seem almost as dangerous as his exceptional fighting skills. It takes a moment for her to pull herself together.

"How did you get across the Great Divide?" she finally asks.

"My patrons... they belong to—they *are*—Andelovian society..." Yong speaks slowly, carefully choosing his words. "For people like that, getting across the Great Divide isn't an issue."

"Do you mean people like Lord Vykroux?" Akari mentions the one Andelovian aristocrat she's heard of.

"Those of that type. They'd run in the same circles."

Given Yong's vague answer, she senses she isn't going to get names from him. "So, it wouldn't be impossible for me to cross the Great Divide?" Akari asks instead.

"Not if you were with me," Yong clarifies with a smile.

So, you just need to know the right people... Akari straightens up, sure that any information will be useful for Salam, but she still has more she needs to find out. "Are you looking for other merchandise here in Cheyvelenia?" she probes.

"Akari," Yong says, taking her pleasantly by surprise. The sound of her name is especially sweet in his deep, velvety voice. "I'm here in the outskirts precisely for that. Once I've found what I'm looking for, I can't linger."

"Right..." she says, pondering when that day will come, and if it will matter to her. Akari shakes off the thought, not wanting to be distracted by his hypnotic presence. "So, what were you doing at the abandoned farmhouse?"

"We were passing by while looking for merchandise in Casserica, but we got caught in the fight." His words sound plausible, but she isn't sure she believes him. His presence when she was at Philippe's mercy seemed an unlikely coincidence.

"You fight well. Very well... Almost too well for a trader..." Akari points out.

"Well, we're the best in our trade. With all the bandits and pirates, we need to take great care to protect our merchandise," Yong replies. She is still debating whether to take his word when he adds, "You're not too bad yourself at fighting. You just don't really seem to have the heart to kill, or even hurt anyone for that matter."

Akari struggles to hide her discomfort. "And do you... have the heart for it?" she asks apprehensively. "Did you always have it?"

Yong hesitates before giving a nonchalant shrug. "I'm not sure. It's hard to say. But when duty calls, I act."

After a long pause, Akari finally musters the courage to ask, "Is that why you said you knew how it felt to hurt a comrade?" Their encounter at the farmhouse plays in front of her.

This time, his eyes dart around nervously, as though he's been caught off guard. "You do pay attention, don't you?"

"Not any more than you do," she counters.

"Well, let's just say there was a time when I was in a position where I had to choose one of my two... comrades to give up."

"Oh..." Akari's eyes widen in shock. She can't imagine how she would react in a similar circumstance. Incapable of finding the right words, she stares down in silence again.

"Are you alright?" Yong asks, his eyes filled with concern. "After the mission, when Zatori returned..."

"Could be better," she admits, taking a deep breath. "That was my first mission."

"It must have been especially hard for you." His voice is empathetic but strained.

Akari registers his pain. "It must have been hard for you too."

"Coming to the decision wasn't hard," Yong says, though his tone is somber. "Following through on it was. And living with it has been the hardest of all."

She looks at him intently, wondering exactly what decision he had to make.

"Well, enough about me," Yong says with a clap. "You've asked too many questions. Now it's my turn..." He pauses for a moment, and then his voice turns tentative as he asks, "What are you going to do now that Zatori and the Harvesters know you're gifted?"

"I'm going to fight them," Akari says shakily. "This time, I'll protect my mother with my own hands. Just as she protected me ten years ago."

Yong's fine features contort into an appalled expression. "Did the two of you encounter Zatori before? Was that during the Great Harvest?"

Akari nods, despite having promised her mother to keep this a secret.

"This is even more dangerous than I expected," Yong murmurs.

"I have the People's Protector with me."

"They can't be with you forever," he counters. "This is ultimately a battle you'll have to fight alone."

"Well, then when the time comes, I guess I'll do what I have to do." Akari speaks with as much conviction as she can muster, although she isn't entirely convinced herself. *I'm still as much a danger to those I love as I am to my enemies.*

Yong seems to read her mind. "You're afraid of your gift, aren't you? And even more so now Zatori's back..."

She looks down once more, afraid of acknowledging her own fear. "I just don't want to hurt anyone again—especially not anyone on my side."

"It's a powerful gift. It's alright to be afraid." Yong's tone has a soothing quality. "But do you really want it gone?"

"No... But I've tried controlling it. It doesn't work, and it's not going to work..." Akari spreads her arms, and almost flings the ring again in frustration.

"Trust me, it will work," he says encouragingly. "But you won't be able to control your gift unless you stop being afraid of it."

"What do *you* know?" she challenges. "Surely you can't be gifted too?"

Yong releases a chuckle. "You do know gifts are incredibly rare, don't you? You're special, Akari."

She just shakes her head. "I'm not..."

"That's the way I see it, at least," Yong replies, smiling. "But anyway, you'd better get going. I don't want to hold you up any longer."

"Right... I hope you find what you're looking for..."

"I'm getting there," he says optimistically. "Till we meet again."

"If we even meet again," she points out.

"We will." Yong flashes a lopsided smile. "You still owe me one for saving your life. Maybe I should start keeping count."

Akari returns a shy smile and heads for the exit.

♦

As soon as the door closes behind her, Yong makes his way to the counter, where Mr. Tinkler is dozing.

"How can I help you today?" the storekeeper asks with a sleepy wink. "Or did you already find what you were looking for?"

Yong's eyes grow wide with surprise, but he doesn't comment, and neither does Mr. Tinkler probe. As a moment of silence ensues, he is unsure if the storekeeper has fallen asleep again.

"That ring the girl just left with—it couldn't have been twenty-two bronzes," Yong finally says, eyeing Mr. Tinkler carefully.

"It wasn't. And I never said that," he clarifies, barely awake. "It was twenty-two silvers."

Yong furrows his brow, unable to comprehend the storekeeper's business sense. "That's two hundred and twenty bronzes. And you let her have it for ten?"

Mr. Tinkler shrugs drowsily. "It belonged to the Miyaharas to begin with... And besides, that girl, Akari—she's special, like you said. I like her. Don't you too, young lad?"

Yong's cheeks flush red as he fumbles for words. But before he can form an answer, Mr. Tinkler has already drifted back into a deep slumber.

◆

It's snowing lightly outside Tinkler's, and all of Cheyvelenia is blanketed in fresh white. Akari makes her way to the very north of this northernmost town, where the land falls away into the ashen cliffs that overlook the frozen ocean and the distant Hollow—an abyss left behind when the White Blaze destroyed Moira Island.

Ty is already waiting for her at the edge of these cliffs, better known as the Verge. They rise in striking formations, their rugged edges softened by layers of snow, their surfaces etched with timeworn striations that whisper of ages past. Though imposing in stature, they aren't unwelcoming, instead standing as steadfast sentinels over the frosted world below.

The Telos Ocean, locked in ice, stretches endlessly toward the horizon in a vast expanse of gray-green and white. This rare phenomenon, made possible by the ocean's extraordinarily low salt levels, transforms the waters into an unbroken, shimmering tundra every winter. It is punctured by the Hollow, its rim framed by the Hollow Falls—great icy cascades formed a decade ago when the ocean froze solid as it gushed in. Strangely, the falls have never melted, not even in summer when the rest of the ocean thaws. Over the years, curious explorers have ventured into the Hollow, eager to uncover the truth of Zatori's supposed demise—but none have ever returned.

"It's been a while since we came here," Akari says, glancing at Ty.

The Verge has always been their special place—a perch above the world where they'd spent countless hours as children talking, playing, laughing, crying, dreaming. They'd once chased each other along the cliffs' edge, their footsteps kicking up frost and dust, their voices echoing into the endless sky. But ever since Ty joined the People's Protector, and especially after Akari followed suit, their visits have grown few and far between. Now, being here together again feels like a rare occurrence, a sliver of solace.

"It seemed like you needed to get away from everything for a bit. From your home, Moonstone, and the Quartz... I thought you might like to come here since you said you missed the old times." Ty grins and lobs a snowball lightly in her direction.

Akari hops to avoid it, and it lands on her boot and crumbles. She kicks some snow back at him, laughing light-heartedly—her first genuine laughter in a while. Eventually, they take their usual seats at the edge of the cliff.

"You won't believe who I just ran into," Akari begins.

"Who? Weilcox? Mole rat and blobfish?" Ty chortles at his own joke.

Akari giggles but shakes her head. "It was the Andelovian boy," she says. "He's here in Cheyvelenia. His name is Yong."

"What is *he* doing here?" Ty asks suspiciously.

"Yong is a trader searching for merchandise in the outskirts for patrons in the capital," Akari shares. "I ran into him at Tinkler's."

"I told you, these can't merely be coincidences! Especially not with Zatori's return." Ty scoops up a snowball and throws it over the cliff. Akari watches it tumble out of sight, imagining it hitting the rocks and crumbling on the way down, each action caused by what came before. "There must be something the Andelovian boy is after. What do you think he's looking for?"

She shrugs. "I don't know. I never thought there would be anything in the outskirts deemed worthy enough by those in the capital. I thought things like that were already in Andelovia."

Ty scratches his head. "Well, Salam wants us to find out what brought the Andelovians to the outskirts. Whatever it is, it can't be for anything good," he concludes presumptuously. "And what were *you* doing at Tinkler's? You haven't decided to really work there now that Zatori has returned, have you?"

Akari scowls at his teasing tone as she pulls out the silver moonstone ring.

"What's that?" he asks.

"Something I got for my mother," she replies. "Do you remember, when I was a lot younger, I promised myself that when I grew up, I'd do everything for my mother that my father couldn't do for her all these years? And now I'm finally able to do something." She twists the ring in her hands, admiring it anew. "It's beautiful, isn't it? And it's something I can imagine her wearing. I know it'll never compare to the ones she used to wear in the capital, but it'll do for now."

Ty takes the silver moonstone ring from Akari, scrutinizing it with squinting eyes. "Is this expensive?"

"Yes, very. I spent half the money Madam Salam gave me on it, but it's worth even more. I got a good deal on it."

"I love expensive things. But what's the point of this?" Ty enquires, genuinely clueless. "It can neither be used nor eaten."

Akari snatches the ring back, rolling her eyes. "Not everything's meant to be used or eaten."

"I didn't know you like these kinds of things." He scratches his head again.

Akari shrugs. "They just remind me a little of Andelovia."

He makes a face at the mention of the capital, but says, "I'm sure Madam Mari will love it. Your mother would love anything you give her."

"I don't want to give her just anything," Akari interjects. "I want to give her something special—something I can be proud of."

"You know you can be! That looks like a pretty good ring to me. It's very shiny," Ty says as reassuringly as he can manage. "Your mother will be proud of you."

"I'm not sure about that. She doesn't even know I'm part of the People's Protector," Akari laments as she puts the ring back into her pocket. "You know, I saw Ethan the other day and he was completely well. My mother healed him using her gift. Apparently, she's been healing the Protectors for a while now... without my knowledge."

"Really?" Ty's ocean blue eyes grow wide with surprise.

"Yes." Akari throws a snowball this time. "My mother, who wouldn't hear of me joining the People's Protector."

"I'm sure Madam Mari meant that she doesn't want you *fighting* for the People's Protector. And she does have a point..."

Akari's gaze drifts down to her boots, dangling over the edge of the cliffs, as the memory of wounding Ethan resurfaces.

"That's not what I meant..." Ty quickly clarifies. "Your mother just wants you to be safe."

"I know..." She lets out a long sigh, gathering more snow and tossing it down the Verge. "Well, I'm safe now that Salam has suspended me from combat missions until she deems fit. She's been training me to control my gift... but it hasn't been going very well..." A frown creeps onto Akari's face as she adds, "I guess it'll be a while before I'm in peril again."

"Don't speak too soon," Ty says light-heartedly. But before she can scowl at him again, he turns serious. "Have you ever thought of searching for your complement? Maybe it could help you control your gift."

"My complement?"

"Yes, a complement is an object that a gifted shares a special connection with. It will enhance its wielder's gift and protect their life," Ty explains, evidently proud of his knowledge. "Possessing a complement will help hone your ability."

"I know what they're supposed to do. But complements just exist in children's stories." She knits her eyebrows.

"No. They exist for real," he maintains. "Don't you know people once thought that gifts only existed in children's stories too?"

"Yes, I've heard about that," Akari concedes. "But how do you know complements exist for real? Have you ever seen a gifted use one before?"

"No, I haven't... But my mother told me about them a long time ago—before... before she turned mad..." he says. "She couldn't have been wrong about it."

Although Akari fully appreciates his intention, she still has some reservations. "How will I know if a particular object is my complement?"

Ty shrugs. "My mother said you're supposed to feel it... although I'm not sure how exactly..."

"And how am I supposed to go about finding it?" she asks.

"That, I have no clue at all..."

They look out at the frozen Telos Ocean in silence for some time, scuffing more snow down the cliff every now and then. *A complement is probably too good to be true*, Akari thinks, although a small flame of hope ignites tenuously at the back of her mind.

"Do you remember how, when we were children, we made a promise that if either of us fell into the Hollow, the other one would come to the rescue?" Ty reminisces after a while.

"Well, I don't have to worry about that. You wouldn't even get anywhere close," Akari teases. "Do you remember when we ice-skated on Telos and raced each other to the Hollow, despite knowing it was too far away by a long shot? It was always you chickening out first, not long after each race had begun!" Her laughter peals through the wintry air.

"I can't help that I'm so tall. It doesn't help with ice-skating," Ty protests, glancing at his awkward, lanky limbs.

"Excuses! You only started chickening out after you claimed to have seen an archivian flying out from the Hollow, forging into his human form as soon as he landed on the ice." Akari nudges him with her elbow. "Don't you know archivians have long been extinct?"

"I swear I did see one!" Ty insists stubbornly.

"You were imagining things!" she counters. "There was nothing when I looked. Nothing! Not a dragon—or even a human!"

"It got all hazy and frosty the moment you looked!"
Akari breaks into fresh laughter.

"You're never going to take me seriously, are you?" He grimaces.

"No," she confirms, only half joking.

"Akari, there's something I've been wanting to tell you," Ty says after a deep inhale.

"What is it?"

He looks into Akari's eyes for an answer, but all she can give him is a worried look which, lately, has been there too often. Flashing a goofy grin, he tosses a snowball at her shoulder, whooping, "I got you!"

He leaps to his feet to make a run for it. Akari hurls a snowball at him, hitting him squarely in the rear. She bursts into giggles. "Thanks for getting me to come to the Verge again today, Ty. I really do miss the old times."

"Is this how you thank someone?" he demands light-heartedly, yet deliberately aiming wide as he lobs a snowball back in her direction.

"Just you," Akari says with a playful smile, but her heart is grateful.

Even if the whole world is changing—even if Zatori is back harvesting gifts, or the Andelovians are infiltrating the outskirts—our friendship is never going to change.

7. Presents

The winter days are short and cold, but snow-draped Cheyvelenia glistens gloriously under the sparing midday sunlight. Akari is perched on a tall stool by the counter in Moonstone Apothecary, meticulously picking out the wilted and discolored leaves from a bundle of herbs.

She looks up as Mari enters, the whites of the snow and ribbon in her hair accentuating the subtle blush on her porcelain cheeks and nose. After waiting all morning for her, Akari jumps up excitedly at her return.

"Mama, I have something for you," she announces brightly as her mother rubs her nose, which twitches in the cold.

Mari makes her way to the counter. "What's the occasion?" she asks, eyeing her daughter curiously.

"It's not the occasion that's special. It's you who's special, Mama," Akari chirps. "You've always been the one giving me everything in life. I want to do the same for you too, especially now I've started earning my keep."

"Oh, Akari, my baby... that's really sweet of you, although you really didn't have to do anything," Mari says with a loving smile. "You know I don't need anything else—I just need you to be safe."

"I know. But I've always wanted to give you something special." Akari pulls out the ring she bought from Tinkler's and holds it out. "I got this present for you."

Mari gasps at the sight of the silver ring with the oval moonstone.

"Try it on, Mama," Akari urges, taking her mother's hand and slipping the ring on her index finger.

The exquisite moonstone ring reflects a soft white glint under the winter sunlight. Mari's gaze fixates on the ring, as though she's in disbelief that such beauty could be hers. After all, it's been ten long years since she has worn anything remotely this beautiful.

"It fits perfectly, like it was always meant to be there." Akari beams proudly. The way the ring sits splendidly on her mother's finger is exactly as she'd pictured.

"Yes, indeed... Thank you, Akari, my baby..." Mari says, her thoughts wandering. When she finally finds her way back to reality, she asks, "Where did you find this?"

"Tinkler's."

"And where did you get the money for something like this?" Akari is unable to tell if her mother is suspicious.

"From working at Tinkler's," she answers, making sure her expression hides any nervousness. "Besides, Mr. Tinkler gave me a good deal."

Mari seems too distracted to notice.

"Mama?" Akari calls out, sensing her mother isn't herself. "Is anything wrong?"

"No, nothing at all. It's perfect... I love it... I can't believe you picked this out... It's... it's beautiful beyond words... I've not seen anything quite like this in a while," Mari gushes, admiring the ring on her hand. She seems ineffably touched, a glimmer of tears skimming her eyes. "Thank you, Akari, my baby. I heart you with all my love." She scoops Akari up in a warm, tight embrace.

"Me too, Mama. I heart you with all my love too," Akari says despite struggling to fathom what's on her mother's mind. There are times she seems so far away, as though she's at the other end of the kingdom, back in Andelovia.

After Mari releases her, Akari watches her mother make her way into the consultation room to set her things down. Mari pauses, casting yet another glance at the ring before finally heading upstairs.

Shaking her head in confusion, Akari resumes her rhythmic plucking of the leaves. Just as she's getting lost in her thoughts, a young farmer boy, whose family owns the most adorable dog Akari has ever seen, bursts into the apothecary in tears.

"Help! Help!"

Akari springs up from behind the counter and rushes to him. "Don't cry," she coaxes, gently patting his back. "What's wrong?"

"It's my grandfather!" he explains between sobs, his eyes laced with fear. "He fell and he can't move."

"I'll get my mother to go with you. She's a healer and she'll help your grandfather," Akari reassures him. When she starts up the stairs, Mari, having heard the commotion, is already making her way down.

"Let me get my things," she says composedly, the razor-sharp focus in her eyes a stark contrast to the distant expression she wore just moments ago.

From the consultation room, Mari grabs her bulging satchel stuffed to the seams with medical supplies and swiftly re-emerges. "I'll go have a look at his grandfather. Akari, please watch the shop in the meantime."

"Yes, Mama," Akari assures with a nod.

"I'll be back as soon as I can. Be safe while I'm gone, alright?" Mari plants a quick kiss on her forehead. Before she can reply, her mother is out the door with the boy.

Akari tiredly plops herself back on the tall stool, ready to resume her work. But another visitor—this time, one who looks glaringly out of place—enters Moonstone Apothecary.

Akari scans him from head to toe, taking in his braided raven hair, dark crescent-moon eyes, and midnight blue cloak. *Yong!*

"What are *you* doing here?" she blurts in surprise, hardly believing her eyes. Of all the places in Cheyvelenia, he has found his way to her mother's apothecary.

Yong lets out a chuckle. "Is *this* how you greet your patrons? Or is this just how you greet me?"

"I've just been seeing a lot of you lately," Akari remarks, trying to act indifferent. "Well... welcome to Moonstone Apothecary. What brings you here today?"

"Moonstone Apothecary..." Yong murmurs as he looks around, carefully taking it all in.

Akari tracks his gaze until it drifts back to meet hers.

"I'm looking for some herbs. These ones, specifically," he says, handing her a list.

Akari glances through it, and then reads it once more, carefully, digging her nails into her palm as she thinks. *This is... These ingredients are...* When she tears her gaze from the writing, the piece of parchment is crumpled where she gripped it too tightly.

"What's wrong?" Yong asks.

Akari takes a hard look at him. "Is someone dying?"

"What do you mean?" His dark eyes go wide with shock.

"These exceedingly rare and potentially life-threatening herbs are used to concoct the yuriq brew, an ancient medicine used to sustain the life of a dying person," she informs him.

"Are you sure?"

"I'm positive," Akari says with quiet confidence. "Judging by the list of herbs, their quantities, and the order they've been written in—which coincides perfectly with the order the herbs are added in this brew—I'm sure I'm right." In fact, she and her mother handpick all these herbs, most of which can only be found in the outskirts, on their monthly herbal treks. With the Great Divide, the Andelovian apothecaries must be hard-pressed to stock them.

"Aren't there other brews that use similar ingredients?" Yong asks anxiously.

"The only other one is its sister concoction, the tanrine brew, another ancient medicine used to rouse an insentient being. They're both incredibly tricky to concoct, but to make the tanrine brew, the last herb would be different." Akari says, glancing at the list again. Mari was the one who taught her everything to know about herbalism, and she has never been wrong. "If these ingredients aren't to keep a dying person alive, what did you think they were for?"

"I didn't assume anything. It's not my place to do that," Yong replies flatly, his expression now carefully neutral.

Akari isn't convinced by his apparent lack of curiosity. "Who is the yuriq brew meant for?"

"A patron." Yong's answer is deliberately ambiguous, and Akari knows she won't get more even if she presses further.

"I'll also take the last herb needed for the second brew you mentioned," he adds as an afterthought. "Who knows? It may come in handy someday."

"Let me warn you, these herbs are going to be expensive," Akari says, but he waves her words away casually.

"Money will be no object."

Why did I even bother saying that to an Andelovian? Unused to this answer—one an outskie would never give—Akari takes another look at Yong's luxurious getup. "I'll get them for you. Please wait a moment."

She picks out different herbs from various drawers and jars, wrapping them in separate brown paper packages. Although her hands are busy, she can't help but ask, "Why would they do this?"

"What do you mean?" Yong asks, a puzzled expression creasing his features.

"Subjecting anyone to such pain would mean a life that's worse than death," Akari says, and shakes her head in bewilderment.

His face blanches.

"I guess you didn't know that..." Akari winces as she wraps another herb. "The yuriq brew sustains the life of a dying person at a cost—they'll suffer unbearable pain for every additional moment they live."

It takes a moment for this to sink in. "I can only guess he's waiting for something—or someone—before he dies..." Yong breathes. "He's still holding on to some kind of hope..."

"Well, I hope whatever—or whoever—it is, is worth the wait," Akari says quietly, unable to imagine what having her life sustained by the yuriq brew would feel like. "And the pain."

"It will be." Yong's voice is both effortlessly assuring and alluring.

Just as Akari is about to reply, the dainty Andelovian girl bursts into the apothecary, her fiery red hair blazing behind her. A cloying scent, with notes of flowers Akari is certain aren't native to the outskirts, drifts in alongside her. This time, she has traded her clunky armor for some egregiously flashy Andelovian-style robe, a shade of mint so striking that it takes the most courageous of souls to wear it. The pleats and gathers on her clothing flutter erratically behind her as she makes her entrance.

"I couldn't find any of the—" she rattles off before catching Yong's warning eye, stopping mid-sentence. She hastily glances over at Akari, who notices but carries on packing the herbs. "I couldn't find... what we were looking for," the girl says instead. "The stores in the outskirts are shockingly poorly stocked. And Cheyvelenia is the smallest and worst of them all. Everything here is old and worthless. They won't have what we're looking for," she exclaims tactlessly, frustration threading through her voice.

"We'll just have to look harder," Yong states simply.

"How do we even know if they're in the outskirts?" she challenges. "Or in Cheyvelenia?"

"Nothing's for sure. We won't know until we've found them. We'll just have to look harder." He speaks with an underlying authority, and the girl throws her hands up.

"Yes, *sir*," she replies exasperatedly. "Did you manage to get the herbs?"

"Yes." Yong nods, glancing at Akari.

When the Andelovian girl finally takes a proper look at her, her emerald eyes flicker in recognition. "Isn't she the girl from the People's Protector... from that night Zatori returned?" she asks with distaste.

She is right here, Akari thinks, as Yong casts the Andelovian girl a pointed look.

"Emeraude, this is Akari Miyahara. Her mother owns Moonstone Apothecary. Akari, this is Emeraude Eleaconde, my assistant trader."

Akari smiles politely at Emeraude, who returns a curt, unsmiling nod. Cold and snobby, the girl embodies everything Akari imagined an Andelovian would be. Without further prompting, she senses right away that Emeraude isn't fond of her—or perhaps anything related to the outskirts. She keeps her head down and her eyes fixated on her hands as she finishes wrapping up the herbs, still feeling Emeraude's icy stare boring through the top of her head.

When Akari is done, she hands the packages of herbs to Yong. His hand momentarily brushes hers, and blood rushes to her cheeks while a tingling sensation spreads through her. He quickly takes the packages and withdraws his hand, seemingly just as aware of Akari's touch. At the side, Emeraude quietly tracks all their interactions with subdued hostility.

Yong doesn't seem to notice as he pays Akari what would usually be several months' earnings for the shop. "Thank you for the herbs."

"I should be the one thanking you." Akari runs a finger over the unfamiliar silver nugget amongst the bronzes. Lately, she has been holding a lot more money than she's used to.

Yong shakes his head. "Till we meet again."

"If we even meet again." Akari isn't so sure this time.

"I've already told you we will." He flashes a lopsided smile. "You still owe me one for saving your life. And just so you know, I've decided to start keeping count."

Without waiting for a response, he turns and heads for the door. Emeraude shifts her glance from Akari to Yong and follows wordlessly behind him.

♦

After what seems like an impossibly long day, Akari is alone in Moonstone Apothecary yet again. She takes time to sweep the floor, clean the counter and shelves, complete a stock-take of the herbs and medical supplies, and finally check the account book. When she's finally done, she falls back onto the stool, slumping across the counter.

Akari has been so preoccupied that she only just notices that her mother hasn't returned, even though the sun is setting. *What's taking Mama so long?* She goes around the counter and looks out into the sleepy street, but Mari is nowhere in sight. After pacing around mindlessly for a bit, she eventually gives up and heads upstairs.

When Akari reaches the landing on the second floor, something catches her eye. The corner of a crisp white envelope peeks out from under the floorboard right outside their bedrooms. She blinks, puzzled, thinking her eyes are playing tricks on her. But after lighting a lamp, she realizes they've made no mistake.

Akari pulls out the envelope with the utmost care, and the floorboard unexpectedly comes loose with it. When she pushes it aside, it reveals a rectangular hole in the floor—a secret hiding place!

Akari gasps. *How is it possible that I've never known about this despite living here for the past ten years? What could possibly be hidden in here?*

When she brings the lamp closer, she's astounded by the sight of a familiar golden box lying within it. *Could this be the very same one?*

Despite her apprehension, Akari picks it up and inspects it thoroughly. The intricate mandala pattern carved on it is exactly as she remembers. Akari's heart palpitates wildly as she lifts the lid. Inside lies a dark gold necklace with a deep red, teardrop-shaped jewel.

She gasps again. *It's the present from Papa for my sixth birthday! But Mama said it was lost when we escaped the White Blaze. Why is it here? Was it never missing this whole time?*

Akari reaches out a trembling hand to touch the jewel. It emanates a soft red glow, and a pulse of energy surges through her body. She recoils, but quickly realizes there's neither pain nor discomfort. On the contrary, she feels invigorated and empowered—the same overwhelming, dizzying rush of energy she experienced during her first-sighting ten years ago. Her eyes grow wide in surprise, her brow furrowing in confusion.

Unable to find an answer to what the necklace is doing to her, Akari shifts her focus. She studies the weighty white envelope, running a finger over its clean edges. The words *Mari Miyahara* have been written in a spidery, cursive script on the back. *Who could this letter be from? I never knew Mama was corresponding with anyone—that she even had anyone to correspond with. Could it be from... Salam?* However, the wiry handwriting doesn't look like it belongs to the bulky bear lady. A knot tightens in Akari's stomach.

She turns the envelope to the front, noticing how the orange wax seal has already been broken. This means two things—Mari has already read the letter and, more importantly, she won't find out if Akari does the same. Although she knows it isn't her place to pry, a rash impulse and a burning curiosity overcome her. She lifts the flap of the envelope and removes the letter, hesitating briefly before reading it.

Dearest Mari,

Every single day I wait to hear from you feels like an eternity. How are you and Akari? I've still been the same after all these years—neither dead nor truly alive.

It seems to me that Akari has grown up well and that she takes after you, for which I'm glad.

I've sent along some telmezia tea with this letter. I hope it helps you seek solace in memory of better times.

Yours truly,
Xavier Vykroux

Akari reels in shock and disbelief. *Xavier Vykroux?*
Isn't Lord Vykroux—an Andelovian, of all people—the
one whose donation revived the People's Protector and
the one whose riches are second to only the king? How
does Mama know him? Why is she in correspondence
with him? Why has she not mentioned him previously?
Who is he to Mama? And to both of us?

She has always known there are things Mari dislikes
talking about—the capital and her father, for instance—
but she has always thought it's because they bring back
memories her mother wishes to forget. Not once has
Akari suspected Mari of keeping any secrets, much less
from her. *Why did Mama have to hide the necklace*—my
necklace—from me? And why hasn't she spoken of her
acquaintance with Lord Vykroux before? What is it that
I shouldn't know?

Cautious as Mari is, Akari realizes that perhaps it isn't
too surprising for her mother to have successfully kept
this hiding place a secret for the past ten years. Had it not
been for the farmer boy's urgent cries for help, Mari
wouldn't have hastily replaced the loose floorboard,
carelessly leaving the envelope peeking out—and Akari
would never have uncovered it.

The sound of the front door opening jolts her from her
thoughts. *Mama must be home!* In a hurry, Akari closes
the lid of the golden box and slides the letter back into
the envelope, before returning them to the secret hiding
place. As quickly and quietly as she can manage, she
replaces the loose floorboard and starts down the stairs.

Snowflakes speckle Mari's hair once again, matching
the white ribbon that holds it all from her face, now
pinker than the cold had made it earlier. As she places her

satchel carefully on the counter, her nose twitches and she rubs it to warm it up. Akari comes to a stop midway as she eyes her mother, trying to figure her out.

Mari lifts her head and catches her watching. "Akari, my baby, what are you doing there? Come on down. I have something for you!" Her excited voice snaps Akari out of her thoughts.

"What is it?" she asks curiously, continuing down the stairs and coming around to the counter.

Mari opens her satchel to reveal the most adorable puppy Akari has ever seen. Bright red fur coats the puppy's body, save for her white paws, snout, and chest. With her curly tail wagging and pointed ears pinned back, she lets out a heartwarming yelp and leaps into Akari's arms.

As she caresses her, the puppy gives her tiny body the mightiest wriggle and tries to lick Akari. She bursts into laughter, letting the puppy do as she pleases, before she sinks her face into the soft, warm fur and takes in the fresh puppy scent. For a moment, Akari forgets all about the necklace and the letter.

"Mama!" she cries gratefully. "I thought you said we were never going to get a dog! What made you change your mind?"

"This was the only payment the old farmer could afford for my visit. Their dog has just given birth to three puppies, and he made me take this one. Her name is Kami," Mari says with a smile.

"Kami..." Akari looks at the puppy's face. Somehow, there doesn't seem to be a more fitting name.

"Kami shall be my present to you for your sixteenth birthday, since it's right around the corner," Mari announces with pride. "She's a special gift for a special person for a special occasion."

"Thank you, Mama! This is the best present ever!" Akari exclaims elatedly before asking, "But didn't you say we might leave Cheyvelenia? What will we do with Kami then?"

"We'll bring her with us when we go, of course. I'm sure she'll prove useful on our journey." Mari embraces her daughter and the puppy tenderly. "I know we don't always agree about everything, but you know I'll always heart you with all my love right, Akari, my baby?"

Akari nods. "I heart you with all my love too, Mama."

When Akari looks from Kami to Mari, she notices, among the white ribbon and white snowflakes on her head, the very first strand of white hair she has seen on her mother. *It seems like age really is catching up with Mama... Where has all the time gone?*

She can't be more grateful to Mari for dedicating her youth to raise her, especially in trying times. But even so, Akari struggles to understand the reason her mother has been hiding secrets from her—even lying to her.

Her mind drifts back to the red jeweled necklace and the letter from Lord Xavier Vykroux, while Mari similarly appears lost in her own thoughts as she stares pensively at the silver moonstone ring on her finger.

8. Andelovians

Akari paces outside the storefront of Heavenly Bakery as she waits for Ty to arrive. He wishes to get a cookie before they head to the Quartz together for yet another day of training.

The door of the bakery swings open. Someone emerges in a hurry, bumps right into Akari, and gives a yelp of annoyance. "Watch where you're going!"

As she whips around, her frilled satin robe in a shocking shade of lime twirls with her dainty body. A trail of fiery red hair sweeps through the air, effusing the same unmistakable cloying Andelovian floral scent. *Emeraude.*

When Emeraude sees Akari, her pointy elfin features twist with shock, but she quickly rearranges her expression to a nonchalant one.

"Aren't you the girl from Moonstone Apothecary? And aren't you also the Protector girl whose ass was saved by Yong?" Emeraude asks, although she already knows the answer. "Fancy running into you again."

"Yes, you're right. They're both me," Akari says levelly, trying not to let her embarrassment show. "What are you doing here?"

"Not much. I was just looking around the bakery as I was passing by." She peers into the store once more before turning back to Akari. "Well, Cheyvelenia *is* the smallest of all the towns in the outskirts. There really isn't much around here," Emeraude remarks, an air of superiority about her.

Akari remembers her mission. *Yong has been closed off for the most part, but maybe I can wring some more information from his assistant.* "What brought you here?" she asks. "Didn't you and Yong come all the way to Cheyvelenia because there's something you want from here?"

"All you need to know is that we're bringing you business," Emeraude says haughtily. "Let me tell you, poking your nose where it doesn't belong is not going to do you any good. There are things you'll never understand."

What kind of things? Akari wonders.

Emeraude uses this opportunity to eye Akari from head to toe, starting with her face before taking in her tattered clothes and battered boots.

"How did you end up like *this*?" she asks, her voice laced with disapproval. "Weren't you originally from Andelovia too? Why would anyone move from the capital to the outskirts?"

"Didn't you just tell me not to poke my nose where it doesn't belong?" Akari counters, raising an eyebrow.

Emeraude narrows her emerald eyes.

"You must have heard that from Yong," Akari surmises, and wonders what else he's told her. "How has he been?"

"He hasn't been himself since he came to Cheyvelenia," Emeraude snaps frustratedly.

"What do you mean?" Akari asks, curious to hear more about what he's usually like. *Just for my mission*, she tells herself.

"Yong used to be such a stickler for the rules. But after coming to the outskirts, he seems to have developed a new penchant for bending them," Emeraude rants with dissatisfaction. "I don't even know who I'm working under anymore."

"You seem to know him very well," Akari notes.

To her surprise, Emeraude's eyes shift nervously and her face flushes almost as red as her hair. In this instant, Akari is positive Emeraude's feelings for Yong surpass mere admiration.

"Well, I've known him for three years now and he's never acted this way till we came to the outskirts," Emeraude says, hastily schooling her expression before she adds with a smirk, "Although, if it weren't for Yong bending the rules, you would certainly have been done for by now."

Akari stares down at her boots, pondering the truth in her words, when Ty finally makes his appearance. Taking just a single look at Akari, he immediately knows something isn't right.

"What's going on here?" he asks, eyeing Emeraude suspiciously. With her bizarre clothing, he needs no introduction to know she hails from the capital.

"Nothing," both Akari and Emeraude say simultaneously. They glance at each other, their eyes locking awkwardly for a brief moment, before quickly turning away.

"Another one that pokes his nose where it doesn't belong..." Emeraude mutters under her breath.

Ty catches a whiff of her nauseatingly sweet fragrance. He narrows his eyes in disgust and asks, "What's that smell?"

"*I* should be the one asking that question," Emeraude shoots back, scrunching up her face as though she's smelled something foul. "Who are you and what's this stench?"

He sniffs himself and reports, "I'm Tyler Kane and I smell normal, unlike you—"

She lets out a mocking bark of laughter. "Do you even know what normal is?"

"I know you're certainly not anything close to it," Ty counters pointedly, eyeing her outfit again.

A taunting smirk spreads across Emeraude's face as she fires back, "And I would say the same about you—by proper Andelovian standards, that is."

Ty takes another whiff of Emeraude and pretends to gag. She rolls her eyes.

"That's because I'm exceptional," she continues, "whereas you... you're not even ordinary."

Ty chortles, never having seen someone so shameless yet bold. He glances at the empty-handed Emeraude, asking, "Couldn't find anything that you like at Heavenly Bakery?"

"Not at all. I much prefer the ones in the capital," she says in a condescending manner. "Everything in here seems a little... scorched."

"That's why they're so good," he points out. "You wouldn't know until you've tried them—"

"You wouldn't think so if you knew better." Emeraude snickers. "Everything I've tried in the outskirts tastes a little... crude."

"Maybe you should try starvation instead, like most of the outskies," Ty snaps. "It can really grow your appetite—"

"And maybe you should try civilization, which is severely lacking in the outskirts," Emeraude shoots back. "It can really refine your taste."

Ty cuts her a glare. "Well, if you'd tried poverty, you would certainly have long been a goner—"

"We have to be on our way. We're late." Akari, eager to break up the squabble, urges her best friend to move with a tug on his sleeve. Emeraude wheels around sharply and heads on her way.

"What taste does the Andelovian girl speak of when she has the most ridiculous clothes?" he spits, thinking Emeraude is out of earshot.

To Ty's surprise, she twists back around and scans him from head to toe, taking in his torn shirt, ill-fitting pants, and holey boots. "What do *you* even know about fashion, outskie boy?"

"I know it can neither be used nor eaten!" he retorts defensively, eliciting a derisive snort from Emeraude before she struts off, the green frills of her robe billowing behind her.

"Come on, let's go." Akari nudges him and they step into the bakery, where the toasty aroma of freshly baked bread wafts toward them in greeting.

"That young lady doesn't seem to like you very much, does she?" Madam Celine, who has witnessed at least some part of their squabble, comments with a cackle.

"She doesn't seem to like your baked goods very much either," Ty spits, still salty from his spat with the Andelovian girl.

"Well, it doesn't matter so long as you do," Madam Celine points out, placing a paper box on the counter. "I have your order ready."

"Well, thank you," Ty mutters as he pays.

"What's in it?" Akari eyes the box curiously, surprised that he isn't getting his usual scorched sea-salt cookie.

"Your birthday cake!" he announces brightly. "Happy birthday, Akari!"

"Oh... Thank you," Akari says, confusion flickering on her face, before it finally sinks in that today is January tenth—her birthday.

"Did you think I would forget what day it is?" Ty asks. "Or did *you* actually forget your own birthday?"

Akari nods with an embarrassed laugh. She has been so preoccupied lately that despite reminders from Mari and Mr. Tinkler, it slipped her mind. "Yes, I did. But thanks for remembering, Ty."

He smiles widely. "You're most welcome."

"Happy birthday, my dear!" Madam Celine chirps.

"Thank you, Madam Celine."

"Time really flies, doesn't it? Has it been ten years since you and your mother came to Cheyvelenia?" she asks.

Akari nods.

"That's around the same time you opened your bakery here, wasn't it?" Ty recalls.

"Yes, indeed. Where has all the time gone?" Madam Celine remarks. "How old are you today, my dear?"

"I just turned sixteen," Akari says.

"What a wonderful age to be! Young, blossoming, ripe..." Madam Celine gushes excitedly.

"Well, thank you..." Akari looks around, anywhere but the baker's eager face. "You don't seem too bad yourself."

"Well, I may not be sixteen, but I do still have a lot to look forward to." Madam Celine gives an airy laugh.

"Are you finally getting hitched?" Ty asks jokingly.

She shoots him daggers. "You'll see, there'll be better things than that. Spring isn't far away, and it'll be the mark of new beginnings."

"It seems your injury is a lot better," Akari remarks, noticing that Madam Celine has done away with the bandage and the patch of tinted skin on her forearm appears to be healing well.

"It wasn't too serious to begin with." She flexes her fingers and quickly moves her arm down behind the counter.

"I'm glad... Well, we better get going. If not, we're going to be late," Akari says.

"Here, take it, Akari! It's for you!" Ty urges, beaming proudly as he puts the box in her hands.

"Thanks, Ty." Akari smiles gratefully, careful to keep it level. "Have a good day, Madam Celine," she says, and he holds the door open.

"I'm looking forward to your wedding!" Ty chimes as they leave, closing the door on Madam Celine's scowl.

As they make their way through the town, Akari asks, "Why can't you just be half decent to Madam Celine?"

"She was the one who started not being decent to me first!" Ty protests, his voice full of grievance.

"When? What has Madam Celine ever done to you?" Akari presses. "Except not let you linger at her storefront when you were a child..."

"She just looks like she could chuck me in her oven any time and scorch me alive," Ty answers with an incommensurate seriousness.

Akari releases an amused snicker. "Oh Ty, when will you ever grow out of it?"

"Never," he says firmly, flashing a goofy grin. "Just wait, one day you'll see I was right about her."

Akari sighs in resignation, turning her focus to the box in her hands. She lifts the lid and sees a ring-shaped cake decorated with icing.

"It's just like the ring you gave your mother, isn't it? Except this one is better. This one can be eaten!" he exclaims.

Akari bursts into laughter, almost rolling her eyes. "Well, I'm going to let you have some of it then!" she squeals playfully.

With lightning speed, she swipes some icing off the cake and blobs it on his nose. Both amused and satisfied with her work, she lets out a bright laugh.

Ty tries to lick the icing, but his tongue doesn't reach his nose. "That's a waste of perfectly good food. I'm going to make sure every bit of this goes into my belly. But before that..." He plants some icing on her nose in return.

Akari giggles and nudges him with her elbow. "Who are you and what have you done with Tyler Kane? He doesn't play with food. He eats it."

"I'm still going to eat it." He sticks his tongue threateningly toward her nose.

"Get away from me!" Akari places the box on the ground and dodges swiftly, before giving him a friendly shove. But a relentless Ty continues with his icing quest.

Peals of laughter ring through the air as they play-wrestle.

Eventually, he lets Akari win and places the box with her birthday cake back in her hands. "Make sure you finish every bit of that! If not, I'll do it for you," Ty warns with another grin that's quickly wiped off his face when something—someone—catches his eye.

When Akari looks up to see what he has noticed, she finds Yong watching them from the window of another antiques store across the street. He stands casually, his arms crossed in front of him. When their gazes meet, Yong smiles, uncrosses his arms, and strides over.

"Tell me that isn't at least a little bit scary," Ty remarks with a grimace.

"Come on, Ty... Yong isn't so bad," she says. "He's not like the other Andelovians."

"Well, we've only seen one other Andelovian around here of late. The girl is all bark and no bite. She may be infinitely more annoying, but the boy is undoubtedly much scarier." Ty grimaces as Yong approaches them. "He looks like he could actually bite."

Akari quietly ponders the truth in his words.

"How long do you think he's been watching us for?" Ty whispers.

"Not for very long," Yong replies as he reaches them, not giving Akari a chance to respond. "And I'm not very scary—at least I don't think so. Nor do I bite—for the most part." He holds out his hand. "I'm Yong Lee, by the way. You're Tyler Kane, aren't you?"

Ty flushes red, mortified that Yong has heard him. "Well, what a coincidence that we've just seen all the Andelovians in Cheyvelenia in one morning!" He ignores

Yong's hand, but Akari knows his bravado is a front to cover up the embarrassment.

"Why, did you see Emeraude too?" Yong asks, overlooking the sarcasm. "I was looking all over for her. She's never where I expect her to be these days."

"We saw her leaving Heavenly Bakery, but we don't know where she was headed," Akari offers, trying to ease the tension between the boys.

"The bakery? That's the last place I thought she'd be," Yong remarks, but doesn't dwell on it. "Is that from there too?" He lets out a chuckle, pointing at the icing on their faces.

"Yes, and as a matter of fact, it's Akari's birthday today," Ty informs him, throwing his arm around her shoulders. Embarrassed by his attempt to prove their friendship, Akari hurriedly wipes the icing off her nose.

Not taking any notice of this, Yong turns to her with a smile that touches his eyes. "Happy birthday, Akari. I wish you many happy returns."

"Thank you." She returns a shy smile, her heart feeling full.

"So, what do you wish for this year?" he asks before adding, half joking, "For the capital and the outskirts never to be apart?"

"The outskirts were abandoned!" Ty cuts in before Akari can respond. "We were left to fend for ourselves after King Alvaro handed the *Register of the Gifteds* to Zatori!" he hollers in resentment, finally having someone from the capital to vent at.

"Stop it, Ty! Yong didn't mean it—" Akari starts but is quickly drowned out.

"Do you know in Andelovia, you could be charged with treason and severely punished for saying this?" Yong stands a bit straighter and squares his shoulders.

"Well, welcome to the outskirts!" Ty exclaims scathingly. "Since the king abandoned us, I'm no longer his subject. He won't be able to punish me!"

"If you ever come to the capital, you should try that excuse and see if it works," Yong warns, his voice dry. "King Alvaro isn't a bad king, but one embroiled in testing circumstances. He has already done everything within his means, but sometimes, everything is still not enough."

Ty raises his eyebrows. "How is handing over the *Register of the Gifteds* to Zatori and giving up the gifteds in the outskirts doing everything within his means? How is building the Great Divide to keep us at bay doing everything within his means?" he challenges, never having met someone who thought of the world so differently to him. "The king has never treated the outskirts like a part of Xylon. He hasn't done everything within his means, and that's why it can never be enough!"

Yong chews his tongue. "He must have had his reasons," he says eventually.

"And what might they be?"

"It's not my place to speak of that."

"Haven't you ever suspected those were only excuses for King Alvaro's misdeeds?" Ty presses. Akari wants to disappear into her birthday cake, but she has to admit he has a point.

"Never," Yong answers with absolute conviction.

"Well, maybe you should learn to question your king!" Ty is shouting now, practically spitting his words.

"Or maybe you should learn to trust your king," Yong suggests levelly.

"He's not *my* king!" Ty spits.

They glare at each other until Yong shifts his gaze to Akari. "I won't hold up the two of you. Enjoy the rest of your birthday." With that, he stalks off before either of them can reply.

How is it possible for him to have such unwavering faith in such a terrible king? she wonders, but knows no one is going to change his mind. With a sigh, Akari trudges off in the opposite direction with Ty, toward the forested foothills outside town on their way to the Quartz.

"Have you started to warm to the Andelovians now?" Ty demands. "Or maybe just the Andelovian boy?"

"What do you mean? He saved my life," Akari says. "I don't want to owe him anything."

"Do you really think it's coincidence the Andelovians were there when Zatori returned? And that they're now here in Cheyvelenia? Have you ever wondered why they've appeared before you so many times lately?" Ty questions, not willing to drop his suspicions.

"They're traders from Andelovia. They're just looking for merchandise from the outskirts for their patrons in the capital." She wipes the bridge of her nose again, suspecting the cake mess is still plain to see despite her efforts to clean up. *Ty may have a point, but is it so wrong to want to trust Yong?* She reasons that his story does make sense.

"I've seen Yong at two antiques stores," she adds. "He must be after something he can't get in the capital, like the herbs he bought at my mother's shop."

149

"Something he can't get in the capital, like you?" Ty asks, stopping and folding his arms.

Akari scowls.

"I don't buy their claims," he continues. "Let me tell you, the two Andelovians can't be up to anything good! That's why Salam wants us to look into them."

"And getting into quarrels with them isn't going to help us find out anything we need to," Akari reminds him. "Ty, I know you hate King Alvaro almost as much as Zatori, but Yong and Emeraude were children like us during the Great Harvest. They didn't wish for the Three Greats either."

"That doesn't make either of them any more likable." Ty starts walking again, kicking fallen sticks to make his sulk more evident.

"I get that you have reservations about them." Akari sighs and follows. "But I have something more important to tell you."

"What is it?" Ty asks as he begins breaking off chunks of birthday cake and stuffing his face.

She tells him about the secret hiding place beneath the loose floorboard, the letter from Lord Vykroux to Mari, and the jeweled necklace her mother claimed had gone missing. When she's done, half the cake is gone.

"Ty, are you even listening? It's my birthday and I haven't even had my birthday cake yet! And now, there's not much of it left," Akari complains, her tone teasing.

"Yes, I'm listening. And the rest of the cake is yours," Ty says remorsefully, between bites. "I'm sorry, I was hungry."

"How are you always hungry?" Akari pretends to be annoyed but finds herself amused instead. When she finally starts eating, it tastes even better than she was expecting, with bits of preserved fruit embedded in the fluffy vanilla cake, topped with a mildly sweet icing.

"Why do you think my mother told me the necklace was lost when we were fleeing from the White Blaze? And why do you think she never mentioned that she's acquainted with Lord Vykroux?" Akari ponders distractedly.

"I haven't a clue," Ty says.

The two walk side by side, polishing off the last bits of the cake, until they reach the edge of the precipice.

"That jeweled necklace you mentioned... is it expensive?" Ty's eyes twinkle with curiosity.

Akari shoots him an incredulous look. "Is this the only thing you're actually curious about?"

He nods fervently, his face breaking into a goofy grin. He lifts his hand and rubs his fingers together as a sign of money.

She breaks out in laughter.

"That's it, Akari. Don't look so down on your birthday," Ty urges, grabbing her hand and jumping off the precipice with her. "Happy birthday!" he exclaims as they take the Leap of Faith.

"Thanks for the cake, Ty. I've got to run," she says, even before her feet touch the dark brown, quartzite floor of the Quartz. With ample experience using the gateway now, she makes a nimble landing, before rushing up the stairs and bounding down the hallways. When she bursts into the den-like office, Salam is already waiting for her.

"I expect greater punctuality from you, especially since time is against us!" her superior growls.

"Yes, Madam Salam! I'm sorry. I won't be late again," Akari says meekly.

"Apology accepted." Salam nods, softening her expression. "Oh, and happy birthday!"

"Thank you..." Akari takes a long breath in and out. Although taken by surprise by Salam's knowledge of her birthday, she's more relieved that she has been let off.

"Well, let's get started. We don't have time to waste," Salam commands.

Without any introduction, Akari is plunged into the realm of darkness once more. Fear grips her all over again. Before her eyes are given a chance to adjust, a bolt of violet lightning streaks through the air, striking her squarely in the chest and flinging her backward. She looks up to see Celestine slinking toward her.

Akari quickly gets to her feet and leaps lithely to avoid a successive bolt of lightning. With a single swift motion, she sidesteps Celestine, passing so close to her that for a moment, their faces are only inches apart. With a skillful slit of her kris, Akari cuts her mask free.

Underneath it, Celestine is so disfigured that Akari can't picture how she might have looked originally. Her entire face is marred by battle scars, leaving not a single patch of good skin. Akari reels in shock, unprepared for this gruesome sight.

"What's wrong? Is my face not what you were expecting? Is my devastating beauty so spellbinding?" Celestine trills with a deranged laugh.

Taking advantage of her lapse in focus, she grabs Akari, pressing her metallic talons against her neck. A bolt of violet lightning erupts from Celestine's talons, shooting through her. Akari is transported back to her first encounter with Celestine on Moira Island. The world starts morphing into a numbing violet blur, and she screams and squeezes her eyes shut.

"Focus!" Salam's gruff voice echoes throughout the illusion.

But Akari finds herself unable to do so. Another bolt of lightning flickers through her eyelids, catching her off guard. Akari snaps her eyes open and tries to dodge, but she isn't quick enough. It strikes her left shoulder, hurls her to the ground, and engulfs her in an inferno eerily reminiscent of the one at the abandoned farmhouse.

"Madam Salam, make it stop, please! Make it stop!" Akari screams as the violet flames crackle over her.

Silence falls in an instant and the fire dies out, giving way to darkness once more. Salam stands opposite her, a worried expression etched on her ursine face. "Why are you so distracted today?"

Thoroughly disappointed in herself, Akari, still trembling, remains quiet, her eyes lowering to her boots. As she stares at them, she racks her brain, searching for a way to better control her gift, and recalls a conversation she had with Ty.

When Akari finally looks up to meet her superior's gaze, she asks, "Do complements really exist?"

Salam's eyes grow wide with surprise, her brow furrowing. "Yes, they do, although they are beyond rare."

"What will happen if a gifted finds one?" Akari asks.

"They will be able to uncover the greatest potential of their gifts," Salam says. "Surely you aren't thinking about finding your complement to get you through the training, are you? While that seems like an easy way out, may I remind you that finding your complement is going to be far more challenging than excelling in your training—provided you focus."

"No... it's not that..." Akari denies anxiously, but her superior flashes a knowing smile, instantly putting her at ease.

"I just... really want to control my gift," she continues, wondering if her desperation is creeping into her strained voice. "I just want to be out there fighting Zatori and the Harvesters rather than doing it in an illusion." The shame and frustration of not being able to participate in combat missions have begun to weigh down on her.

"I know," Salam says empathetically. "But I can only let you go when you've proven that you're ready. I cannot simply send you to your death."

Akari sighs, her mind drifting to her real distraction. "Do you know Lord Xavier Vykroux?" she manages to ask.

This question seems to take Salam by even greater surprise. "King Alvaro's former grand advisor? The aristocrat from Andelovia whose donation revived the People's Protector?"

Akari nods.

"Well, I wouldn't say I know him, but I saw him around during my days in the Royal Regiment."

"What was he like?" Akari probes.

"The Vykrouxes have served the kings of the Ashgenov Empire for generations. Lord Xavier Vykroux was the childhood friend of King Alvaro. Growing up, they were inseparable—closer than blood brothers," Salam recalls. "But all of that was ruined when King Alvaro gave up the

Register of the Gifteds to Zatori ten years ago, causing Lord Vykroux to lose his wife and daughter during the Great Harvest. After that, things were never the same between them and they've since been nothing more than strangers."

The hairs on the back of Akari's neck stand on end. *Could Lord Vykroux possibly be my father? Could the wife and daughter he lost in the Great Harvest be Mama and me? Is Papa alive and well in Andelovia? Why did he abandon us in the outskirts? Why don't they want me to know who he is? Why do they want me to believe he's dead?* Endless questions run through her mind.

"What's become of him now?" Akari presses breathlessly.

"I've been gone from Andelovia for too long to know, but I've heard that following the death of his wife and daughter, he has grown reclusive, and few have seen him since," Salam answers.

"He's still alive then? In the capital?" she asks, struggling to contain her nervousness.

"I should think so."

"And are you certain his wife and daughter are dead?"

"There's no reason to believe otherwise," Salam replies, her brow furrowing. "Why are you asking all this?"

"I was wondering if Lord Vykroux could be one of the patrons whom the Andelovians in the outskirts are serving," Akari answers carefully, her words measured, as she finds herself treading close to dishonesty. "It seems they're traders sourcing merchandise in the outskirts for their patrons in the capital."

Salam ponders Akari's findings. "Is that why the Andelovians are here? I hear they've found their way to Cheyvelenia."

"Yes, I've seen them in town," Akari confirms. "They bought herbs from my mother's apothecary too—herbs for the yuriq brew. And the tanrine brew."

"Aren't these brews for those on the brink of death?" Akari nods.

"And aren't the herbs for those brews exorbitant?" She nods again.

"I guess that shouldn't come as a surprise, since they have very wealthy Andelovian patrons who can pay for those combat skills. The way they fight is highly unusual for mere traders though." Salam's claws clatter against each other as she tries to make sense of it all.

"They claim to be the best in their trade," Akari says. "And despite everything, there doesn't seem to be anything odd about the Andelovians."

"That's exactly the problem. The less suspicious they appear to be, the more suspicious they seem to me."

"What do you mean?" Akari asks.

"There haven't been any Andelovians in the outskirts in ten years. They must be here for something—something of significance," Salam remarks. "Getting across the Great Divide would have been difficult, even for them. We can't trust them without learning more. Do you know what else the Andelovians are looking for?"

"No, they won't say." Akari sighs before adding, "But I saw Yong, the Andelovian boy, in two antiques stores in Cheyvelenia. He has to be searching for an antique of some sort, although I have no idea what it might be."

"Then you'll have to find out," Salam says simply.

"But how do I do that?" Akari asks, frustration seeping through her voice. "I've tried asking but their lips are sealed."

"I never said anything about asking." Salam unleashes a rambunctious laugh.

"What am I supposed to do, then?"

"I have a mission for you, Akari," Salam announces, catching her completely off guard.

Akari's expression brightens up. "Does this mean I'm not suspended anymore?"

"No. You're still suspended from combat missions," her superior clarifies matter-of-factly. "But this one, I think you and Tyler can help with—with utmost discretion."

The light in Akari's face dims. "What do we have to do?" she asks warily.

"I hear the Andelovians are staying at the Colossal Inn in Hazenfeld," Salam says, enunciating her words carefully so there's no chance Akari will misunderstand her. "Your mission is to search their rooms."

9. Childhood Playmates

The sun sets a little later each day and the snow seems less relentless than before. Ty is on a mission in Yuxenia, an outskie town not too far from the Quartz, and Akari is alone with Kami today.

Since she's been suspended from combat missions, Ty has continued to go, and one thing has been crystal clear—since Zatori's return, the Harvesters have been steadily making their way northward through the outskirts. It seems like only a matter of time before they reach Cheyvelenia. However, Zatori himself has yet to make another appearance.

The suspense has been keeping the outskies on edge, any news of Zatori and the Harvesters throwing them into a state of frenzy. Each time Ty heads out on a mission, Akari worries that something might happen to him. But to her relief, he's made it back in one piece every time thus far.

Eager to get some peace and quiet, she takes Kami to the Verge. But when they get there, Akari sees someone sitting in her usual spot, his back to her. Surprised at the intrusion, she stops in her tracks and Kami instinctively follows suit. This is Akari and Ty's special place, and barely anyone comes here, especially not during the freezing winter.

Akari takes in the figure. He is wearing a familiar midnight blue cloak and his hood is up. Sensing her presence, he turns his head around slowly. Even though the hood blocks his face, Akari has a good idea who he might be. For a moment, she contemplates whether to take her usual seat or return another time.

When the figure stands up and wheels around, she sees those crescent-moon eyes smiling at her. *Yong. Is this happenstance, coincidence, or fate?* Akari ponders, but she's quickly reminded of her mission to search his and Emeraude's rooms. *As long as it isn't enemy action...*

Before she can sort out her thoughts, Akari finds herself making her way over, as though she's being drawn in magnetically. Kami prances along beside her, leaving a set of pawprints in the snow beside her footprints.

"I see you've brought along your real puppy today for a change." Yong chuckles as he takes a couple of gigantic swipes to clear the spot beside him of snow.

Akari purses her lips. "Ty isn't my puppy."

Yong is still grinning as he sits back down. Akari rolls her eyes and takes her seat beside him. Unwilling to lie in the snow, Kami settles herself comfortably on her lap.

"You must be disappointed it's just me today," Akari says sarcastically.

Yong mutters something under his breath before reaching over to pet Kami's head. With a wagging tail and pinned-back ears, she evidently takes to him well. "She's adorable," he says. "What's her name?"

"Kami," Akari informs him with a small smile. "She seems to like you. She usually barks at strangers."

Yong smiles back. When their eyes meet, her face flushes.

"So... what do you have against Ty?" Akari asks quickly, hoping he won't notice.

He shakes his head nonchalantly. "Nothing, really. On the contrary, Tyler Kane seems to have something against me."

"He distrusts Andelovians," Akari explains. "Just as many of the outskies do after the Three Greats."

"You actually mean 'dislike', don't you?" Yong clarifies. "And even so, that's only half of the whole truth, isn't it?"

"What do you mean?" she asks, her brow scrunched in confusion.

"You really are oblivious, aren't you?" he remarks with a lopsided smile. "Well, you can dislike everything about the capital, but you can't dislike me. I saved your life."

"I don't dislike you," Akari blurts. "Ty's just worried about me."

"Right, so it's true then. Tyler Kane doesn't like the capital or me very much," Yong notes.

"And Emeraude Eleaconde doesn't like the outskirts or me very much either," Akari points out.

"I guess not," he says. "But at least not all of us hate each other."

She lets on a shy smile. "Though I can't say it's that way for Ty and Emeraude."

"Haven't you heard, sometimes there's an imperceptibly thin line between love and hate..." he remarks with a knowing chuckle.

Before Akari can decide what to make of this, Kami hops onto Yong and curls up in his lap. He lets her stay, smiling adoringly at her as he scratches her neck. Seeing Yong and Kami, Akari thinks, *Maybe we aren't so different after all. Maybe the Andelovians and the outskies can stand on the same side. Maybe we can be comrades—even friends...* Lost in her own thoughts, she stares into the distance. Yong joins her.

For a while, they both take in the spectacular view in silence. The Telos Ocean is still frozen over, its unending expanse punctured by the deep dark Hollow, framed by the jagged icy shards of the perpetually frozen Hollow Falls.

"The Great Harvest ended there, didn't it? That's where the White Blaze happened..." Yong speaks softly, as though to himself.

Akari nods.

"I've heard so much about this place, but this is the first time I've seen it for myself," he says. "What do you think caused the White Blaze?"

"It's always been a mystery, hasn't it?" Akari gives a seemingly nonchalant shrug.

"Sure, but there are stories going around, theories even." Yong gazes into her eyes. For a moment, Akari wonders if he knows the truth, but she's certain this can't be possible. The Miyaharas have been very protective of their past.

"And what's yours?" she asks innocently. "What do *you* think brought about the White Blaze?"

"A gifted—one of Zatori's harvestees," Yong replies with inexplicable confidence.

Although shocked and impressed by how close he is to the truth, Akari makes sure to hide any expression. "How did you come up with that?" she asks.

"By elimination," he says. "It's the only thing that still makes sense."

"What were the other theories?" Akari wonders, curious.

"Earthquake, lightning, or a combination of both... The magnitude of the White Blaze is comparable to those, except it was too coincidental and deliberate... And it couldn't have been Zatori's own doing, putting himself out of action for ten whole years... So, the only theory left standing is a gifted who was potentially Zatori's harvestee," Yong concludes. "And if the White Blaze didn't destroy that gifted as well, they would be the best bet at defeating him."

Is this true? Is Mama the best bet at defeating Zatori? But she wants us to stay safe, lie low, and keep out of trouble. Is this really a battle we have to fight? Akari is unable to wrap her head around all of this. "And why do you think the force that was great enough to destroy Moira Island wasn't able to destroy Zatori and the Harvesters?" she asks.

Yong shrugs. "I've no clue how it's possible some of them escaped. Their nequilouses were found somewhere else without a trace of the Harvesters in sight. With the White Blaze, there was no other way out unless they vanished into thin air. Despite being incredibly powerful, surviving the White Blaze would have been an unattainable feat even for Zatori and the Harvesters. And yet, they did."

Akari nods along, not knowing how else to think. Eventually, she asks, pointing to the Telos Ocean, "Shall we go closer?"

"I didn't know we could get down there," Yong says, curiosity flickering in his eyes.

"Of course we can," she assures him.

"But won't we slip on the ice?"

"You'll see." Akari gives a knowing smile.

She heads to the start of the steep, snow-laden trail that leads down to the shore. Even though Kami has never been this way before, she descends first, sure-footed on her four paws. She scouts ahead, looking back every now and then to make sure Akari is still within sight.

Yong goes next. After taking a few steps, he turns around and offers her a hand.

"That's alright, I can manage—" But no sooner have the words left her mouth than she slips on the snowy slope, falling face-first toward the ground. Before she crashes, Yong swiftly grabs her waist, steadying her.

Akari quickly stands back up, reassuring him, "I'm fine... I'm alright..."

He chuckles. "You'd be much better off if you listen to me—at least sometimes." Without asking this time, he takes Akari's hand in his, sending a tingling sensation rippling through her. "Just bear with me until we hit the shore."

Akari nods abashedly.

They tread down the trail together, their boots sinking into the fresh powder with each cautious step. Their grip on each other remains firm—particularly Yong's on Akari's—steadying her as they navigate the slippery path together. When they finally reach the shore, she retrieves some ice skates from a hole inside a fallen log and places them before him.

"You can try these on. They're Ty's."

Yong eyes the skates apprehensively. "I've never done this before," he admits.

"It's Kami's first time on the ice as well. Are you worried she might do better than you?" Akari teases as she pulls on her own skates.

Yong lets out a chuckle, his crescent-moon eyes beaming. "Not at all."

She flashes a smile in return. "Well, then put them on. We can skate around the shore for a start."

"Do you do this a lot?" He slips his feet into Ty's skates, which seem to fit. There's a slight deliberation before he adds, "With Tyler Kane?"

"A fair bit," Akari says. "Ty and I have skated here every winter since we became friends."

"He's lucky to have grown up with you," Yong remarks with a tinge of wistfulness. She isn't sure if it's envy she also senses in his voice.

At the start of winter, out of convenience, Akari and Ty would hide their skates inside a fallen log by the shore. They would return every week for a skate—at least before they joined the People's Protector—until the frozen ocean began to thaw. Their ice skates, fashioned from leather pieces Akari had cut from Zephy's worn-out saddles and metal bits Ty had forged when he worked as a blacksmith, were a symbol of their friendship.

Although it's been a while since she last skated, years of experience have Akari gliding on the ice with effortless grace, completely in her element. To her, ice-skating is second only to flying in its sensation of freedom.

When she circles back to the shore, Akari gently places an excited Kami on the ice. At first, Kami wobbles on her four paws, her tail whirling to keep balance. Her legs slip out from under her in every direction, sending her tumbling to the ice every few steps. However, clever as always, she quickly adjusts, frolicking across the ice in no time.

Somewhere further ahead, Yong skillfully propels himself forward with a smooth push of alternating feet, gliding steadily across the ice. His balance is as impeccable as his combat skills, which comes as no surprise. Akari soon catches up and extends a hand toward him. Although he doesn't need the support, he takes her hand as they skate across the frozen expanse of the Telos Ocean.

"Kami seems to be getting on really well," Akari chimes proudly. "And you're not too bad for your first time as well." *Why is he good at everything?*

As they turn toward the Hollow, Akari shares, "When we were children, Ty and I made a promise that if either of us fell into the Hollow, the other one would come to the rescue."

"You know, I'd come for you too." Yong's lips curl into a lopsided smile.

She lets out a radiant laugh that seems to warm the brisk air.

"The outskirts are different from what I thought they would be," Yong remarks.

"What did you think they would be?" Akari asks, curious.

He stays quiet, struggling to find the right words.

"Not-so-good things, I suppose..." Akari quickly realizes.

"I thought they'd be sprawling with rebels who are plotting to overthrow the Ashgenov Empire and outskies full of resentment for Andelovia," Yong admits. "While there's distrust and dislike—not unfounded—I also see people healing their wounds, earning their keep, and going about their lives. For a long time, I could only imagine what the outskirts would be like until I finally made it here." He speaks with an unfiltered candor this time. There's a slight pause before he asks, "And what do you think of Andelovia?"

Emeraude's cold, haughty self seems to sum up the capital exceptionally well, Akari can't help but think. *And her flamboyant clothes.* "Well, they make everything in the capital bigger, brighter, and better," she says with a playful smile, before turning serious. "Actually... I was from Andelovia too. But I don't remember much of it." Although Akari tends not to talk about herself, she feels a strong urge—an impulse—to open up to Yong. "Since my father didn't make it out of the Great Harvest alive, my mother saw no reason to stay in the capital. She wanted a fresh start for us both and made the outskirts our home."

"Oh... I'm sorry to hear that." Yong's charming features soften with surprise. "Do you miss him?"

Akari nods. "Without him, it feels like a part of me is missing." She skates after Kami, suddenly longing to run her fingers through her soft, comforting fur. "But as my memory of him gets hazier, I get more afraid that I'll forget his face altogether."

A lingering silence ensues as Yong becomes lost in his thoughts.

"What is it?" she asks softly.

"Well, it's fortunate that you remember at least some things about your father. I don't have any memories of either of my parents. They passed away when I was two."

"Oh... I'm sorry to hear that too," Akari whispers, slowing to a halt. She hesitates slightly before asking, "What happened to them?"

"There was an accident when they were flying," he answers in a strained voice as he comes to a stop beside her. "They... their nequilouses were shot down by accident."

Akari studies Yong's eyes to see if she can find any trace of sadness or longing, but she can't be sure.

"Well... at least, since I don't remember, it doesn't hurt," he continues with a nonchalant shrug. "I can't miss people I don't have memories of."

Akari glances at Yong with a mix of commiseration and admiration, unsure how she should react.

"Don't look at me like that," he says with a nervous laugh.

"I'm not looking at you in any way..." She gives an encouraging smile, and he eases up. "If anything, I think you've done well for yourself."

"Well, the credit all goes to my nanny, Nana Eleanor. Because I didn't have any other family, I was sent to live with my mother's childhood friend after my parents' deaths. But I was really raised by her servants and Nana Eleanor. As it turned out, I got very lucky with her."

"Well, she must be an amazing lady. The two of you must be very close," Akari says.

"Almost as close as you and your mother," Yong answers with a warm smile. He skates in a circle and lifts one foot off the ice, balancing as if he has done it thousands of times. "There was something Nana Eleanor taught me whenever I was afraid. I thought it might help you control your gift..."

"You don't understand. My gift isn't a gift at all. It's a curse," Akari interjects. "I've hurt people because of it—not just my enemies, but also my comrade. I've even been suspended from combat missions."

"I understand, Akari..." Yong speaks with empathy, his tone softening. "But you didn't hurt that Protector boy intentionally."

"Intentional or not, it doesn't change the fact that a comrade got hurt because of my gift," she rebuts. "How can you understand? I wouldn't expect anyone to."

"I don't need to be gifted to know what guilt feels like," he replies. "It'll eat into you if you aren't careful... And you should never let that happen..."

Akari shrugs. "It's not that easy. Given a choice, I'd rather not use my gift again for the rest of my life. I can't bear the thought of hurting anyone again."

"If this is the case, all the more reason not to be afraid of your ability," Yong advises. He begins jumping and twirling, landing perfectly each time. "If you fear your gift, you'll never be able to control it, and you may end up hurting even more people."

"What should I do then?" she asks in a small voice.

Yong takes a deep breath before saying, "When I was younger, I used to be afraid a lot more..."

"Really?" Akari blurts in disbelief. She finds it exceedingly difficult to imagine someone so strong, so fast, so skilled at fighting, and so good at everything, being intimidated by anything at all.

"Yes. I may not look like it now, but I was..." Yong admits in a quiet voice. But it becomes full and deep again as he shares, "And this was what Nana Eleanor told me back then. Whenever you're afraid, close your eyes and count to three. One, forget the world. Two, forget your fears. And three, never forget yourself."

Their eyes lock for a moment, the reassurance in his gaze giving her strength.

"Your compassion, wisdom, and courage... Remember not to let your fears overshadow them," he eventually continues. "Now, shall we give it a go?"

Akari nods.

Yong lets go of her hand, skates behind her, and places both of his hands over her eyes.

"Are you ready?" he asks.

"Yes." Akari closes her eyes, feeling the soothing warmth of his hands on her eyelids.

"Here we go."

Their voices blend into one another as they count in unison. "One..." For a moment, Akari forgets that she's skating on the frozen Telos Ocean. She finds herself cocooned by the realm of darkness, much like the one in Salam's illusion. Except this time, it comforts rather than scares her.

"Two..." A sense of tranquility washes over Akari, dissolving the chains of fear of her own gift that had shackled her so tightly. Although the memory of hurting Ethan lingers, it no longer consumes her.

"Three..." Finally, the defining moments in her fledging life come to mind. Akari vividly recalls the premature first-sighting of her gift ten years ago, when she'd unintentionally deflected Zephy's wounds onto Philippe. That first time had been out of fear. A year later, she deflected Ty's wounds back onto Hanwell. Though still unintentional, the second time was out of compassion. However minute, there had been growth. Akari finds solace and strength in this.

"Now, how do you feel?" Yong's voice is disarmingly soothing.

With her eyes still closed, Akari says with an unprecedented calmness, "Light, powerful..."

"And are you afraid?"

She shakes her head.

"Now, I want you to remember how you're feeling in this exact moment," he gently instructs as he removes his hands from her eyes. "This is how you should feel when you wield your gift."

Akari nods, trying to capture her emotions.

"Remember, Akari, you're infinitely more powerful than you imagine."

"Thank you," she says with immense gratitude, wondering how he manages to be so convincing.

"You have a good heart. Sometimes, too good," Yong says, their gazes locking for a heartbeat. "You've been compassionate toward a lot of people—family, friends, comrades, even enemies... But don't forget that you need to start by being compassionate toward yourself."

Akari nods, smiling. As their voices continue chiming in unison inside her head, she's unsure if she is imagining Yong's face inching closer to hers with every count. The insides of her entire being flutter with nervousness until she finally pulls herself away, her face flushed, her breathing heavy.

Yong seems to feel the exact same way. He skates away, creating some space between them.

When Akari finally comes round and catches up with Yong, she finds him hunched over a slab of snow-covered ice. She peers over his shoulder with curiosity. His fingers fly across the surface too quickly for her eyes to follow, and the unmistakable image he is drawing begins to take shape.

Painted with snow on ice, it's Akari, Yong, and Kami on the vast canvas of the frozen Telos Ocean. He stands behind her, his hands covering her eyes, mirroring the moment earlier when they were counting to three. Both their lips are curved into soft smiles, their hair swept by the wind. The ominous Hollow looms behind them, while the inviting shoreline meanders ahead.

"Wow... It's beautiful..." Akari lets out breathlessly, thoroughly in awe. *Yong really is good at everything.*

"Well, thank you," he says proudly, yet shyly.

"How did you learn to draw like that?"

"I started when I was given a drawing of my parents," Yong recalls. "That was the first time I got to see how they looked. I spent days and nights drawing copy after copy until I could replicate it perfectly by memory. From then on, I knew I'd never forget their faces." He pauses before adding, "Now, I draw whenever there's something, or someone, worth remembering. I haven't drawn in a while, but I thought I'd want to remember today."

Heat pools inside Akari as she studies Yong—his dark eyes, delicate nose, and subtle cheekbones. When she turns to the drawing again, she doesn't miss the closeness in the image he has created of them. She taps the ice beneath her with the toe pick of one skate, as if to ensure the warmth he's imbued his art with isn't going to melt the ocean, or even the Hollow Falls.

"If you ever have the chance to go to Andelovia, you'll know what I mean." Yong's voice recaptures her attention. He takes in the wintry splendor all around them before locking onto Akari. "You'll never find anything like this there."

"With the Great Divide, I guess I'll never find out if that's true," she says softly, unable to peel her eyes from his hypnotic gaze.

"If only you'd never left Andelovia." Yong breaks into a wistful smile. "We could have been friends," he adds before skating ahead.

We might actually *have been friends...* Akari is momentarily lost in her thoughts, but mentally shakes herself and skates after him. "Have you heard of Lord Xavier Vykroux?" she asks when she catches up.

"Yes, all Andelovians know who he is," Yong says. "Lord Vykroux used to serve as the grand advisor to King Alvaro. But after the Great Harvest, during which his wife and daughter perished, he disappeared from the public eye. Later, his donation revived the People's Protector."

Yong comes to an abrupt halt, an air of somberness settling over him. Akari stops in tandem. "Is something wrong?" she asks carefully.

"I had two childhood playmates when I was growing up. Lord Vykroux's daughter was one of them," Yong replies, his tone grave. "We used to play hide-and-seek together."

Akari gasps. *Was I his childhood playmate? Could my hunches really be true?*

Everything fits in her mind. The dark gold necklace with the deep red, teardrop-shaped jewel... The letter from Lord Vykroux... And then, something Zatori said. "Lady Mari..." *Lord and lady... Lord Xavier Vykroux and Lady Mari Miyahara... Is it really possible?*

"Lord Vykroux's wife and daughter... are you sure they're dead?" Akari asks, trying to keep her voice even.

"Yes," Yong answers solemnly. "She and her mother have been gone for ten years now."

Even though he isn't aware they survived, at least Akari now knows for sure that there's truth to her dream about the young boy with the crescent-moon eyes. *Yong's my childhood playmate. We used to play hide-and-seek together. We have more in common than I thought. He isn't a total stranger. He just doesn't recognize me... He thinks that I'm dead...*

This time, Akari skates ahead, wanting to be alone with her thoughts. With one foot pushing the other, she propels herself forward mindlessly. But she doesn't notice the jutting frozen wave until the toe pick of her left skate kicks it. Akari comes crashing down toward the ground. She reaches out her right hand to break the fall, but it hits the jagged ice so hard she hears her wrist snap. Blood flows from a deep cut on her palm. Akari screams.

Yong is by her side before she knows it, his usual lightning reflexes barely slowed by the ice. As she struggles to stand up, he lifts her from under her arms, helping her back to her feet. But even before she has the chance to count to three, Akari finds herself deflecting her wounds onto him.

Yong groans as his right wrist snaps, his palm turning into an excruciating, bloody mess. Meanwhile, the pain vanishes from Akari. She doesn't have to look to know her hand is as good as new.

"Yong! I'm so, so sorry," Akari gasps guiltily as she examines his wound, her face twisting into a grimace. "I wanted to warn you, but you were too fast, or I was too slow... I forgot about counting to three..."

"It takes practice, and practice takes... time," Yong reassures her, his jaws tensing as he grits his teeth to suppress a grimace. "It was the same for me too. What was on your mind?"

"Nothing." Akari's eyes veer down to find her boots.

"Are you alright?" he asks, concerned, despite being the one who's hurt.

"Yes. And you?" she checks in a small voice.

"Nothing to worry about," Yong assures her, glancing nonchalantly at his bloodied, broken wrist. "I'm glad you're fine."

"I'm fine only because you got hurt in my stead." Akari sighs and clenches the hand that would otherwise be injured into a fist, letting her nails dig into her palm.

"Don't you worry. I heal quick. I'll just have to add this one to the count," he declares blithely. "In return, promise me you won't put yourself in peril again. You didn't promise the last time I asked."

"I promise I'll try my best, but you'll have to let my mother look at you," Akari says, loosening her grip the slightest. "She's a healer and she'll fix you. When you see her, you'll know what it actually means to heal quick."

"Oh no, it's fine... I'm fine..." Yong tries to protest, but Akari is adamant. She can't bear the thought of someone else being hurt in her stead *again*, especially not someone who's a comrade, or a friend—not to mention an old friend.

"Oh yes, let's head back to Moonstone. My mother will heal the wound and you'll be as good as new," Akari insists, calling out into the distance, "Kami, come here! We're going home!"

From across the ice, Kami runs back to Akari and Yong, trailing them as they skate back to the shore. Behind them, the sunset splashes vivid shades of pink, purple, and orange in the sky. The whole way home, Akari is lost in thought about her father, while Yong follows quietly behind her, well aware that her mind is preoccupied but clueless as to why.

When they reach Moonstone Apothecary, Akari stops outside, and Yong comes to a halt beside her. Through the window, she sees Mari and Ty chatting over the counter, awaiting her return. She feels a pang of guilt toward them both. Akari knows neither Mari nor Ty will be happy to see her with Yong.

"I want to give you fair warning that my mother, like Ty, isn't too... comfortable around Andelovians... despite having come from the capital herself," Akari informs Yong. "Don't get me wrong, she doesn't hate Andelovians, she's just... cautious. Very cautious."

"I've traveled around the outskirts long enough to know this much," Yong says with a shrug. "But, you know, we don't have to see your mother. Like I said, I heal quick."

"Don't even think about it," Akari maintains as she reaches for the door. "Regardless, my mother is a healer. And when she's doing her job, she treats all her patients fairly. You'll be fine—especially because that wound was supposed to be on me."

When Akari opens the front door, Mari and Ty look up simultaneously. Akari enters as naturally as she can manage and Yong slips in quietly behind her. In stark contrast, Kami prances inside gaily.

Although Mari doesn't speak, her expression is telling. She stiffens at the sight of Yong, the color draining from her. She scrutinizes his face, then eyes him from head to toe, taking in every bit of the Andelovianness that was once all too familiar to her. It's bad enough seeing him at her doorstep, but even worse seeing him with her daughter.

Meanwhile, Yong glances at Mari, an unspeakable intensity roiling in his eyes, before dropping his gaze nervously, his head almost descending into a bow.

Ty glances from Yong to Akari, asking, "What are you doing with *him*?"

"I... I was near the shore with Kami, and I fell..." Akari explains.

Her mother's eyes finally dip to their matching bloodied hands and the cut on Yong's palm, worry flickering in them. "Come over here." Mari beckons him to take her seat at the counter.

As soon as he sits down, she reaches for his hand and examines the wound. "The cut looks messy. How did this happen?" Mari asks, concerned yet distant.

Yong's hand trembles when she takes it.

Before he can form a reply, Akari answers on his behalf. "He tried to help me, but I deflected the wound onto him by accident. Can you heal him, please, Mama?"

Mari nods, her eyes still trained on the Andelovian who's suddenly appeared in her shop—a walking reminder of her worries. "Let me heal you."

She places her hand with the silver moonstone ring on his wound. Just as Yong takes a sharp inhale, his wrist clacks back into place. When Mari removes her hand, the deep cut on his palm has disappeared and his hand is as good as new.

"Thank you," he whispers, in awe of her gift of healing.

"No, thank you for helping Akari," Mari says. "I'm glad she brought you to me."

"Well, it's getting late, and I should take my leave. Have a good night." Yong bows to her, nods at Ty, and smiles at Akari, before striding out.

Even before the door closes behind him, Ty asks, "Madam Mari, why did you heal him? I thought you didn't like Andelovians."

"Those were Akari's wounds. I had to heal him, just as I would Akari—or anyone, really," Mari explains. "But that doesn't mean I want to have anything to do with him. Nor do I want *you* to be anywhere near him," she adds, shooting her daughter a threatening look.

Ty gives a smug smile and Akari scowls at him.

"Akari, my baby, you should steer clear of the Andelovian boy. It's not going to do you any good hanging around him," Mari warns.

"I know, Mama," Akari replies, sighing. "You've already made this very clear..."

"Alright then, I'll leave the two of you to yourselves. Ty's been waiting for you," Mari says as she prepares to retire for the night. "Lock up for me, will you, Akari?"

"Yes, Mama. Goodnight."

"Goodnight, Madam Mari," Ty chimes in.

Mari smiles at the duo before heading up the stairs. Kami patters after her.

Turning to Ty, Akari asks, "Why were you waiting for me?"

"To show you I've gotten back from the mission in Yuxenia in one piece. Besides, I've been coming by here this whole time without a reason, haven't I?" There's a tinge of bitterness in Ty's voice.

"I'm glad you got back safe—"

"So, why were you *really* with him?" Ty interrupts.

"Yong and I met at the Verge by coincidence—*really*..." Akari emphasizes.

"Playing it down just means there's something to hide." Ty's tone is teasing, but she detects the discontent he's trying to cover up. The Verge has always been their special place.

"We were ice-skating on Telos, and I fell," Akari recounts. "Yong helped me and my wound ended up being deflected onto him."

"The Andelovian boy ice-skates?" Ty asks sourly. Ice-skating on the frozen Telos Ocean has also exclusively been their favorite pastime.

"It was his first time today," Akari says. "I lent him your ice skates."

"*My* ice skates?" Ty's voice rises a notch. "You lent the Andelovian boy the skates *we* made together?"

Realizing her explanations seem to be working against her, Akari's eyes veer downward, then back to Ty. "Will you let me get to the important part?" She sighs, aware he won't like what she's about to say. "You know how I told you I saw Yong in the dreams I get sometimes about the children I used to play with when I lived in the capital? And that I think he was one of my childhood playmates? Well, today, he told me that Lord Vykroux's daughter was his childhood playmate. I can't help thinking that the wife and daughter Lord Vykroux lost during the Great Harvest... are... they're my mother and me..."

"Really?" Ty questions skeptically.

Akari knows he isn't fond of the idea that she and Yong were friends before they were, but she can't help acknowledging the truth laid before her. "I can't think of another explanation for all this, especially with the necklace and Lord Vykroux's letter... You don't believe me, do you?"

Ty shrugs. "Honestly Akari, what are the odds? If you claim Lord Vykroux to be your father, that's almost as farfetched as saying that King Alvaro is your father," he says with a light sarcasm. "Not that I want him to be."

"I know. I wouldn't either." Akari sighs again as she starts tidying the shop and preparing to close it for the day. "But you can't deny this is the way things look right now—that my father isn't dead, but alive and well in the capital. And Lord Vykroux's wife and daughter aren't dead either, but alive and well—or just alive, at least—in the outskirts."

"Alright, even if Lord Vykroux is really your father and he's in correspondence with your mother, how could they knowingly keep their family apart? Wouldn't they want to be reunited?" Ty asks as he lends Akari a hand, putting the herbs into the right drawers.

Akari shrugs. "This is why I want to go to Andelovia. To find out the truth," she says with complete seriousness. "I want to find out why my father wants me to think him dead."

"Over your mother's dead body!" Ty exclaims disapprovingly.

She cuts him a glare.

"Are you out of your mind?" He stares back incredulously. "Shouldn't you at least ask Madam Mari about it first?"

"If I ask her, both of us know she won't let me go," Akari retorts. "Besides, the truth's already been laid out before us. I don't need her validation..."

"And how will you get across the Great Divide?" Ty challenges.

"I don't know yet... But Yong said it wouldn't be impossible if I were with him. If he can make it out, I can find a way in."

"What kind of ideas has the Andelovian boy been feeding you?" Ty raises his voice, throwing his hands up in the air frustratedly.

"This is *my* idea!" Akari replies with exasperation. She takes it out on a drawer, cramming a bunch of herbs in and slamming it shut.

"You didn't have ideas like this before you met him!" Ty points out heatedly as he leans against the counter, glowering.

"And you weren't like this before Yong came to the outskirts!" she fires back, shooing him away from the counter and arranging the jars on its surface.

They fall silent, both pretending to be absorbed in their chores. In all the years they've known each other, they have never had an argument. But now their friendship stands at a crossroads, they're both unsure where it will take them. Although neither wants their friendship to change, Ty seems especially afraid of it.

"You don't have to be bothered with Yong," Akari tries to reassure him. With all the things on her mind lately, she certainly doesn't need a rift with Ty to add to them. "We've been best friends long before he ever came to the outskirts. And nothing is going to change that."

"Don't you see, though? You're so much more than a best friend to me. You're a gifted, you're my savior, and you're family... You're everything to me—everything I've never had and everything I've ever wanted." Ty looks into Akari's eyes, trying to search for an answer. But he finds nothing—nothing he wants to see.

"Ty..." Akari's tone softens as she grasps the weight of his words. *Does Ty... like me? Does he want to be more than just friends? But I don't feel the same way he does... He's my best friend and the last thing I want is to hurt him... What do I do?* She busies herself with jars that are already neat, avoiding his wounded gaze.

"That's alright. I shouldn't have said anything at all." Ty smiles weakly, shaking his head as if to brush off the entire conversation. "It's getting late. I should go. Goodnight, Akari."

"Goodnight, Ty," Akari whispers as she lifts her chin, only to see he's already slipped out of the apothecary.

10. Room Search

Akari and Ty haven't seen each other since their argument, but under Salam's command, they convene at the Colossal Inn to search Yong's and Emeraude's rooms. While the awkwardness casts an unusual silence between them, it also gives them the opportunity to take in their surroundings in greater detail.

The Colossal Inn, the fanciest accommodation in Cheyvelenia, is nestled in Hazenfeld. Situated in North Cheyvelenia, it's the most bourgeois part of town and caters to travelers from all over the outskirts—and now, Andelovia—as well as a handful of wealthy local folks. Its ostentatious yellow and green exterior complements the tall bright buildings in Hazenfeld, which are uncharacteristic of Cheyvelenia.

Neither Akari nor Ty is familiar with this part of town. Upon stepping into the inn, they are welcomed by a spectacular foyer, more opulent than anything they've seen before. An ancient grandfather clock ticks in the corner, while plush yellow and green velvet couches invite patrons to unwind in the sitting area. Fine art decorates the walls, enhancing the atmosphere of refined luxury. The grand double staircase, with its sweeping curves, frames the entrance to the inn's dining area—the renowned Cavalier Restaurant.

The guests of the Colossal Inn display a wide spectrum of clothing choices, from the neutral color scheme of the outskirts to the conspicuous clash of tones and textures closer to the Andelovian style.

Unused to such diversity and vibrancy, Akari feels uncomfortably out of place. Ty's slack jaw suggests he feels the same. With every step they take, their worn boots clunk loudly against the colorful tiles, making her even more self-conscious. *It's just in our heads*, she tells herself. *No one is paying us any attention.*

"Try not to worry," she mutters to Ty. "From our intelligence, we know Yong's and Emeraude's room numbers, and that they usually head out in the late afternoon. Once they're gone, we'll swipe the spare keys from reception and sneak up to their rooms."

He nods with an unusual quietness.

"Let's go into the restaurant to wait," Akari proposes. "From there, we'll be able to see them when they leave, but they won't be able to see us as easily."

"How about we just sit out here?" Ty suggests. He bites his lip as he glances at the fancy Cavalier Restaurant, seemingly intimidated by the idea of setting foot in there.

"And wave to Yong and Emeraude as they come down those stairs?" she asks sarcastically.

"Well... maybe we *should* head in," he concedes, but with no small measure of reluctance.

Fortunately, they are seated at a table to the back of the restaurant where they can get a good view of the foyer. Almost as soon as they settle down, the bell inside the grandfather clock strikes four. Yong descends from one of the staircases and heads out of the Colossal Inn.

Akari tracks him—her gaze almost longing—until he nearly disappears, then nudges Ty with her elbow, saying, "Look, one down. Now we'll just have to wait for Emeraude."

However, Ty's eyes are fixed elsewhere. He nudges her back, his focus unshifting as he whispers, "The Andelovian girl is over there."

Akari traces Ty's line of vision, spotting Emeraude's fiery red hair amidst the crowd. She is seated alone at a table in the corner, her face buried in the menu. With her back toward Akari and Ty, Emeraude doesn't notice them, or anyone else for that matter.

Akari props up her menu and hides herself behind it, beckoning Ty to do the same. The two of them peek out at Emeraude until a beefy waitress steps into their view.

"What can I get for you?" she demands, eyeing their surreptitious behavior with suspicion.

"Give me a second..." Akari fumbles through the menu, quickly coming to a decision. "I'll get the potato soup."

The waitress nods curtly, her glare shifting to Ty. "And you?"

"I'm good," he says without meeting her eyes.

"We have a minimum order here, sir," the waitress informs him with disdain.

Ty turns to Akari, whispering, "Was yours the cheapest option?"

She nods, embarrassed.

"I'll get the same one," he mumbles.

The waitress glowers at them and tries to collect the menus, but both Akari and Ty hold on to them too tightly. With a sharp sigh, she rolls her eyes and marches away.

From behind her cover, Akari resumes scanning Emeraude's surroundings. Surprise flickers in her eyes as she catches sight of three other people she recognizes.

"Look who's at the table behind her," she whispers, nudging Ty again.

Hanwell, Prisci, and Aloy sit at the table behind Emeraude's, their backs facing hers.

"What do you think they're doing here?" Ty asks.

"Well, Hanwell's father is the mayor, so it isn't surprising he frequents places like this—"

The beefy waitress returns and deposits two bowls of potato soup on their table, throwing them a judging look before marching away again.

Without any prompting, Ty digs in heartily. He takes a generous scoop of piping hot soup, together with large chunks of potatoes, carrots, and onions, and shovels it into his mouth, spoonful after spoonful.

Beside him, Akari sips in silence, keeping her eye on Emeraude, Hanwell, and his cronies.

Within minutes, Ty finishes his soup and plonks his spoon victoriously into the empty bowl. In contrast, Akari's remains nearly untouched.

"We didn't come here to eat," she reminds him, a mix of frustration and amusement evident in her voice.

Ty makes a sheepish attempt to explain himself. "I'm sorry, I was—"

"Hungry," they say simultaneously, both trying to stifle their laughter.

"That's your excuse every time." Akari finds the corners of her lips curving upward. For a moment, it's as though things have gone back to how they were, and she clings to the fleeting feeling.

"It's really good! You should have more. It's better than any of the soups I've ever had anywhere else—although I'm not sure if it's worth thirteen times the price." Ty eyes her bowl with a goofy grin. "But if you can't finish it, I can help you—"

Emeraude sets down the menu, places a few bronze nuggets on the table and turns to go, leaving an almost full cup of tea on the table. Akari and Ty quickly duck back down behind their menus, but Emeraude isn't paying attention to anything as she struts out of the restaurant and the inn.

Just as they re-emerge from behind the menus, Hanwell rises, Prisci and Aloy immediately following suit. Akari and Ty promptly hide themselves again. Peeking out from above their menus, they see Hanwell leaving some money on the table before the trio heads for the door.

"Ty, your hair is sticking out! Will you hide yourself properly?" Akari whispers anxiously.

"I can't help that I'm so tall," Ty retorts, quickly adjusting himself.

"And what good is that now?" Akari shoots back.

"I—"

He knocks over her soup. It spills all over the table, flowing off the edge, and the bowl hits the floor with a dull thud. Both of them spring from their seats, but some hot soup still splashes on Ty's crotch.

"Ow! Ow! Ow!" He jumps up and down, desperately trying to brush it off.

The commotion catches the trio's attention, and they make their way over.

"Tyler Kane!" Akari sighs exasperatedly as Hanwell, Prisci, and Aloy reach their table.

"What are the two of you doing here in Hazenfeld?" Hanwell demands, evidently surprised.

"Why do you care, Weilcox?" Ty retorts.

"Are we intruding on a secret date?" Prisci scoffs at the pair.

At the exact same time, Ty vehemently denies it, saying, "No!" while Akari grabs his hand and declares, "Yes!"

He turns to look at her and then at their linked hands. Although his heart skips a beat, Ty quickly catches on to Akari's intention. This convenient lie is perhaps the most plausible explanation for them being at the Cavalier Restaurant in the Colossal Inn. While enduring the pain of his scalded crotch, he wraps his arm around her waist to make their lovers act look convincing. The trio is neither surprised nor suspicious. Instead, they appear bored and unimpressed.

"What happened over here?" Hanwell mocks, pointing a taunting finger at the splotch on Ty's pants. Behind him, Prisci and Aloy snicker in amusement.

"After all this time, have you still not grown out of wetting your pants?" Aloy sneers nastily.

Ty flushes brick-red as he steps awkwardly behind Akari.

Akari grips Ty's and Hanwell's forearms and closes her eyes, concentrating hard. Hanwell's knees quake, then collapse inward. He bobs up and down helplessly, both hands over his crotch. "Owww! Miyahara! You..."

Realizing he's been put out of his misery, Ty turns to Akari, a mix of surprise and pride written on his face. When their eyes meet, they burst into laughter, shaking uncontrollably till their stomachs hurt. All the tension that's built up between them vanishes in an instant. For a moment, Akari is seven and Ty is eight all over again— just like the very day they first met.

"Did you just use your gift, Miyahara?" a fuming Aloy seethes, looking like he wants revenge but is too afraid to come any closer. "You're getting all cocky now that Salam's got your back, aren't you?"

"Perhaps," Akari says, her voice steeped in newfound confidence. "Madam Salam did tell me not to be afraid of my own gift."

Prisci narrows her eyes, also appearing like she wants to jump on Akari but is scared of her gift as well. "Wait till Sir Maximus hear about this!" she hisses.

Hanwell lets out an unintelligible groan.

"We aren't in the Quartz now," Ty reminds them with a huge, annoying grin. "There's no one here for you to complain to about Akari's accident."

"Except it wasn't an accident this time," Akari emphasizes with a small smile and takes his hand. "Let's go!"

"The bill's on them!" Ty announces triumphantly, pointing at the trio as they take off from the restaurant.

Hand in hand, they keep running until they reach a courtyard, where they finally decide they're far enough from Hanwell and his cronies. It's framed by colossal yellow and green columns, and interspersed with exotic plants and sculptures of creatures from children's stories. Powdery snowflakes fall lightly on them, coating every inch of exposed surface. Akari can't shake the feeling that they're within an ornamental snow globe, much like the meticulously crafted ones that belong in Tinkler's.

Yet, amidst an almost otherworldly beauty, Ty's animated voice draws her back to reality. "If I knew that was going to happen, I'd have ordered everything on the menu!"

Akari's laughter ricochets around the courtyard as she rejoices that they're finally back to normal. "Thanks to you, I didn't even get to enjoy my potato soup," she reminds him light-heartedly.

"If you really want to, we can come here again in the future... on another occasion..." Ty suggests.

Akari simply smiles, not quite knowing what to say.

"I miss us... from before..." he continues. "I don't ever want to argue with you again."

"Me neither," she concurs. "I'm sorry, Ty."

"I'm sorry, too," he says. "The Andelovians remind me too much of what happened to my parents during the Great Harvest."

But they both know there's more to it. Guilt thrums through Akari for not returning Ty's feelings.

"I know the Andelovians bother you..." She chooses her words carefully. *Especially Yong,* Akari thinks, not wanting to touch Ty's raw nerve.

"But they'll return to the capital sooner or later, and everything will go back to normal," he says, reassuring himself more than her.

Although Akari nods along, her heart sinks when she hears this. *If only the Andelovians—Yong—could stay in*

Cheyvelenia for a little longer. I haven't seen him in ten long years and haven't had a chance to tell him about our—

"What are you thinking about?" Ty asks.

Akari looks all around the courtyard, then at him. "I was just thinking how beautiful this place is," she answers diplomatically, loathing how she isn't completely honest with him, but dreading even more the prospect of another argument.

"Don't be deceived by its beauty," he warns, making a face. "Hazenfeld feels so artificial and disconcerting... It's what I'd imagine the capital to be. I honestly much prefer the slums. It feels so much more comfortable and real—like home."

"You don't seem to have a problem with the food here though," Akari points out.

"I don't have a problem with food anywhere," he clarifies with a shrug, his voice turning sharp. "You know, Akari, you're one of the rare few in Cheyvelenia who didn't grow up starving. If you had, you'd know what it means to be perpetually hungry!"

Akari purses her lips. "I thought we agreed not to argue again."

He immediately softens his tone. "We're not arguing. We're discussing," he says with a grin. "Now let's go get the keys to the Andelovians' rooms."

After they head back to the foyer, it doesn't take long for Ty to distract the receptionist and for Akari to swipe the spare keys, before they race up the grand double staircase and make their way to Room 412.

"This one is Emeraude's," Ty whispers, picking out the key labeled with the right room number, only to have it slip through his clumsy fingers and hit the floor with a loud clang.

They both jump, looking around to see if they've attracted any unwanted attention, but the hallway remains silent.

"Seriously, Ty..." Akari hisses, exasperated. "Now isn't the time for this."

"I know, I know..." he says, his head hanging low. "Let's just get on with it."

Akari swiftly picks up the key, sticks it in the keyhole, and unlocks the heavy walnut door. She looks to Ty, who gives her a reassuring nod, before pushing it open. As quietly as they can, they slide into the room, relocking the door behind them.

They are met with an earthy smell fused with the signature cloying Andelovian floral scent of Emeraude. The sizable room, featuring striking mahogany furniture, looks dated but well maintained. A large bed, adorned with plush yellow and green velvet cushions, occupies the heart of the room.

"Shall we begin?" Akari prompts after a quick scan. "I'll look inside the wardrobe, and you can start with the bed."

Ty nods, and the search commences.

Akari opens Emeraude's wardrobe to reveal a packed but meticulously organized collection of clothes. On the row of hangers are cloaks, robes, dresses, blouses, skirts, and pants arranged by item, then color. Akari sees on display the full range of outfits Emeraude has brought with her, consisting of a mix of bright reds, pinks, yellows, greens—a lot of greens—and blues, flaunting artisanship of origins far beyond the outskirts. Their vast variety of fabrics and designs are unfamiliar to Akari, leaving her impressed yet unsurprised.

Emeraude must have brought these clothes without realizing how much they would make her stand out. As part of her not-so-great attempt to blend in with the outskies, Akari realizes she's actually been wearing the least brazen of the outfits she owns. Yet, Emeraude still sticks out like a sore thumb.

With no time to lose, Akari quickly gets to work. She searches the linings and pockets of the clothes, as well as every nook and cranny of the wardrobe itself, careful not to leave any signs that she's been through them.

Meanwhile, Ty checks the bed. He flips over the pillows and quilt, feeling the pillowcases and quilt cover to see if anything is hidden inside them. While the bed yields nothing unusual, Ty finds Emeraude's arsenal of incredibly well-made daggers, darts, throwing stars, and needles on a leather baldric slung on her bedpost. Her spear leans on the wall by her bed.

Ty picks it up and examines it. The spearhead gives off a glint in the late afternoon light, flaunting its defined edges that have been crafted to kill. The shorter-than-usual shaft, tailored to Emeraude's petite build, feels remarkably light, yet with no compromise to its strength.

Ty has always thought the weapons distributed by the People's Protector are already far superior to the ones made by the Cheyvelenian blacksmith he used to work under. But when he feels the way this spear cuts the air, he knows instantly that the Protectors' weapons are no match for these.

While wishing he could own a weapon of this make, Ty reluctantly returns the spear to its original spot.

Unable to find anything suspicious, or even any clues as to what the Andelovians are looking for, he moves on to Emeraude's dresser.

On the dresser stand a few strange-looking diffusers holding the fragrance that smells just like her. Beside them, a tray holds numerous dazzling jewelry pieces with multicolored gemstones and sparkling crystals, as well as exquisite hairpieces made of gold, silver, jade, and lustrous pearls. All of these are far more ostentatious than the selection available at Tinkler's Oddities and Antiquities.

"Look at all of this shininess! I *love* expensive things!" Ty gasps in awe, randomly picking up an earring with a purple gemstone the size of a grape. "How long do you think I can feed my family for with this one?"

Akari, finally done with Emeraude's wardrobe but finding nothing out of the ordinary, looks up at him. "For several years, maybe? Decades, even? I don't know."

Ty's lips curl into a goofy grin as he slides the earring into his shirt.

"Don't you dare, Ty! Put it back! Emeraude is going to know if you take something," Akari warns before pointing out, "And just so you know, taking only one earring isn't going to do you much good. They're supposed to come in pairs." She walks over, gaping at the many mesmerizing pieces, unable to imagine the wealth Emeraude's patrons live in.

Ty holds the earring up against Akari's face, looking on admiringly. "All of these would look so much better on you than on any of the Andelovians."

Akari turns to the mirror. Even with just one shiny, gaudy earring dangling by her face, her reflection feels unfamiliar—strange, foreign, not quite her. *Is this how I'd appear if I'd never left the capital?* The jewelry feels excessive, too much—too Andelovian.

Ty seems to sense it too.

"I won't wear anything like that," Akari declares, and pushes his hand away. "Maybe something simpler," she adds quietly.

"You don't need any of these ridiculous things to look beautiful anyway," he proclaims, returning the grape-like earring to its place.

Akari gives a slight smile but says nothing.

Turning back to the dresser, Ty opens an intricately carved wooden jewelry box. Its plush black velvet interior encases a necklace that's a lot plainer than the ones on the tray. Hanging from a silver chain, the pendant, which resembles a fang, is of an off-white substance much like ivory, but with a subtle iridescent sheen. To Ty's untrained eyes, it pales in comparison to the other jewelry he's just seen. He is about to close the box when Akari catches a glimpse of the creamy, pearl-like necklace.

"This can't be..." she gasps, reaching for it.

"I thought you told me not to take anything..." Ty reminds her playfully. But Akari seems too preoccupied to hear him.

She holds out the necklace where it catches the light. The rays of the sun hit the pendant, revealing its translucency. Akari touches its cold, smooth surface and observes its length, approximately that of her pinky. Although she's no expert, her eyes flicker with recognition. "This is an archivian fang—an archivian milk fang, to be exact."

Ty peers at it curiously. "As in the milk teeth that baby archivians lose as they grow into an adult?"

Akari nods. "I've read about archivian fangs from my mother's books on mythical medicine but, just like archivians, I never thought they'd actually exist in real life," she shares. "Not only do they have medicinal properties, but they're also made into jewelry and ornaments for their beauty and rarity. Above all, they are one of the most resistant materials around, able to withstand the frost archivians breathe."

She twists the necklace round and admires it further. "Archivian fangs are uncommon enough, but their milk fangs are almost unheard of. The younger an archivian fang, the more translucent, the more beautiful, the more valuable, and the stronger its medicinal properties. This one is a real treasure. And in your form of measurement, it could feed your family for their entire lifetime—several lifetimes, even."

Ty gasps. After her words sink in, he asks, "Exactly how rich are those Andelovian patrons? I wonder if they're anything like Lord Vykroux..."

Akari shrugs.

"After seeing these expensive things, I was thinking maybe you *should* go to the capital to look for him," Ty jokes, flashing a goofy grin.

She gives him a scowl. Lord Vykroux's wealth is most certainly not among the reasons that push her to look for her father.

Ty ignores her response. Pointing at the fang, he cheekily suggests, "Alright... So, change of plans. Let's just take this baby tooth, run away, and live a life of luxury. Forget everything and everyone else."

This elicits a laugh from Akari, but she quickly remembers that they are on a mission and need to move quickly and quietly. "Alright, stop joking around, Ty. We aren't here to have fun," she reminds him.

He turns serious. "Do you think it's this that brought the Andelovians to the outskirts? Besides the herbs from Moonstone?"

"Possibly. It could be one of the things, but there must be something else they have yet to find, although I have no clue what," Akari replies. "Yong told me that once they've found what they're looking for, they'll have to return to the capital right away." She returns the necklace to the box and moves to search the desk.

Ty gives the archivian milk fang another glance before he reluctantly goes on to scour the drawers of the dresser. Like the wardrobe, the dresser contains more pieces of clothing that showcase Emeraude's ridiculous taste in fashion but reveal nothing that might make her or Yong look suspicious.

"Haven't you already covered the wardrobe? Why are there more clothes here?" Ty complains as he rummages through them. "This girl has more clothes than all the outskies combined!"

Mid-laughter, Akari notices a bronze badge lying on the desk.

"Look, it's Zephy! It's a zephanerix!" she says excitedly as she picks up the badge and inspects it. The engraving is of decent craftsmanship, doing its job of depicting the majestic beast, from the curve of its horns to the softness of its feathers. The warm patina on its surface hints that the badge is well-worn.

"Do you mean your giant horned bird I've yet to meet?" Ty takes the bronze zephanerix badge and gives it a quick scan, but appears unimpressed. It's clearly nothing as immaculate as the jewelry they've just seen.

"That's the one," Akari confirms. "I wasn't expecting to see it here."

"I know zephanerixes are supposed to be very rare like dragons, but this badge doesn't look nearly as expensive as the other colorful things around here," Ty concludes uninterestedly, placing it back on the desk.

Akari can't help but agree. "If there's nothing here, let's move on to Yong's room," she suggests.

As they head toward the door, Akari spots a crumpled ball of paper in the wastepaper basket beneath the desk. Curiosity piqued, she retrieves it and smooths out the creases. The message scrawled across the paper reads— *Meet me at the Cavalier Restaurant at four in the afternoon today.*

Ty peers at the note over Akari's shoulder. "But we *were* there around four today. Emeraude was seated alone at the table when we saw her..."

"What if this isn't from today?" Akari asks.

"It has to be. The maids at these places clean the rooms every day. One of my sisters used to work at an inn, though not quite as fancy," Ty explains. "Who do you think wrote it? And why do you think they didn't show up?"

Akari shrugs and tucks the note into her pocket.

"I thought you said not to take anything!" Ty interjects.

"This shouldn't matter. Emeraude will think the maids cleaned the room anyway," Akari surmises. "I'm going to take this to Salam to see if she can make anything out of it."

Ty nods in agreement. "Let's get out of here."

They leave Emeraude's room, lock the door, and head across the hallway to Room 413. As Akari stands outside Yong's door, her heart begins to race. She isn't sure whether she's more afraid of what she might find, or betraying Yong's trust. After taking a deep breath, Akari unlocks the door and steps into his room.

She is greeted with the same earthy smell as Emeraude's room, this time combined with Yong's scent, which reminds her of crisp mountain air. His room has the same layout as Emeraude's, except with far fewer things, making their job much easier. Just as before, Akari and Ty search through the wardrobe, dresser, and desk, albeit with far quicker progress.

Yong's clothes, mostly shades of dark or muted blue, prove no less fine in quality. Although they're much less conspicuous compared to Emeraude's, they are still eye-catching by the outskirts' standards. Akari goes through them, finding more than a few nuggets—even gold ones—in some of the pockets, but nothing to cause alarm.

Like Emeraude, Yong has his weapons on a sword belt hung on his bedpost. His arsenal is surprisingly small for how well he fights. He sticks to elevated essentials—an impeccably crafted sword and a few deadly daggers.

Noticing that Yong hasn't taken his sword out with him, Akari draws the impressive weapon from its sheath and examines it. The gleaming, freshly sharpened blade of the weighty sword is longer than average to match Yong's height, giving him an edge over his opponents—not that he needs it. She shudders, wondering how many lives this blade has taken.

"I already warned you against hanging around him so much," Ty seizes the opportunity to say, as if reading her mind. "After we're done with this mission, you should steer clear of them."

He takes Yong's sword from her, giving it a thorough inspection before swinging it around haphazardly. "Holy... Akari! Look at this blade." Ty swishes it again with an approving nod. "What kind of blacksmith do you think it takes to craft something like this?"

Akari glances at him, sighing. "Ty, we don't have time for this. In case you need me to remind you, we aren't really supposed to be here. We need to be gone as soon as possible."

"You know, among the blacksmiths, there have been stories that a legendary blade exists, of the most ancient craftsmanship." Ty admires the hilt, then carefully runs a finger along the flat of the weapon. "Do you know how to test if a blade is legendary? You blow a strand of hair against it and see if it can be cut in two."

He pulls out a strand of his own hair and blows it against the sword. But it falls to the ground intact, leaving him disappointed.

"Maybe the capital-made goods aren't as superior as they look," Ty says in contempt, reveling in any opportunity to scorn the capital.

"And were you expecting to find the legendary blade here?" Akari asks with a raised eyebrow.

"Who knows?" Ty shrugs, half joking, sheathing the sword and returning it to its original spot.

He goes on to check the bed, only to discover another dagger underneath Yong's pillow.

"It seems your Andelovian boy has sleep problems," Ty remarks mockingly. "I wonder what he dreams of at night."

Akari scowls. "He's not *my* Andelovian boy."

Ty ignores her. He draws the dagger and flails it around in huge, exaggerated movements, as though he's slaying some sort of terrifying monster.

"Stop that!" She snatches the dagger from Ty's hand just as he's about to blow a strand of hair against it. "We don't have any time to waste." Akari sheathes the dagger and replaces it under the pillow.

He makes a face and searches the dresser, but unlike Emeraude's, Yong's is practically empty.

Meanwhile, Akari moves to the desk, discovering several unopened packages of herbs from Moonstone Apothecary along with a zephanerix badge identical to the one she found in Emeraude's room.

"Look, Yong has one of these too!" she exclaims, picking it up for a closer look. "I wonder if it means anything..."

"Maybe the badge is a token of their love," Ty blabbers as he closes the drawers of the dresser.

Akari's heart sinks a little.

"Or maybe people in the capital just like these giant horned birds," Ty adds mindlessly.

Unable to figure out which is true, Akari replaces the zephanerix badge before picking up the notebook beside it. A piece of parchment slips out and falls to the floor. When she bends to retrieve it, she sees her own face staring back at her.

The drawing brings Akari to life—from her straight silky hair and smooth oval face, to her inquisitive almond eyes, lightly arched eyebrows, and soft ample lips. *How long and how closely has its artist been observing me to recreate my face this vividly?*

Akari doesn't have any doubt who's done it. *But why... why would Yong draw a picture of... me?* And she recalls his deep, velvety voice. *I draw whenever there's something, or someone, worth remembering.*

However, Yong's words aren't why Akari can't peel her eyes from the image. In the drawing, she is wearing the jeweled necklace her father gave her a decade ago. Although she was six years old the last time she had it on, the drawing shows her face as it is now, not of her as a child. And Akari's father only gave her the necklace *after* the last time she saw Yong in the capital, later the very same day in fact—the day of her sixth birthday. *How is it possible he knows of a necklace he's never seen before?*

Akari's long silence draws Ty's attention. "What are you looking at?" he asks.

"Nothing," she says, shutting the notebook with the drawing sandwiched inside.

Although Akari has never kept secrets from Ty, it somehow feels wrong to let him see Yong's drawing of her. It's too personal, something not meant for anyone else's eyes—perhaps not even hers.

Just as Ty walks over, looking suspicious, a rap on the door jolts both of them.

"Yong! Yong, are you in there? It's me." Emeraude's voice reverberates through the room, sending shockwaves through Akari and Ty.

"They're back early!" he whispers frantically. "What should we do—"

Akari shushes him, tiptoes to the door, and looks through the peephole. "It's only Emeraude," she whispers back. "She can't come in without Yong..."

"Yong? Yong!" Emeraude knocks impatiently on the door again, exclaiming, "He's never where I expect him to be these days!" Without waiting for a reply, she struts off in frustration.

They heave a sigh of relief. When the coast is clear, they creep out of Yong's room, lock the door behind them, return the spare keys, and slip out of the inn as discreetly as they can.

All this time, Akari remains fixated on the drawing of herself. *If Yong doesn't recognize me as his childhood playmate, why would he think I'm worth remembering? And if I'm really worth remembering, why doesn't he recognize me as his childhood playmate?*

Despite coming to the Colossal Inn in search of answers, Akari finds herself leaving with even more questions.

11. Intruder

Night has already fallen, and a brisk late winter chill lingers in the air despite spring approaching. After searching the Andelovians' rooms, Ty accompanies Akari on her walk home.

When they approach the shophouse, Akari notes that the windows are dark and figures her mother isn't home yet. Just as they're about to step into Moonstone Apothecary, Akari notices the front door has been left ajar, its doorknob broken. Mari would never be careless enough to leave the door unlocked or open if she were out, and the lamps would be lit if she were home.

A wave of unease washes over her. Akari and Ty exchange looks. Without either having to say a word, she knows he senses something amiss as well.

She pushes open the front door and slips into the shop as stealthily as she can, Ty following close behind. As she tries to make out her surroundings in the darkness, Kami rushes up to greet them with licks and nuzzles. Just as Akari thinks nothing seems out of place, they hear movement upstairs. There is someone in her home— someone who doesn't belong.

The hairs on the back of Akari's neck stand on end. In all her time in Cheyvelenia, her house has never been broken into. She flies up the stairs to find a masked figure in black setting down her golden box on the table. *My necklace!* Akari's heart lurches.

Staying concealed between the darkness and shadow, the figure tilts his head just enough to ascertain her presence, before twisting around and leaping out of the window in one swift motion.

"Stop there!" Akari cries and rushes to the window, left swinging open in the chilly night air. Without turning back, the intruder races along the narrow strip of shingles with inhuman speed and jumps down to the ground below. Without the slightest hesitation, Akari climbs out of the window and gives chase.

"Akari! Stop! It's dangerous!" Ty yells as he tries to grab hold of her, but he's too late. She is already on the ground, in relentless pursuit.

Sensing someone on his heels, the intruder picks up his already inconceivable pace, weaving through the alleys and bolting down the streets. But Akari keeps him in constant sight, taking shortcuts whenever possible. Her familiarity with this part of Cheyvelenia compensates for their difference in speed.

The intruder turns into a narrow alley, only to realize it's a dead end. He stops in his tracks and swivels around, looking for an escape route. But she's already standing between him and his only way out, kris drawn and ready to attack.

"Return the necklace! Take off your mask!" Akari commands as she steps toward him. *Could he be a petty thief? Or... could he be with Zatori? Could he be one of the Harvesters?*

When the intruder doesn't comply, she advances

slowly, poising her weapon for a fight. He backs up, seeking to buy time and put distance between them.

"Don't move!" Akari cries. "And I said, return the necklace!"

"I didn't take it," he claims, his voice quiet, gruff. His back almost touches the wall behind him, leaving him cornered, with nowhere to run except in her direction. "Go home now," he urges. "You'll find it there."

She doesn't believe him for a moment. "Don't lie—"

The intruder whips out a dagger, swiping Akari's kris aside. He darts around her, attempting to flee, but she leaps forward and swings her weapon toward his torso. With effortless elegance, the intruder dodges and parries her blow.

"I'm not lying," he asserts tightly.

"Did you also take the letter?" Akari presses, eyes locked on her opponent, prepared to strike again.

"There was no letter to take—" Before he can finish, she lunges at him.

It quickly becomes clear who the superior fighter is. The intruder moves with supple grace, gliding easily on his feet, his dagger carving through the air with artful precision. He fends off all her attacks with ease, each movement light and liquid, yet every blow weighty and solid.

Knowing full well she's on the losing end, Akari grows increasingly reckless, her bold, desperate moves only leaving her more vulnerable. In a rapid counter, the intruder's dagger slashes her left arm, sending a blinding pain streaking through her. A piercing scream escapes her, and he inhales sharply. Grasping her wound, Akari's fingers meet warm, sticky blood. She falters, stunned, and he exploits this.

In one fluid motion, the intruder ducks around Akari and makes a break for the opening of the alley. He nearly escapes, but she whirls around, seizing the tail of his cloak and yanking it with all her strength, halting him in his tracks.

Unable to shake her off, the intruder drives Akari against a wall in a swift countermove. With a powerful twist, he wrenches her wrist until her kris slips from her grip. Before it hits the ground, he catches it with one hand, smoothly sheathing his own dagger with the other.

This time, the intruder has Akari cornered. His trembling hand grips her collar, lifting her off her feet and hoisting her up against the wall. The fabric digs into her throat, choking her with each passing second. She claws at his hand, desperately trying to create even the smallest gap for air, but her efforts are futile.

In that harrowing moment, the intruder raises her kris, its blade aimed directly at her. With no way to free herself, Akari squeezes her eyes shut, steeling herself for the fatal blow.

A deafening crash erupts right beside her left ear. Her eyes snap open in shock, her head whipping toward the source. To Akari's astonishment, her kris is deeply embedded in the wall, driven in by an unthinkable force, pinning her by the collar with unnerving precision. She freezes, paralyzed by the moment, utterly baffled. It would have been so easy to end her life—to plunge the blade straight into her heart. Yet, the intruder hadn't.

He releases Akari, his hand loosening from her kris. Then, he casts one final, lingering glance at her before dashing out of the alley, disappearing into the night.

Still pinned to the wall, Akari lets out a frustrated scream, knowing she's failed to apprehend the intruder, reclaim her necklace, or uncover his identity. She wriggles desperately, allowing the kris to shred her collar as she struggles. But by the time she frees herself, he's long gone, making any pursuit pointless. With a sigh of exasperation, she extracts her weapon from the wall and slides it back into its sheath.

As the searing pain sets in, Akari glances down at her arm. Her sleeve, now stained with blood, is cleanly sliced, as is the wound beneath. She stumbles toward the opening of the alley, clutching her arm tightly. Blood trickles between her fingers and drips to the ground, leaving a fresh trail behind her.

Akari totters down the street toward home. The cold claws at her bones, seeping through her torn sleeve and leaving her shivering. Her wound throbs with every step, a relentless pulse of pain that has her gritting her teeth so hard her jaw aches. She doesn't know how much time has passed when she vaguely makes out a tall figure sprinting in her direction.

"Ty?" Akari squints to see in the darkness.

"Akari!" A deep, velvety voice calls out to her as a sinewy silhouette comes into view.

"Yong?" Akari's heart stirs.

In a few fluid strides, he's by her side. "Are you alright?" Yong asks anxiously as he peels Akari's hand from her arm and rolls up her bloodied sleeve. At the sight of the fresh wound, he squeezes his eyes shut and releases a long sigh. His warm touch sends flutters through Akari, momentarily distracting her from the pain.

"I'm fine," she insists weakly. "How did you know I was here?"

"I heard a fight and came over. What happened?" he asks without looking up. As Akari recounts her encounter with the intruder, he's barely listening, his focus solely on her wound.

"The cut is deep," Yong notes darkly, his touch lingering.

"It's nothing permanent," Akari reassures him, brushing off his hand, worried she might deflect her wound onto him. She takes a deep breath, intent on controlling her gift. *One... two... three...* Akari still feels the pain gnawing at her arm. *It worked! I did it!*

A frown creeps onto Yong's face as he firms his grip. "You're trying to control your gift, aren't you?"

Realizing what he's trying to do, her eyes grow wide in bewilderment. "And you're trying to make me deflect my wound onto you, aren't you?"

Akari tries to pull away, but each tug tears her injury wider—deeper—sending a sharp pain shooting through her arm. Despite her struggle, Yong's iron grip holds her in place, unable to budge.

With his intentions exposed, he lets out another long sigh. "You're only controlling your gift so well because of what I taught you. But can't you use your gift just this once?" he pleads darkly, a profound intensity whorling in his eyes.

Akari shakes her head. But Yong tightens his fist around her arm even more.

"Let me go!" she cries. "You're hurting me!"

"Then stop squirming about!" Yong raises his voice, his anger reminiscent of the night Zatori returned. But she has a feeling it isn't entirely directed at her this time. "You promised not to put yourself in peril again, but you still did. When you see someone dangerous, you're supposed to put as much distance between yourself and them, not go after them!"

With full knowledge that she hasn't upheld her end of the promise, Akari stays silent and stares at her boots.

Yong loosens his grip the slightest. "So, will you not be so stubborn just this once?" He is almost begging now, his anger overshadowed by desperation. "Will you deflect your wound onto me?"

"No." Akari is adamant. "Why are you doing this?" She looks up at him. "Why do you want to be hurt in my stead?"

There's a monumental silence before Yong finally finds his words. "Because it pains me immensely to see you hurt—even more so than if I were hurt myself. I can't bear to see you in peril, Akari. Because... because I like you," he confesses as he reaches for her hand, his touch sending heart-palpitating shockwaves through her. "Actually, I think I love you, Akari. No, I'm sure I love you. And I don't ever want you to be in peril again." He takes a deep breath when he finishes, as though relieved to finally get this off his chest.

The confession catches Akari completely off guard, leaving her utterly speechless. Her thoughts immediately drift to the drawing she found in his room. Had all the intricate details been captured through the eyes of an admirer? Amidst the confusion and disbelief, a warm sensation stirs within her chest. *Yong likes me... He loves me... He feels the same way I do...* As her heart swells, Akari's focus falters for just a split second.

The wound on her arm stops hurting, replaced by a dull numbness that draws her back to reality. Akari realizes right away that she's done it again— she has deflected her wounds to Yong for the second time. His sharp inhale confirms he's now feeling the same blinding pain she experienced just moments before.

"Yong!" Akari cries out, a pang of guilt hitting her squarely in the gut.

"I'm fine. Don't worry about me," he reassures her as his left sleeve stains red. "I told you before, I heal quick." Yong tries to act nonchalant.

"I'm sorry," Akari says, stuttering. "I didn't mean to... I... You... Whatever you taught me worked until..."

"Don't apologize," he insists, offering a comforting smile despite the pain. "I was asking for it. I wanted it this way."

She shakes her head, bemoaning her gift anew. Yong's feelings—love—for her make his pain weigh even more heavily on her conscience.

Akari takes his left arm worriedly, rolling up the sleeve of his billowy, eggshell-blue shirt to reveal a deep but clean cut. She grimaces.

"It looks really bad. Why would you do this?"

"It looked worse on you..." Yong says blithely. His attempt to lighten the mood seems to work, somewhat, tugging the corners of Akari's mouth up the slightest.

"You're going to add this one to the count again, aren't you?" she says tentatively, half joking.

But Yong turns serious instead. "Not this time," he replies with an unexpected solemnity, his eyes avoiding hers. "Well, I'd better be on my way then."

"Where are you going?" Akari asks worriedly.

"Back to the inn." He glances at his injured arm. "I'm going to get this wrapped up."

"No, you're not," she says firmly. "You're coming back with me to Moonstone. I'll get my mother to heal you. She should be home any time—"

"Your mother won't want to see us together again," he interjects. "Besides, if she sees this mess and learns it was on you before, she'll be very upset."

Yong's consideration both touches and infuriates her. She shakes her head stubbornly. "Leave my mother out of this. Don't you realize it upsets me too, seeing you hurt?" she challenges, her voice quivering, almost breaking.

"I... I..." He falters when he sees Akari's pained expression, as though she's still carrying the wound herself. With a long sigh, he finally relents. "Alright, I'll come with you."

Akari gives a relieved smile, but she can't unfurrow her brow. She unties her cloak and places it on his shoulders. "You're wearing awfully little for such a chilly night. You need to keep yourself warm."

"No... I don't need it," Yong claims as he tries to return the cloak, but she doesn't let him.

"I'm from the northernmost town of the outskirts while you're from the capital down south. I'm much more used to the cold than you are," Akari insists. "You took my wound. Now, at least take my cloak in return."

"Let's compromise, shall we?" Yong wraps his uninjured arm around her shoulder, pulling her to his side and draping her cloak over them both.

Akari nods shyly, nestling into Yong's chest. With his arm still around her shoulder, they make their way back toward Moonstone Apothecary together. The whole time, her mind is inundated with thoughts of his drawing and confession, and the intruder's identity and intention...

"Did you really mean it?" she eventually asks, her voice quiet. "When you said you love me?"

Yong stops in his tracks, bringing Akari to a halt beside him. Turning to look at her, his crescent-moon eyes ablaze with sincerity. "Every word," he confirms.

The cloak is suddenly very warm, and she knows her cheeks are burning. *He's truly, deeply in love with me— like I am with him.* A sprig of happiness blooms in her chest, and she nestles even closer.

"Akari, I know it's not the best time to ask this, but I'm afraid there aren't many chances left." Yong speaks with purpose—and a certain earnestness—showing no trace of pain from the injury. "Will you meet me outside Tinkler's Oddities and Antiquities at noon on the last day of winter?"

"What for?" Akari blurts.

"No particular reason." His nervousness is exceedingly rare, but he quickly plays it down with a lopsided smile. "Or you can take it as repaying me for saving your life."

But they both know it's really a date.

As butterflies flutter in her stomach, Akari manages to answer, "Yes..."

Yong locks her in a tight embrace, her cloak wrapping them in a cocoon. "I've been waiting so long for this!" he exclaims, his dark eyes sparkling with joy.

Akari smiles radiantly, wondering if the sprig of happiness will burst into a tree right there. "I hope it was worth the wait."

"Every moment," he declares.

When Yong loosens his arm from around Akari's back, their eyes meet with an impassioned intensity that renders all her questions inconsequential. Under the cloak that shields them from the world outside, they revel thoroughly in each other's presence, momentarily forgetting everything else.

Yong's fingers curl around Akari's shoulders, pulling her in as he inches forward, his lips closing in on hers. Completely inexperienced and utterly surprised, she freezes, unsure whether to lean in or pull away. Just as their lips are about to touch, a blaring voice interrupts them.

"Akari! Is that you?"

Akari and Yong pull away, looking up into the foggy night to see Ty bounding toward them. Yong gives a tiny shake of his head, accompanied by a small sigh. Beside him, Akari shows no perceivable expression despite the guilt churning in her gut.

Although she's flustered, Akari quickly pulls herself together, calling back to Ty, "Yes, it's me."

When he reaches them, Ty begins fussing over her, completely passing over Yong. "Akari! I've finally found you! Where have you been? Are you alright?" he gasps worriedly at the sight of the bloody mess. Ty hastily pulls up Akari's sleeve to inspect the wound, immeasurably relieved to find the skin beneath it intact despite the blood. Without further prompting, he knows she must have deflected her wound onto someone else.

"Yes, I'm fine. Is the necklace still at home?" Akari asks, naively holding on to the slightest glimmer of hope that there could be some truth in the intruder's words.

"I don't know. I didn't check. I ran after you immediately, but lost you halfway," Ty admits sheepishly. "What happened?"

"I had the intruder cornered, but he attacked me and got away," she says.

Ty finally twists to Yong, eyeing him suspiciously. "What are *you* doing here?"

"I heard the fight and—" he begins again, but this time, Akari finishes explaining for him.

"Yong found me and my wound ended up being deflected onto him." She doesn't mention that he'd wanted it this way. "We're going to get my mother to heal him."

When Ty's gaze lands on Yong's matching bloodied sleeve, his tone softens slightly. "We'd better get the wound healed. Let's head back to Moonstone. It's freezing out here."

Yong nods reluctantly, placing Akari's cloak back over her shoulders. This time, she lets him, while Ty quietly tracks their exchange.

Under the pale moonlight, the trio makes its way toward Moonstone Apothecary. As Akari glances from Yong to Ty, it strikes her, disconcertingly, that they've both fallen for her—and at some point, she must have an answer for each of them.

Yong and I may feel the same way about each other, but what will ever come out of it? We're both from the capital and knew each other as children, but now the Great Divide stands between us. As for Ty, he's my best friend—family, even—but I can't help that I don't feel the way he does. I love them both in different ways and I don't ever want to hurt either of them...

But Akari isn't the only one who's preoccupied. Flanking her, Yong and Ty both seem lost in their own thoughts, none of them uttering a word until they return to the shophouse.

"My mother still isn't back yet. Let me help you tend to your wound," Akari says, lighting a lamp to see Kami prancing up to greet them again, her tail wagging and ears pinned back.

"Why don't you check on the necklace first?" Yong suggests, knowing it must be important to her, while stooping to pet Kami's head.

Ty nods, for once in agreement with the Andelovian boy. "I can help him with his wound," he offers, surprising both Akari and Yong, before giving Kami a hearty scratch.

Akari eyes the boys worriedly, hoping they won't tear each other apart. If that happened, she knows who'd undoubtedly be on the losing end.

"I'll try not to hurt him," Ty assures her with baseless overconfidence, but falls short of sounding convincing.

Yong lets out a chuckle. "Go ahead, Akari. I'll be fine."

"Ty, you know where everything you need is, right?" she checks.

"Yes, yes... I've been around here long enough now." He waves her away.

Akari flies up the stairs and sees the golden box on the table, exactly where the intruder left it. With dread, she lifts its lid.

To her utter disbelief, the dark gold necklace with the deep red, teardrop-shaped jewel lies safely inside the box. She inhales sharply and reaches out a trembling hand, gingerly brushing the jewel. At her touch, it glows a soft red. *This is all I have left to remind me of my father.* She can only imagine the devastation she'd feel if she lost it again.

It seems the intruder is neither a thief nor a liar... But Akari's realization leaves her exceedingly befuddled. *Wasn't he after the necklace? Why didn't he take it when he obviously could have? And how did he know of the secret hiding place I didn't even know existed until recently?*

She closes the lid and returns the golden box into its hiding place, no longer a secret to only her and her mother. Then, she notices that the letter from Lord Vykroux is indeed nowhere to be found. *Has Mama destroyed it? Is that what she's been doing all this time with other letters? That one can't have been the first from Lord Vykroux...* Akari purses her lips and replaces the loose floorboard, seamlessly concealing the hiding place.

She gives it a last look, closes the window the intruder escaped from, and makes her way back downstairs. Midway, she informs the boys, "The necklace *is* still there..."

"Thank goodness!" Ty exclaims as he holds a bandage to Yong's arm, applying pressure to the wound—perhaps a little more than he needs to. As she nears, Akari is quite sure she hears him mutter begrudgingly, "Why did I volunteer for this?"

"I'm just as glad. I never thought the intruder would be telling the truth." She heaves a sigh of relief as she re-joins the boys, thankful they haven't torn each other apart.

"I guess he had no reason to lie," Yong says, hesitating briefly before he adds, "Not with how the fight unfolded."

"Perhaps," Akari concedes reluctantly. "But why didn't he take the necklace when he obviously could have? And if he wasn't out to steal, then what *was* he after?"

"Well, if the intruder didn't take anything, you either interrupted him before he had the chance, or... he was looking to learn something instead..." Ty surmises.

Akari and Yong turn toward him, both impressed by his unexpected flash of acuity. *Just like when we searched Yong's and Emeraude's rooms,* she realizes, knowing her best friend is thinking the same.

"What could that possibly be?" Akari asks.

"How would I know when you don't?" Ty scratches his head before announcing smugly, "I've stopped the bleeding."

When Akari looks, she notes that he hasn't done too shabby a job.

"Well, thank you," Yong says, retracting his arm.

"I still need to dress the wound," Ty reminds him flatly.

But Yong pulls his sleeve back down, maintaining, "This'll do—"

The door swings open, and Mari steps into the apothecary. She is met with Kami's warm welcome and the trio's quiet gazes.

"What's going on here?" she asks as she catches sight of Akari's and Yong's matching bloodied sleeves. "What happened?"

She rushes up to Akari, lifting her sleeve anxiously, only to find her unscathed. Mari's eyes then veer to meet Yong's with a look that is both concerned and questioning.

He drops his gaze, and Mari rolls up his sleeve to inspect the wound. "It looks clean, but deep. Is this from my daughter again?"

"It wasn't her fault. I wanted it this way," Yong explains, heat pooling in Akari as he defends her. Ty raises an eyebrow at her, and she quickly glances downward.

Mari doesn't comment on this, simply saying in a quiet voice, "Let me heal you."

She closes her eyes and touches the wound with the hand adorned by the silver moonstone ring. Yong clenches his teeth, a muscle feathering in his jaw, while Akari and Ty watch on silently. When Mari finally removes her hand, his arm shows no sign of ever having been hurt.

"Thank you." Yong dips his head to a bow.

"It's the least I can do," Mari replies before adding, "It's getting late. You boys better head home."

Taking her cue, Yong and Ty say their goodnights and turn to leave.

Once they are out through the front door, Mari asks, "Akari, my baby, are you alright? Tell me what happened."

"An intruder broke into our house, but thankfully he didn't take anything," Akari informs her as calmly as she can, knowing her mother will panic.

Sure enough, Mari's dark, almond eyes grow wide with hysteria. "Did they hurt you? Was that the wound that was deflected onto the Andelovian boy?"

"Yes, but I'm fine now. We both are," Akari assures her.

"Didn't I ask you to steer clear of him?" Mari chides. "I told you it's not going to do you any good hanging around him."

"Yong was the one who found me when I was hurt! I ended up deflecting my wound onto him." There's a hint of defiance in her words as she rushes to his defense. "If anything, it's not doing him any good hanging around me!"

"And do you really think this was all coincidence?" Mari challenges, her voice rising a notch.

Akari falls silent, her eyebrows scrunching in confusion. "Are you saying it wasn't?" she asks after a pause.

Mari lets out a long sigh. "What I'm saying is that you need to stay safe, lie low, and keep out of trouble, Akari."

"I know, Mama. You've said that too many times now." She leans against the counter and lets her indignation simmer. "I also know you still have the necklace—the one from Papa. I saw the intruder looking at it, but he didn't take it."

A gasp escapes Mari's lips, horror shadowing her eyes before they grow distant. Akari isn't sure which unsettles her mother more—that she's seen it, or the intruder.

"Mama... why did you hide it from me? Why did you tell me it was lost?" she demands. "The necklace was the only keepsake to remember Papa by!" Tears begin to brim Akari's eyes, but she steels herself, refusing to let them fall.

Mari hesitates, a pained expression twisting her delicate features, before she takes her daughter's hand and leads her upstairs.

With trembling hands, she removes the loose floorboard and retrieves the golden box. Akari notes her mother makes no mention of the letter as she sets it down on the table where the intruder had left it earlier. After opening the box, Mari gazes at the jeweled necklace briefly before beckoning her daughter over. "Come to me, Akari, my baby."

Akari makes her way over apprehensively, stopping before her mother.

"Now, turn around," Mari says, her voice especially quiet, yet quavering with emotion, as she fastens the necklace around Akari's neck.

When she turns back around, Mari takes in her beautiful daughter wearing the beautiful jewelry and locks her in a warm embrace.

"It's yours now," Mari pronounces when she finally releases Akari. "It's always been yours."

Akari holds up the jewel, marveling at it in disbelief. By now, there's no holding back the tears. "Thank you, Mama," she whispers.

Mari strokes her daughter's cheeks before her fingers trace Akari's neck down to her collarbone, and eventually to the jewel. "Promise to keep it safe, will you?"

Akari nods.

"I've always wanted to return it to you when the time was right, but it just never seemed to be," Mari explains solemnly. "I've kept this necklace hidden from you to keep you safe, Akari, my baby. Possessing it... it's dangerous... You aren't ready for such consequences..."

"What do you mean?" Akari asks. *What haven't you told me?*

When Mari looks her in the eye, she realizes her daughter is no longer the fearful six-year-old with round rosy cheeks and soft baby hands. For the very first time, she sees in Akari a strong young woman—a fighter and a survivor. It strikes her that the time has finally come to entrust her daughter with the truth.

"There's been blood spilled and lives lost over this necklace, and I couldn't allow anything to happen to you," Mari says tightly after drawing in a long, deep breath. "King Alvaro and the Royal Regiment, as well as Zatori and the Harvesters... all these people will kill to possess it."

"Why?" Akari asks. But a chill runs down her spine as she realizes she already has an inkling of the truth—and her mother's words prove her right.

"This necklace around your neck—the jewel on it—is one of the three missing royal regalia. This is the Jewel of Compassion."

12. Revelations

At bedtime, Akari curls up with Kami by Mari's side instead of sleeping in her own room. She doesn't want to be alone again tonight, and her mother's presence gives her immense comfort.

As Akari fiddles with the Jewel of Compassion, she still struggles to grapple with the revelation that a royal regalia is in *her* possession. *The Jewel of Compassion... One of the three missing royal regalia... Here in Cheyvelenia, the smallest town of the outskirts... Previously hidden under our floorboard... And now hanging from my neck...* Endless thoughts race through Akari's mind until a sudden realization strikes her. *Yong's drawing shows me wearing the Jewel of Compassion! Could he possibly know what it is?*

"Do you know what the three royal regalia are?" Mari eventually asks. Although she's taken care never to mention them, she has a hunch that her daughter is aware of their significance.

Akari nods.

Mari frowns. "How did you—"

"Besides the intruder, are there others who've laid eyes on the royal regalia lately?" Akari blurts, interrupting her mother.

"No... Not since they went missing—well, the Mirror of Wisdom and the Sword of Courage at least," Mari says. "As for the Jewel of Compassion, it's been sitting beneath our floorboard for the last ten years."

"Does this mean only two of the three royal regalia really went missing? And the last one has always been in our possession?" Akari checks, stunned at how far she—and everyone else—has been from the truth.

Mari nods.

Akari furrows her brow. Still preoccupied with Yong's drawing of her and the Jewel of Compassion, she can't help but wonder if he's ever seen it, under what circumstances he's done so, and if he knows what it is.

"Many seek the three royal regalia for their incredible powers," Mari continues.

Akari lets out a soft gasp. "They possess powers?"

"Yes, indeed," Mari confirms. "They've been said to hold powers so unfathomable they can bestow legitimacy to the throne. That's why so many seek to unite them."

Akari picks up the Jewel of Compassion, examining it for the umpteenth time that night. "How does one wield these powers?"

"No one knows that..." Mari glances lovingly at her daughter, saying, "Akari, my baby, promise me one more thing, will you?"

"What is it?" she asks.

"You have to keep the Jewel of Compassion a secret," Mari instructs her. "It'll be extremely dangerous if anyone else knows about it."

"But... but I... I've already told Ty about it," Akari confesses. "And now, Yong has come to know too..."

Mari groans. "Akari! How many times have I told you that you need to be careful with your secrets?"

"I know, Mama. But not even with Ty?" she protests. "He's my best friend and you like him! Besides, you can't blame me for telling him about the necklace. I've only just learned that it's the Jewel of Compassion."

Mari sighs exasperatedly. "Although I have absolutely no doubt Ty has the best of intentions, his reliability is a whole other story. You shouldn't have even told him about Zephy!"

"I still don't get why you won't let Ty see Zephy since he already knows about him..." Akari points out as solemnly as she can, although she can't help laughing at the way her mother speaks of Ty.

"Zephy is a rare creature that will attract unwanted attention," she explains. "The fewer who have seen him, the better. It'll be safer for Zephy as well."

"Alright... alright..." Akari sighs and scratches the top of Kami's head. *I was never going to be allowed a dog. If I can change her mind about that, maybe I can get Ty to meet Zephy at some point too.*

"Akari, we live in dark times now. With the intruder, it's frightening to think that the Jewel of Compassion is possibly safer hanging from your neck than it is in a secret hiding place under our floorboard. And now Zatori has returned, I'm too afraid to think of the consequences if he finds us or this royal regalia..." Mari's worries have always been excessive, but especially of late.

"Mama, you can trust me. I'm no longer a child," Akari reassures her bravely. "It's my turn to protect you."

Mari shakes her head. "All I ask is for you to stay safe."

"I know... I know..." Akari says. She's heard the words too many times now, and they've lost the impact they had when she was younger.

"You know, your father was right about you," Mari says with a distant look in her eyes. "He gave you the Jewel of Compassion because he saw compassion in you."

This has been the one and only time Mari has brought up her father without Akari asking first. Now her mother has raised the subject, she can't help but probe, "Mama, how did Papa get hold of this royal regalia?"

Mari shakes her head again, and Akari can almost hear a door slamming in her mind. "Akari, I don't want you digging into history and bearing the burdens of the past, be it mine or your father's," she says, her firm voice belying her sorrow. "He's gone now, and we should let the past be gone with him."

Despite her mother's response, Akari is more convinced than ever that her father is Lord Vykroux. *Besides King Alvaro himself, who else would be able to get close enough to lay hands on the royal regalia?*

She's dying to ask about her father, but she's well aware any mention of him always causes Mari sadness. Even so, she tries a roundabout way. "Mama, was Papa your first love?" Her thoughts unconsciously drift to Yong.

"Oh Akari..." Mari is half surprised and half embarrassed by the question. "Yes, he was—my first, last, and only love... But first love doesn't usually last..."

Although she's been occupied, Mari hasn't been completely oblivious to Akari and Yong's interactions. On the contrary, her observations of the pair have left her worried and uneasy. But she hasn't been quite sure how to broach the matter.

"Were the two of you happy together?"

"Yes, there was a time we were." It dawns on Mari that she's been so absorbed in ensuring her daughter's safety that she hasn't once considered her happiness. And without realizing, she's forgotten all about this with time.

"Did you love him very much?" Akari presses.

"Yes, I did." Mari recalls a time when she was young and reckless, plunging head-first into love without a care in the world. She hadn't been much older than Akari is now when she met her father.

"And how about now?" Akari wonders, caressing Kami's soft fur and imagining how her mother would have been if she were unburdened by the threat of Zatori.

"I've learned to let him go." Mari's brief answer understates the turmoil she's endured to come anywhere close to finding peace within herself.

"Isn't it painful to let someone go?" Akari holds her breath, as though bracing herself.

"It is. But sometimes, if you already see the end of it all, it's less painful to let someone go than to keep them in your heart."

Yong has to return to the capital eventually and it'll all come to an end. I'll have to let him go. I'll have to let Yong go from my heart... Akari thinks hopelessly, terrified at the prospect of having to bear such insurmountable pain.

"But still, wasn't it hard?" She finds herself wincing.

"It was. Letting go of your father was one of the hardest things I had to do," Mari admits. "But sometimes, you have to do what's best for both of you and let time take care of everything else." She lets out a long sigh, relieved to have finally put the past behind her.

Akari nods, despite being doubtful she'll ever be able to let Yong go when her feelings for him are so intense— overwhelming, even. "Mama, was it difficult to forget Papa?" she asks.

Her heart sinks at the thought that her father, who was once the sun Mari joyfully revolved around, has long since become seemingly inconsequential. Waves of sadness overcome her when she envisions a future where she and Yong are no more than strangers to each other.

However, Mari's answer isn't what she expects. "Akari, my baby... I haven't forgotten him... I've let your father go, but I'll never forget him. Even though he doesn't live in my heart, he still lives in my memory."

A single tear rolls down Mari's usually stoic porcelain face, unraveling a decade's worth of bottled-up hardship. This whole time, Akari has naively equated her mother's few words about her father with how little she thought of him, not realizing the full magnitude of the pain she must have been suppressing.

"Oh, Mama..." Akari puts her arms protectively around Mari, carefully caressing her back. Her heart wrenches at her mother's vulnerability, laid bare before her. In all her life, she's only seen Mari cry once—ten years ago after escaping the White Blaze.

Without a place to stay, they spent their first night in the outskirts, huddled up by the sidewalk. Before falling asleep in her mother's lap, Akari saw her weeping silently.

Mari had just seen Akari's father for the last time, narrowly escaped Zatori's clutches, and faced the prospect of having to single-handedly raise her daughter in a completely unfamiliar place. But for the following decade, she has managed to do so, creating a new life for them both in Cheyvelenia—although not without hardship and sacrifice along the way.

"But it's all worth it... Nothing matters more than you, Akari. You know I'd give up anything in the world for you—even your father. I'll do everything I can to keep you safe." Mari's resilience comes through in her voice.

When Akari loosens her arms from around her mother, she sees a woman who has given—given up—everything to raise her. Despite her burning curiosity, she can't bring herself to ask about Lord Vykroux and reopen old wounds. *Whether I like it or not, everything Mama's done is to keep me safe, and the least I can do is not hurt her.*

"I know, Mama," she simply says. "And you know I heart you with all my love."

"I heart you with all my love too, Akari, my baby," Mari replies, squeezing her daughter tightly, still wanting to protect her but not knowing how much longer she can.

That night, Akari falls fast asleep in the safety of her mother's arms, thoroughly exhausted from the long day. Beside her, Kami has already begun snoring intermittently.

Mari looks at her daughter, her soft gaze brimming with immeasurable love. She plants a gentle kiss on her forehead and slips out of bed, careful not to wake her.

Mari sits in the living area till daybreak, sipping on a cup of powder-pink telmezia tea, lost in her own thoughts. Although she doesn't sleep a wink that night, at least she doesn't shed more tears.

With dark times looming, she's well aware this isn't the time to cry—there are more crucial things to be done.

♦

Back in the Quartz, Akari is about to turn into the hallway leading to Salam's office when she hears raised voices at the other end. She quickly hides herself behind a wall, perking up her ears. Maximus and Salam don't sound too pleased with each other.

"How could you plant spies in the capital without first running it by me? We're supposed to lead the People's Protector together, not hide things from each other!" Salam growls. "Even now, I still don't know the identities of our insiders in Andelovia. It seems the traitor who's been compromising us and feeding our intelligence to Zatori isn't one of the Protectors—that leaves the spies you've planted. One of them could very well be a double-crosser!"

"Salam, even though you have every reason to be angry, you can't assume this. But rest assured, I'll personally eradicate the traitor," Maximus says calmly. "Just as Zatori has planted a spy among us to feed him intelligence on the People's Protector, we need to get intelligence about the capital too. The reason I haven't told you about the spies is because you don't see what I see yet. I planted them in the capital so they could be of use to *both of us* when we eventually move there to achieve greater things."

"I don't intend to move back to Andelovia, thank you," Salam rebuts. "I very much enjoy the fresh air and freedom of the outskirts."

Akari peers round the corner for a moment, relieved they haven't noticed her. Salam towers over Maximus, but he shows no sign of fear at her bared teeth, shooting back a glower of his own. Akari ducks back behind the wall as his head turns slightly, her heart a drum against the blood in her ears.

"You still don't see it, Salam. We can't possibly have done this much for the People's Protector just to stay in the outskirts forever," Maximus continues. "Alvaro is too weak to be king and he doesn't have an heir. The throne has been unstable for too long. If a king capable of protecting the people had been on the throne a decade ago, the outskirts might not have been abandoned. Replacing him can only happen when we go to the capital."

"And the capable king you speak of, are you referring to yourself, Maximus?" Fury boils in Salam's voice. "Are you seeking the throne? And are you planning to reunite the three royal regalia?"

"Yes," Maximus admits without a single shred of hesitation.

Akari grips the Jewel of Compassion through her clothes and slumps against the wall. A chill runs down her spine. There's yet another contender who wants the royal regalia hanging from her neck. Petrified, she looks down to ensure the Jewel of Compassion is still hidden from view. *What would Sir Maximus do to get this? Would he kill me for it?*

Akari is beginning to understand why her mother chose to keep the royal regalia hidden all this time. *But it is still hidden.* She forces her nerves to the back of her mind, then straightens and peeks out again.

Salam ruffles her fur, exasperated. "Maximus, let me make this clear. The current state of affairs is caused by Zatori. It's his thirst for power that brought about the Great Harvest. You need to know who the real enemy is. It's greed—Zatori's greed, and now yours. It consumes people and leads them to destruction."

Maximus shakes his silver head in dissent. "The real enemy right now isn't greed, but inadequacy. If Alvaro stays on the throne, we can expect another Great Harvest in the near future. If we replace the inadequate king with a competent one, we'll be saving more lives in the grand scheme of things. Together, we can make Xylon a better place for all."

"No!" Salam barks, her shadow almost eclipsing him as she stands even taller. "When I joined the People's Protector, we had an agreement never to let ourselves be involved in another rebellion, or any matters relating to the capital. I only agreed to lead so I could protect the Xylonians, not seek to take King Alvaro's place. The king is only as strong as the people who support him. What good is any king alone? This is the time he needs the support of the People's Protector, in addition to the Andelovian Army."

There's a pause as Maximus mulls over Salam's words. "Are you still holding on to your old ties to the Royal Regiment and Alvaro?"

"It's not those ties I'm holding on to, but rather the promise I made to myself—to protect all Xylonians, be they gifteds or nulluses, in the capital or the outskirts." Salam's voice is unwavering.

"In that case, when the time comes for me to be king, this is all the more reason I need you right by my side, in the capacity of grand advisor, a position second to none," Maximus asserts. "We can rule Xylon together, hand in hand, just as Alvaro and Vykroux once did."

"And look where they are now," Salam retorts. His jaw tenses, and she asks, "And if I refuse to do as you say?"

"In that case you can leave, but you'll go as you came— with nothing." Maximus's silver eyes are hollow and dead.

Salam unleashes a feral growl. "Are you saying you won't reconsider your stance?"

"I see that you won't either." He shakes his head in disappointment. "I genuinely hoped there would be a way to show you what I see."

"The way I see it, you're risking the lives of Protectors because of a traitor," Salam roars, enraged. "And you're risking the lives of the Protectors so you can sit on the throne."

"Every cause comes at a cost. Aren't you also risking the lives of the Protectors for a cause you believe in? If not, why have you led so many Protectors to their deaths in the hope of defeating Zatori?" Maximus challenges, leaving Salam speechless. "That's because you think their lives will be lost for a greater good." With that, he turns and starts down the hallway in Akari's direction.

Pretending she's just arrived, Akari strides toward Salam's office as indifferently as she can manage. "Sir Maximus!" She comes to a stop, saluting him when their paths cross. Maximus slows, the fire in his silver eyes blazing as he scrutinizes her. She shifts nervously under his watch.

"You're Akari Miyahara, aren't you?" he asks in a stone-cold voice.

"Yes, Sir Maximus," Akari says, surprised that the all-important Maximus Fontan knows her name.

"I heard that you're training to control your gift with Salam," he continues.

"Yes, sir," Akari replies tightly.

"Well, good luck. We'd like to have you back on combat missions soon." Maximus flashes an unsettling smile before disappearing behind the wall.

Unsure of what to make of her brief interaction with him, Akari continues down the hallway.

"You're early today!" Salam comments in surprise, her ruffled fur and exposed claws suggesting she's still riled by the argument. She tries to compose herself, hastily smoothing her fur and retracting her claws.

Akari salutes her. "Madam Salam! I promised you the last time I wouldn't be late again," she says as naturally as she can manage, hoping her superior doesn't suspect she overheard them.

When Salam gives a small nod, then opens the door and ushers her into the office, her stomach unclenches slightly.

"Ty and I searched the Andelovians' rooms in the Colossal Inn but found nothing suspicious," Akari promptly reports.

"Tell me what you saw," Salam says as she takes her seat by the desk.

While deliberately omitting Yong's drawing of her with the Jewel of Compassion, Akari recounts everything else. "We found some fancy pieces of jewelry in the Andelovian girl's room that looked incredibly expensive. I even saw an archivian milk fang for the first time in my life. Emeraude isn't lacking in clothes. She seems to have them in every single color of the rainbow, with a disproportionate amount of green. Meanwhile, Yong's room is rather bare. Nothing appears out of the ordinary, although he sleeps with a dagger under his pillow. Both of them have an arsenal of very fine weapons and identical bronze badges with a zephanerix engraved on them."

Salam's ears twitch as Akari finishes her description.

"What do you think of it?" Akari asks.

"Hmmm... archivian milk fangs are extremely hard to come by these days. They've all typically been bought up by collectors eons ago," Salam answers tentatively. "But then again, their patrons are incredibly wealthy, so anything is possible, really."

From Salam's taut shoulders, Akari wonders if there's more than she is letting on. "Is there anything suspicious about the Andelovians?" she probes.

"Nothing concrete just yet," Salam concludes stiffly. "But I'd stay away from them if I were you."

"Why does everyone tell me that?" Akari wonders out loud.

"Did your mother say that too?" Salam's hearty laughter seems to release all her tension.

Akari nods. "And Ty as well," she adds with a sigh. "He hates them."

Salam continues laughing. "It's probably for your own good."

"I know..." Akari says. "And guess who else we saw in the Colossal Inn?" Without waiting for Salam's reply, she continues, "We saw Hanwell, Prisci, and Aloy at the Cavalier Restaurant before our search."

"I'm not surprised if the trio frequents that sort of place," Salam remarks.

"We also saw Emeraude in the restaurant, but on a different table. She was waiting for someone, but they never showed up," Akari recalls.

Salam raises her eyebrows. "How do you know that?"

"I saw this note in her wastepaper basket." Akari pulls it out and hands it to Salam. "She was supposed to meet someone at four, but she was alone the whole time. I wasn't sure if it was going to be important, but I took it anyway."

Salam examines the note and sniffs it thoroughly. "It smells like a bit of everything," she remarks with a growl.

"What do you mean?" Akari asks.

"I'm not too sure what it means myself," she admits, giving the note one last perplexed sniff before placing it in a drawer.

Akari watches her, wondering if there *is* anything about the Andelovians she needs to be wary of. *But Yong loves me... He couldn't possibly—*

"We have no time to lose," Salam continues, as a realm of darkness descends upon them again. "Now, let's get to our training."

This time, Akari doesn't see anyone else. She whirls around several times but finds herself all alone in the illusion. Then, just above her, she sees a sinister, sunken black left eye and white right eye looking down at her. *Zatori!* Akari finds herself rooted to the spot once more, paralyzed by fear.

The rest of Zatori slowly comes into sight. Akari looks up at him, only reaching the height of his waist. His artificially uniform hair is black with white streaks, like it was ten years ago. When she looks down at her soft tiny hands, she realizes she's six years old again.

Zatori bends down so their eyes are level. The proximity of his face unhinges Akari. After taking a moment to examine her, he reaches out his icy hand and places it on her warm cheek. Akari flinches, remembering all too well how her face burned cold at his touch. She lets out an ear-piercing scream, flailing and trying to pull away.

But then Yong's voice echoes in her mind, as though they were back ice-skating together on the frozen Telos Ocean. *Whenever you're afraid, close your eyes and count to three. One, forget the world. Two, forget your fears. And three, never forget yourself.*

Akari squeezes her eyes shut and begins counting. "One..." Momentarily forgetting that she's in an illusion, she allows the realm of darkness to envelop her. Compared to the ones before, which were isolating and intimidating, this makes her feel safe and calm.

"Two..." Akari imagines Zatori before her, just as he was mere moments ago—except this time, she has grown a lot taller. Not only has she reached the height of his shoulders, Zatori's hair has also become white with black streaks. Abandoning her fear to the past, she looks into the haunting eyes that once terrified her.

"Three..." Akari recalls the times she used her gift. Her deflecting Zephy's wounds onto Philippe ultimately enabled her and her mother's escape during the White Blaze. And her subsequent deflection of Ty's wounds onto Hanwell put an end to the bullying. These thoughts give her confidence to use her gift for good. She feels light and powerful, and a surge of energy gushes through her.

When Akari's eyes fly open, she directs all her power at Zatori with an outstretched palm, deflecting the cold burn in her body back onto him and banishing him to the darkness beyond. Beneath her clothes, the Jewel of Compassion emanates a pulsing red glow.

"I did it! I managed to control my gift!" Akari exclaims triumphantly, staring at her hand in disbelief. After the seemingly endless training with Salam, she finally savors the sweet taste of success.

The illusion dissipates around her, and she finds herself back in the den-like office. Salam stands opposite her, a look of surprise and elation lighting up her ursine face.

Akari leaps forward and hugs her in a warm embrace, but she's unable to reach around Salam's gigantic body. In turn, Salam wraps her massive arms around Akari, engulfing her in a ball of fur.

"Thank you for believing me all this time, even when I doubted myself," Akari says gratefully. Her voice turns excited as she asks, "Now, can I get back on combat missions?"

Salam stays silent, her expression shifting. She looks down at Akari's expectant face in a way that appears like she's afraid to disappoint her.

"No." Salam shakes her bear head vehemently, releasing Akari from her arms. "You're still not ready yet."

Akari's eyebrows scrunch in confusion. "But, Salam, I did it..." She speaks slowly, not understanding why her superior hasn't been convinced of the feat she just achieved. "I managed to overcome my fear and control my gift. I'm ready to fight Zatori and the Harvesters!"

"No, Akari," Salam maintains. "Doing it this once in practice isn't enough, for goodness gracious sake. You need to do it at least a hundred—thousand—times before you can get back on combat missions."

"Is it because of Sir Maximus?" Akari dares ask despite the fear of incurring her wrath. "Are you... trying to protect me?"

"Did you eavesdrop on us?" Salam roars furiously. "Do you know you could be punished for this?"

"I didn't mean to," Akari explains meekly. "The two of you weren't keeping it down at all."

Salam growls, exasperated. "It's Maximus and Zatori. I'm trying to protect you from them both."

"Does this mean I actually did alright back there?" Akari asks, her voice hopeful.

"You're right, you did amazing. I've always believed in you, and I'm so proud of you," Salam concedes, pausing briefly before adding, "But with the traitor still among us, it's far too dangerous a time for me to put you back on combat missions. And now Zatori has returned, I can't serve a gifted to him to be harvested! I can't send you to your death!"

"But the rest of the Protectors will still be going on missions," Akari retorts. "I want to fight alongside them."

"No, Akari. I will not allow this." Salam's tone is gentler but still firm.

"Is this because of my mother?" Akari asks.

She hesitates before nodding. "Your mother and I have known each other for a long time, and she saved my life. I'll do anything for her, and that includes protecting you. Even if I can't save the rest of the Protectors, I have to save you."

"But that's not fair," Akari points out indignantly.

"Nothing is fair in this world except death. We're born unequal, live amidst inequality, but are only equal in death—and this is precisely why I'm not putting you before it," Salam concludes with finality. "Besides, didn't you promise me that self-preservation will always be your priority?"

Akari lets out a sigh of resignation, knowing it's pointless to argue further. "What do you plan to do about Sir Maximus?"

"Nothing. I will do all I can for the People's Protector until the day there's nothing left for me to do. And when that time comes, I'll leave," Salam says as casually as she can manage.

"You can't leave!" Akari cries. "The People's Protector won't *be* the People's Protector without you! You can't leave us in the hands of Sir Maximus."

"But don't you see, Akari, all of us are already in the hands of Maximus Fontan."

Akari clutches the Jewel of Compassion through her clothes to quell the chill scuttling along her spine.

Salam doesn't seem to notice. "Or you could leave the People's Protector too," she says on a lighter note. "Your mother would be very happy about it."

"No! The outskirts need us. The people need us. We can't just leave—"

The deafening beating of drums reverberates throughout the Quartz. Akari and Salam glance at each other, both disconcerted, before making their way to the Goethite Hall, where most of the Protectors have already assembled.

From the stairs, Akari's gaze fixes on what everyone has been called to witness. Blood drains from her face and she feels faint. Never before has Akari seen anything like this during her time at the People's Protector. Behind her, Salam reveals no expression whatsoever as she places a protective paw on her shoulder.

Ethan sways on the platform before them, his body a patchwork of green and purple, his damp hair clinging to his temples. Barely conscious, he stands limply on an elevated wooden trapdoor, mouth gagged and hands bound behind his back. Akari's eyes widen in horror as they lock onto the noose cinched around his neck, tethered to a high beam. *Ethan Cook is facing execution!*

Maximus steps forward, and the hushed whispers turn into a pin-drop silence. "We have found the traitor responsible for betraying us to Zatori! He shall pay for the deaths of our comrades with his own! May Ethan Cook die with shame!"

"No!" Akari cries, leaping down the stairs. *That's impossible! Ethan's the last person who would be a traitor! He served the People's Protector with all his heart, and he saved my life. There has to be a mistake. We can't execute him!*

But before she reaches the bottom, Salam grabs her and clasps a paw over her mouth, forcing Akari to still—succumb—as the weight of the moment presses down on her. Even as her heart pounds erratically within Salam's hold, Akari can do nothing but watch in agonizing helplessness.

When Maximus raises his hand, the wooden trapdoor beneath Ethan's feet opens. Right before his body free-falls and the rope around his neck goes taut, he looks in Akari's direction, his hazel, doe-like eyes sad but unafraid.

Akari thrashes desperately in Salam's iron grip, her muffled screams drowned out by the echo of the last words Ethan spoke to her. *You can make sure Zatori's really gone forever this time. And don't forget your promise to stay alive longer than me.* Although Akari is likely to outlive her comrade at this rate, she's wrought with a debilitating fear that she'll never be able to defeat Zatori. *But I have to try... for Ethan...*

Without much fight left in his already mangled body, he writhes briefly before becoming dead still. As Ethan hangs lifelessly from the rope, a deafening silence lingers in the main hall. The Protectors stand frozen in their spots, incapacitated by horror.

When Maximus speaks again, there's no hint that an execution—a murder—has just taken place, or that a life—an innocent life—has just been lost. With a stone-cold voice, he addresses the crowd before him.

"We have intelligence on Zatori's plans. There will be a mission tomorrow night, when we will destroy Zatori and the Harvesters! Every single one of you who's combat-fit will participate. There will be no exceptions." His silver eyes whip toward Akari and Salam before he takes his leave from the platform.

"Ethan's execution is a warning—a warning to me," Salam explains in a hushed whisper, the fury raging in her jet-black eyes undeniable. "Maximus Fontan is trying to show me what the outcome of defying him will be."

Akari's legs go weak and her chest grows tight. As she stares at the emblem of the People's Protector above Ethan's body—at the two-headed lynx—a revelation crashes down on her.

One of the heads has already begun biting the other.

13. Repayment

Amidst the grimness of Ethan's execution and the hopelessness of the conversation with Mari that first love doesn't usually last, there's still a part of Akari's heart that flutters at the thought of seeing Yong for "no particular reason"—or rather, for "repayment".

It's almost noon on the last day of winter. Akari, who's spent far too much time primping, makes her way to Tinkler's Oddities and Antiquities as quickly as her legs can take her. She is wearing her best woolen tunic and skirt, both in burnt sienna, with her faded maroon cloak draped over the top.

Yong is already waiting outside the antiques store with an expectant expression as he paces around to kill time, his usual midnight blue cloak fluttering behind him, revealing a crisp cobalt robe underneath. He beams when he catches sight of Akari and eagerly makes his way over.

"I was worried you'd forget about today..." He heaves a sigh of relief.

Akari shakes her head, a shy smile creeping onto her face. "Of course not. I still have a debt to repay."

"Right..." Yong nods, as if to remind himself of the excuse he gave to ask her out. "Today shall be the day you start repaying me for all the times I saved your life," he declares with a playful smile.

"And how exactly should I go about doing that?" Akari asks cautiously.

"Hmmm..." He pretends to ponder, but the sparkle in his eyes shows he already has something in mind. "For starters, how about a tour of Cheyvelenia?"

"There's not much to see around here," she remarks.

"I'm sure there is," Yong replies. "How about your favorite place growing up?"

"You've already been to the Verge," Akari points out.

"And your next favorite place?" Yong asks.

"That'd be the town square. Have you been there?"

"I've passed by without paying too much attention. Let's go visit, shall we?"

Akari nods, starting down the street that leads to the square. Yong follows closely behind.

"And on the way, I can show you the bakery Ty and I frequent. That's also where we ran into Emeraude the last time," Akari says, taking her new mission a little too seriously. "You can try their famous scorched sea-salt cookie."

"Is that also the bakery where the icing on your face was from?" he asks with a lopsided smile.

"That's the one," Akari admits, slightly embarrassed.

"Maybe I'll try their cake instead." Yong chuckles to himself.

She pretends to scowl.

"How about the place you went for your first date? Or had your first kiss?" he asks, half joking, although there's a hint of genuine curiosity in his voice.

As their conversation takes a turn in a whole other direction, Akari finds herself caught by surprise—and even more embarrassed now. "I... I've never had either of those," she answers quietly, wondering what Yong will make of it.

"I don't believe you." His tone is soft but surprised, yet his eyes seem to brighten.

This time, it's Akari who isn't sure what to make of it.

As they walk on, they attract numerous glances.

"Don't you see how they look at you?" Yong asks.

She shakes her head. "It's *you* they're looking at. You're the one who's from out of town. Don't you see how they look at *you*?"

"In most of the outskies, I see dislike and distrust—fear, even," Yong observes.

"I was referring to the girls our age," Akari says, noting several adolescent girls gazing at him with covetous eyes.

He chuckles, now his turn to be embarrassed. "I've been too preoccupied to notice," Yong claims as he glances her way, his crescent-moon eyes beaming.

"And don't you see how they look at *us*?" Akari continues as she eyes the scratchy fabric of her outfit self-consciously. Despite being decent by the standards in the outskirts, it looks miserably battered beside Yong's. "They all see what I'm seeing—that I'm down here and you're up here." She places her left hand in front of her chest and her right hand at her eye.

He seems utterly taken aback to hear this. "If only you knew... You don't see yourself very well at all, do you?"

"There's not much to see," Akari says with a shrug.

"Well, even if that's really the case—which I completely disagree with—I'll bring you to me," he offers, taking her left hand and lifting it so it's level with her right.

Yong's touch never fails to set off fireworks inside Akari. She gives a nervous smile.

"You, of all people, shouldn't have to care," he reassures her.

"Why is that?" The difference in status and appearance still bothers her, and she isn't sure she'll be able to let it go anytime soon.

"Because you're special, Akari." There isn't a shred of doubt in his eyes. "You have been and will always be special."

"Thank you, but I doubt it..." Akari barely manages to say. The compliment seems almost consolatory, coming from someone like Yong, who seems exceptional in almost every way.

"Well, like I said, I beg to differ," he maintains. "And how about the boys our age? There were plenty looking your way..."

Akari hesitates, hovering between surprise and disbelief. "That can't be... We don't talk. If they know about my gift, they stay away from me. And if they don't, I stay away from them. I don't want to hurt anyone else by accident."

"And is Tyler Kane the exception to all of this?" he asks. "Is he the only one you let hang around you?" Akari isn't sure if she catches a trace of jealousy in his tone.

"Well, Ty is my best friend," she explains.

"To you, maybe," he says, his eyebrows rising with a hint of amusement. "Surely you must know he likes you."

Akari lets out a small sigh. "I... I figured..."

"Seems like you aren't that oblivious after all..." Yong remarks with a lopsided smile.

"But with Ty, we're always going to be best friends," she insists. "That's all it's ever been, and all it's ever going to be."

"Our poor friend... Tyler Kane..." he says dryly.

"And how about Emeraude?" Akari blurts as a lingering thought about their matching zephanerix badges comes to mind. She ponders their significance, but knows she can't ask him about them without giving herself away.

Yong's face turns serious. "Emeraude to me is much like Tyler Kane is to you—a great friend and companion—no less, but also no more."

"You must know she likes you too," Akari says in a small voice, her thoughts drifting to Emeraude's flamboyant but beautiful outfits. She wonders what he sees in her and her shabby clothes.

"I don't know that for sure—"

"But you're almost certain—"

"Regardless, it's forbidden in our line of work," Yong concludes, and she doesn't miss his haste to brush off her suggestion.

There's a small pause before Akari asks, "How about in the capital? There has to be someone waiting for you back home."

"If you knew how occupied with work I am when I'm back in Andelovia, you wouldn't even have to ask this," he assures her. "There's no one at all."

"I don't believe that you've never had a first love," she says doubtfully.

Yong chews his tongue. "I did... Eons ago, I fell in love with a princess..."

"A princess?" Akari gasps despite a tinge of jealousy welling inside her. "I see you're very ambitious, future King of Xylon," she teases in an attempt to hide it.

"Yes, but the princess's husband only becomes a prince, not the king."

"Oh... I didn't know Xylon has a princess, though." She tries to cover up the embarrassment from her lack of capital-related knowledge. "I thought there weren't any heirs to the throne..."

This time, Yong seems surprised—impressed, even—by the bit of knowl edge Akari has demonstrated. "She's not exactly the direct heir to the throne, but she may well be if Queen Jocelin doesn't bear King Alvaro a child," he explains.

"That princess... was she beautiful?" Akari asks, curious.

He smiles, somewhat nervously, before answering, "Very much. She was more beautiful than anyone could imagine..."

Akari's heart twinges. Somehow, his earlier compliment seems to hold less value now. "And were you her first love too?" she probes.

Yong shakes his head. "It was one-sided. She didn't even know about it. But it's been a long time. That's all in the past... And now is what matters," he says as they reach the edge of the town square. "Right now, I'm looking at the person I love." He gazes into Akari's eyes, then fleetingly at her lips.

His dark eyes twinkle as he lets on a shy smile. As casually as he can manage, Yong sweeps the loose strands from Akari's face and caresses her hair. His hand comes to rest at the back of her neck, stirring a warm sensation within her. He leans in unbearably slowly.

Akari closes her eyes, fists clenched, heart racing wildly. For a moment, she forgets all about letting him go. Just as Yong's lips are about to touch hers, she senses him come to a standstill.

"Akari, I'm leaving," he announces, dread lacing his words. "I have to go back to Andelovia."

Akari's stomach, full of butterflies just a moment ago, feels severely winded. Her eyes fly open, only to find Yong's face an inch from hers. He releases his touch and backs away, putting some distance between them.

"I thought I should tell you... before we... I..." he tries to explain.

Akari is utterly shattered, completely at a loss. It takes her a while to regain her composure. "When?" she finally asks, her voice barely a whisper scraping the back of her throat.

"Tomorrow. The first day of spring."

Akari's heart plunges. "So soon?"

"Yes," he replies. "I have to report back to the capital after completing my mission."

"Does this mean you've found the merchandise you're looking for?"

"Yes," Yong says, his jaw tensing.

"You still won't say what it is, will you?" she asks teasingly, an attempt to cover up her disappointment at the prospect of him leaving.

"You know I can't..."

"I know... It's fine," she says with an unconvincing half-smile. After all, she has secrets of her own too.

As if able to read her mind, Yong asks, "Do you know that feeling, when you have an urge to open all of yourself up to someone—wholly, completely, and unrestrainedly?"

Surprised by how aptly he's described one of her deepest desires, she looks him in the eye and nods fervently. *Stay safe, lie low, and keep out of trouble.* Akari has always known this feeling.

He gazes magnetically at her. "I feel that way, but I'm bound by duty..." he admits. For a moment, Yong seems desolately fragile, wearing a look of vulnerability that's unlike him.

"How about Nana Eleanor?" Akari offers, hoping to make him feel better.

Yong smiles at the mention of his nanny. "She comes very close. Having brought me up, she knows me better than I know myself," he says. "And you? Have you ever had someone you didn't have any secrets with? That you could be completely yourself with?" After a slight deliberation, he adds, "Is Tyler Kane that person for you?"

"He was... until recently..." Akari concedes.

"Why is that?"

She hesitates briefly, wondering how to explain. "Ty doesn't like hearing about you very much—or us," she admits, deciding to be upfront. Yong doesn't seem surprised to hear this. However, this isn't what's bothering her. "I also thought I had that with my mother too... until recently..."

"Why? What changed?"

Through her clothes, Akari clutches the Jewel of Compassion tightly before her eyes veer down to stare at her boots. Although Mari has kept secrets from her, Akari knows she's guilty of the same. *Who am I to blame then?*

"What is it?" Yong presses.

"Do you know anything about the missing royal regalia?" she asks, her voice tentative.

"I know reuniting them would pave the way to the throne." Yong's answer is terse.

"And coming from the capital, have you seen them before?" Akari probes.

"The royal regalia are not something just anyone can lay eyes on. Besides, they've been missing for years." There's a slight pause before he adds, "But I've seen drawings of them..."

So, Yong knows what the Jewel of Compassion looks like! But why did he draw me wearing it? Does he know I have it?

"Why do you ask?" Yong eyes her suspiciously.

"I was just curious..." Akari says as Heavenly Bakery comes into sight. To her surprise, it seems closed. "That's odd. The bakery is usually open at this time of the day..."

Akari and Yong cup their hands around their eyes, peering through the glass windows of the storefront. But neither Madam Celine nor the usual array of baked goods can be seen.

"That's a pity. I was looking forward to trying some of their cake," Yong says with a mildly disappointed shrug.

They continue on their way until they reach the town square. Set in the heart of Cheyvelenia, the square, though quaint and ordinary, serves as a place of congregation for all events, big or small. A defaced stone statue of King Alvaro stands erect in the middle, its once-regal features chipped beyond recognition.

To the north, the square is bordered by faded stores, their signs dulled and peeling, yet still the pride of the town. To the south, the air reeks of poverty, where the homeless—with their gaunt faces and hollow eyes—beg for scraps, as though they know better than to cross over. The segregated layout of the square reflects the divide in Cheyvelenia—Hazenfeld in North Cheyvelenia, its relative wealth and prosperity enjoyed by only a select few, and the slums in South Cheyvelenia, where the masses are left to scrape by.

The town square is especially busy today. The older ladies are huddled in groups, their hands working fast on thin wooden strips and paper.

"What are they doing?" Yong asks.

"They're making paper lanterns," Akari informs him. "The annual Lantern Festival is tonight." She has been so preoccupied that she's nearly forgotten about the upcoming celebrations.

"What is this Lantern Festival?"

"It takes place on the last night of winter to mark the start of spring and new beginnings. Cheyvelenians gather in the town square with their loved ones to write wishes on paper lanterns, light them, and send them up into the air. If their lanterns touch the sky, their wishes will come true," Akari explains. "Don't you have this in the capital?"

"No. In Andelovia, we have the Festival of Colors instead, although it isn't until spring has begun," Yong shares. With twinkling eyes, he suggests, "Shall we go to the Lantern Festival together tonight?"

Yes! But duty punctures Akari's excitement with a spear of disappointment. "I can't..." she says with regret before dropping to a whisper. "I have a mission tonight."

"Are you going to fight Zatori?" he asks, concern eddying in his dark eyes.

Akari doesn't respond, but her silence is answer enough.

"I thought you were suspended from combat missions?" he recalls with a frown.

"There was a command for the participation of all combat-fit Protectors in this mission... Besides, the method you taught me to overcome my fear worked and I managed to control my gift during training," Akari states, pride evident despite her disappointment. "I've been wanting to thank you. Thank you, Yong."

"My pleasure. This seems like a cause for celebration," he says, though his voice is tight. Worry—perhaps even a hint of regret—is etched on his face.

"I'll be alright," she attempts to reassure him, sensing his unease. "The People's Protector is well prepared this time. We'll destroy Zatori and the Harvesters tonight."

"Be careful. And remember, you promised not to put yourself in peril again," Yong reminds her, his tone heavy.

"I'm not sure how that's going to work when I'm on a combat mission," Akari points out meekly, finding the Jewel of Compassion again and gripping it tightly.

He lets out a long sigh. "Let's get some lanterns to write our wishes on, shall we?"

"It doesn't work that way," she tells him. "We'd have to light our lantern and send it up into the sky for our wishes to come true."

"I'll send it up for both of us tonight," he offers as he walks over to the old ladies and buys two white paper lanterns.

"People usually share a lantern with their loved ones—or friends..." Akari interjects, but she's too late.

"Oh..." Yong breathes, evidently unaware of this. "That's fine. I'll hold on to the extra one as a keepsake."

She nods and takes a seat on the steps, across from the statue of King Alvaro. He settles next to her, close enough that his knee skims hers. Akari's insides flutter.

Yong takes a poignant look at the defaced statue. "Why didn't they fix it?"

"It's King Alvaro," Akari replies as if that's explanation enough. "No one would bother to."

"How long has it been like this for?"

"Since the Great Rebellion."

"Ten whole years?" Yong exclaims in shock. "Anything similar in the capital would have been fixed within the day." It dawns on him just how deep-seated the resentment toward the king is in the outskirts.

Akari simply nods as she glances at the statue, realizing she doesn't know the face of the man so many outskies have come to loathe.

Just as she wonders what he looks like, Yong asks worriedly, "Do you, by any chance, share Tyler Kane's views on the king?"

"We hold similar views, but to varying degrees, as do most of the outskies," Akari says. "To me, King Alvaro is so far away that there's no point in hatred. We have nothing to do with him and I want it to stay that way."

Yong looks at her, speechless.

"But to Ty, the pain has hit too close to home," Akari continues. "If you understood what he went through, you'd understand his hatred for King Alvaro as well."

"I don't blame him," Yong concedes after hearing about Ty's predicament. "But what if King Alvaro's side of the story provides a different perspective? What if the truth you know about him isn't the whole truth? And what if he had challenges to overcome and people to protect?"

"What challenges is the king not able to overcome? And who is the king not able to protect?" Akari questions skeptically.

"He's still only human," Yong says with an exasperated chuckle. "Won't you give him another chance?"

"I'll decide if I ever get to hear what he has to say," she declares, flashing a playful smile.

"Alright, alright..." Yong holds out the folded paper lantern to her, along with a quill and some ink. "Here you go. You can write your wish first."

Akari quickly pushes the lantern back toward him. "No, you should start on it first. I haven't decided what to write," she says. "And don't forget, you're only allowed to write one wish—the one single thing you want most in the entire world."

"Alright." Without any hesitation, Yong begins working on one side of the lantern.

Ten years ago, Akari attended her first Lantern Festival with her mother shortly after moving to Cheyvelenia. However, Mari didn't seem to favor the crowds or enjoy the festival, and never went again. Fortunately, Ty came along soon after, and Akari has been going with him ever since.

Throughout the years, they have written all there is to wish for—taller, wiser, fuller, healthier, richer, happier.... Akari recalls that when she was fourteen, she wished to join the People's Protector. The very next year, she did.

What should I wish for this year? she wonders. Her wish this year seems especially difficult to choose— especially precious. *For Zatori and the Harvesters to be defeated by the People's Protector? For me to be reunited with my father? Or for me to have a chance with Yong?*

A tiny smile skims across Akari's face but quickly disappears. *But after tomorrow, I'll never see him again...* She looks up to find Yong gazing intently at her, a hint of amusement flecking his face.

"What kind of wish are you thinking about to have you smiling and frowning like that?" he asks.

"I'm not telling. It's a secret." Slightly embarrassed, Akari quickly rearranges her expression. "Are you already done?"

"Yes," he answers proudly.

Akari realizes she hasn't managed to catch even a glimpse of the wish he penned. Yong has already flipped the lantern blank side up and placed it in front of her.

He looks at her expectantly. When she doesn't start writing, he asks, "Have you not decided what to wish for?"

Akari shakes her head. "Not yet. Let me see yours," she says, attempting to flip over the folded lantern.

But with his inhuman reflexes, Yong catches her wrist before she can touch it. "I'm not showing. It's a secret."

"That's not fair," Akari protests. "You'll get to see mine when you send the lantern into the sky."

"That's what I get for helping our wishes come true," he says with a lopsided smile. "Now it's time for you to work on yours."

Before deciding which wish to write down, Akari feels the need to ask, "So, is this it then? Is this the last time I'll be seeing you? Is this when we have to say our farewells?"

He shifts in his spot, his voice tentative as he says, "I'll drop by Moonstone Apothecary tomorrow to pick something up before I leave." He seems to be stalling for some reason she isn't able to grasp. "I'll see you again then."

"And after tomorrow?" she presses.

"Till we meet again," Yong answers simply.

"If we even meet again." Akari sighs.

"I'm sure we will." He speaks with conviction. "Especially now I owe you one for the tour of Cheyvelenia you gave me today."

"How will we?" she challenges. "There are a hundred-odd towns in the outskirts. Yet of all places, you have to go back to the capital. With the Great Divide, how do you suppose you're going to repay me with a tour of Andelovia?"

"I told you, it wouldn't be impossible to get you across the Great Divide if you were with me," Yong says, smiling.

"Are you asking me to go to the capital with you?" Akari is bewildered by the flicker of hope she feels at the idea.

"Will you go if I ask?" This time, his dark eyes are more serious than they should be. "I can take you if you want to."

Yong's offer is exceedingly enticing. Akari has already had thoughts about visiting the capital in search of Lord

Vykroux. She also wants to see Andelovia, the home she doesn't quite remember and the city where she spent her early childhood. While she's at it, she is curious to know how Sage has been. And now, Akari's feelings for Yong—and his for her—are the most compelling reason of all.

Yet, she knows Mari will never let her go, and she doesn't have the heart to leave without telling her mother. Besides, Ty would be utterly shattered if she left. Despite the many reasons drawing her to the capital, Akari can't just abandon everything she knows and everyone she loves. With a long resigned sigh, she forces herself to give up any hope of going to Andelovia—and inadvertently, any hope of a future with Yong.

"My mother's harder to get past than the Great Divide," Akari states simply. "I'll never be able to set foot in the capital."

Yong's brow furrows, his lips curving into a frown.

"What's wrong?" she asks.

"Nothing..." Yong claims, quickly composing his expression. "It's just... Sometimes, I wonder what it would be like if you'd never left Andelovia. How things... how things could be different... even, or especially, between us..."

Akari smiles wistfully. She wants, so badly, to let him know she's his childhood playmate and Lord Vykroux's daughter—that she didn't die in the Great Harvest and, in a twist of fate, ended up at the opposite end of Xylon. As a child, Yong, believing he'd lost a childhood playmate after losing both parents, mustn't have had it easy. Akari wishes to tell him that his childhood wasn't only defined by losses. *This is the one thing I can do for him before he leaves for Andelovia.*

However, this would mean exposing her and her mother. Not having had the chance to ask Mari about Lord Vykroux, Akari wants to be sure about her father's identity before revealing her own to Yong. Although she's been afraid to broach the subject, she is determined this time.

I'll ask Mama about Lord Vykroux first thing tomorrow, so when Yong drops by Moonstone, I can tell him we were childhood playmates and that we've known each other for more than a decade. We'll get to bid each other a proper final farewell when we part this time. And then I'll let him go... Akari tries to convince herself.

After a long while, she eventually writes her wish. *I wish for us to be safe and happy, even when we are apart.* It feels remarkably simple, but it's what she truly wants.

"I'm finally done..." she says, handing the lantern back to Yong.

He tucks it into his robe, promising, "I'll see to it that our wishes come true."

"Are you going to add this to the count too?" Akari asks.

"Maybe I should, now that you've reminded me..." Yong pretends to toy with the idea. "I was originally only going to keep count of the number of times I have had to save your life."

"And what's it at now?" Akari wonders, her brow furrowing.

"More than you can keep count," he goads her, giving his usual lopsided smile.

She purses her lips. "How am I going to repay you for the rest of the times I owe you now that you're leaving tomorrow? I don't like being in debt."

Yong gazes at her with a profound intensity, his eyes twinkling with ardent anticipation. "We can fix that," he says with a playful smile that poorly masks his nervousness.

Without warning, he leans in until his lips land softly on hers. They skim lightly over each other in a delicate dance. Yong's hand finds Akari's waist, pulling her closer, as her fingers trace his cheek and slide to the nape of his neck, their touch tender but electrifying. Lost in the moment, they become oblivious to the world around them.

After an imperceptible amount of time, when they eventually come apart, their breathing is quickened, their faces flushed. Their eyes lock, a silent reminder that their time together is dwindling.

"I didn't realize *this* counts as paying you back," Akari says with a coy smile.

"I accept this form of repayment any day," Yong declares, chuckling light-heartedly.

She lets on a pretend scowl. "You really do follow your own advice, don't you?"

"What advice?" he asks, puzzled.

"To not hesitate when you go in for a kill."

"Oh, that..." he recalls, smiling. "I guess you can say so. You really do pay attention, don't you?"

"I've told you, not any more than you do," she counters with a laugh, but it quickly melts into a sigh. "I never thought our first kiss would be a goodbye kiss..."

"Before, I didn't even dare hope that we'd have a first kiss..." Yong admits. "But now, I'm sure it's not goodbye for us. It won't be our last..."

Akari smiles although she doesn't believe him. "I guess the town square has just become the place where I've had both my first date and my first kiss. In case I ever need to bring anyone in the future," she jests.

"Who else are you planning on giving a tour of Cheyvelenia to?" Yong asks, now his turn to give a pretend scowl. He pulls Akari in, gently locking her between his arms.

"No one in particular," she says meekly as the smell of crisp mountain air envelops her. Even after their first kiss, his touch still sends shockwaves through her entire being.

Tucking her head under his chin, Yong presses his nose to the top of her head and inhales deeply to take in the fragrance of her hair. "Stay safe during your mission, alright?" His voice is earnest, pleading.

Akari, her face resting on his sturdy chest, nods. "I'll try my best."

"And I still stand by my advice. Don't hesitate when you go in for the kill," Yong says, his expression serious. "I don't want to have to add to the count—although I do accept our established form of repayment," he adds to lighten the mood.

It works. Akari lets out a radiant peal of laughter.

He studies her intently with his beaming crescent-moon eyes. "Akari..." he says softly.

"Yes?"

Just as Yong thinks he cannot possibly fall deeper in love with her, she proves him wrong. "Akari, I love you..." he confesses once again, as though unable to contain his emotions.

Regrettably, Akari doesn't say these words back, but not because she doesn't feel the same way about him. In fact, she does—much more than she realized before. But she's immensely afraid that professing her love will be akin to sealing her fate, making it even harder to see him leave.

It dawns on her that she has sunk a lot deeper in love than she ever thought possible. Although her mind had been resolved the night before to let him go, her heart now wavers.

After countless attempts to bury her feelings, Akari finally plucks up the courage to admit to herself that she is irredeemably in love—with an Andelovian boy from the opposite end of Xylon, who's about to leave for the capital the very next day.

14. Confrontations

Akari returns to Moonstone Apothecary later than she intended. She'll have to pick up her kris, well hidden beneath her mattress, and hurry to the Quartz in order to make it on time.

The new doorknob catches her off guard—its unfamiliar, polished shine starkly out of place on the worn front door. As soon as she steps through, she senses an unspoken tension hanging in the air. Mari sits quietly at the counter, perfectly still and in deep thought. When she lifts her head, Akari sees a devastating look of hurt, anger, and worry etched on her mother's face.

"Akari Miyahara! Did you join the People's Protector?" Mari demands, confronting her daughter as she rises from her seat. She enunciates every word excruciatingly slowly, her voice quavering with the agony of betrayal.

Guilty as charged, Akari's heart takes a plunge. *So, is this it? Is this how it feels to disappoint someone you love? Is this how it feels to disappoint someone who loves you?* She can't be sure—she has never disappointed her mother before. But whatever this feeling is, she detests it. Akari has always wanted so badly to make her mother proud, but she seems to be slipping further with every passing moment.

"I... I... I did..." she stutters, finding herself at a hopeless loss for words, completely unable to conjure some blatant lie or lame excuse. "How... how do you know? How did you find out?" Akari thought she'd been careful enough to hide this secret well.

"I went to Tinkler's. You weren't working there. You never have." Mari is fuming as she makes her way around the counter, stopping before her daughter.

Well aware her lie has been exposed, Akari is unable to look her mother in the eye. *What brought Mama to Tinkler's—*

"How could you join the People's Protector? You know I've always been so against the idea!" Mari's expression is dead serious—desperate, even.

"Mama, you know all I've ever wanted is to protect you with my own hands, with my gift, with my everything... just like you did ten years ago..." Akari desperately wants her mother to understand, but her words feel inadequate. She crumples under Mari's gaze, bracing for an onslaught of chastisement.

But Mari is stunned speechless. A decade ago, she'd been willing to sacrifice everything to save her daughter. The last thing she ever wanted was for Akari to face the same fate. Yet, she never imagined that, for this very reason, Akari would admire her—let alone aspire to emulate her.

"Akari—"

"Mama, I just want to be useful!" Akari cries impassionedly.

Mari's face stiffens and her jaw tightens. "Useful?" This word jolts her, bringing back the memory of when Zatori had uttered it with his dreadful drawl.

She grits her teeth. "I don't ever want to hear any of this again! Do you hear me? I don't ever want you to be useful to anybody! This is the only way you can be safe!"

Indignant tears well up in Akari's eyes. She knows her mother means well, but she can't help but disagree with inaction. "Mama, this is a battle we have to fight ourselves. We can't wait on somebody else to fight it for us!"

"We fought plenty ten years ago! After that, all I've asked from you is to stay safe, lie low, and keep out of trouble! Why couldn't you just stay away from the People's Protector? How could you hide it from me? How could you lie to me about it?" Mari admonishes.

The grievance Akari has been nursing eventually overcomes her. While Mari's accusations hold true, she is also equally guilty. When Akari plucks up her courage and looks her mother straight in the eye, anger has already taken over. It's her turn to confront Mari.

"How could you fault me for all the things you've done yourself? You, too, have hidden secrets from me and lied to me!" Akari finally erupts, having held it all in for too long. "I know *you've* been helping to heal the wounded at the People's Protector!"

Taken by surprise, Mari's breath catches, her eyes shifting guiltily. "That's... that's different! I wasn't out there fighting—"

Akari doesn't stop to listen. "Why did you lie to me about losing the Jewel of Compassion? Why did you hide what it was from me?"

"I explained to you before! It was too dangerous! You weren't ready—"

"Where do you get your telmezia tea from? They don't have that anywhere in the outskirts!"

"I... I..." Mari struggles to find the right words. "Akari, my baby—"

"I'm not a child anymore, Mama! I know things! You can't keep me in the dark like you've done all my life!" Akari fires at her mother, her resentment rising.

Mari falls silent, knowing any of the reasons she provides will fall on deaf ears.

Akari stills for a moment, save for the heaving of her chest, breathless. Then, with a resolute shake of her head, she concludes, "None of these questions matter now. I have to go."

"Where are you going? Are you going to the Lantern Festival?" Mari demands, concerned.

"No... I have a mission tonight—with the People's Protector," Akari answers quietly before heading upstairs, conveniently avoiding the look of consternation on her mother's face.

"Zatori?" Mari asks in a horrified whisper. She barely steadies herself before trailing up the stairs behind her daughter.

"Yes," Akari answers as nonchalantly as she can manage while she retrieves the kris from beneath her mattress.

"You're not going anywhere tonight! And you're not ever returning to the People's Protector!" Mari exclaims frantically, her voice rising a notch. "I forbid you to go! We need to leave Cheyvelenia now! We need to run!"

Akari shakes her head adamantly. "There's no point in stopping me, Mama. Zatori already knows about me—us—by now."

"They've seen you?" Mari gasps, her wide eyes swirling with terror.

"Yes, on the night Zatori returned," Akari informs her mother quietly, trying her best to contain any trace of emotion. "I was on that mission as well."

Mari gasps again, her face blanching. "That's all the more reason we need to go—"

"If the People's Protector doesn't destroy him tonight, he *will* come for us. We have to stop Zatori. I have to stop him. Like you did ten years ago," Akari declares.

"Ten years ago, we were cornered! I'm not going to let you walk right up to him for harvesting now!" her mother cries. "Do you know how much I've given up to keep you safe? I'd give up my life to keep you alive!"

"Mama..." Akari sighs, exasperated.

Mari clutches her head between her hands, her breathing growing erratic. "Please, Akari, I'm begging you! Don't leave! Tonight is not the night for you to go!"

"I have to," Akari maintains.

"There's so much I have to tell you. If you stay, I'll tell you everything there is for you to know," Mari offers, desperate.

"You're now willing to tell me all your secrets, so I won't go on the mission?" Akari asks incredulously.

Of all the secrets Mari has hidden from her, the most hurtful one—but also the one she has the least courage to ask her mother about—has always been her father's identity. And now, she is about to tear the scab off the most painful wound of all.

Akari looks into her dark, almond eyes, steeling herself to confront her mother about the most unbroachable subject. "Why don't you tell me about Papa?"

Mari's features first twist in utter shock, then unfurl into a profound sadness. "What do you want to know about him?" she asks cautiously, deliberately avoiding her daughter's gaze.

Akari sighs, knowing all too well that she's leveraging her mother's greatest weakness, that it isn't a fair fight. "Actually, I don't even need you to tell me about him. I already know what there is to know."

"What do you know, Akari?" Mari asks anxiously.

"Everything. Why didn't you tell me who Papa is?" Akari begins. She grips her necklace to steady her shaking hand. "And why didn't you tell me that Papa's still alive and well in the capital?"

The remaining color drains rapidly from Mari's porcelain face, leaving her ghostly pale. Her throat tightens, growing dry and hoarse, as though she's swallowed sand, and her mind blanks completely. For what seems like an eternity, she's incapacitated, until she eventually breaks down, sobbing softly into her palms.

Akari's heart wrenches as she watches her mother, but she doesn't allow it to show. *It's time I learned the truth.*

It takes her mother a near insurmountable effort to regain some control. Between sobs, she struggles with coherence, barely managing to ask, "Akari, my baby... how... how do you know? How did you find out?"

"So, it's true then." Akari sighs softly, her voice cold.

When their eyes meet, there's a maturity in Akari's gaze that's unfamiliar to Mari. Her daughter has grown up so much—so fast.

"Regardless, that doesn't matter." Akari shakes her head sadly. Her iciness begins to melt and her eyes brim with tears. "What matters is you lied to me and kept secrets from me. But now I know them all."

"Akari, please hear me out. I have something to tell you." Mari wheezes suddenly as she collapses into a chair, her breathing painfully strained. "Do you remember the fortune teller—"

"Mama, I need to go." Akari barely hears her mother as she checks the clock anxiously.

"I don't feel well... I don't have much time left..." Mari gasps breathlessly.

Akari fixes her mother with a long stare, then dismisses her words as a ruse to prevent her from leaving. "You'll be fine. You can heal yourself."

What if Mama's really unwell? a small voice in the back of her mind asks. *Do you believe what you just said, or are you convincing yourself more than her?* But Akari quickly brushes these thoughts aside. With her hand clenched around her kris, she firms her resolve and starts down the stairs.

"Akari... Akari!" Mari rises and pants after her daughter breathlessly. "Don't go... Not tonight!"

From the middle of the stairs, Akari turns back to look at her mother. Her face is ashen and her pupils are dilated with fear. Akari's heart sinks.

"I'll be back soon, and I promise to stay safe," she reassures Mari despite anger and hurt simmering inside her. Even so, she has never doubted that there's also love—there always has been and there always will be.

Akari feels an aching impulse to rush up the stairs and give her mother a hug, but she knows there's no time. She'll have to save it for later.

Before leaving, Akari says, "Mama, you know despite everything, I still heart you with all my love, right?" With that, she flies down the steps without waiting for her mother's reply.

"Akari, my baby... Akari Miyahara!" Mari calls after her daughter with the little remaining strength she manages to summon.

But Akari is already gone.

♦

Night is approaching on the eve of spring, and the crisp air is soothed by an occasional warm breeze. Akari pauses briefly and turns to take a fleeting look at the modest wood and stone shophouse she and her mother have lived in for most of her life.

For a moment, a crippling fear that something untoward might befall her mother grips her, but she quickly quells her worries. *Mama has the gift of healing. She'll be fine—she always has been.*

With little time to lose, Akari takes hurried strides to the Quartz. When she arrives at the headquarters, most of the Protectors have already begun preparing for their mission. She hastily throws on the dirt-brown uniform of the People's Protector before polishing her armor and sharpening her kris.

Already clad in uniform, Ty has been glancing around anxiously every few seconds while running a whetstone along the blade of his battle-ax. He heaves a sigh of relief when he spots her in the crowd and immediately makes his way over.

"Akari! Is everything alright?" he asks, concerned. "Where were you? You're almost late."

"My mother found out. She went to Tinkler's," Akari says as she slips on her armor.

Without much elaboration, Ty knows exactly what she means. As his ocean blue eyes widen in trepidation, his first thoughts are of self-preservation. "Your mother knows I brought you here, doesn't she? Is she going to slaughter me? Did you tell her that you forced me to bring you?"

Despite Akari's unease, Ty's misguided response puts an amused half-smile on her face. "Don't worry. My mother didn't mention you even once," she replies with a roll of her eyes.

"Oh... Thank goodness!" He heaves a huge sigh of relief. "How did she take it?"

"Not well. She was very shaken. She wasn't in a good state when I left... especially knowing where I left for..." Akari's expression shifts, her face shadowed by the weight of the immense disappointment she recalls in her mother's eyes. "But she'll be alright... She always manages somehow..." she says in a small voice, again more to convince herself than Ty.

He gives her shoulder a reassuring squeeze. "Let's focus on the mission for now," he suggests before plucking up the courage to offer, "I'll go with you to see Madam Mari later. Hopefully she'll be less angry by then."

Akari smiles gratefully, knowing how much it took for him to say this. "Thanks, Ty—"

The deafening beating of drums ends their conversation, prompting the Protectors to assemble in the Goethite Hall, in front of the platform where Ethan was executed. This time, Maximus and Salam take the stage together, portraying a united front to the rest of the People's Protector, reinforcing the significance of this mission.

"Tonight, we'll determine the future of the outskirts and the future of Xylon," Maximus begins, punctuating his words by slamming his fist into his other hand. "Even long before the Great Harvest, Zatori has been harvesting gifts in the outskirts and will continue if we don't stop him."

He sweeps the hall with his gaze. "Although he's yet to make another appearance since his return, we've learned that Zatori himself will lead the Harvesters to our neighboring town of Yilina tonight. This time, we'll make them pay for what they did to us. Tonight is the night we'll destroy them! Never again will we live at their mercy!"

The crowd erupts into cheers, their emotions running high. The Protectors, acutely aware of the heavy losses they've suffered, are anxious how this mission will unfold.

"Since this is our biggest and most important mission, Salam Esquenald and I will be leading it together," Maximus continues, and the crowd falls silent, tension sizzling in the air. "We'll split the Protectors into two groups, which will flank Yilina from both sides as we close in on Zatori and the Harvesters.

Salam will now explain the formation and strategy for tonight."

There isn't even so much as a fleeting moment of eye contact between Maximus and Salam when he passes the baton to her to speak. By the looks of it, their relationship has become irreparably strained. But the rest of the People's Protector seems oblivious to it.

Salam opens her briefing with a deep growl. "Maximus will be leading Units One to Ten, taking the gateway leading to the north of Yilina. I'll be leading Units Eleven to Twenty-One, and we'll be hiking up from Cheyvelenia to the southwest of Yilina. It's said that Zatori and the Harvesters plan to enter the town from the northwest. When they're in, we'll ambush them from both sides, leaving them no route for retreat."

Her eyes land on Akari in the crowd, offering her a look of encouragement. Akari knows all too well that, if given the choice, Salam would prefer she sit this mission out.

Yet, even the second-in-command of the People's Protector is powerless against the first-in-command.

♦

Under Salam's lead, Units Eleven to Twenty-One set up an ambush amongst the trees and shrubberies of the forested foothills between Cheyvelenia and Yilina after sundown. The prospect of facing Zatori again has the Protectors waiting in uneasy silence.

From between the branches, Akari has a good view overlooking Cheyvelenia on one side and Yilina on the other, from which a bright light is supposed to signal to them to begin their attack. Although most of the Protectors have their eyes on Yilina, Akari can't help but be mesmerized by the night view of Cheyvelenia—a speckle of lights across town glittering against the dark sky.

To the north, Hazenfeld stands apart with its characteristic bright lights and tall buildings. In stark contrast, the squat, dimly lit slums—Ty's home—lie on the other side of town. Between them sits the town square, especially lively tonight, bustling with local folks making merry at the Lantern Festival. Akari wonders where Yong is among them.

The first wave of paper lanterns ascends into the night sky. From her vantage point, she watches the warm flickering lights rise toward her before drifting far beyond. The dreamlike splendor of this view, so unlike the one from the square, makes her wonder if the world has always seemed more beautiful from above.

"Do you remember the first time we went to the Lantern Festival together?" Ty whispers. "You burned your finger while lighting the lantern. After that, you became so afraid of fire that I had to light the lanterns every year after."

Akari laughs softly. "And do you remember the time when you set Madam Celine's skirt on fire by accident? I still remember the look on her face. She looked like she was going to scorch you alive—just like her cookies."

As she tries to stifle her laughter, Ty pales at the remembered threat. "Madam Celine still often looks at me that way—"

"Will you two love-mutts stop with the sweet nothings?" Hanwell shushes them harshly. "I don't want to puke before the mission!"

Embarrassed, Akari and Ty immediately go quiet.

While waiting for the signal, which is taking longer than expected, Akari tries to make out the wishes on the lanterns that fly by. *Food. Food. Money. Food. Love. Happiness. Money. Money. Food. Family. Health. Food. Money. Peace. Love.* This last one is reminiscent of her own wish this year. *I wish for us to be safe and happy, even when we are apart,* Akari thinks to herself, her heart twinging.

This wish also reminds her of the one her mother wrote during the first and only Lantern Festival they attended together. *I wish for us to be safe.* Akari can almost hear Mari's gentle, measured voice reciting these words, which have long been etched in her mind. Despite the difficult confrontation they had earlier, she knows her mother's love for her is beyond measure.

Raw guilt washes over Akari when she recalls how they parted. *I'll make it up to her when I'm back. Tomorrow is the first day of spring and the mark of new beginnings. I'll give Mama my time—assuage her fears, convince her to let me remain in the People's Protector, and ask her about Lord Vykroux. At least she's willing to share all her secrets with me now.* Akari finds some comfort in the thought that, perhaps, everything between them will soon be back to normal.

A lantern with a dash of ink across one side catches her attention. Instead of words, she vaguely sees a picture on it. *Who draws on their lanterns? You're supposed to write your wish, not doodle*—Akari's thoughts are interrupted when she makes out the image. Without further prompting, she realizes who its artist is.

The flame within the lantern casts a soft glow against Yong's drawing. Akari sees them standing side by side, each with an arm wrapped around each other. Her head, resting where Yong's shoulder meets his chest, is tilted up to meet his smiling gaze. However, this isn't what surprises her the most.

It's the three children with them that catch her completely off guard. In the drawing, Akari has her free hand on the shoulder of a little girl with crescent-moon eyes, who stands beside a little boy with almond eyes. Behind him, a pudgy toddler girl is nestled in Yong's other arm.

Akari's brow furrows as she tries to interpret this picture in all possible ways, but there's ultimately only one logical explanation. *Yong wishes to have a family with me...*

A strange, overwhelming mix of feelings—from delight to shock—surges through her. Although her heart is warm, her thoughts are cold. *What is he thinking? I'm never going to see him again after tomorrow!*

As their lantern drifts up toward the sky, it continues twirling gently in the breeze. On the other side of the lantern, Akari sees the wish she has written—except it has been edited. *I wish for us to be safe and happy; ~~even when~~ we ^ will never again be ~~are~~ apart.*

Akari is thoroughly taken aback. *He's not allowed to do that! He's broken all the rules with this lantern.* As it disappears between the clouds, she's unsure what to make of it. Beside her, Ty, who's been staring off in another direction, doesn't seem to have noticed anything.

After what seems like far too long, the People's Protector begins to question if something's wrong. According to their intelligence, Zatori and the Harvesters should have reached Yilina a while ago, but there's yet to be a signal to launch an attack. A wave of worried whispers ripples through the Protectors.

"Do you think Zatori might not be harvesting tonight?" Aloy asks. "Or do you think we've got the place wrong?"

"Or could we have been fed inaccurate intelligence again?" Prisci suggests. "Like we were when Zatori returned?"

"That's impossible," Hanwell says, although there seems to be a note of uncertainty as he dismisses their speculations. "The traitor has been executed. Ethan Cook died right before our eyes."

Another lantern suddenly catches Akari's eye, a violet flare among the twinkling white specks peppering the inky sky—the very shade of Celestine's lightning. She can just make out the words scrawled on it—*A new realm under Zatori Valakhan.*

She stiffens, and her eyes widen in fear. Cold beads of sweat form on her forehead, trickling down as fragments of harrowing memories surge through her mind. Akari grips Ty's arm tightly, her voice caught in her throat.

"Ow! You're hurting me!" he yelps, trying to pull free, but to no avail. His protest fades when he notices her fearful expression. Concern clouds his eyes. "What's wrong?"

"Look at that lantern! The violet one! It's Celestine! Zatori's Harvester!" Akari lets out a strained gasp, her eyes trained in the distance.

Ty traces her line of sight, his gaze landing on the luminous violet lantern. Before he can grasp its implications, Akari spells it out for him—and the rest of the People's Protector.

"This mission is a decoy! Whatever intelligence the People's Protector received is a lie! We're waiting for nothing! Zatori isn't coming to Yilina. The Harvesters are in Cheyvelenia. They're after my mother!"

15. Doom

Ten years ago...

It hadn't been long since Akari and Mari moved to Cheyvelenia. Six-year-old Akari skipped into Moonstone Apothecary cheerfully, finding her mother exactly where she wanted her to be. Mari was sitting at the counter, plucking the dried leaves off some herbs.

"Mama, can we go to the Lantern Festival?" Akari was bubbling with excitement. After hearing the other children speak of it, she was eager to see the celebrations with her own eyes.

Mari looked up nervously when she heard the question. "So there really is a Lantern Festival..." she muttered under her breath, her eyes growing distant.

"Mama..." Akari called to regain her mother's attention.

"Yes, Akari, my baby?" Mari spoke levelly as she looked her daughter's way, trying not to let her anxiety show. "What's the Lantern Festival?"

"It's a festival where we can write our wishes on a lantern, light it, and send it up into the air. If our lantern reaches the sky, our wishes will come true!" Little Akari was already ahead of herself, running through in her mind all the wishes she could possibly write. She was finding it extremely challenging to pick just one.

"Oh..." Mari said, a slight inflection in her tone. "When is it?"

"Tonight!" Akari was bursting with anticipation. "Mama, can we go, please?"

Mari hesitated briefly before answering, "Sure, we can..."

"Thank you, Mama! I heart you with all my love, Mama!" Akari exclaimed, too exhilarated to notice any of her mother's apprehension.

"I heart you with all my love too, Akari, my baby," Mari answered, but her mind was elsewhere.

After nightfall, they headed to the town square, where all of Cheyvelenia had gathered for the Lantern Festival. Mari hadn't been around so many people since she left Andelovia, and the crowd made her immensely uneasy for two reasons.

Firstly, she was afraid of standing out. During their early years in Andelovia, fitting in was something Mari paid much attention to. While it was tough for little Akari to adapt, it was even more difficult for her mother. To compensate for that, Mari kept her head down more than she needed to.

Secondly, she was afraid of losing Akari. As they wove their way through the swarm of Cheyvelenians, Mari squeezed her hand, signaling for her to follow closely. Akari returned the squeeze, obediently trailing behind her mother.

After procuring a white paper lantern, they settled on the steps. Sitting among all the other local folks in the town square, Mari felt, for the first time, that Cheyvelenia could really be their home. Never had she been at ease after the Great Harvest—not until this very moment. She let on a rare smile as she watched her daughter struggle to decide on a wish before writing with a shaky quill and some diluted ink, *Mama and I will be together forever.*

When Akari was done, Mari blew lightly on the lantern to dry the ink and flipped it to the opposite side. She didn't so much as deliberate before she wrote in an elegant script, *I wish for us to be safe.*

By the time they'd finished, many Cheyvelenians had begun lighting their lanterns and sending them up to the sky. Mari and Akari headed down the steps to join them. After taking a pensive glance at the defaced statue of King Alvaro, Mari lit their lantern, allowing the hot air to fill up its interior until they felt it pull upward. Then, they released it, allowing the lantern to drift toward the sky.

They looked up, their smiling almond eyes fixed on their lantern. It began making its ascent, edging further and further away from them. But, for no apparent reason, it suddenly burst into flames.

Mari and Akari stared helplessly at the fireball, as though their wishes were incinerated right before their eyes. With anxious tears rolling down her cheeks, Akari looked to her mother for validation. "Mama, does this mean we won't be together forever?"

Mari herself was unsure of the answer as another question that was arguably even more pertinent plagued her mind. *Does this mean we won't be safe?* She couldn't determine if the fire was caused by her lack of experience in handling the lantern, or whether their wishes were truly destined for doom.

Either way, Mari never attended a single Lantern Festival thereafter.

✦

Celestine's violet light has made a twisted joke of the signal they've been waiting for. Following Akari's outcry, all the Protectors look from her to the violet lantern in shock. While everyone is still at a loss, Akari shoots to her feet and makes a run for it.

Her actions would have revealed the location of the ambush they were setting up, except she's right—the People's Protector is indeed waiting for nothing. The mission is merely a diversion for the harvesting about to happen in Cheyvelenia.

With the violet lantern serving as the North Star of doom, Akari keeps her eye on it as she weaves through the trees, darting down the dirt path toward Cheyvelenia. She can vaguely hear the Protectors hollering behind her, some hurling profanities and others calling after her in concern or confusion.

"Akari!" Ty, in rapid pursuit, neither tells her to stop nor wait. He just wants her to know that he's behind her—that she isn't alone.

Akari also hears Salam roaring, "Akari Miyahara! Stop there right now!"

But she keeps running from the forested foothills, not once pausing or looking back. Confronted with the imminent possibility of losing her mother, even the prospect of severe punishment for disobeying military orders seems insignificant by comparison.

She doesn't stop until the shophouse is in sight. From the alley across the street, she sees its front door wide open, the new doorknob mangled beyond use. Akari has no doubt her home has been broken into—again. She's certain the intruder hasn't come just to learn something this time. Fear seizes her. Somewhere around, Kami's barks echo through the night.

Barely recovering from shock, Akari is about to make a dash for the apothecary when Ty appears out of nowhere, grabs her by the arm, and drags her behind some junk abandoned in the alley. The duo has barely managed to hide when a dozen-odd masked figures in long black cloaks emerge from Moonstone Apothecary. Akari lets out a horrified gasp, but Ty instantly clasps his hand over her mouth.

"What should we do now Lady Mari is gone?" one of the Harvesters asks.

Akari's heart plunges. *I've let Mama down.* Her knees give way, and Ty grabs her just in time, preventing her from hitting the ground.

"And what do we do about the missing deflector?" another Harvester adds.

"It seems she isn't outside of Yilina with the rest of the People's Protector," a third says. "They must have found out by now it's only a diversion."

"She's not in the town square either," a shrill female voice chimes in. "I was there earlier."

Is that... Celestine? A panicked Akari isn't quite able to place the voice.

"The Jewel of Compassion is missing too. The deflector has probably disappeared with it," a Harvester who sounds like Philippe says.

"Then find her!" comes a reply in a cold, deep drawl. *Zatori.* This time, Akari has no doubt who it belongs to.

With that, the Harvesters swiftly reorganize themselves and head off in various directions. Zatori lingers briefly, as though to gather his thoughts, before sauntering into an alley parallel to the one Akari and Ty are hiding in.

Once Zatori and the Harvesters are out of sight, Ty whispers, still in shock, "Is the necklace you mentioned the Jewel of Compassion?"

Akari nods, clutching the jewel through her clothes.

"Why didn't you tell me?" he demands.

"My mother wanted to keep it a secret," Akari explains.

"Just like that giant horned bird?" Ty scratches his head. "Regardless, is it on you?" he asks, eyeing her clenched fist.

Akari nods again.

"Then we should leave now," he says decisively, his words hushed but urgent.

"No." Despite her quavering voice, Akari is adamant. "I need to see my mother."

Ty sighs, knowing he won't be able to convince her otherwise. "Then we need to be quick—"

Before he finishes, Akari has already made her way across the street, past the front door of the apothecary. Ty follows hastily.

The air inside Moonstone Apothecary seems unusually and unbearably frigid. The dread that Zatori and the Harvesters have just invaded her home and killed her mother licks at her bone, adding to the cold. Although she's on the verge of falling apart, Akari drags her trembling body toward the second floor.

It seems to take an eternity to climb those stairs she'd so callously flown down as she bade Mari her final farewell earlier. Guilt consumes Akari. As she makes her way up, she wishes over and over again that she's wrong about her mother's fate, that perhaps Mari has somehow been able to heal herself. If not, she'd deflect her mother's wounds onto her own self in a heartbeat. But all these thoughts seem to have come too late.

When she's a couple of steps from the second floor, Akari sees her mother's body sprawled motionless outside their bedrooms, exactly where she last saw her. Beside her, the loose floorboard has been displaced to reveal the hiding place with nothing but an open, empty golden box.

Horror and devastation paralyze Akari. She collapses on the stairs, at a complete loss. Ty quickly rushes to her side.

When she regains some strength, Akari crawls up the final few steps and kneels beside her mother's body. With no wounds inflicted and no blood spilled, Mari's demise must have been caused by a gift. *Zatori must have harvested Mama's gift and killed her!* Yet, with her eyes closed, the expression on Mari's face seems unusually calm, as though she's at ease with her fate.

Never having laid hands on a dead person, Akari gingerly reaches out her fingers and grazes the cool surface of her mother's blood-drained cheek, a glaring contrast to her usually luminous porcelain face. Mari's body has rapidly begun to lose warmth and color. Akari bursts into uncontrollable sobs. She takes her mother's cold, lifeless hand and squeezes it, hoping to get any kind of response. But Mari remains still.

Akari nudges her mother's shoulder, pleading desperately, "Mama, Mama... can you hear me? Talk to me, say something—*anything*. I never should have left you alone. I'm sorry. I'm so sorry. Mama, please come back to me..."

Ty kneels beside them, taking an anxious glance at Akari before looking at Mari. Even when he turns back to his best friend, he's still unsure how to comfort her.

Wrapping his arm around her, he says, "I'm so sorry for your loss, Akari."

"Ty... how did this happen? I thought Mama could heal herself... I thought she'd never be hurt... I thought..." Thoroughly broken, Akari alternates between violent sobbing and mindless spluttering. "My mother died because of me. If only I had listened to her and stayed... If only I hadn't left for the mission tonight... If only I'd never joined the People's Protector..."

"You didn't know, Akari. You couldn't have known," Ty tries to console her, but to no avail.

"I should have known... I should have listened to her..." Akari's voice is steeped in regret. "I need to save my mother!"

"You need to save yourself, Akari," Ty reminds her gently. "This is what your mother would have wanted—"

The stairs creak as footsteps approach. *Is it Zatori? Or the Harvesters?* The thought grips Akari with a mix of panic and anger. Their eyes meet before Ty hurriedly shoves her into one of the bedrooms, signaling for her to hide. Drawing his battle-ax, he positions himself behind the wall by the landing, poised to attack.

As soon as the swift, steady footsteps reach the second floor, Ty jumps on the newcomer. But before his weapon can be put to use, a familiar midnight blue cloak sweeps through the air, and he's haplessly tackled to the ground in one seamless countermove.

"Ow! Ow! Ow!" Ty howls.

Akari springs from her hiding place, ready to take on the newcomer. But she freezes when she beholds those crescent-moon eyes.

"It's me, Akari," Yong says quietly.

"And me," Emeraude adds as she emerges from the stairs, clad in the darkest shade of green.

Momentarily forgetting that he has Ty pinned to the ground, Yong brims with concern as he checks on Akari. "Are you alright?"

"I'm not!" Ty yelps from underneath him. "Let me go! I only attacked because I thought you were a Harvester!"

"Oh, I'm sorry. I didn't mean to hurt you." Yong releases Ty without so much as glancing at him, his worried eyes still trained on Akari.

"Yong... I... My mother..." Between sobs, she struggles to put into words the pain and grief she herself has barely begun to process. She squeezes her eyes shut, brushing away her tears.

"Let's go," Yong says levelly, placing a hand on Akari's arm. "We can't afford to stay any longer."

"No, I can't leave my mother." Akari sinks down beside Mari, hugging her longingly, frantically. "I need to save her."

Yong says nothing, allowing Akari to spend the last few moments with her mother.

"What should I do? What *can* I do?" As the words spill out, a sudden thought strikes Akari, hard and sharp.

Although there's no wound to deflect, there is something else—death itself. Akari doesn't know if it's within her powers, or even possible, but she tries anyway. She squeezes her eyes shut and grips her mother's hand even more tightly, as if willing the warmth—the life—to return. Again and again, she grasps at any trace of her gift to deflect her mother's death onto herself.

But it doesn't work. Death doesn't claim her. Akari feels nothing—no surge of power, no flicker of energy. Her body is hollow, empty, drained. There's a massive void inside her, and no matter how desperately she tries to reach for that strength, it eludes her, leaving her utterly helpless.

No one else seems to realize what she's attempting—or that it's all in vain. It's a moment Akari forever wants to keep to herself... and her mother. She buries her face in Mari's still chest and weeps.

"Mama... please wake up... please..." But she knows there's nothing more she can do. Only doom awaits.

As Yong watches Akari, a tear rolls down his cheek. After a long while, when she remains crouched over her mother, refusing to budge, he bends over and embraces her.

"This is all my fault... I should be the one dead... Mama... she didn't have to die..." Akari's voice trembles with despair. She buries her face in Yong's chest, tears flowing freely.

"Hush, Akari... Don't say that..." he coaxes soothingly as he caresses her hair. "It's not your fault."

Behind them, neither Ty nor Emeraude says a word.

Yong eventually gives Akari a tight squeeze before releasing her. "Akari, will you listen to me just this once?" he implores, taking her hand in his. Despite the softness in his voice, there's an air of authority to it.

"I need you to pull yourself together. We need to leave right away. It's extremely dangerous to linger."

Akari nods reluctantly. She grabs a satchel, hastily throwing in some money and other belongings, consisting of a few articles of clothing, an array of herbs and medical supplies, and the empty golden box.

Just as she finishes packing, more footsteps scurry up the stairs, so incredibly light-footed that they sound distinctively inhuman. Ty is about to hide himself once more in preparation for a sneak attack when Kami makes an entrance.

The moment she reaches the landing, Akari notices her usually playful gaze has been replaced with one of inexplicable steadiness, as though she's suddenly garnered experiences that far exceed her young life. After taking a long look at Mari, Kami makes her way to Akari.

Akari drops to her knees so she's level with Kami, who rubs her soft furry face endearingly on hers in greeting. The familiar white ribbon that usually held up Mari's hair has been tied around Kami's neck, the silver moonstone ring hanging from it.

Perplexed, Akari wonders why her mother left the ring with Kami, but there isn't time to ponder this. She quickly undoes the ribbon from Kami's neck and ties it in her hair, then slides the silver moonstone ring onto her finger. Akari feels a tug on her clothes and looks down to find Kami pulling firmly with her teeth, as if she wants to take her somewhere.

Akari gets to her feet, glances at her mother's body one last time, and lets herself be led down the stairs by Kami. Ty trails closely behind her, followed by Emeraude.

After they begin their descent, none of them see Yong place his right hand over his heart, drop his right knee onto the ground, and bow down to Mari before he, too, takes his leave.

16. Capture

Kami darts forward, then circles back to make sure that Akari, Yong, Ty, and Emeraude are still following. With a soft but urgent yelp, she calls to them to make haste. She leads them out of town, up some forested foothills, and down a dirt path. Akari finds the route all too familiar.

It doesn't take long for them to reach Havenswill. After coming to a stop, Kami's nose twitches in the chilly air. She rubs it with a paw to warm it up.

As they step into the meadow, they notice that the lanterns have risen high amongst the clouds. It seems the wishes of many Cheyvelenians will come true. Yet, among the warm white lanterns that illuminate the dark sky, the violet one is nowhere to be seen.

"What are we doing here?" Ty asks.

Before he can get an answer, an instinct calls out to Akari to start kulning. As soon as she cups her hands around her mouth, the ethereal melody of the 'Summoning Song' surrounds them. The usually mellifluous tune now evokes a haunting quality as it echoes through the night.

Yong, Ty, and Emeraude gaze at Akari in awe. None of them have witnessed her—or anyone else for that matter—kuln before. After all, it is an ancient technique used to summon wild zephanerixes. Few even know about kulning, let alone have heard it with their own ears.

Ty is especially surprised there's a side to Akari he hasn't seen, and he's equally baffled by the purpose of the kulning. Beside him, Emeraude contains her brimming curiosity, a single glance from Yong quelling any budding questions. Meanwhile, he watches on quietly, his expression undecipherable.

As Akari continues, a teardrop rolls down her cheek. It feels painfully different to be kulning alone for the very first time. Memories of her mother flood her mind, inundating her with a profound grief that manifests in her voice.

Zephy seems to sense this. Akari, Yong, Ty, and Emeraude hear a melancholic cawing in the distance. When they look up, a gigantic shadow is circling above the lanterns. After ascertaining the origin of the kulning, the zephanerix makes a nosedive for Havenswill. He descends swiftly, glowing champagne-gold amidst the sea of lanterns.

"Zephy!" Akari bounds toward him. As she touches her forehead to his beak, the zephanerix provides her with immense comfort, allowing her to feel closer to Mari, somehow.

While Yong and Emeraude let on little to no emotion, Ty is shocked and excited—even scared—by Zephy's presence. He instinctively backs off, putting some distance between them.

"Holy... Akari!" Ty cries, his eyes firmly locked onto the zephanerix. "Is this your giant horned bird?"

She nods. "This is Zephy."

"You're not supposed to refer to zephanerixes that way," Yong says quietly.

"So, he *is* real!" Ty exclaims, ignoring him. "He's a lot bigger than I thought he'd be."

"Zephy's very gentle," Akari says, stroking the beast's neck.

With a mix of eagerness and caution, Ty approaches and touches his beak gingerly. The zephanerix coos softly in response. Although Ty has heard much about Zephy, seeing him in person is a different experience altogether. "He's beautiful," he gasps in awe.

While Ty continues marveling, Akari retrieves the tack from the burrow and begins saddling and bridling Zephy. Yong steps forward to help, fastening the buckles and tightening the straps with quick hands. Sensing their urgency, Zephy tries his best to cooperate by keeping still.

As though formulating plans to procure one himself, Ty asks, "How did you and your mother come to own—"

"The deflector is over there!" A woman's scream pierces the night sky, her voice unsettlingly familiar.

Before Akari can ponder its origin, a bolt of violet lightning shoots from between the trees, hitting her squarely in the chest, flinging her to the ground. *Celestine!*

"Akari!" Yong and Ty cry out at the same time, both rushing to help her back to her feet. Drawing their weapons, they stand guard over her.

"It's Zatori and the Harvesters!" Yong yells as they emerge in scores from between the trees.

Akari feels a sharp pain stabbing at her chest, albeit overshadowed by the rage burning within her. She glares at the Harvesters, surveying them, her eyes eventually locking in on the figure in the center of the pack—the only maskless one. Before Yong and Ty realize what Akari is planning, she lunges at him, howling, "You murderer!"

A red flash of light erupts from her palm, striking Zatori in the chest. The pain she felt dissipates as the wound inflicted by Celestine is deflected onto him. Underneath her clothes, the Jewel of Compassion emits a red glow.

"My gift will let you have a taste of your own medicine!" Akari screams as Zatori clutches at his chest, staggering backward in surprise. Her anger has nearly blinded her to the significance of the blow she's just dealt to the most powerful and dangerous gifted in the entire kingdom.

However, this doesn't go unnoticed by Zatori. He has always been untouchable—almost.

"It seems like you have grown up well, little deflector. And you have honed your gift well too," Zatori drawls as he composes himself. "Deflecting wounds without direct contact! You're a lot more powerful than I expected... and a lot more useful than before..." he muses, now seeing Akari in a new light.

"Don't even think about it," she warns. "Over my dead body!"

Zatori laughs. "It seems that's all that is left of your poor mother."

"You murderer! I'll end you with my own hands!" Akari's blood boils at the mention of Mari.

"I didn't kill your mother," Zatori retorts calmly.

But she doesn't believe him even for a moment.

"We've already had a long night. Let's make it quick, shall we?" he continues before ordering, "Get them!"

The Harvesters quickly surround Akari, Yong, Ty, and Emeraude. The four stand with their backs together, weapons drawn and ready to fight.

A split second before the Harvesters launch into attack, Yong leaps into the air and begins taking them out. He deals lethal blows and deftly fends off every move of the Harvesters, playing their attacks against each other, as though he's toying with them. The Harvesters seem thoroughly taken by surprise. To one side, Zatori looks on wordlessly.

Somewhere amidst the chaos, Ty charges at the Harvesters, swinging his battle-ax heavy-handedly. Although his fighting—actually, anyone's—pales in comparison to Yong's, his effort more than makes up for it. Ty takes on more Harvesters than he can handle, so fewer of them have a chance to get to Akari.

Instead of putting her at a disadvantage, Emeraude's petite frame lends her an exceptional nimbleness, enhancing her impressive combat skills. Armed with her spear, she moves with an extraordinary lightness, lithely dodging attacks and viciously counterattacking.

Akari raises her kris and springs into action, letting her thirst for revenge consume her. Now she's lost her mother, she seems to have no qualms about fighting. This time, heeding Yong's advice, she doesn't hesitate when she goes in for the kill.

However, anger has clouded her judgment. Akari miscalculates several maneuvers and gets hurt numerous times—a stab to her arm, a slash at her shin, a graze on her cheek—but she instinctively deflects all these injuries back onto the Harvesters. As she fights, an unprecedented surge of energy gushes through her, enhancing her gift beyond imagination, surprising even herself.

Yet, even with their respective strengths, the four of them are still vastly outnumbered. *I don't think all of us are making it out tonight...* Akari thinks grimly as Ty narrowly avoids the thrust of a Harvester's sword. Just when despair threatens to settle heavy on her shoulders, a thundering war cry sends the meadow quaking.

"Charge! Kill Zatori! Get the Harvesters!"

Salam surges into Havenswill with a roar. The rest of Units Eleven to Twenty-One are close behind her. All ready to take down Zatori and the Harvesters, the Protectors draw their weapons and charge toward them.

Zatori remains unperturbed. "Capture the deflector and kill the rest!" he commands as he prowls toward Akari. But Salam quickly intercepts him, slamming her massive body against his.

She spares Akari a quick glance before diverting her attention entirely to Zatori. Salam is a formidable opponent, but even her sheer size and power don't intimidate him. With his arsenal of harvested gifts, Zatori has the upper hand in this duel.

Akari starts toward them, but Philippe blocks her path, closing in with his bloodied spear. Akari shakes involuntarily at the sight of him, but she quickly pushes her fear aside, slashing at Philippe with her kris. However, he parries her attacks as though it's child's play.

Yong leaps between them, breaking up their fight. Philippe immediately recognizes him, needing no reminder of how skilled an opponent he is.

"It's you again, young lad," Philippe remarks. "Always interrupting our fight."

"I warned you not to touch her again!" Yong seethes.

Philippe lunges at him. "I didn't promise anything, unfortunately..." He thrusts his spear at Yong's head and then his heart, but he fends off the attacks faster than Philippe can deal them.

Akari raises her kris to help, but Celestine takes Philippe's place. She claws wildly with her metallic talons, not allowing any reprieve. But, incensed by the grief of losing her mother, Akari strikes back just as relentlessly. She lashes out, each move more lethal than the last, until one cuts Celestine's mask free, sending it flying from her face.

The sight leaves Akari debilitated by shock. The rumors couldn't be further from the truth—Celestine isn't disfigured in the slightest.

Madam Celine, the baker, stands before Akari with a deranged smile, the gleaming metallic talons on her fingertips ready to strike another blow. Her mousy brown hair isn't tucked neatly behind her ears, but instead spiking out in every direction.

Madam Celine—Celestine—seems unfazed that her disguise has been exposed. "What's wrong? Is my face not what you were expecting? Is my devastating beauty so spellbinding?" she trills tauntingly.

A chill runs down Akari's spine. "Madam Celine?" she squints, checking if her eyes are playing tricks on her.

"Yes, my dear! That's the boring version of me! The one that had been watching you and your mother in that boring little town for the past ten years!" Celestine shrieks. Exploiting Akari's shock, she fires a bolt of violet lightning at her.

Akari tries to dodge, but she isn't quick enough. The lightning strikes her on the left shoulder, hurling her to the grass. But before she hits the ground, Akari has already deflected the electric shock back onto Celestine.

"You've become feisty, little deflector," Celestine screeches as she steadies herself. "It seems like you've learned how to grow a spine from your mother. Your father wasn't half as gutsy."

"You knew my father?" Akari's tone is tinged with surprise.

"Everyone knows your father," Celestine replies with a cryptic smile.

Right... Of course, everyone knows Lord Xavier Vykroux. "Then prove it," Akari demands anyway. "Tell me who he is!"

"Where's the fun if I tell you?" Celestine chirps. "Hasn't your mother been hiding his identity from you this whole time? And now she's gone! Even before saying a word!" She laughs like a maniac. "Mari Miyahara caused us so much damage with the White Blaze. But she's dead now, so you'll have to be the one to pay for it!"

Celestine fires another bolt of violet lightning at Akari. But this time, Kami jumps up to intercept it, shielding her from the blow.

"Kami!" Akari cries as her treasured companion flumps to the ground. To her relief, Kami crawls back to her feet, baring her teeth at the Harvester in a furious snarl.

Taking advantage of Akari's distraction, Celestine knocks her over. She grasps Akari's neck with her metallic talons, pinning her firmly on the ground. More lightning streaks through her, and she writhes in agony.

"It seems your body still remembers the pain from ten years ago." Celestine lets out a grating laugh, her face just inches away.

But this time, Akari refuses to show any sign of weakness. She grits her teeth to stop herself from screaming.

Dissatisfied by the lack of submission, Celestine sinks her talons into her supple skin. As thick, warm blood leaks from Akari's punctured neck, her eyes gleam in wild, sadistic delight.

"Since you take after your mother so much, why not follow her footsteps in death?" Celestine suggests with a shrill giggle. "But not before my sire harvests your gift!"

The mention of her mother fires Akari up. But in her hapless state, she's unable to retaliate. Akari tenses her jaw and clenches her fists so tightly that her nails leave marks in her palms.

Just as she thinks she can't bite back a scream any longer, Ty grabs Celestine from behind, flinging her off of Akari. "I knew you were a nasty one!"

Akari moans as the tips of Celestine's metallic talons are extracted roughly from her neck. Blood spills freely from the perforations, and she gasps for air. Ty scrambles toward her to help her up.

But all it takes is a lapse in concentration. Blood pours from Ty's neck as soon as he touches Akari. He clutches at his new wounds, reeling backward. From beneath her clothes, the Jewel of Compassion emanates a red glow.

"No! Ty!" Akari screams, knowing what she has done—again. Somewhere around them, Celestine cackles hysterically.

Yong, leaving some other Protectors to take on Philippe, rushes worriedly to Akari's side. "Are you alright?" he asks, quickly realizing the skin on her neck is now intact despite the bloody mess, while Ty is quickly losing blood.

"Tyler Kane?" Yong calls out anxiously.

Before Ty can respond, Celestine slashes him directly below his left collarbone with a metallic talon, narrowly missing his heart. As she does so, a bolt of violet jolts his entire being, catapulting him backward.

"I'm going to scorch you like I scorch those cookies you love so much, you stupid boy. Would you like to be toasted golden or scorched brown? Or *burnt black*, this time?" Celestine shrieks, bursting into manic giggles. "Do you know how long I've been waiting for this day?"

"This is exactly why I never liked you," Ty spits stubbornly despite gasping in pain.

Although he can barely stand his ground, he raises his battle-ax and staggers in front of Akari and Yong, placing himself between them and the Harvesters.

Aware that the People's Protector can't hold out for much longer, Salam calls for retreat. Even as the Protectors begin withdrawing from the meadow, the Harvesters continue attacking in an endless swarm.

"Akari, hurry!" Salam roars from the far end of Havenswill.

"Akari, go! Now!" Ty, eyes ignited with a firm resolution, commands with an authority Akari has never seen him possess. "We won't make it if I go along."

"No, Ty. I can't..." She refuses to budge as she doggedly checks the wounds on his neck and chest. Akari desperately tries to deflect Ty's wounds onto any Harvester—and even herself—but fails miserably.

"Go now!" Ty squeezes his eyes shut and brushes her off roughly. "Yong, take her!"

Even before he finishes speaking, Yong seizes Akari by the arm and peels her away. "We need to go, Akari," he says, dragging her toward Zephy. "Any later and we won't make it out!"

"No! I can't leave Ty behind!" Akari screams. "Not after what I've done to him!" She struggles vehemently, clawing at Yong's iron grip, but to no avail.

He lifts her off her feet, carrying her over his shoulder as he bolts toward Zephy.

"Emeraude!" Yong hollers, the sound of her name a command.

With just a single word, Emeraude knows exactly what's expected of her. She sprints to Ty's side, both of them fending off multiple Harvesters simultaneously. Even then, they're barely able to prevent the Harvesters from getting to Akari and Yong.

Just a few feet away, Yong tosses Akari unceremoniously onto Zephy's back—where Kami is already waiting—before leaping on. As soon as he steadies himself, he kicks his legs and spurs Zephy into the night sky.

♦

Amidst the anarchic battle in Havenswill, Ty rolls his eyes at Emeraude as she fights alongside him with evident unwillingness.

"Why am I stuck with you?" Ty complains, swinging his battle-ax at a Harvester but missing entirely. The profuse bleeding is numbing his senses.

"Do you actually think I want to? Yong ordered me." Emeraude gives an exasperated snort as she thrusts her spear at the same Harvester, cutting his arm and causing him to stumble backward. "But don't worry. I'll ditch you soon."

"Go ahead! I don't need you here anyway," Ty claims proudly as he blocks a blow another Harvester aimed at Emeraude.

She throws him a look of surprise. "Why did you do that? You can hardly fend for yourself," Emeraude hisses as she swiftly aids Ty in taking the Harvester down.

He shrugs indifferently. "With my wounds, I'm a goner regardless. If you can make it out, you should go." This time, Ty speaks as if he means it.

For the first time, he sees a shred of hesitation on Emeraude's usual nonchalant, haughty face. She wavers momentarily, unsure of her next step.

"Go!" he barks, as if to help her make up her mind.

Emeraude takes one last look at him, an inexplicable expression on her face, before disappearing into the forest.

"Don't kill the boy! Capture him alive!" Zatori's command erupts from a distance. "If you have him, the deflector will come to us. And so will the Jewel of Compassion!"

♦

From the safety of Zephy's back, Akari looks on in horror as the Harvesters spring on Ty while the Protectors scurry to retreat. He hasn't thought twice before putting his life on the line for her, aiding her escape from the mayhem. While he seems braver than he'd previously let on, she's ashamed of her own cowardice.

As the one-sided fight unfolds, Ty, with his dulled reflexes, loses grip of his battle-ax. Akari knows instantly that he's done for. She shudders, wishing to do something—*anything*—to help, but knowing there's nothing she can actually do.

"Ty! Ty!" she screams desperately, but he doesn't hear her. "We have to go back! Zatori and the Harvesters have him!" She wrestles for the reins, but Yong doesn't budge.

"We can't go back. It's too dangerous." He speaks with a level-headedness that infuriates her. "We have to get you out of here."

"We left Ty to fend for himself, and now Emeraude has left him too!" Akari yells. "He's fallen into Zatori's hands. He's going to die in my stead!"

"If Emeraude made a run for it, then there must have been no other way out," Yong simply says.

"Then I should have been the one who stood with Ty!" Akari cries, her voice quavering.

A long silence ensues between them as they gain elevation. They find themselves among the lanterns in the sky, which cast an unearthly glow on their faces.

Yong flies Zephy almost as well as Akari. On any other day, despite his propensity to be good at everything, Akari would be surprised at his flying abilities, considering that she and Mari were the only two people whom she knows to have even seen a zephanerix, let alone fly one. But tonight, her mind is lost somewhere between the fight in the meadow and the lanterns in the sky.

Not having to steer Zephy provides her with the chance to register Mari's death and Ty's capture. *I lost everyone tonight. If only I had listened to Mama and not gone on the mission, I could have been with her when Zatori and the Harvesters came. Maybe she wouldn't have died. And maybe Ty wouldn't be headed for the same fate.* Grief and anger begin eating Akari from the inside. Tears stain her face.

Sensing her pain, Yong puts a comforting hand on her shoulder, but she pulls away brusquely.

"Are you mad at me?" he asks softly, finally breaking the silence.

"I'm mad at myself!" Akari exclaims, her voice cracking. Her shoulders tremble as she breaks into sobs. Not wanting him to see her cry, she fixes her stare straight ahead.

"It's alright... You can be mad at me instead..." Yong murmurs, caressing her arm gently. This time, she lets him, his touch bringing her some solace, however slight.

Eventually, Akari turns to meet his worried gaze. He studies her in silence, her moist eyes and damp cheeks gleaming under the lantern light.

"I know I shouldn't be mad... I know I should be grateful that you got me out alive..." Akari shudders between weeping, quickly turning back to the front to avoid his eyes.

"That's alright. You don't have to explain," Yong says quietly.

"It's just that I've lost my mother and my best friend in one night..." She barely manages a whisper, her voice strained.

"I know I'll never compare to either of them, but just let me be here for you—for however long you need." Yong pauses slightly before he adds, "There'll be light at the end of the tunnel."

Akari's eyes are lifeless as she peers out into the distant darkness, beyond all the lanterns floating around them. She releases a long, lamenting sigh. "But Yong, what if I only see darkness?"

"Maybe you don't see it yet, Akari..." He leans forward, his lips inches from her ear as he declares, softly but reassuringly, "But *you* are light in the darkness."

She swivels around to face him, her eyes wide with surprise but her heart full of gratitude. As a little bubble of hope wells within her, she forces a weak smile and whispers, "Thank you, Yong."

Yong gently wraps his arms around Akari from behind her. In the warmth of his embrace, she leans her head back on his chest, hiding from the chaos around them. But it doesn't take long for Kami to wriggle her way between them, settling comfortably in their midst. They gaze at each other, smiling briefly.

"Where are we headed?" she asks.

"To Andelovia." Yong enunciates his words slowly, allowing them to sink in.

Akari sits bolt upright. "To the capital?"

"Yes."

"No, I can't... I don't want to... I—" she protests weakly.

"Andelovia is our safest bet," Yong assures her.

"But there are so many other towns in the outskirts that are a lot closer than the capital. Why don't we go to one of them?"

"Since Zatori and the Harvesters are all the way up north here in Cheyvelenia, seeking refuge down south in Andelovia would put us at the greatest distance from them," Yong explains. "The capital is the last place Zatori will expect you to be."

Akari knows the capital is also the last place her mother would want her to be. Yet, among the many reasons to stay away, there's one that draws her there. *Lord Xavier Vykroux.* But at this point, this ghost of a father seems inconsequential compared to Mari and Ty.

"Besides, I know a safe house in Andelovia we can stay at," Yong adds, trying to soothe her worries. "We can get some rest there before planning our next step."

Akari, thoroughly worn out, stops putting up a fight. She nods tiredly, resting her head on his chest again. "Are you certain you can get us through the Great Divide?"

"You don't have to worry," Yong says. "Even if I can't, Zephy can. His name is 'Zephy', right?"

Akari nods, puzzled. "But what does it have to do with him?"

"Zephanerixes will never get shot down," Yong says, as though that's explanation enough.

"Why?" She's still perplexed.

"They're the royal emblem of Xylon."

Akari snaps her head around, shock and confusion written on her face, only to meet a look of seriousness in Yong's dark, crescent-moon eyes. "Zephanerixes? The royal emblem of Xylon? Zephy, too?" she asks, bewildered.

"Yes," he says quietly. "But I guess this isn't common knowledge in the outskirts."

"Then... surely, my mother must have known this..." Akari shakes her head and lets out a long sigh, the Jewel of Compassion clutched tightly in her hand.

What were all the things Mama wanted to tell me before I left? I should've stayed and listened. But now, I'll never have a chance to hear from her...

17. Betrayals

When Akari wakes up, she doesn't see the familiar aged wooden beams of her bare bedroom, nor does she feel the stiff mattress beneath her. Instead, she gazes up at a foreign ivory-colored plaster ceiling adorned with ornate patterns as she rests on an unusually large and comfortable bed, with Kami curled up cozily at her feet. Judging by the light streaming through the tall windows, it must be late morning, perhaps even noon.

In the refuge of the safe house, Akari's hazy memory comes into focus. She recalls the recent events—Mari's death, Ty's capture, her return to Andelovia—all of them surreal. *How did so many things change overnight?*

She looks down to see a rough but dependable hand clasping her small, supple one. It seems to have held hers through everything lately. Her gaze follows the hand upward, tracing the arm to where Yong sits at the edge of her bed, his back against one side of the headboard, fast asleep.

He looks younger in his sleep, bearing a much stronger resemblance to the eight-year-old boy she remembers as her childhood playmate. Akari takes in his dark hair, eyebrows, and lashes, as well as his delicate nose and full lips. Somehow, Yong seems poised even as he rests.

His eyelids flutter, brow furrowing and unfurrowing quickly. *Is he dreaming?* Akari wonders as she sits herself up slowly, taking care not to wake him.

She isn't sure how long it's been since she was last jolted from her nightmare, having woken umpteen times during her turbulent, interrupted sleep.

◆

That time, she awoke screaming. It was still pitch-black outside. Within seconds, she heard a soft knock on her door.

"Akari, are you alright?" a deep, velvety voice asked, both concerned and comforting. "Can I come in?"

"Yes..." she whispered into the darkness. It was all Akari could muster.

Yong opened the door and slipped lithely into the room.

"Did I wake you?" she asked, embarrassed by her own screaming.

"No, I was already awake," he assured her. Yong walked over and knelt by Akari's bed, his eyes level with hers as he studied her. "Were you having nightmares?"

She nodded self-consciously. No one else besides her mother had seen her in this state before.

He reached for her hand. "Don't worry, you're not alone. I'm no stranger to nightmares either." While his presence calmed Akari's nerves, his touch sent her heart racing.

"Go on, close your eyes. I'll stay with you tonight," he murmured softly, soothingly, before he swept her hair from her face and planted a kiss on her clammy forehead. "Sleep tight, Akari."

She flashed Yong a weak but grateful smile.

For the rest of the night, he perched at the edge of Akari's bed, holding her hand in his. Under his watch, it didn't take her long to drift into a deep slumber.

She didn't have another nightmare, nor did she wake again until now.

♦

Akari takes the opportunity to scan her surroundings. The bedroom is spacious, larger than the entire shophouse she lived in. Each piece of furniture exudes exceptional refinement. The wardrobe, desk, vanity, and full-length mirror share a matching ivory hue, intricately embellished with what she suspects to be archivian fangs. She gasps at the opulence. This room surpasses even the elegance of those in the Colossal Inn, previously the most exquisite Akari had ever seen.

Yong stirs, pulling his hand from Akari's to rub his eyes. "Are you feeling better?" he asks, turning to her.

She nods. "How long was I out for?"

"You were sleeping for a day," he informs her.

"One entire day? You should have woken me earlier!" Akari tries to jump up, flustered by the time she has lost and its implications for her best friend. "I need to save Ty now! It's been nine days since he's been in Zatori's hands!"

"You needed rest, Akari." Yong places a reassuring hand on her shoulder. "But I promise, I'll help you save Tyler Kane."

"When will we go?" she asks anxiously, her voice trembling.

"As soon as we get intelligence," he replies with a calmness that is infuriating.

Her hands ball into fists. "We can't afford to wait! We're losing time!" Akari's heart races, her mind smothered by panic. "He... he could..." Her voice cracks, and she exhales shakily, struggling to regain control. *He could already be dead!*

Yong's grip on her shoulder firms just a fraction, his eyes darkening but steady. "Akari, I understand. But we need to know where to go, and going in blind will only put us at greater risk. That's the last thing Tyler Kane would want."

"I don't care about risks. I care about him!" She grits her teeth, frustration simmering. "I just want him to be alright. He needs to be alright!"

"I know, I know," Yong says, his tone pacifying, comforting. "I promise, I'll inform you once I hear something."

Akari stares at the floor, her thoughts a chaotic whirlwind. She forces herself to loosen her fists and unclench her jaw, but the gnawing sense of urgency doesn't fade.

After a long pause, she sighs, her shoulders slumping with the weight of helplessness. "Fine," she concedes in a reluctant whisper. She just hopes Ty's time hasn't— won't—run out.

Akari climbs out of bed and eventually finds herself absorbed by the elaborate decor around her. As she inspects her surroundings, Yong's eyes track her unfailingly.

The iridescent embellishments on the furniture catch her eye. She leans in, watching how the sunlight filters through them, revealing their translucency. Running her fingers over their cold, smooth surface, she feels a chill of recognition, her suspicions confirmed. They are indeed archivian fangs—not milk fangs, but still incredibly valuable.

She wheels around to face Yong, her eyes wide with awe. "Where exactly are we? Isn't it a little too... nice for a safe house?"

"This is the guestroom... of the Lee Residence. It was my parents' place—and my home for the first two years of my life—until they passed away," he says, trying to keep his tone light. "It's mine now, although I don't come back here as often as I'd like."

"Oh..." Akari isn't quite sure how to respond. It isn't the answer she was expecting. "It's beautiful," she remarks after a short pause. "It's nothing like Cheyvelenia, not even Hazenfeld. This is the most beautiful place I've ever seen."

As Yong looks around, expressionless, Akari is unable to fathom what's on his mind. *Is he thinking about his parents? Or something else entirely?* But he simply gives an unimpressed shrug, as though he's used to seeing far grander things.

"Yong..." Akari makes her way back to the bed, stopping before him.

"Yes?" Their eyes lock as he rises from his seat.

"I wanted to thank you," Akari says with a shy smile. "Thank you, Yong."

"What for?" he asks, puzzled.

"For all of this." She gestures to the splendid room. "For providing me with a roof over my head and for... for being there for me last night."

"My pleasure. That's the least I can do." Yong returns a warm smile. "I hope you're comfortable here."

"Yes, very much so." Akari glances around the room once more before she looks down, immersed in her thoughts.

"What's on your mind?" he asks.

"That night when we were fighting Zatori and the Harvesters, my gift felt completely different from before..." Akari struggles to relay something she barely grasps. "It's as though there was this unspeakably immense force, some kind of greater energy, flowing into and then overflowing—almost exploding—out of me... so much so that I lost control again and deflected my wound onto Ty..." She stoops to scratch Kami as the memory replays in her mind. "Just as I thought I had my gift under control, it suddenly became uncontrollable all over again..."

Yong looks deep in thought for a moment, and then he meets Akari's gaze, his expression as serious as his tone. "It has to be your complement."

"My complement?" Akari straightens up, surprise and apprehension threading through her voice. "But they're even rarer than gifts..."

"Yes, they are. But having one isn't entirely impossible," Yong replies. "And that seems to be the only explanation for all of this..."

Akari struggles to imagine what her complement could possibly be, but then her eyes land on the silver moonstone ring sitting on her finger. "Could this be it?" Her heart twinges as she's reminded of Mari's death.

Yong barely glances at the ring before giving a firm shake of the head. "That isn't it." There's a brief silence before he adds, "For an object to be your complement, you'll feel a special connection to it. Once that happens, it will shape the way energy flows in your body and enhance your gift."

Through her clothes, Akari clutches the Jewel of Compassion.

Yong's words couldn't be more accurate a description of her experience. During her last encounter with Zatori and the Harvesters, she felt the jewel channeling some sort of energy into her whenever she used her gift, magnifying her power so much that it became uncontrollable.

Even so, she shakes her head in absolute disbelief. *This has to be pure coincidence. How can the Jewel of Compassion possibly be my complement? The implications would be too much to bear—*

"What's on your mind again?" Yong's deep, velvety voice interrupts Akari's thoughts. He sits her on the edge of the bed, settling beside her.

She hesitates, conscious of her promise to Mari to keep the necklace a secret. She knows she needs to be cautious, to not let her feelings get in the way of judgment. However, now that her mother's gone, Akari needs, more than ever, someone to talk to.

I'm sure Yong knows more about the Jewel of Compassion than I do—and I need to know all there is to know. Besides, he's already aware I have the necklace. How else would he have been able to draw me wearing it? Most importantly, from the bottom of her heart, Akari wants to trust Yong—and her gut feeling tells her she can.

"My father gave me a present for my sixth birthday, and it's the only thing I have to remember him by," Akari says. "My mother told me it was lost while we were fleeing from the White Blaze, until I recently found out she'd been hiding it from me all this time..."

"You were there when it happened?" Yong seems more alarmed by her mention of the White Blaze.

"Yes, my mother caused it," Akari informs him, summing up her encounter with Zatori and the Harvesters during the Great Harvest.

"My theory was right," Yong says to himself. "So, your mother was the gifted who conjured the White Blaze..." Reverence comes through in his voice.

Akari nods.

"And what of the present your father gave you?" Yong asks, in a manner that implies he already knows the answer.

She glances at him before slowly pulling out the Jewel of Compassion from under her clothes. As she touches the jewel, it glows a soft red. A pulse of energy flows through her. "Here it is. Could this possibly be... *it*?" She still struggles to believe her hunch.

When Yong's eyes land on the dark gold necklace with the deep red, teardrop-shaped jewel, they narrow in focus. Although he doesn't reveal much, from the subtle changes in his expression—a muscle feathering in his jaw, a spark glinting in his eye—Akari has no doubt he recognizes the necklace as the Jewel of Compassion.

"You know what this is, don't you?" Akari is aware she still needs to tread carefully, making sure not to mention the drawing she found in his room and compromise the People's Protector.

"Yes, unmistakably so. This is the Jewel of Compassion, one of the three royal regalia," Yong says levelly, with no hint of awe or surprise, as she would have anticipated from anyone else. "You know what this is too, don't you?" he checks.

Akari nods. "I learned this from my mother... rather recently."

"Then you must know of the implicit dangers of being in possession of it," he continues. "Your mother was just trying to keep you safe."

Akari lets out a deep sigh, clutching the Jewel of Compassion. *I should have been the one to keep her safe...*

Yong eyes Akari's clenched fist before shifting his gaze to her. "Would you mind if I take a closer look at it?"

She shakes her head and unfurls her fingers, allowing the Jewel of Compassion to hang over her clothes, in full view. He reaches for it, brushing her collarbone ever so lightly as he does.

"Compassion..." Yong murmurs, thoroughly engrossed in his inspection of the royal regalia. "I can see that..."

Akari scrunches her eyebrows. "What do you mean? Is the Jewel of Compassion really my complement?"

"Yes, it is," he confirms, lifting his gaze to meet hers. "And as its name suggests, it thrives on and magnifies compassion. It's not sheer chance that it chose you, Akari, and I believe for good reason. Compassion is your greatest strength, and you have to use it well."

"Compassion is my greatest strength?" Akari's tone is skeptical.

"Yes, indeed," Yong confirms as he gently releases the Jewel of Compassion, letting it fall back against her.

Akari holds it away from her chest for a moment. The jewel dangles in the sunlight, reflecting every possible shade of red. She watches it, transfixed, until it eventually comes to a stop.

"You know the Jewel of Compassion has been missing for years, don't you?" Yong continues, also enthralled by the necklace.

"Yes, but this was a present from my father for my sixth birthday..." Akari points out.

"Well, it seems he left it in your care—and your mother's," he says.

Did Lord Vykroux really do that? she wonders. *Why would he leave the Jewel of Compassion with me, and want me to think him dead?*

"It seems your father had great foresight," Yong adds. "This red jewel is garnet—the birthstone of January. And you, coming into the world in the dead of winter, are light in the darkness. You were born to wield this royal regalia."

"I was born to wield the Jewel of Compassion?" Akari gasps, bewildered. "That can't be possible..."

"Why not?" Yong counters, his face unspeakably solemn. "Akari, do you know what it means?" His dark, crescent-moon eyes search her honey-colored, almond ones for an answer, but their blankness tells him she's unaware. "It means you're the future of Xylon."

Akari blinks in utter shock. "Me? Of all people? I can't possibly be. I'm not strong or powerful..." She tries to undo the clasp of the necklace, but he catches her hand.

"Taking it off won't change anything. It's already yours. I've told you before, Akari, you're infinitely more powerful than you imagine."

"Haven't you already seen for yourself? My gift is a curse. First Ethan, and now Ty." She pulls her hand away. "What good is a complement—a royal regalia, at that—if I keep hurting the people I love?"

Yong shakes his head firmly. "Your gift is in no way a curse. In fact, it's a blessing that the gift of deflection has been bestowed on someone with great compassion. Your gift isn't simply the ability to deflect wounds, but also to defend the people you love. This gift is incredibly powerful, and thus incredibly hard to control—even more so since you regained possession of your complement. You'll need to practice how to wield your gift, alongside your complement, all over again. And when you do, you'll be powerful beyond imagination."

Akari's breath catches as she struggles to take it all in. "And when that time comes, what do I do?" she asks anxiously. "Become the future of Xylon? What does that even entail?"

"I don't have those answers, but I know someone who might," Yong replies slowly, cryptically.

"And who might that be?" Akari's curiosity is piqued.

"King Alvaro..." he discloses with a deep breath, fully aware of her feelings about the king.

Before she can organize her scattered thoughts and form a coherent response, Yong continues, his voice laced with apprehension, "There's something I've been meaning to tell you. I... I'm not a trader... I'm part of the Royal Regiment, and I serve King Alvaro. Among other things, Emeraude and I were sent to the outskirts in search of the missing royal regalia."

Yong's words are a dagger of betrayal that stabs at Akari's heart. "You serve King Alvaro?" She enunciates every word with simmering anger. "You serve the king who abandoned us?"

He nods breathlessly. "Yes. But listen, it's not like that—"

"Why... How..." Akari falters, her voice cracking. Now that she thinks back, everything starts falling into place. *The zephanerix badges are symbols of their service to the royal family, not tokens of love... But is it the Jewel of Compassion, rather than me, that Yong thinks is worth remembering?*

"Akari, give me a chance to explain—"

"The Jewel of Compassion was the merchandise you were tasked with bringing back to the capital..." As Akari tries to make sense of it all, there's something else she struggles to understand. "But... how did you know I have it? I only just showed it to you..." This couldn't have been possible when her mother had hidden the necklace away from the world for the past decade.

Yong remains suspiciously quiet. An uncomfortable silence stretches between them before the truth finally crashes down on her.

Akari feels a second stab of betrayal. *Yong was the intruder! Just as Ty guessed, he hadn't come to our house to steal, but to check if the Jewel of Compassion was still in our possession. He searched my house the same day I searched his and Emeraude's rooms. How could I not have realized earlier?*

In hindsight, it seems so obvious. *Kami not barking... The intruder fleeing without taking anything... His fluid movements and effortless dueling... Yong's shirt—undershirt—that was far too thin in the cold... His begging for my wound to be deflected back onto him...*

Akari glares at Yong furiously. "You... you searched my house? You were the intruder who cut my arm in the fight? And then came back to check on me, pretending it was pure coincidence that you were in the vicinity?" She is fuming, speaking aloud questions whose answers she already knows, as if to cut him with guilt. Akari doesn't care that she's just as guilty of trespassing. She can't help but feel betrayed.

Yong avoids her eyes, his silence confession enough.

"How did you know there was a secret hiding place under the floorboard?" she demands.

"It sounded hollow," he claims. "It was rather obvious..."

Akari stares at him, speechless. It hadn't been obvious to *her* during the ten years she lived in the shophouse.

"I'm sorry..." Yong says quietly. "I would have told you earlier if I could. I wanted to tell you so many times, to not have anything standing between us, but I couldn't... until now."

"Why now?" she asks, anxiously gripping the Jewel of Compassion as she braces herself for something she knows she'll dread hearing.

"Now I've confirmed that the Jewel of Compassion is in your hands, I have to bring you to King Alvaro."

Anger boils within Akari. "Is that why you brought me to the capital?"

"Partly," Yong admits tightly.

"And if I refuse to go?" She stands and plants her feet, her fury escalating.

"I'm afraid you don't have a choice," he replies with a certain authority, his expressionless face unfathomable.

"So, this whole time, you've been planning to hand me over to King Alvaro?" Akari's voice trembles as she glares down at him. "Is this why you saved me and sacrificed Ty? Did you do this so you can accomplish your mission? So you can deliver your trophies to the king?"

"No, Akari! You have no idea!" Yong exclaims incredulously with a vehement shake of his head.

"Is this why you appeared before me so many times in the outskirts by 'coincidence'? Is this why you asked me out? Is this why you kissed me? Is this why you claimed you loved me? Were you just trying to get close to me because you've been eyeing the Jewel of Compassion all this time?" Akari hurls a stream of accusations, even though her fury can't mask the betrayal ripping her apart inside.

Yong is lost for words.

"All this time, here I was thinking that you helped me—even saved me—because... because... we were... friends. Comrades at the very least. I thought we were standing on the same side." Akari tries to appear cold, schooling her expression to stop the hurt from showing.

"We've always been on the same side, from the very beginning." Yong also rises as he tries to explain himself. "Even now."

"And all this time, here I was thinking you truly wanted to be... more than friends with me... that you genuinely loved me..." Akari's voice breaks.

"My love for you is real. And everything I've ever wanted with you has always been from the bottom of my heart." Yong holds his arms out to her, but she takes a step back.

"No! I don't believe you!" Akari yells, tears welling up in her eyes. Now Mari and Ty are no longer by her side, it doesn't take much to rile her. Not only is her anger directed at Yong, but also at herself for being so naive.

"Akari... please..." He inches toward her, flustered by her tears—ones that are falling because of him. "I was trying to protect you. And I still am." Yong's expression morphs into one of worry as he places a hand on her shoulder.

Akari brushes it away roughly. "There's no one on my side anymore!" she cries, and rushes from the room.

"Akari!" he calls after her.

But she doesn't look back, instead running as far as she can from the Lee Residence.

18. Solitude

It's a lot warmer in the capital. Akari doesn't know how long she's been running for until beads of perspiration roll down her forehead. Eventually, she comes to a stop at a marketplace.

It's nothing like the one in Cheyvelenia. Innumerable sturdy wooden stalls with multi-colored fabric roofs sprawl across an enormous stone-paved plaza—at least ten times the size of Cheyvelenia's town square—even branching into the surrounding streets and alleys. The vast array of spices, herbs, textiles, furniture, jewelry, and other trinkets far exceeds Akari's imagination. Everything is bigger, brighter, and bolder.

Throughout the bustling marketplace, sellers tout passionately and buyers bargain aggressively, markedly different from the typically cordial outskie manner she's used to. Despite having lived in Andelovia during her early childhood, the capital evokes an unsettling unfamiliarity within her.

The Andelovians—one with shocking purple lips and garish blue booties, and another with an excessively ruffled yellow silk robe and orange hair braided like a spiral seashell—don't shy away from colors or textures. Looking around, Akari can now picture how Emeraude's flamboyant wardrobe would fit in perfectly here.

In comparison, Yong's getup seems relatively understated. She feels conspicuously out of place in the capital, just as the Andelovians were in the outskirts. Her hair is too disheveled, her face too bare, her clothes too shabby, and her boots too weathered.

As Akari roams the streets of Andelovia, she receives stares from all directions. The Andelovians whisper to each other, probably discussing her origins. After reaching the safe house, Akari swapped her People's Protector uniform for some fraying, dark burgundy, linen tunic and pants she'd brought along. Although she looks normal, even comfortable, by the standards of the outskirts, she looks more like the homeless in the capital, except they stay in the shadows—out of sight and out of mind.

Seeking solitude, Akari slips into an alley that meanders away from the marketplace. The crowd gets sparser the further she goes, allowing her to become increasingly immersed in her thoughts.

I'm sorry, Mama. I'm truly sorry. If only I could go back in time, I would have stayed with you till the very end. The sounds of the capital fade away, and Akari is back with her mother.

The last time she saw Mari alive, Akari had callously left her behind despite her desperate pleas. She slumps against the side of the alley. *Perhaps I'm still six after all.* Her mother was invincible in her eyes—an everlasting figure in a naive child's life. But she hadn't been. In fact, she'd evidently been unwell. But Akari had so thoughtlessly reminded her that she could heal herself before turning to leave. She stares ahead, the tears that have sprung to her eyes making the world look distorted, unreal—more than the capital already is.

There was something Mari had wanted to tell her. *Was it about the fortune teller? Or was it about Papa?* Akari wonders hopelessly, harboring a deep regret that she'll never have the chance to hear any of it from her mother.

Her shoulder has long been numb when she eventually stands and traipses away. Akari wanders through the maze of alleys, and her thoughts drift to Yong.

He's part of the Royal Regiment. He serves King Alvaro! The clues had been there all along, but I failed to see them. Just as Salam and I thought, his fighting skills would have been wasted on a mere trader... And the bronze zephanerix badge shows where his allegiance lies...

She isn't so upset because Yong's work kept him from opening up to her—she understands that. It's the realization that it places them on opposing sides. Now, they can't even be comrades, let alone friends—or possibly more. This shatters Akari.

He's from Andelovia, part of the Royal Regiment, and on King Alvaro's side. I'm from the outskirts, part of the People's Protector, and... on the side of the people the king abandoned... With all this standing between us, how could our love ever hold up? Akari wishes she had never felt for Yong, of all people. *I need to put my feelings aside... I need to let him go... I need to let him go from my heart...*

She then thinks of Ty. Her best friend gave himself up to Zatori for her freedom, yet all she gave him were her wounds. *I'll rescue him, bring him home at all costs!* Akari vows, clenching her fists in determination. *Otherwise, I'll never forgive myself.*

Aware that Yong is no longer on her side, she knows she can't—and doesn't want to—count on him to save Ty. She won't give him any further reason to add to the count, to burden her with an even larger debt to repay. *But how am I supposed to go up against Zatori and the Harvesters, and rescue Ty, all by myself?*

A tap on her shoulder draws Akari back to reality. She wheels around to see a figure with flat, oil-slicked hair standing before her.

"Hanwell?" Akari gasps, wiping her eyes to make sure they're working properly. "How did you get here? How did you find me?"

Unexpectedly, it gives her some relief to see a familiar face despite it being someone she dislikes. However detestable, Hanwell reminds her of home.

He gestures to Akari to be quiet and leads her into a smaller and more deserted alley. There's an odd look in his beady eyes as he gives her a once-over.

"Via the gateways and then by flight, of course," he replies curtly. "The People's Protector has eyes and ears everywhere—and you stick out like a sore thumb here."

"Did Ty really end up in Zatori's hands? Did he really not manage to escape?" Akari asks anxiously despite the bleak prospects.

"Zatori has Kane. You ran for your life with your new Andelovian lackey and left him behind. You can't possibly have expected us to save him for you, can you?" Hanwell's tone is gloating, taunting.

Despite knowing this was likely, her heart still plunges. "We need to save him," Akari says desperately. "And how is Madam Salam?"

"She suffered some injuries, but she's fine," Hanwell replies stiffly before informing her, "Anyway, I've come today with orders for you from Sir Maximus."

"What sort of orders?" Akari asks, her thoughts still occupied by her best friend. "Whatever it is, I need to save Ty first."

"Miyahara, I know you have great difficulty following instructions, so let me remind you that, as part of the People's Protector, your actions aren't your call," Hanwell snaps harshly. "I'm not here to comfort you or mourn your loss. I'm here to deliver a mission."

Any feelings of relief Akari felt have dissipated. Even though she hadn't expected much from Hanwell, she'd at least hoped for a sliver of kindness. But even that seems too much for him.

Hanwell doesn't seem to care. "Your Andelovian friend will soon bring you to the White Palace to seek an audience with King Alvaro. When you see the king, you are to assassinate him."

Akari blinks in disbelief. "You want me... to kill King Alvaro?" she checks, not quite believing her ears. For as long as she can remember, the purpose of the People's Protector has always been to protect, not to rebel, and never to kill. Furthermore, there had been an agreement that they'd never again participate in any uprisings or any other capital-related matters.

"Yes," Hanwell confirms.

"Why would the People's Protector want that?" Before the words are out of her mouth, Akari realizes she already knows the answer. *Sir Maximus Fontan. He wants to replace King Alvaro on the throne.*

"We've been made aware that you have a royal regalia in your possession, giving you the rare opportunity to stand before the king—one we must seize. As the leader of the assassination mission, the responsibility falls on me to ensure its success. After we get rid of King Alvaro, Sir Maximus will accede to the throne and establish a realm where all Xylonians will receive equal protection."

Fear grips Akari. *Does Sir Maximus expect me to assassinate King Alvaro and hand over the Jewel of Compassion to him?* "I... I can't do this," she says, her tone quavering. "You, of all people, know I don't... don't do well with killing."

"Well, you'll have to this time, Miyahara. This is an order. And if you succeed, the People's Protector will help you rescue Kane." Hanwell speaks slowly to ensure every word sinks in. He steps toward her but takes care to maintain some distance, still fearing her gift. In his slimy voice, he informs her, "Killing King Alvaro is the only way to get your lover boy back."

Akari nods weakly, sickness spreading through her stomach. This time, she grits her teeth and bears it. "I'll do it," she whispers shakily. *I'll do anything to get Ty back.*

"Good. There'll be other Protectors—myself included—who'll be carrying out the mission with you. When you enter the palace, you won't be allowed to bring any weapons, but we have an insider planted within the White Palace to provide you with one. They'll identify themselves on the day," Hanwell instructs.

Akari nods again. "So... after I kill King Alvaro, will Sir Maximus become the new King of Xylon?" She's unable to quite picture this.

"Yes," he replies. "And in that new realm, Zatori will have to pay for all his harvestings, and the Xylonians will no longer have to live in fear."

Is that true? Will Xylon really be a better place? And can that justify taking a life? Even if it's the life of an unworthy king? Akari is so inundated with doubt she barely notices Hanwell disappearing into the maze of alleys.

After he's gone, she continues wandering aimlessly through the twisting alleys, trying to find her way back to the marketplace. To her frustration, she keeps retracing her steps, walking the same path over and over, completely disoriented in the labyrinth. The more Akari attempts to figure her way out, the more lost she becomes. Eventually, she stops to catch her breath, defeated.

When she looks up, her gaze lands on a breathtaking edifice in the distance, which she guesses must be the White Palace. The opulent white marble structure stands grandly against the majestic mountains, its domed turrets piercing the fluffy white clouds. She marvels at its beauty, unlike anything she's ever seen in the outskirts.

Perched upon them are gigantic, life-sized sculptures of zephanerixes, with real ones weaving their way between them. The sight staggers her. Zephanerixes are rare, but she supposes she shouldn't be surprised the king has so many at his beck and call. Akari can't help but wonder where Zephy is now, and if he's among them.

When she finally peels her eyes away from the palace, Akari is quickly drawn back into her thoughts. The assassination mission weighs heavily on her mind, adding to all her other worries. She keeps her head down and places one foot in front of the other mindlessly, heading in no particular direction.

Just as she takes a left turn into yet another alley, something hard hits her chest with a thud. Jolting back to reality, Akari looks down to see an old lady she's knocked over sprawled on the ground, her walking stick flung a few feet behind her. Before she can extend her hand to help her up, half a dozen guards materialize from nowhere, forming a line of protection between them.

They are well built and quick-footed, their coordination impeccable. Every one of them seems ready to pounce if Akari shows—even in the slightest way—that she might mean harm. However, even with this formidable assemblage, the presence of the old lady is not to be overshadowed.

"That's enough." She waves the guards away idly after taking the sandalwood walking stick one of them hands her.

As they recede behind her, she reaches a hand toward Akari. When she helps the old lady up, Akari is surprised at how light she is. Barely reaching her shoulders, she is inconceivably tiny. Her sleek, snow white hair is pulled back into a perfect low bun, without a single loose strand in sight. She casually straightens her dusky lilac robe and lifts her head. While the old lady's regal, albeit aged, beauty is undeniable, it's her striking opalescent eyes that leaves Akari in shock. The old lady is blind.

Before Akari can react, she asks, "Do they scare you? My eyes..."

"No... no... not one bit. I'm so sorry. I wasn't looking where I was walking," Akari says quickly. "Are you hurt?"

"No, I'm quite fine. Nothing to cause alarm over," she replies in a stately manner, waving her worries away. She stands completely still for a moment, as though taking the time to examine Akari with her unseeing eyes. "You must be lost, my child."

Akari furrows her brow, wondering how she knows this. "I'm afraid so, madam. All these alleys look the same to me. It's like a maze here."

"Indeed, it's quite confusing down here, my child, especially when you stand at a crossroads. But let me warn you—your eyes aren't always the best guide. They can easily be misled," the old lady says cryptically. "You try too much to look into the future when, ironically, that's not your gift."

Akari looks at her quizzically, contemplating the possibility she isn't in her right mind. Before she can come to any conclusion, the old lady offers her hand. "Come with me, my child. I'll lead you back to the main street."

Not knowing a better way out, Akari takes her hand. The old lady interlaces her crinkled fingers between Akari's supple ones and leads the way. The guards trail silently behind them.

While the old lady relies on Akari to steady herself, she doesn't need any help with navigation. Although Akari can't imagine how she can figure her way around, she doesn't question her authority.

As if reading her mind, the old lady explains, "I've been around here for more than half a century, even back when my eyes didn't fail me."

Akari nods. She has absolute faith in her sense of direction, somehow.

"You've come a long way to get back here," the old lady notes.

Once again, Akari wonders how she knows this. For anyone who can see, it's obvious she doesn't belong in Andelovia. But that clearly doesn't apply here. "How can you tell?" she asks.

"I see better this way," the old lady says, blinking her blind opalescent eyes, as if that's explanation enough.

Akari scrunches her eyebrows, asking, "What do you mean by that?"

"Now I don't see with my eyes, I'm not blinded by other distractions."

Confused yet intrigued by the elusive answers, Akari continues with her questions. "And what do you mean when you said I try to look too much into the future?"

"Oh, my child... because you're feeling lost, you've been trying so hard to look into the future for an answer—for some sort of guidance on what you should do," the old lady replies. "But what you don't realize is that your current decisions and actions are what will determine your future."

Akari isn't sure she fully understands, or if she ever will. "Then what should I do?" she asks anyway.

The old lady stops in her tracks, pulling Akari to a halt. She turns toward her, as if studying her. "My child, while you may not be able to see the future, you're still able to forge the future. Remember, that's a gift in itself."

Akari nods hesitantly, although she is filled with gratitude. Somehow, the words of a complete stranger are able to provide some degree of solace and enlightenment.

The old lady resumes leading the way. Akari follows beside her, their hands still linked.

"So, are there gifteds who can see the future? Fortune tellers perhaps?" Akari asks, the fortune teller she met as a child coming to mind.

"I'm sure such gifteds exist, although they are undoubtedly a rarity," she replies. "But even so, I can bet that anyone with a gift of seeing the future would steer clear of being a fortune teller. No one would want to bear the burden of defining someone's destiny. That's a tricky job."

Well, none of the things the fortune teller said made any sense to me anyway... Akari thinks. *Surely, they can't define my destiny...*

"Unless... unless..." the old lady suddenly adds, but stops as abruptly as she started. Her mind seems to be elsewhere.

"What is it?"

"Unless... they're from the future themselves," she qualifies. By now, Akari is quite certain she isn't in her right mind.

The old lady gives her a pointed look before continuing, "But remember, no matter what any fortune teller says, you have control over your destiny, my child. Even if you can't escape it."

"Yes, madam." Akari nods along despite her skepticism.

Eventually, they emerge from the labyrinth of alleys, returning to the busy main street.

"Is there somewhere you want to go?" the old lady asks.

"The Vykroux Residence," Akari blurts without giving much thought.

"Xavier Vykroux?" she checks, her tone questioning. "Vykroux may not be the person you're seeking, but you should go anyway," she advises before adding, "Although he isn't really someone you can just meet as you please..."

"I know, but that's alright. I'll find a way," Akari says as she prepares to take her leave.

"Well, today is your lucky day," the old lady remarks, smiling. "If you walk down this main street, you'll find the Vykroux Residence at the very end of it. Take one of my guards with you and Xavier Vykroux will grant you an audience if he's present."

"Thank you, madam," Akari says gratefully.

The old lady waves her hand once more and peers into Akari's eyes. "You don't have to thank me. Farewell for now, my child."

With that, she and the rest of her guards disappear back into the maze of alleys, leaving one behind to accompany Akari to the Vykroux Residence. He leads Akari down the main street until they arrive at a gated estate enclosed by high granite walls.

From between the rusted black iron railings of the gate, she glimpses a once-magnificent mansion standing beyond a sprawling, overgrown garden. Age has softened its grandeur. Ivy coils around the stone facade, its carvings worn smooth by the elements. Yet, the sheer presence of fortress-like property still commands an air of quiet authority. *This has to be the Vykroux Residence!*

Akari's breath catches. It's as though she's waited an entire lifetime to return.

After the guard exchanges whispers with one at the entrance, the former takes his leave while the latter opens the gate and escorts Akari into the mansion. After weaving through a series of bleak passages and echoing chambers, she's finally shown to a grand, musty sitting room.

The air reeks of time and neglect, perhaps proof that it hasn't seen guests in too long. The faded velvet curtains hang heavily, nearly drawn shut, allowing only slivers of feeble sunlight to filter through. The pale beams cast long dusty streaks across the room, barely illuminating the dull ebony furniture that blends into the murky shadows. All alone in the vast space sits Lord Vykroux, shrouded in a certain emptiness.

As Akari steps into the sitting room, her stomach twists in knots and her heart pounds against her ribs. Every sound—her footsteps, her breathing—seems magnified. She swallows, but her throat is dry.

Lord Vykroux squints, surveying her thoroughly as she nears. His brow furrows in confusion, as if trying to place the familiar stranger before him.

When Akari reaches him, she casts him a glance, taking in his stately but repressed demeanor and his sandstone-colored robe, well-worn yet unmistakably lavish. The silence between them stretches long, and her eyes veer down to her own battered boots, marking the stark dissonance between the two of them.

"Mari?" Lord Vykroux's voice cracks, raw with emotion. His face twitches spasmodically, and his eyes have a faraway look to them. He seems completely lost in thought, as if his mind is lingering in another time—another life.

A shiver runs down Akari's spine as she watches the former grand advisor fall into a moment of oblivion.

The years alone—without family—have clearly fractured him in ways she can barely understand. Having been drawn into seclusion for too long, his penchant for solitude has made him forget how to be around people.

Perplexed, Akari takes a deep breath, trying to steady her racing pulse, then forces herself to meet his eyes. She knows she needs to speak, but the words feel heavy in her mouth. "I'm not Mari..." she informs him softly—carefully—afraid to burst his bubble. "I'm Akari, her daughter..."

For an agonizingly long moment, Lord Vykroux doesn't respond, his eyes wide, as if struggling to process her words. Then, as if the realization finally hits him, his face morphs from confusion to shock.

"Akari?" he murmurs, his tone tight and uncertain, almost as if testing the name that hasn't touched his tongue in a decade. His eyes rove over her again, a mix of wonder and disbelief whorling in them. "You've grown so, so much... It's been a while since I last saw you... I've lost track of how much time has passed..." His voice trails off and his gaze becomes distant again, as though he's but a mere shadow of the past.

Lord Vykroux examines her intently again, albeit a little more soberly this time. His lips finally curl into a weary half-smile. "You do, very much, take after your mother, for which I'm glad."

Akari grazes her teeth with her tongue, unsure how to respond.

After a long empty pause, he finally seems to pull himself together. "Have a seat." He gestures weakly to a sagging armchair.

Akari gingerly takes her seat.

"Would you like something to drink? Some telmezia tea, perhaps?" Lord Vykroux looks lost and pensive once again, withdrawing back into his memories. Then, as he glances back at her, his eyes flicker with a sudden burst of clarity. "It was your mother's favorite..."

Akari hesitates, then nods politely. "Sure, thank you."

As he instructs a maid in apricot garb to prepare some refreshments, Akari notices, self-consciously, that even the servant's uniform in the capital is fancier than the shabby clothes on her back.

"Your return to Andelovia means only one thing." Lord Vykroux's urgent, fearful tone recaptures Akari's attention. She looks up at him anxiously, expecting him to bring up their relationship. "It's true, isn't it?" he asks between labored gasps, as though it hurts to breathe—to say the words. "That Mari is gone?"

The mention of her mother wrings Akari's guts. She lowers her head, fighting back tears. "Yes," she whispers without looking up, her voice quavering. "Just over a week ago. Zatori killed her. He has returned."

Lord Vykroux's face twists into a grimace before he buries it in his palms, momentarily lost in thought again. When he finally looks up, the expression on his face seems to be caught between devastation and fury. "Zatori! That murderer. I will personally see to it that he meets his end this time!" Lord Vykroux cries, pain searing his words.

A tear slips from Akari's eye, and before she can stop it, another follows.

He places a trembling hand on her shoulder to comfort her. "However hard it is for me to accept this, it must be infinitely harder for you. I'm so sorry for your loss."

Akari nods slowly, brushing her tears away and forcing herself to take a deep breath.

After they've both taken a moment to compose themselves, Lord Vykroux says, "What matters is that you're safe now. This is all your mother would have wanted..."

When the maid returns with a tray, she carries a tall silver teapot with intricate telmezias detailing it, two matching teacups, and some butter cookies. She pours a stream of powder-pink liquid with a graceful tip of her hand, then bows and takes her leave silently.

Akari steals a glance at Lord Vykroux and finds him already starting on the pink tea. Catching her gaze, he shifts his eyes from her to her untouched cup. "Please help yourself. Do make yourself at home."

Avoiding the discomfort of his scrutiny, Akari busies herself, sniffing and sipping the telmezia tea. She first tastes the flowery sweetness that lingers on the tip of her tongue before the bitterness sets in, bringing back memories of her mother. Her chest contracts, her breathing becoming strained.

Lord Vykroux seems to share the same sentiment. "I haven't had this in a while. It reminds me very much of Mari," he recollects in a daze.

"So, how did you come to know my mother?" Akari finally asks. *And what was she to you?* She hasn't mustered the courage to voice her true question.

"I first met her around two decades ago when I frequented the palace," Lord Vykroux recalls between sips, his gaze distant.

"When you were on good terms with King Alvaro?" Akari probes.

His entire being stiffens at her mention of the king. "Yes, but that's history. So much has changed since then." The air is suddenly thick with tension. "Back then, your mother must have been around your age. She was training to become a royal physician to the Ashgenovs, which she eventually did a few years later."

Akari's eyes grow wide with surprise. *Mama was a royal physician? She knew the Ashgenovs?* Never had Mari mentioned that she used to work in the White Palace, much less directly for the royal family. In fact, she seemed to want nothing to do with them. *Is this how Mama got hold of Zephy when we were escaping from Andelovia?*

Despite his state, Lord Vykroux marks the change in Akari's expression and gathers that this is news to her. "Your mother never spoke of her time in Andelovia, did she?"

Akari shakes her head. "She never liked to, although she did tell me she worked as a healer when we lived in the capital." *Healer was quite an understatement,* she realizes.

"Well, it seems I've already said too much," Lord Vykroux notes with a brooding frown. "So, are you a physician or a healer like your mother?"

"Throughout the years, my mother taught me everything she knew, but I don't work as a healer," Akari informs him. "I'm... I'm part of the People's Protector."

"You joined the People's Protector?" Lord Vykroux exclaims in surprise, his tone steeped in disapproval, like that of Mari's when Akari had mentioned enlisting. "Your mother wouldn't have allowed that! Did you hide it from her?"

Akari nods guiltily. "Yes, my mother didn't know... She wouldn't have let me... But I wanted to protect the people who were abandoned by King Alvaro."

"There are other Protectors who can do that!" Lord Vykroux rebukes worriedly. "Although I contributed to the rebuilding of the People's Protector, I agree with your mother. Joining them is too dangerous for you! Haven't you forgotten what happened a decade ago? Especially now Zatori and the Harvesters are back, the last thing she'd want would be for you to be anywhere near them." Like Mari, Lord Vykroux's protectiveness of Akari is undeniable—fatherly, even.

From his reaction, it's clear he's unaware that Akari has been ordered to assassinate King Alvaro—perhaps even of the whole assassination mission. And she knows better than to mention it. For Ty's sake, she can't risk this mission failing—even with her aversion to taking lives.

"Do you think King Alvaro is no longer worthy of the throne?" Akari wonders out loud.

"It's been a long time since he proved fit to be king!" Lord Vykroux snarls in distaste.

"Why is that?" Akari's voice drops to a nervous whisper.

"Because of King Alvaro, Zatori tried to harvest my gift, causing me to lose my wife and daughter." Lord Vykroux's words are laced with anguish, the memories clearly still fresh in his mind.

His answer leaves Akari thoroughly disconcerted. "But you knew where we were all this while! I saw your letter to my mother! Why didn't you come to look for us? Why did you abandon us in the outskirts?"

Her unexpected outburst catches him off guard. "No, no, no! Your mother and I were friends—good old friends, but nothing more," Lord Vykroux clarifies anxiously, evidently taken aback by her presumption. "Akari, I'm afraid you've got it all wrong... I'm not your father..."

19. Memories

Akari lets her heart settle before taking a proper look at Lord Vykroux. His straight blond hair is swept back from his pale haggard face, which seems worn with grief yet almost untouched by time. As she stares into his aquamarine blue eyes, she's now certain they aren't related. He doesn't have her honey-colored eyes, or the bronze skin and wavy hair she remembers on her father.

Although the signs have been obvious from the onset, from the moment Akari set foot in the Vykroux Residence, she had only seen what she'd wanted to see—a protective and loving father to help soften the loss of her mother. She longed to believe she had found her father—that she had family again. No wonder she hadn't realized earlier what's now crystal clear—her father is someone else. A strange mix of embarrassment, frustration, and disappointment overcomes her all at once.

"I'm... I'm sorry... Your letter... The telmezia tea... I thought—" Akari is unable to find the right words. Her mind is in chaos. *I've had it wrong this whole time...*

"It's alright, Akari," Lord Vykroux hushes her gently, as though she's still six years old.

"My mother told me that my father died in the Great Harvest. But lately, I've begun to have my doubts. After I saw your letter and heard you lost your wife and your daughter in the Great Harvest, I thought... I thought that you could be my father..." Akari takes a long breath, feeling lost all over again. *So, who is my father? Is he already long gone, as Mama said? Or is he still alive and well?*

"Is that why you came to me today?" Lord Vykroux asks, shadows eddying in his eyes. "Are you here to find your father?"

She nods.

"I'm sorry I'm not who you're looking for, but I'm glad you came," he says, his face twitching again. "I've always wondered what Sage would be like if she were still around. Seeing you, in some ways, answered that for me. Perhaps seeing me might have done the same for you too."

"Sage... Sage was your daughter? The girl Yong and I played with as children?" Akari doesn't know how much more shock she can take.

"Yes, that's my little girl." Lord Vykroux's face grows solemn.

"Sage is... dead? She died during the Great Harvest?" Akari asks, still in disbelief. This whole time, she'd falsely assumed she was his so-called dead daughter while Sage had been alive and well. *So, Yong's childhood playmate, who was Lord Vykroux's daughter, really did die...*

Pain sears Lord Vykroux's eyes.

"I still think of the times the three of us played hide-and-seek together. Sage was always so lively and clever. I wish she could be here with us," Akari laments. *The Great Harvest destroyed so many lives—those who perished, as well as those of us left behind.*

"I do, too. Both Sage and my wife, Miriam. As well as your mother..." Lord Vykroux says quietly.

When their eyes meet, there's an unspoken understanding of their shared pain of having lost family. The passings of Mari, Lady Miriam, and Sage have left a gaping void in their lives. Lord Vykroux refills their teacups with more telmezia tea, and they sip in silence between bites of butter cookies, mourning in the comfort of each other's company.

"Speaking of Yong, he's grown into a fine young man," Lord Vykroux eventually continues. "Although it's a pity he now serves King Alvaro. His talent could be put to much better use elsewhere, such as the People's Protector. Salam could groom him to be the next leader." From the looks of it, the former grand advisor seems oblivious to the current power struggle between Maximus and Salam.

"I've met him," Akari shares. "Yong's the one who brought me back to the capital."

Lord Vykroux's features twist with shock. His mind seems to be racing, his eyes darting wildly in their sockets.

"What's wrong?" Akari asks.

"Nothing," he says as he attempts to compose his expression. "Didn't you come today looking for your father?"

Akari nods, her heart pumping in anticipation. "Do you know who he is? Is he still alive? Is he here in the capital?"

"Why don't I show you instead?" Lord Vykroux offers as he finishes up his tea.

"Sure!" She shoots up eagerly. "How will you do that?"

"By visiting my memory." Lord Vykroux speaks as though this is the most obvious answer ever.

Akari peers at him incredulously. Everyone she's met today doesn't quite seem to be in their right mind. "And how are we supposed to do that?" she asks skeptically, contemplating whether his seclusion has pushed him past sanity.

"Using my gift," he answers with a sad smile.

Without warning, Lord Vykroux lifts his arm, lobbing something invisible into the air. For an instant Akari isn't sure if he threw anything at all, until she sees what looks like a phantasm of a glowing rope unfurling down the sitting room.

With a nervous laugh, he asks, "Are you ready?"

But before she can answer, Lord Vykroux takes her hand and pulls on the rope. Their surroundings blur into a swirling haze.

When clarity returns, Akari finds them back in the same sitting room, though it has transformed. While the musty air has been replaced by the fresh scent of Andelovian flowers, the ebony furniture remains, albeit shiny and new, as though it has yet to withstand the test of time. The vibrant velvet curtains are now drawn wide, letting in streams of sunlight that bathe the room. Outside, the veranda stretches into view, bright and inviting.

The sound of metal clanging takes Akari by surprise. She instinctively twists to face its source. A second Lord Vykroux, clad in vivid persimmon, stands before her. Despite seeming only a tad younger, he possesses an animated charisma that has yet to be worn away by grief or seclusion. He's on the veranda, fencing with a blond-haired, blue-eyed boy of about ten who bears a striking resemblance to him.

They each have a piece of colored chalk attached to the tip of their foils, so every successful attack is made visible by a mark left on the opponent's clothes. An evidently skilled fencer, Lord Vykroux trains the young boy with a deliberate balance between challenging him with unpredictable moves and letting him win at times. Even then, the boy's clothes are peppered with chalk marks while those on Lord Vykroux's robe are few and far between.

Beside them, a pair of brown-haired, brown-eyed adolescent boys fence with an impassioned vigor, a lot more evenly matched. The taller, presumably older of the two thrusts his sword at the other boy, who manages to parry the blow. Akari sees a bit of Lord Vykroux in them both as well.

Just as the older two finish their match, the middle boy wheels around and prods the youngest in the rear with his foil.

"Hey! That's cheating!" he protests sullenly, his flushed face wrought with displeasure. "That's not fair!"

"There's no fairness in battle," the middle boy reminds him with a mischievous smile. "Don't you want to join the Royal Regiment in the future? Do you need me to remind you of the saying they live by? *Kill or be killed.*"

Is this saying specific to the Royal Regiment rather than simply the capital? Akari wonders. Both people who've mentioned it to her—Salam and Yong—are affiliated to that elite troop.

The youngest is about to fire back when Lord Vykroux playfully lunges at the middle boy, attempting to prod him in the rear with his foil, almost catching him off guard. But he has quite the reflexes and fends off the advances in time, much to the dismay of the youngest.

"Shall we do two against two? Sven and I against the two of you?" Lord Vykroux suggests as he continues sparring with the middle boy, occasionally directing blows at the eldest.

Sven, the youngest, whoops excitedly, pleased to finally have Lord Vykroux on his side after a long and tough training session.

As the four of them spar, Akari carefully makes her way toward them. But she elicits no response as they continue with their fencing, completely oblivious to her presence.

"Welcome to my memory," present-day Lord Vykroux announces somewhat proudly, yet jadedly, from behind her.

Akari jumps, having momentarily forgotten his existence. "Where are we?" she asks. "Or rather, *when* are we?"

"This must have been about sixteen years ago," Lord Vykroux answers, his face twitching spasmodically.

"Are they your three sons?"

"Yes. That's Seth, my firstborn, Skye, my second son, and Sven, my youngest boy—"

The joyful peal of a child's laughter captures Akari's attention. She whirls around to see a lady with a toddler girl on her lap, sitting in the armchair that she occupied just moments earlier. It's plush in the memory, untouched by neglect.

The top half of the lady's face sprouts an array of brown and cream feathers, framing her bright brown eyes and blending into her wavy brown hair. Her nose and mouth curve into a prominent black beak. More feathers peek out from the sleeves of her brocaded coral kirtle, covering parts of her hands and arms, and are fully showcased on the large wings extending from her back. She looks uncannily like an owl—to be exact, she is an owl hybreed.

The two-year-old girl is undoubtedly her and Lord Vykroux's daughter. Her baby feathers are a fluffy fuzz of beige and cream and her beak is a tiny white hook. As she lets out a radiant laugh, her curly blonde hair bounces and her bright blue eyes twinkle. Akari instantly recognizes the little owlet in the buttercup frock. She's none other than Sage, her childhood playmate. And the owl lady must be Lady Miriam Vykroux.

"I didn't realize Lady Miriam was a..." Akari stops as quickly as she starts, realizing she may have sounded impolite. "I mean, I should have known. Not that it matters in any way... I don't care at all... I just... didn't consider it..."

Evidently not the first time he's been faced with such a response, Lord Vykroux shares, "My side of the family was initially opposed to Miriam because she was a hybreed. We didn't care what anyone else thought and got married secretly. Eventually, they came around when they saw how warm-hearted and intelligent she was. As time passed, even though we had three wonderful sons together, both of us still wanted a daughter very much. Everyone told us we should stop, to be content with our lot. None of our sons manifested as hybreeds and that was the best outcome we could have hoped for.

"But eight years after having our youngest boy, we finally had Sage. Her manifestation as a hybreed didn't lessen our joy one bit. In fact, I was elated to have a daughter who took after her mother. Although Miriam was initially ridden with guilt, it gradually wore away when she saw how genuinely happy I was. Both of us and our three sons loved Sage with all our hearts. At that time, my life was complete—there was nothing more I wanted."

For the brief duration that Lord Vykroux speaks of the happiest period in his life, he reverts to his old, charming ways. His current, reclusive self seems like a lifetime away. However, this fleeting moment vanishes as quickly as it came.

"Mama, I already know the result. Skye won today," two-year-old Sage announces, her full sentences capturing Akari's attention.

"How do you know?" Lady Miriam asks as Lord Vykroux and the boys slide into the sitting room while counting the chalk marks on each other.

"I counted," Sage says, eyeing her father and brothers. "Papa has twenty-three, Seth has eighteen, Skye has seventeen, and Sven has sixty-nine—seventy, if you count the one on his buttocks."

"But *they* haven't even finished counting," Lady Miriam points out, her tone soft but surprised.

When the boys are done, they start tallying the number of chalk marks on each person.

"Papa has twenty-three," Seth begins. "And I have..."

"Seventeen," Sven replies.

"Skye has seventeen as well," Seth continues. "And you have..."

"Sixty-nine." There's a hint of disappointment in Sven's voice.

"How did you do that, Sage?" Lord Vykroux asks, amazed, her three brothers proudly watching her.

"I can count too!" she points out with a frown. "Just quicker!"

"You're so clever!" Seth beams as he picks up his little sister from their mother's lap and twirls her around. "I can't believe you're so close. And so quick too."

"So, it's a tie then?" Skye checks. "Seth and I both have seventeen each."

"No, you missed out this one on Seth when you were counting," Sage informs her family as she points to the faint chalk mark on his neck. "Seth has eighteen. And this last one would have been fatal. It's not a tie. Skye won." Her face breaks into a triumphant little smile.

Lord Vykroux and Lady Miriam look at each other, then at their daughter in awe. Skye pats Sage on the head while Sven gives her hand a gentle squeeze.

Lady Miriam gushes with pride, planting a kiss on her cheek. "You really are a special child!"

"A genius! A prodigy!" Lord Vykroux adds proudly before planting another kiss on Sage's forehead.

In her peripheral vision, Akari glimpses someone walking into the sitting room. When she turns toward the newcomer, she freezes. Just a few steps beyond her reach, a younger version of Mari cradles a tiny bundle as she makes her way to the Vykroux family.

Young Mari looks so achingly familiar, yet so painfully different. In place of her usual unassuming garments is a soft pink robe with intricate beading covering the entire surface of the silky fabric. Her shiny black hair is done up in elaborate twists and braids, topped off with crystals and jewels. Her porcelain face, a little fuller and a little more radiant, is made up to perfection, highlighting all her beautiful features. The most striking of all is young Mari's dark, almond eyes that seem to give off a certain tenderness—naivety, even—which Akari hasn't seen in her mother for as long as she can remember.

Tears well up in Akari's eyes. She runs up to Mari and embraces her, but finds herself grasping thin air as her arms sweep through her mother's body. Oblivious to present-day Akari, young Mari continues through the sitting room.

"She's just a memory," present-day Lord Vykroux reminds Akari gently, as though he has practiced this himself countless times. "Even so, being able to be around the loved ones you've lost is better than losing them completely. This is why I spend more time here than in the real world." And why he hasn't aged much—time doesn't flow within memories.

"Do you think it's better to live like this?" Akari wonders as she falls into step with Mari, an attempt to establish any semblance of closeness with her mother. *Would I rather stay in a memory with Mama or go back to a real world without her?* She doesn't know the answer.

But Lord Vykroux does. "My memory has long been a better place than my reality... because some of the people who gave me the happiest memories have themselves become memories... If I hadn't lived this way for the past decade, I might not have lived at all."

As Akari mulls over his words, an idea strikes her. "If you can go back in time, why didn't you try to change the past? Then maybe Lady Miriam, Sage, and my mother wouldn't have to lose their lives."

"Unfortunately, I don't have that gift. If I did, I would have done everything to bring them back. However, this isn't time travel, but rather a trip down memory lane. We don't exist to the people here—they can neither see nor hear us. If you actually went back in time, you'd exist in that time period and be able to interact with the people from then."

"Right..." Akari nods slowly, taking in his words. "But even so, I've never heard of a gift like this before," she remarks in awe.

"Not all gifts are for combat," Lord Vykroux points out as he turns toward young Mari.

When Akari does the same, she realizes the bundle her mother's carrying is a baby—baby Akari. She must have been only about a month old.

"This was the day I first saw you," Lord Vykroux says. "I've never seen Mari happier. You were everything to her."

Tears roll down Akari's cheeks as she continues watching the memory unfold before her.

Lady Miriam warmly invites Mari to sit with her, and the three boys resume fencing on the veranda.

"I can't believe I'm finally getting to meet her," she says exuberantly. "Can I hold her?"

"Of course!" Mari smiles, carefully passing baby Akari across.

"She looks just like you. She's beautiful," Lady Miriam gushes. "What's her name?"

"Akari. It means light," Mari informs her proudly as Sage climbs onto her lap to get a closer look.

"Her name is just as beautiful as her," Lady Miriam coos, rocking her arms rhythmically.

Sage studies the baby curiously, softly touches her face, and smiles. Baby Akari bubbles with giggles. "Akari..." Sage muses to herself.

"They seem to like each other," Mari remarks.

"Sage is the only girl among all the boys in the family," Lady Miriam says. "She'll love Akari's company for a change."

"I'm sure they'll grow up to be like sisters, just like the two of you," Lord Vykroux concludes as he strokes baby Akari's cheeks.

Lady Miriam and Mari lock eyes and laugh.

The scene touches Akari, but she reminds herself it isn't why she's here. "Where's my father? I thought you said I'd be able to see him."

"He didn't visit my residence on this day..." Present-day Lord Vykroux's glance shifts surreptitiously as he backs away, creating some space between them. His face twitches spasmodically once again.

"Then when will I get to see him?" she asks, perplexed. "I thought you'd show him to me."

"For your own sake, don't be curious about him," he beseeches her. "He hasn't existed in your life for such a long time, and you should let it stay this way. Your mother moved to the outskirts not only to hide you from Zatori, but also your father."

"What do you mean?" Akari demands. "Does this mean he's still alive and here in the capital?"

"Forget about him, Akari! Pretend he never existed," Lord Vykroux implores as he puts even more distance between them. "After all, you've lived all this while as if he didn't."

Akari finally senses something amiss. "Where are you going?" Her words are steeped in panic.

"I'm sorry. You have to stay here until I've found a way to get you back to the outskirts," Lord Vykroux says, spreading his arms apologetically, and with yet another twitch of his face. When he raises his hand, the phantasm of the glowing rope rematerializes. "I won't be long."

Dread overcomes Akari when Lord Vykroux's true intention dawns on her. He doesn't—never did—plan to show her who her father is. Instead, he wants her trapped in his memory and removed from the capital.

"If it was up to me, I'd rather Sage stuck here—safe and alive—than dead in the real world..."

Akari dashes toward him. But she is too late.

Lord Vykroux tugs hard on the rope, hastily drawing it toward himself. When Akari reaches for him, her hands pass through his body as they did with Mari's. He has already begun dematerializing.

"No! Don't leave me here! Let me out!" she cries, desperately grabbing the air in front of her.

As Lord Vykroux evanesces, he says, "This is what Mari would have wanted... She never wanted you to know your father..." Then he vanishes completely, leaving behind the fading echoes of his voice, followed by absolute silence.

As an emptiness engulfs her, Akari tries to calm herself. She realizes Lord Vykroux's last words confirm something her mother had already suggested—her father is alive and well. *But if he isn't Lord Vykroux, who could he possibly be?*

She clutches the Jewel of Compassion, anxiously pacing back and forth around the sitting room. *I need to get out. I can't just stay here waiting to be sent back to the outskirts after I've come this far. But how can I escape this memory?*

As if in response to her thoughts, the Jewel of Compassion emanates a soft red glow. Akari releases it exasperatedly. *What's the use of having a gift and a complement when I'm stuck here—*

"Do you want to play hide-and-seek?" The voice of a child breaks the silence.

Akari looks up and finds Sage staring directly at her. Bordering between shock and disbelief, she asks, "Are you... talking to me? You can... see me?"

Meanwhile, Lord Vykroux and Lady Miriam peer puzzledly in the direction of present-day Akari, but she remains invisible to them. In fact, no one seems to be able to see her except the little owlet.

Lady Miriam furrows her brow, asking, "Who are you talking to, Sage?"

"Akari," she replies.

Lady Miriam appears baffled as she glances at baby Akari, now fast asleep in her arms. "She's too young. You'll have to wait a couple of years for that."

Sage shakes her head vehemently. "No. Let's go now!"

Before Akari can respond, Sage hops off Mari's lap and darts out of the sitting room as quickly as her tiny legs can carry her. The skirt of her bright yellow frock flutters behind her, vanishing around the corner.

"Sage! Come back, Sage!" Mari calls after her.

"Don't mind her," Lord Vykroux says as a maid in the same apricot uniform promptly appears and chases after her dutifully.

Mari bursts into laughter, her eyes following the maid until she disappears. "That will be me in a few years..." she notes, giving baby Akari a smile.

Present-day Akari takes one last glance at young Mari before making after her childhood playmate.

"Wait for me, Mistress Sage. Where are you going?" the maid calls out.

Sage comes to a stop in an arched hallway, allowing both Akari and the maid to catch up with her. "Will you play hide-and-seek with me, please?" she asks the servant, putting on her most angelic smile, her bouncy blonde curls and twinkling blue eyes deceptively beguiling.

"Anything you wish, my little lady," the maid duly complies.

"Can you close your eyes and count to a hundred? I'll hide and you can seek," Sage instructs, and the maid obeys.

As soon as she shuts her eyes, Sage takes Akari's hand, quietly beckoning her to follow.

Once they are out of earshot, Akari whispers, "Why can you see me?"

"*You* were the one who created an intervention," Sage says as she makes her way through another wing of the Vykroux Residence, into the expansive back garden.

"What's an intervention?" Akari asks while walking alongside the two-year-old.

"Now is not the time for this," she replies tersely. "We have more important things to do."

"How did I create an intervention?" Akari presses.

"We don't have time for this either. Don't you want to get out?" Sage gives her a pointed look, her piercing aquamarine blue eyes an exact replica of her father's.

Akari's face melts into a smile. The little owlet before her is the same Sage she remembers—intelligent and incisive. But the smile quickly disappears when she recalls that Sage is now gone. *How could she only have six short years of her life left?* Akari looks at her childhood playmate with a melancholic gaze.

"There's no need to look at me like I'm going to die soon," Sage says as she picks up speed, her fluffy feathers ruffled by the wind. "Let's hurry."

Akari's eyes widen. "You know you're going to die... young? How's that possible?"

"I just know things," she states simply, leading Akari into a hidden tunnel behind a thick curtain of hanging plants. "This tunnel has long been forgotten, but I like to use it sometimes."

Akari nods as she keeps pace.

"We're leaving the Vykroux Residence," Sage announces after a while.

"Where are we going?" Akari asks, peering about.

"Somewhere we both know. You'll see when we get there." Sage grins, and Akari wonders if she's ever met an Andelovian who doesn't give cryptic answers.

She raises her eyebrows. "Why are you helping me?"

"What goes around comes around," Sage says with conviction. "That's how it is between friends."

Akari sighs, knowing full well that her childhood playmate will have died before she gets to repay any of her kindness. However, there's no way she has the heart to mention this to a two-year-old.

She switches to a more light-hearted tone, asking, "Aren't you afraid your father will find out?"

"He loves me too much. I'll get away with anything," Sage claims with a smug little shrug. "Besides, he doesn't have to know."

Akari's lips curve upward in amusement.

After they emerge from the long tunnel, it doesn't take long before they end up at the bottom of an oddly familiar stair turret. This is where eight-year-old Sage brought six-year-old Akari to hide when they were playing hide-and-seek ten years ago.

Akari releases her hand, steps into the middle, and looks up to see how high the narrow spiral stairs will take her. Just as she remembers, there seems to be almost no end.

"We're now on the periphery of the White Palace," Sage informs her.

"The White Palace?" Akari asks, horrified. She has taken a shortcut to yet more danger. However, she quickly reminds herself that no one besides Sage can see her.

"Remember, just do what you need to do. Don't change anything," the toddler warns, her eloquent speech both endearing and jarring. "Hurry, we'll come soon!"

"What do you mean by that? What do I need to do?" Akari blinks, confused. But when she opens her eyes, the wise little owlet has already disappeared. The Jewel of Compassion glows softly once more.

"Sage? Sage?" Akari calls out but receives no response.

She glances around before making her way up the spiral stairs, a little less bravely than she did a decade ago. She ascends carefully, for a single misstep could cause her to fall to her death. Eventually, Akari sees a wooden door. She takes a deep breath and enters the room, closing the door behind her.

Just as Akari expects, she is in a circular room with a high domed ceiling. The tall curved walls with eight evenly spaced windows are lined with endless shelves containing books, vases, crystals, and other ornaments of all sorts. She recognizes this place right away. It's the room where she met the fortune teller.

But what do I need to do here? Akari ponders Sage's ambiguous instructions. She walks around the room, examining the different trinkets on the shelves but not daring to lay a finger on any of them.

The voile curtains which obscure a segment of the room seem inviting but mysterious. She approaches with caution and peeks between the curtains, half expecting to see the fortune teller, but no one is there. She steps between them, into the area she was previously not made privy to.

Suddenly, the wooden door creaks as it opens and closes gently. Footsteps patter lightly into the room. Akari jolts in surprise, hitting her hand on the desk.

"Is anyone there?" A child's voice reverberates through the room. But it doesn't belong to Sage.

Akari freezes in panic when she realizes someone else can hear her. *At least it's only a child,* she tells herself as she quickly gives a reply. "Well... yes, yes..."

"Who are you?" the child asks, their tone bright and innocent, as they make their way toward the voile curtains.

"I'm... I'm a fortune teller," Akari says, making up an answer hastily.

The child doesn't seem to realize she doesn't belong here.

They try to hold up the curtain to peek. But with a response so swift it surprises even herself, Akari grabs the child's hand to prevent herself from being seen, as though she already has a hunch that this is going to happen.

For a split second, through the slit between the voile curtains, Akari takes in what she can see of the child. The little girl has a light bronze face, silky ash-brown hair, and inquisitive honey-colored eyes. Although the moment is exceptionally brief, Akari has absolutely no doubt that before her stands six-year-old Akari. In fact, this is the day of her sixth birthday.

And present-day Akari *is* the fortune teller.

20. Reunions

Akari is in a daze. *Have I gone back to the past? Or was I already part of the past? Am I changing the past? Or have I already changed the past?* She isn't sure, but her own voice draws herself back to the task Sage entrusted her with.

"You don't get to see me," present-day Akari says, carefully releasing little Akari's hand. As the warmth from their touch lingers, she realizes she must have traveled back in time.

"Why?" little Akari probes.

"Because neither of us should be here," she states plainly.

"Are you hiding too?"

"Not exactly."

"Then can you read my fortune, please?" Little Akari is brimming with curiosity.

"I could... for you... just this once," Akari says, recalling Sage's last words before vanishing. *Remember, just do what you need to do. Don't change anything.*

Akari knows the role she needs to fulfill in this time and place is that of the fortune teller. *But... I can't exactly remember the reading from when I was six... What do I say? What do I tell her?* She rummages through the piles of parchments worriedly, looking for a clue to the reading for little Akari. Somehow, it's as though she knows to look there.

Akari snaps out of her thoughts when she sees a piece of parchment with the *Prophecy of a New Realm* written in an elegant script. *This is it! This is the reading I received ten years ago!*

"Give me your hand," Akari finally says.

Little Akari extends a hand between the voile curtains, and she takes it in hers. After clearing her throat, Akari recites the prophecy.

"Compassion rises from the north,
Wisdom hails from across the Great Divide,
And from beyond the end of land
Comes courage—forgotten but not lost.
Only their treacherous reunion
Shall bring peace of a new realm."

There's a small pause before little Akari asks, "What does that mean?"

"Well... that's something you'll have to mull over," Akari says, a reminder to herself to ponder the meaning of the prophecy. When she does, it strikes her that the Jewel of Compassion has already been found in the northernmost town of the outskirts. Akari gasps.

Compassion, wisdom, and courage—these three virtues must refer to the three royal regalia which symbolize them! And the three royal regalia must in turn be reunited for the stability of the throne. But what does a new realm refer to? Even present-day Akari has yet to figure all of it out.

"And remember," Akari continues, diving back into the task, "this is an inextricable part of your destiny."

"How do you know?" Little Akari is full of questions, and present-day Akari has to stop from laughing at the irony that she's running her own explanations dry.

"Well, Akari, I'm older than you are, so naturally, I know more than you do..."

Taken by surprise, little Akari asks, "How do you know my name?"

She kicks herself for the slip of her tongue. "As I said... I'm a fortune teller," she says, unable to think of a better answer. "There's one more thing, Akari... Promise me you'll tell your mama that you heart her with all your love?"

"You said it wrong," little Akari is quick to point out. "It should be 'I love you with all my heart.'"

Akari lets out a wistful laugh. "No, it's meant to be said this way... Promise me you'll say it like this?" she insists.

"Alright—"

The wooden door swings open and another set of footsteps approaches. Both Akaris fall quiet. Trepidation grips present-day Akari, as she knows exactly who has made an entrance.

Mari's voice breaks the silence. "Akari! Where have you been, my baby? I've been looking all over for you! Thankfully, Sage told me you went this way." Akari's heart pounds rapidly when she hears her mother calling her name, despite knowing it isn't meant for her.

"Does this mean I've managed to stay hidden longer than Sage? Does this mean I've won?" little Akari asks excitedly before informing her mother, "I've been hiding here the whole time, Mama. The fortune teller just gave me a reading."

"A fortune teller?" young Mari asks, but quickly recalls her reason for being there. "Alright, enough playing around. Your papa will be back any moment now and we have your birthday to celebrate." Turning toward the voile curtains, she says, "We're sorry for disturbing you."

As Mari ushers little Akari away, a million thoughts flood present-day Akari's mind. *I don't remember much beyond this point. I don't know what happens after. What if I change something by accident? What if... what if I can change something?* This thought exhilarates but scares her. *Since I've traveled back in time, can I change the past? If I can, is there any way... any way at all... that I can save Mama from death?*

Before they can reach the door, Akari calls after her mother, "May I read your fortune as well?" Although she struggles to hide her fervent longing, Mari doesn't seem to notice.

"I guess you could... Thank you for offering..." Mari's tone is tentative but polite. "Akari, will you wait for me right outside? I'll be with you in a moment," she says before heading back toward the curtains.

Little Akari nods and hops out of the room obediently.

"During the Lantern Festival ten years from now, on the day you find out that your daughter has joined the People's Protector, Zatori will come for you," present-day Akari warns urgently as little Akari closes the door behind her. "You'll have to stop her from leaving for her mission and the two of you will need to flee Cheyvelenia together."

"What's the Lantern Festival? Where's Cheyvelenia? And why would Akari be part of the People's Protector?"

Mari asks, puzzled. At this point, she has yet to set foot beyond the capital. "What do you mean by all of this?"

"I don't have time to explain. But believe me, will you? Please remember what I've said," Akari says, struggling to keep the desperation from seeping into her tone.

"Alright. And what if I can't stop her?" Even back then, Mari seems to know her daughter all too well.

"Don't worry about her—she'll be safe. You need to escape by yourself. Don't stay at home. Go as far as you can," Akari implores her.

"And if I fail—" Mari asks, as though she half expects this.

"You'll die." Devastation ripples through Akari's voice.

The moment of silence seems extraordinarily long as young Mari considers her words.

"Is this the future you foresee?" she asks eventually. Mari doesn't seem to betray a hint of fear despite hearing of her own death. Instead, her mind appears to be working quickly, as though she's already planning for the future.

"Yes," Akari confirms with a solemn nod, wondering if her mother truly understands the gravity of the situation.

"And in this future, is Akari safe?"

"Even at this point—in the face of your own death— you're worried about someone else's life?" Akari questions in disbelief—anger, almost.

"It's not just anyone else's life. It's my daughter's life. It's more important than my own," Mari replies quietly. "Now, will you please answer my question?"

"Yes. In this future, she is safe."

"Then it's enough for me." Young Mari's conclusion is disconcertingly straightforward.

This drives Akari to frustration. "No, you don't get it. If you don't do as I say, you'll lose your own life!" She enunciates slowly, allowing her words to sink in.

However, Mari's answer is not one she expects. "No, it's you who doesn't get it. Be it now or in the future, I live for Akari—and I'd die for her too." Her unconditional love puts Akari to shame.

"She will be fine! You need to look out for yourself!" Akari's anger is now directed at herself.

"You know, I'm sure your mother, too, would have wanted you safe more than anything else in the world." Mari speaks gently, as though she's talking to her daughter.

Akari's head hangs low, her body trembling with guilt. *How could I have so carelessly disregarded Mama's selflessness? And caused her to be the one to pay the price for my selfishness...*

"It's alright, my baby," Mari consoles her.

Akari freezes, then looks up. "Do you... do you know who I am?"

"Yes, you're a fortune teller," young Mari says before warning gravely, "So, you should know you can only change the future, not the past."

"Do you know *exactly* who I am?" From behind the voile curtains, Akari can barely make out her mother's expression.

"Yes, Akari. And I also know you're not supposed to be here. It's time for you to go back to where—

when—you come from." This time, she knows the sound of her name in Mari's voice is meant for her.

"How did you know? How could you have recognized me?" Akari gasps, reeling with shock.

"I'm your mother, Akari. I'd recognize you anywhere, anytime." There's no doubt in Mari's words.

"Mama," Akari calls out, desperate for the love she can no longer have in the real world. Tears well up in her eyes as she tries to grasp on to every moment of their miraculous reunion.

"Yes, Akari, my baby?"

Her heart wrenches in a blend of grief and guilt. There's so much more she wants to tell her mother, but as Akari fights to hold her emotions in, she only manages to whisper, "I heart you with all my love, Mama."

Although this is the very last time she uses this expression with her mother, it's Mari's first time hearing it.

"That's a funny way of saying it... But I heart you with all my love too, Akari, my baby," Mari says. "Remember, even if I'm gone, a part of me will always live in you. And even if I'm not there with you, I'll never stop loving you."

Her words open floodgates. Akari sobs hopelessly, the weight of her mother's inexorable death weighing too heavily upon her conscience. Apprehensively, she reaches her hand through the slit between the curtains.

Just as Akari is about to caress Mari's face, the silver moonstone ring slips from her finger, clinking as it hits the floor and rolls beneath the piles of parchments. At the same time, the Jewel of Compassion emanates a soft red glow. Instead of her mother's cheek, Akari's hand touches thin air.

She hastily pulls open the voile curtains, her heart pounding in her chest. But Mari is gone. Their short-lived reunion is over.

From the window, Akari sees the setting sun radiate brilliant rays, casting a golden glow all around. Dust particles dance in the scintillating light. In an instant, the circular room seems to have aged a decade. The ornaments on the shelves bear signs of wear, while the piles of parchments are yellowed and crinkled. She has returned to the present.

Dropping to her knees, Akari rummages through the endless piles of paper scattered across the floor, but the silver moonstone ring is nowhere to be found. Neither is the piece of parchment with the *Prophecy of a New Realm*. Thoroughly exhausted, she eventually gives up, forcing herself to accept that the ring—like her mother—is gone.

Kneeling in the shadows of the sun-soaked room, Akari brushes away her tears as she grapples with the surrealness of the memory and time travel. She's still in utter disbelief that all of this has been real.

Did Mama know all this time when and how she was going to die? Why didn't she do anything about it? Or did she? Even though Akari has endless questions, she knows this isn't the time for them. She needs to find a way out of the White Palace first.

Fortunately, the periphery of the palace seems sparsely guarded and deserted enough, allowing her to sneak out undetected. With no better place to go, she tries to find the way she came from. She grits her teeth and ventures back into the maze of alleys with dread.

After nightfall, the alleys are even less recognizable than before. Akari quickly loses her sense of direction.

Any attempts to retrace her steps soon prove futile, and it doesn't take long for her to regret re-entering the labyrinth. But it's too late.

To add insult to injury, Akari finds herself at the mercy of the biting wind, her linen garments doing little to shield her. Despite being in the south of Xylon, Andelovia still gets chilly at night. She hadn't thought to bring her cloak when she bolted from Yong's residence earlier. Now, she's left with only her own arms wrapped around her body to warm herself up.

Akari has never felt more alone than in this moment—lost in the dark, disorienting alleys of the capital. With Mari dead, Ty captured, and Yong—well, Akari ran from him—there isn't a single familiar face around. She's even managed to lose the silver moonstone ring. In desperation, she grips the Jewel of Compassion tightly, hoping to derive some consolation from it. With only herself to depend on, she puts one foot in front of the other, trudging along as bravely as she can.

Akari doesn't know how much time has passed when she glimpses a glimmer of hope. A white paper lantern—the exact same kind as the ones at the Lantern Festival—hovers in the distant darkness, emitting a gentle glow. She blinks, not quite believing her eyes. But the paper lantern makes its way to her, slowly but surely.

Eventually, Akari manages to make out the bearer. Yong's worried face is illuminated by the light from the lantern he carries in one hand, while the other grasps her cloak—the very same one they shared after he'd broken into her house. Despite their last exchange, the sight of him brings Akari immeasurable comfort.

His dark, crescent-moon eyes glance up and down anxiously to ascertain she hasn't been hurt. Heaving a sigh of relief, he drapes the cloak over her shoulders and pulls her into his arms, warming both her body and heart. Suddenly, it doesn't seem so cold or dark after all.

"No matter where you are, I promised I'd find you," Yong breathes, resting his chin on her head and letting out another lengthy sigh.

In turn, Akari leans her head tiredly on his sturdy chest, listening as his heavy breathing and rapid heartbeat gradually return to their usual states. They stay wrapped in a tight embrace, momentarily forgetting each other's faults and the harsh realities of the world.

When Yong finally releases her, he simply says, "Let's go home, shall we?"

Although it isn't home for her, Akari nods anyway.

Yong doesn't seem to have even a sliver of doubt as he navigates the confusing maze, leading them through the alleys. Akari falls into step beside him, wondering if she would be just as sure of her way if she'd never left the capital.

"I've been worried sick. You don't even know your way around here," Yong says quietly. "Didn't you promise me that you wouldn't put yourself in peril again?"

"I wasn't exactly in peril..." she claims a tad defensively before her eyes veer down to her boots.

He exhales sharply as he comes to an abrupt halt. "You could've been captured by slave hunters!" he exclaims, concern threading through his voice.

Akari's gaze snaps upward in shock as she stops beside him, then drops back down just as quickly.

"Where have you been all day?" he asks, softening his tone.

"The Vykroux Residence," Akari answers without looking up, worried what he'll think.

Sure enough, surprise flickers in Yong's eyes. "What were you doing there?" he presses. "Did you see Lord Vykroux? No one has seen him in ages."

As they continue their way through the labyrinth, Akari recounts her encounter with the former grand advisor—her visit to his memory, his attempt to trap her there, and her time travel back to her early childhood.

"So, it's true then," Yong says. "I've heard of how he spends his time in solitude."

Akari nods. "To him, his memories are better than his reality." She ponders if it will be the same for her, now her mother is gone.

"Lord Vykroux blamed King Alvaro for the loss of his wife and daughter, but deep down, he always felt responsible for their deaths," Yong informs her. "When Zatori attempted to harvest his gift during the Great Harvest, he held his ground, taking out many Harvesters. But Zatori found Lady Miriam and Sage, and threatened him with their lives. When Lord Vykroux didn't yield, they were killed right before him, one after the other. It broke him. Although he survived the Great Harvest, Lord Vykroux was never the same again. Since then, he's been living in seclusion, spending most of his time in his memories."

"I never should have gone to him!" Akari remarks heatedly, although the anger belies sympathy. After all, she, of all people, knows the anguish of losing a loved one. *Escaping from reality into his memory must have helped take some of the pain away. Maybe if I had his gift, that would be how I'd live for the rest of my life after Mama's death.*

"Why did you go to Lord Vykroux in the first place?" Yong asks, perplexed.

"I... I thought that... that he was my father," Akari admits with a sigh, her face flushing with embarrassment.

Yong seems appalled to hear this. "Why... How... What made you think that? I thought you believed your father is dead."

Akari tells him about the letter from Lord Vykroux she'd found alongside the Jewel of Compassion. "Besides, *you* were another reason I thought he was my father!" she adds.

"Me?" he sputters, baffled.

"Yes. When I saw you in Cheyvelenia, I recalled that... that you... were my childhood playmate. And when you said your childhood playmate was Lord Vykroux's daughter, who passed away alongside his wife during the Great Harvest, I thought they had to be me and my mother! Only today, I learned you were referring to Sage and Lady Miriam..."

"So, you knew this whole time that I was your childhood playmate?" Yong gasps.

"And you, too, knew this whole time that I was yours?" Akari is just as surprised.

"Why didn't you say anything!" they say simultaneously before breaking into awkward laughter.

"I knew who you were from the very first time I laid eyes on you in the outskirts, but I didn't think you'd remember me," Yong admits.

"Well, although I had some recollection of you—your eyes—I wasn't sure at first," Akari shares, heat pooling inside her at the mention of this. "Until you told me you were childhood playmates with Lord Vykroux's daughter. That confirmed we were indeed friends as children, except with a different father from the one you were thinking of."

"So, you do remember after all!" Yong exclaims, beaming as he rejoices. "I thought after all this time—after moving to Cheyvelenia and befriending Ty—you'd have forgotten me."

Akari shakes her head firmly. "Although some memories from my early childhood have begun getting hazier, I still try to hold on to them, as much as I can."

"Well, at least now we finally have our reunion," he says, giving her a warm hug.

She nods with a weak smile. "After ten whole years..."

"Everyone else said that you and your mother, like Sage and hers, had died in the Great Harvest too, but I never believed it. I knew I'd be reunited with you someday," Yong says, adding tightly, "Although the wait was painful, it was worth it..."

"I'm sorry for putting you through that," Akari says in a small voice.

"It's not your fault," Yong assures her, his tone soothing.

There's a pause before she asks, "How did you know we weren't dead?"

"With Sage and Lady Miriam, the two of them were killed right before Lord Vykroux's eyes. But with you and your mother, you both disappeared overnight. Despite what everyone else claimed, I knew you weren't dead," he explains. "I just had to keep faith."

Akari wonders if she, too, should have kept faith that her father has been alive all along instead of believing him to be dead. "Yong, my father is alive—he's here in the capital. He isn't dead, like my mother wanted me to believe all this time. Since we were childhood playmates, do you know who my father is?"

"I wish I could tell you," Yong says as he continues weaving through the maze of alleys. "I remember your mother from back then, but I never saw your father around."

Akari releases a long sigh. "I'm starting to forget his face and I don't even know his name," she laments. "For as long as I can remember, I've always taken my mother's last name."

Yong puts a comforting hand around her shoulder. "Don't worry, Akari. I'm sure you'll find him soon."

"I hope so..." she says solemnly.

A long silence follows, save for the regular rhythm of their footsteps.

Yong eventually breaks it. "How did you move from Lord Vykroux's memory back to the past?"

"I don't know," Akari says with a shrug. "Sage said it was an intervention. Do you know what that is?"

He shakes his head. "I've never heard of that before."

"There's no chance that what I did when I went back in time changed anything about my mother's death, is there?" she asks despite knowing the answer isn't what she wants to hear.

"No." Yong draws her in closer with his arm. "It seems you going back in time was part of the past as we know it to be. You were simply doing what you had to do, just as Sage said. Sage was always right, wasn't she?"

"Yes... But did my mother really know this whole time that she was going to die? Why didn't she do anything to prevent it? Why didn't she tell me?"

"Your mother must already have tried everything within her means. She knew not to let you join the People's Protector, she knew to stop you from going on your mission, and she knew Zatori would come for her. But even then, she couldn't escape death. She didn't want to worry you. She wanted to protect you."

Akari looks down guiltily. "Maybe this is why my mother couldn't trust me..."

"No. She must have trusted you wholeheartedly to take the advice you gave as a fortune teller," Yong says. He takes a deep breath before adding, "You should take solace that you've tried *everything* you can to avert your mother's death."

He noticed. From the glint in his crescent-moon eyes, Akari instantly knows Yong is referring to her attempt to deflect her mother's death onto herself. "You... you knew?" she breathes, her words a strained whisper. She hadn't meant for anyone else to uncover what she'd intended to be a deeply—painfully—private moment.

Yong nods empathetically, as if he understands— would have done the same. "But I realized later than I should have. Thankfully, your complement kept you from giving up your life." This time, he doesn't rebuke her for putting herself in peril.

"So, it's possible then?" Akari asks quietly. "To deflect... death?"

"I don't know," Yong answers with an uneasy shrug. "And I hope I'll never have to find out."

She stays quiet, Mari's death still weighing heavily on her.

"You've been a good daughter, Akari," he says softly, gently. "Your mother's inevitable end isn't yours to bear."

His words bring immense comfort to Akari, but even so, she isn't sure what to think.

"So, your day spanned sixteen years?" Yong asks with a lopsided smile, an attempt to lighten the mood. "Here I am thinking that I've had a long day..."

"What *have* you been doing all day?" Akari asks, her brows arching.

"Searching for you."

Akari looks at him with grateful eyes.

"I'm sorry," they say together, and break into more awkward laughter.

"Are you not mad at me anymore?" Yong asks softly.

Akari's tongue grazes her teeth. "I'm not sure I have the right to be mad about anything..." she says. "I guess I should have known that you aren't a mere trader... that you serve King Alvaro... that you're part of the Royal Regiment... that you broke into my house to check on the Jewel of Compassion..."

"Do you remember when I asked you about having an urge to open all of yourself up to someone—wholly, completely, and unrestrainedly?" Yong asks.

Akari nods, recalling their first date.

"I still want that with you, even if I need more time." His words calm her nerves yet stir her heart.

She gives him a warm smile, asking light-heartedly, "Does this mean you still have other secrets I should know about?"

Yong chuckles to himself. "All I can say is time will be in our favor."

With the paper lantern lighting the way, they eventually emerge from the labyrinth of alleys.

"Isn't that the lantern you bought in Cheyvelenia?" Akari asks, gazing at the one familiar thing that reminds her of home.

"Yes. I initially intended for it to be a keepsake from Cheyvelenia but thought it would help you recognize me in the dark," Yong says with a smile.

"I saw our paper lantern in the sky, the one with our wishes—yours, rather..." she tells him. "It made it up high."

"You did? I guess you saw... all of it?" he asks with a hint of self-consciousness.

Akari nods, still not knowing what to make of it. She knows he didn't intend for her to see his work of art or the amendments to her wish.

"That's the future I want with you, Akari—that will never change." Yong appears slightly flustered, but it touches her that he's standing faithfully by his wish.

A warm sensation ripples through her before she's quickly dragged back to harsh reality.

As the Lee Residence comes into sight, Yong says, "The annual Festival of Colors will be held in the White Palace tomorrow night to celebrate the season of spring. Will you come with me to meet King Alvaro? He'll be able to answer your questions."

Recalling the assassination mission she was assigned, Akari nods slowly, taking care not to appear too keen. An unsuspecting Yong gives her a smile, taking her hand in his as they walk the last stretch home. But her mind is elsewhere.

I'm sorry that your wishes will never come true. After I assassinate King Alvaro, you won't want to have anything to do with me, let alone have a future with me like the one you drew.

Tomorrow, we'll be more than miles apart—we'll be on opposing sides. I'll be attempting to assassinate the king while you'll still be serving him—and to protect him, you'll be seeking to kill me, which I'm confident your skills will make possible. This is the last night we'll be on the same side.

Despite this, as her supple hand nestles within his rough but dependable one, there's still a part of Akari that yearns for Yong and naively wishes that this night would never end.

21. Distractions

Yong's lips curl into a seductive smile, his crescent-moon eyes sparkling in the glorious evening light as he takes in the sight of Akari.

She stands at the top of the stairs in the Lee Residence, draped in scarlet. A low-back, off-the-shoulder chiffon top clings to her frame, its sheer sleeves gripping her arms before flaring dramatically at the elbows. The matching skirt hugs her hips and fans out from her knees, cascading fluidly to the floor.

The Jewel of Compassion rests against her skin, safely hidden beneath her clothes. Dark gold, garnet earrings dangle from her ears, perfectly complementing the unseen necklace.

In all sixteen years of her young life, Akari has never felt more unlike herself.

◆

Under the sharp eye of Nana Eleanor, three maids worked on Akari tirelessly for most of the afternoon to get her ready for the Festival of Colors. As they scrubbed her thoroughly, dressed her impeccably, and did her hair and makeup in the signature, over-the-top, Andelovian style, Yong's overly friendly nanny chattered away between dishing out precise instructions.

"Has your stay been pleasant?" Nana Eleanor asked after excusing the maids. Although she was graying, that didn't stop her from seeming like a ball of sunshine.

Akari nodded. "It's more than I can ask for. This place is beautiful."

"Master Yong has never brought anyone back to the Lee Residence before," Nana Eleanor informed Akari as she adjusted her outfit. "In fact, he hasn't even spent much time here himself. This place reminds him of the childhood he didn't get to have."

Akari smiled tentatively, feeling honored despite a trace of sadness. "Yong is so kind to put me up in the guestroom. I never meant to intrude upon his parents' residence or any memories of them."

"Master Yong has mentioned his parents' passings to you?" Surprise flashed in Nana Eleanor's gray-blue eyes before she quickly resumed applying the finishing touches to Akari's face. "He never used to speak about them to anyone. Master Yong must trust you a lot."

A twinge of guilt hit Akari. Soon, she'd be betraying that trust with an assassination attempt. *I'm sorry, Yong. Maybe you shouldn't have trusted me. We were never meant to be on the same side...*

"Although this residence doesn't hold many memories for Master Yong, it carries much sentimental value." Nana Eleanor glanced around the room, her gray bobbed hair swaying by her weathered face. "He used to live here with his parents until they passed away."

"What were they like?" Akari asked in a small voice.

"I don't know. Master Yong only came under my care after they were gone," Nana Eleanor said as she fidgeted fixatedly with Akari's hair, giving her chatty self a break for the first time. When her wrinkly fingers finally relaxed, she started arranging the wisps of hair framing Akari's face, quickly continuing, "But I know it takes a lot for Master Yong to share this much with you—his past, his parents... I've been looking after him since he was two and I know him like the back of my hand. Master Yong must like you very much."

Akari blushed, unsure how to respond. While a warm sensation bloomed inside her chest, she felt her stomach sinking. *This was never meant to be. We were only going to end up hurting each other... And I'm only going to end up hurting you...*

When Akari finally spoke again, she asked, "So... what was Yong like when he was under your care?" Her childhood memories of him were fuzzy at best.

"Master Yong was a quiet, careful child who kept to himself, but he finally opened up when he met his playmates. The two of you brought out the child in him—his mischievous side, the side of him that yearned to be loved, the side of him he had hidden when he tried to be a grown-up too early... When the three of you were playing together, I saw Master Yong smiling from his heart for the very first time. But after you and Mistress Sage were gone, he became even more withdrawn than before, building his walls high so he'd never be hurt again."

"Withdrawn? But Yong wasn't... isn't like that at all..." Akari blurted in surprise. His nanny seemed to be describing someone else altogether.

"Yes, he was that way for quite a while after losing all the people who were once close to him..." Nana Eleanor explained.

Akari couldn't even begin to fathom how shattered Yong must have been to lose both his parents and both his childhood playmates so early in life. Although it wasn't her fault, it weighed on her conscience that her departure must have broken him. Akari was unable to bear the thought that she'd once again hurt Yong this very night.

"Thereafter, Master Yong turned to swordplay to relieve the pain in him and grew incredibly proficient at it," Nana Eleanor recalled. "The day he turned thirteen, he joined the Royal Regiment, determined it would somehow lead him to you. Last year, he became the youngest vice commander the Royal Regiment has ever seen. Now he's returned with the Jewel of Compassion, it seems like he might make the youngest commander of the Royal Regiment!

"But more importantly, Master Yong returned here with you. Somehow, you slipped through the cracks in the walls he built, or maybe, even as he built his walls around him, you were always within them. Regardless, I'm so glad you managed to bring out his inner child again. I've not seen him this happy since the time you all were playing hide-and-seek together as children!" Yong's nanny spoke like a proud grandmother.

Do I really make him happy? Akari pondered but found fear gripping her instead. *What if I cause Yong to retreat within those walls again?*

Before she could straighten out her thoughts, Nana Eleanor interrupted her and brought her before the full-length mirror. "We're finally done," she announced with a proud smile as she waited for Akari to admire the work she and the maids had put in to make her look at least presentable—by Andelovian standards. "There, you look dazzling, my lady..."

Akari blinked, not recognizing herself. Instead, in her reflection, she saw young Mari, not too different from the one in Lord Vykroux's memory.

"You look just like your mother." Nana Eleanor reaffirmed Akari's thoughts as she noticed her scrutinizing herself. "She was the most beautiful lady I'd ever come across..."

"You knew my mother?" Akari asked in surprise, her wide eyes meeting Nana Eleanor's in the mirror.

"Not particularly. But I did see her around back then," Nana Eleanor clarified, her voice turning heavy. "I heard what happened to her. I'm sorry for your loss, my lady."

Akari stayed quiet for a while as she stared at young Mari's lookalike in the reflection.

"I don't look like myself at all," she proclaimed eventually, examining her defined eyebrows, highlighted cheekbones, and contoured jawline—all of these foreign to her. Akari's eyes had never been this shimmery or feline-like. Her hair had been pulled back into an elaborate, twisted half updo which reminded her somewhat of Emeraude.

She shifted uncomfortably in her outfit as she tugged on the splendid, scarlet skirt. Never had she worn anything this conspicuous before, much less on a mission—and much, much less for an assassination. Although Akari was worried she'd stand out in the crowd, she quickly reminded herself that this was Andelovia—and that almost nothing would ever be too much here.

As Nana Eleanor had her make a dramatic entrance down the stairs, Akari found some consolation in it all. *At least I won't look like myself when I take King Alvaro's life.*

♦

After taking a few steps, Akari sees Yong, all dressed up for the Festival of Colors as well, waiting at the bottom. He wears a slate gray ceremonial uniform with pleats and bronze trimmings, flaunting the bronze zephanerix badge on his heart as a symbol of the Royal Regiment and a pledge of his allegiance to the royal family of Xylon. He looks incredibly dashing in the uniform, which accentuates his imposing height, lithe physique, and those dark, magnetic eyes that take in every inch of Akari as she descends.

When their gazes lock, the burden of her mission seems to vanish, her self-consciousness fading into nothingness. His presence, so hypnotic and comforting, replaces the weight of her worries with a surreal sense of bliss, allowing her to believe—even if just for a moment—that she could be desirable. For the entire span of the staircase, time seems to have come to a standstill for her—for them.

"You look unbelievably beautiful," Yong breathes when she finally reaches him.

"Thank you... You don't look too bad yourself either..." Akari admits as a shy smile touches her honey-colored eyes.

"I could stand here and look at you all day, but we do have to go," he says with regret, the lopsided smile she's come to adore spreading across his face. "Shall we?" He offers her a hand.

Akari nods and takes it. Yong leads her outside, where an ornate olive-colored carriage is waiting. It's attached to four poised nequilouses—two in front and two behind—while a sturdy coachman sits at the box seat, ready to take them to the White Palace.

Before they leave, Nana Eleanor fusses incessantly over Akari's hair and clothes, tirelessly rearranging them to perfection. "Now, we have here the most beautiful lady I've ever come across," she declares proudly, giving Akari a warm hug.

"Thank you, Nana Eleanor." Akari can't express enough her utmost gratitude for the efforts to doll her up, so she can at least appear to fit into Andelovian society.

Nana Eleanor releases Akari, then wraps Yong in a long embrace. When he returns a peck on the cheek, she whispers something in his ear and they both laugh— hers an unbridled, vivacious chortle, while his an awkward, restrained chuckle. He casts Akari a nervous glance.

"Enjoy yourselves tonight!" Nana Eleanor gives them a wink and waves at them to go.

Yong opens the carriage door and helps Akari in, gesturing for her to take the front-facing seat before settling himself opposite her. As soon as the door closes, the coachman issues a resounding command. With a rumbling neigh, the nequilouses take flight, hoisting the carriage into the air.

After they take off, Akari peers out of the window. The Lee Residence shrinks as they gain height, allowing more of the sprawling city of Andelovia beneath her to come into view. The capital is so large, she can barely see where it ends. However, somewhere in the foggy distance, she still manages to catch sight of the towering Great Divide.

They sit quietly for a while, casting furtive but admiring glances at each other's atypical getup.

Finally, Yong breaks the silence. "Nana Eleanor likes you."

"The feeling is mutual. She's been so kind to me." Akari pauses briefly before asking, "What did she whisper to you as we were leaving?"

"A silly speculation." His elusive answer is complemented by a shy smile.

"What was it?" Akari's curiosity is piqued.

"It's a secret," Yong says, but adds, "I'll tell you when it comes true."

"Do you think it will?"

"Probably," he answers with a small chuckle. "Nana knows me better than I know myself."

The two of them go back to their thoughts and the looming assassination mission begins to weigh heavily on Akari.

"What's on your mind?" Yong asks after a while. "You're unusually quiet today."

"Not much," she replies tersely.

"Are you nervous?"

"No. Why should I be?" Akari sounds a tad more defensive than intended, but Yong doesn't seem to notice.

"Because you're going to meet King Alvaro?" he reminds her.

"Right... that..." Akari taps her fingers against the top of her other hand rapidly.

"You don't have to worry," Yong reassures her. "After the last dance of the Festival of Colors concludes, the king will retire to the main palace. I'll accompany you to seek his audience then."

Akari nods, but she barely registers any of it. Thoughts of the assassination mission wholly consume her. Not until now does she wish the statue of King Alvaro in Cheyvelenia's town square wasn't defaced, so she'd at least know the face of the man she's been tasked to kill. But she supposes she'll be able to identify him some other way.

For the umpteenth time, Akari runs through the instructions from Hanwell. The insider planted in the White Palace by the People's Protector will identify themselves and provide her with a weapon. She'll then have to await the signal during the last dance to indicate the right moment to assassinate King Alvaro.

Despite preparing herself as thoroughly as she can for what's to come, the hardest part is convincing herself to do it. As much as Akari resents the king—and as much as she wants to rescue Ty—the thought of having to take a life weighs heavily on her conscience.

The carriage rattles, and Akari realizes they have flown high above the clouds. Several magnificent zephanerixes in varying shades of gold soar alongside them, some just inches from their carriage. Besides Zephy, Akari has never seen another one up close before. A wave of nostalgia sweeps over her as she realizes how much she misses him, particularly flying him with her mother.

For the rest of the journey, Akari stares out of the window blankly as the sun sets before her eyes, while Yong looks quietly at her. When the carriage tilts down, she wishes she could stay in the air forever, away from reality—away from her mission.

Without warning, the nequilouses neigh loudly and the carriage comes to a sudden halt. Akari is jolted out of her seat and straight into Yong. As her face lands on his chest, she catches a whiff of his crisp mountain air scent. With lightning speed, his arms wrap around her protectively, lingering for a while longer than necessary.

When Akari finally dares to look up at Yong, a slight smile flashes across his face before he releases her and gently plants her back on her seat. From the window, they see that their carriage has joined the slow-moving line waiting to drop off their passengers.

"We've arrived," he informs her.

After a considerable wait, a guard finally opens their door. Yong hops out before offering his hand to help Akari down.

Up close, the White Palace is even grander than when she saw it from afar. Under the lilac and amber sky, the splendacious edifice basks in the evening sun, the behemoth white marble structure reflecting the warm rose gold light from the last rays of the day. Some of the domed turrets are built so high that the sculptures of zephanerixes perching on them are only fleetingly visible as the clouds roll past. The White Palace stands tall in its lonely glory, having witnessed the rise and fall of its occupants. And it's about to do so again tonight.

"The palace looks unreal... It seems like a world away..." Akari gasps in awe.

"It's been around since the time of the archivians. The sky is their natural habitat," Yong explains. "The sculptures of the zephanerixes were only added during the Ashgenov Empire when the humans took over."

Yet, even in its imposing magnificence, the White Palace still exudes a certain familiarity. After all, Akari now knows she played hide-and-seek with Yong and Sage there during her early childhood.

Akari and Yong make their way up a mighty flight of stairs before they are perfunctorily stopped by the Royal Regiment guards, who immediately recognize and salute him. Yong returns the salute.

"You have to go that way," he informs her, gesturing to the hallway on the right. "Ladies have to go that side and gentlemen the other side."

"What for?" Akari asks skittishly.

"For a body search. To make sure we don't have any weapons on us. No one except the Royal Regiment guards is allowed to carry weapons in the palace," Yong says. "But since I'm not on duty today, I'll have to go through the check as well. I'll meet you again on the other side."

Akari nods, trying not to let her nervousness show. She heads over, joining a line where several Andelovian ladies are standing. They have on dresses in every color of the rainbow, paired with gaudy accessories and outlandish makeup. Thankfully, with Nana Eleanor's effort to doll her up in capital-appropriate style, she doesn't look out of place in Andelovia for the first time. Yet, Akari still manages to turn heads—but this time, due to sheer beauty.

Although she keeps her eyes on her embroidered silk shoes to try and steer clear of attention, she can't help but notice the fiery red hair of the Royal Regiment guard conducting the body search. *Emeraude!*

The last time Akari saw her was during Ty's capture, and she has burning questions. Although it doesn't come as a surprise that Emeraude is also a Royal Regiment guard rather than a trader, she wasn't expecting to run into her today.

Instead of her usual flashy outfits, Emeraude is dressed in a slate gray Royal Regiment uniform similar to Yong's, bearing the same zephanerix badge, but without the pleats and bronze trimmings of the ceremonial one. Over her uniform, she has on her clunky armor that seems to swallow her petite frame, and a leather belt that holds her spear and daggers.

"Next!" Emeraude commands.

Akari walks over and stops before her.

"I can't believe you're in Andelovia, and least of all, the White Palace." Emeraude's voice is edged with distaste.

"Neither can I," Akari admits. There's barely a pause before she demands, her tone accusing, "Why did you leave Ty to be captured by Zatori? Weren't you supposed to protect him?"

"Don't look at me like that. I have no obligation to Tyler Kane. All I was supposed to do was hold the fort until you and Yong made your escape," Emeraude says dryly. "Besides, Tyler Kane was the one who told me to go. What a kind-hearted fool!"

Akari seethes, unable to comprehend how Emeraude doesn't seem even the slightest bit grateful for it. Anger wells inside her. "Is this how you speak of someone who saved you? What a shame you're incapable of appreciating a selfless act."

"He didn't save me. *I* saved myself!" Emeraude clarifies self-righteously. "I just didn't save him—that wasn't part of my mission."

"Are the actions of the Royal Regiment guards dictated solely by the missions they're tasked with carrying out?" Akari asks in disbelief.

"That sums it up pretty well. Besides, *you* were the one who deflected your wounds onto Tyler Kane. He was too injured to have made it out anyway, and I wasn't going to sacrifice myself for him," Emeraude spits with brutal honesty.

The words render Akari speechless.

"Well, let's not waste time," Emeraude continues without waiting for a response. "I need to proceed with the body search. Stay nice and still."

Emeraude runs her hands along Akari's shoulders and neck, before yanking out the Jewel of Compassion and inspecting it. "Even though I knew you were originally from the capital, I can't imagine how a royal regalia could fall into the possession of someone like you." She releases the jewel with a contemptuous snort, leaving it to dangle over Akari's clothes.

Akari hastily tucks it back under her top. "Weren't you the one who told me not to poke my nose where it doesn't belong?" she shoots back.

Emeraude ignores her and continues with the body search, this time checking her arms and legs.

"Do you know these are *my* clothes you're wearing? Yong borrowed them from me," she reveals with a smirk.

Caught unaware, Akari feels even smaller in front of Emeraude. Her face flushes the same shade as the scarlet ensemble she self-consciously looks down at. Akari wonders if she'd seen it when searching Emeraude's room in the Colossal Inn. But she can't be sure. There were too many pieces to remember.

"You didn't know this, did you?" Emeraude says despite knowing the answer, her emerald eyes taunting. "I took the liberty of picking this outfit, thinking it might flatter you. But the Andelovian look really doesn't suit you."

Akari shifts uncomfortably under her gaze, painfully aware of every inch of the flowy fabric against her soft skin.

"Besides, doesn't Tyler Kane despise this sort of fashion?" Emeraude continues without waiting for a response. "I wonder what he'd say if he saw you in this getup—except he's unable to be with us today, unfortunately."

Akari clenches her fists as a surge of fury rises inside her. But before she can do anything with them, Emeraude suddenly slides her hand across her torso in a movement so fluid she almost misses it. When she retracts her hand, Akari unmistakably feels a thin, cool object tucked beneath the waistline of her skirt, directly below her left rib. It's a dagger—one she is supposed to assassinate King Alvaro with.

Emeraude blinks smugly as Akari's eyes widen in shock, taking pleasure in her appalling revelation.

Images of Emeraude sitting back to back with Hanwell at the Cavalier Restaurant flash through Akari's mind. They must have been liaising even if they didn't appear to be. *Hanwell and his cronies were who Emeraude was supposed to meet that day! She's the insider the People's*

Protector planted in the capital! Emeraude Eleaconde is a double-crosser!

"Does... does Yong know—" Akari struggles to find her words but is quickly cut off. "Of course not," Emeraude snaps. "Does he know what *you* plan to do tonight?"

"No..." Akari is stumped. "It's just... I just can't believe that you, of all people, would be secretly working for the People's Protector. I thought you hate the outskirts and love the capital."

"Keep your voice down," Emeraude hisses. "You're right though. Mostly."

"Then why are you doing this?" Akari whispers, unable to comprehend *anything* about her.

"Don't poke your nose where it doesn't belong," Emeraude reminds her, still pretending to check her clothes. "Now, listen up. *It* will happen during the last dance of the night..." Her face turns serious as she urgently dishes out some crucial final instructions to Akari.

Akari listens nervously, her attention undivided. Everything feels a lot more *real* now she has the means to do the deed. After too little time to steel herself—if that were even possible—she finds Emeraude concluding her 'search'.

"Remember, better to die with honor than to live with shame. Now, go finish what you came here to do—or die trying," Emeraude says in a low voice and signals for her to leave. "Next!" Without even another glance in Akari's direction, she beckons the following lady to come forward.

When Akari finally continues on her way, she finds Yong leaning on one of the countless white marble columns, waiting for her.

"Is everything alright?" he asks. "You took much longer than expected."

"Yes... everything is fine..." she answers as nonchalantly as possible, taking care to school her expression. "I saw Emeraude. She was conducting the body search."

"Oh, I didn't realize she'd be on duty tonight," Yong remarks. He looks like he might ask if they'd argued since Emeraude had abandoned Ty, but Akari manages to muster a pointed look that cuts him off. "Well, regardless, let's head in," he says instead.

Yong leads the way through the White Palace, and she follows behind in silence, taking in the intricacies of its architecture and interior. They pass arched bridges connecting gothic towers, tea pavilions floating atop reflection pools, and pillared verandas overlooking the staggering palace grounds, until they finally arrive at their destination. Yet, nothing prepares Akari for the splendor of the Iris Courtyard—the heart of the palace—known simply as the Iris.

Thousands of red, yellow, and blue lanterns, far more brilliant than the plain white ones of Cheyvelenia, shimmer across the Iris, casting a scintillating kaleidoscopic glow that drenches the entire space in every color of the rainbow. The lanterns drift like stars above, mirrored in the delicate streams that wind through the courtyard, while minuscule fish weave through rippling waters, their scales glistening in a graceful dance. Ornamental fountains at the edges add a soft crystalline murmur, infusing the spring air with a tranquil melody.

A plush gold carpet stretches down the length of the courtyard, starting from where Akari stands and flowing up the magnificent white marble staircase that ascends to the main palace. Flanking the carpet, four rows of long tables are draped in luscious fabrics, their surfaces adorned with lush red, yellow, and blue Andelovian flowers, alongside candles that match the lanterns above. Each table is lined with a row of seats facing the center of the Iris, where a suspended, gleaming marble statue of a zephanerix presides over it all.

"Wow..." Akari gasps, at a loss for words to fully capture the living work of art. The capital is more breathtaking than she'd ever imagined.

Yong gazes at the decor in admiration. "The Iris is always done up beautifully for the Festival of Colors," he says before adding as an afterthought, "though I think this year is the best yet."

"Why is that?" Akari asks.

"Because King Alvaro is expecting a very special guest this year," Yong informs her, smiling.

"Who is it?" Akari wonders if the king will still be alive to meet this special guest.

"You'll find out soon enough," Yong replies cryptically. Changing the subject, he points at the colorful paper lanterns overhead. "Look at these lanterns. They're quite different from the ones in the outskirts."

"I've never seen ones this vibrant before," Akari remarks. "Is this because they're for the Festival of Colors?"

"Yes. And do you know what the colors represent?"

Akari shakes her head.

"Well, red is for compassion, yellow is for wisdom, and blue is for courage. They coincide with the—"

"Three royal regalia..." she finishes for him, wondering if this was something she'd learned during her early childhood, tucked away at the back of her mind for the past decade.

"Yes, that's right..." Yong says in a soft voice. "Well, let's get seated, shall we?" he suggests before strolling down the right side of the courtyard.

As Akari follows along, she takes in the hundreds of resplendently dressed guests flowing into the courtyard, until she realizes she's fallen far behind. She immediately quickens her pace to match Yong's long strides. "How do you know where we're supposed to be seated?" Akari asks when she has caught up with him.

"First, by status. The two inner rows of tables are solely for members of Andelovian society—aristocrats," he explains, ushering her along the rightmost row. "And then, by rank. The higher your rank, the closer you'll be to King Alvaro and Queen Jocelin—they'll be seated above those stairs."

"And how about us?" Akari looks around distractedly, wondering if her father will be among all these people and if she will still recognize him. *Since Mama was a royal physician, Papa might be serving the royal family as well...*

"About here." Yong stops after they've covered more than three-quarters of the Iris's length. "It took me five years to get here, but I'll always remain on the outer rows," he says with a pensive smile. He pulls out a chair and gestures for Akari to sit, before taking his place beside her. Soon after, the guests fill up the remaining seats.

Although there's already an obscene amount of food—more than Akari has ever seen in her entire life—covering every inch of every table, the palace maids, dressed in neat dove-gray uniforms, continue to serve an endless array of cuisines. The tables groan under the weight of golden roasted meats, steaming platters of fresh-caught seafood, and vibrant fruit arrangements glistening like jewels. Tureens brim with rich aromatic stews, while towers of fragrant breads and pastries stand beside a selection of fine cheeses, pickled vegetables, and honey-drizzled confections. The sight is nothing short of a culinary paradise.

As Akari surveys the extravagant spread, her thoughts inevitably drift to Ty. There's no one who loves food like he does—and he's always hungry. *He would give anything to be here. Ty could devour all of this without batting an eyelid.* Her heart twinges with a bittersweet ache, fortifying her resolve to assassinate the king in a desperate bid to save her best friend. Despite the scrumptious feast laid before Akari, a wave of anxiety washes away her appetite.

"Are you alright?" Yong asks, concerned. "You've seemed out of sorts all day."

Thankfully, she doesn't have to come up with an answer. Their conversation is interrupted by a tremendous fanfare.

Two elegant figures emerge from the main palace. Ethereal white capes cascade gracefully around them and gleaming gold crowns rest upon their heads. King Alvaro Ashgenov and Queen Jocelin Ashgenov of Xylon, stand at the top of the marble stairs, exuding regality as they overlook the entire Iris.

The guests instantly fall silent and rise to their feet. Akari follows their lead, but before she can fully process the proceedings, everyone around her moves in perfect unison—placing their right hands over their hearts, dropping their right knees onto the ground, and bowing down. "Long live King Alvaro and Queen Jocelin," they chant in reverence.

Akari remains standing, frozen in place, an unintentional outlier in the sea of kneeling guests. As the king and queen sweep their gazes across the crowd, their eyes land on her almost immediately.

"Oh no! I forgot to teach you the customary bow!" Yong mutters under his breath as he pulls Akari to the ground behind him, angling his body to block her from their view.

Realizing her misdemeanor, she crouches even lower, hastily looking down to avoid their gazes.

As though nothing out of the ordinary has caught their eye, the king and queen wave to the crowd ceremoniously, beckoning them to rise. The guests get to their feet and resume their seats at the long tables. Akari quickly follows suit, trying her best to blend in.

"Thank you for gathering here today to celebrate the Festival of Colors." King Alvaro addresses the crowd, his voice deep and authoritative, yet worn with fatigue. "It's been yet another year of victories and defeats. Unfortunately, the rumors are true. Zatori is not dead—he has returned and is harvesting again in the outskirts. We will be putting our best defenses at the Great Divide to protect the people of Andelovia. The Harvesters won't be able to set foot in the capital again. Now that spring has arrived, new life shall begin and new hope shall bloom. May the Festival of Colors commence. Enjoy the celebrations!"

As soon as the king finishes speaking, the crowd bursts into cheers and digs in eagerly. No one seems to notice him collapsing back onto his throne as Queen Jocelin takes her seat beside him with impeccable poise.

"I'm sorry... It slipped my mind that you aren't accustomed with the proper etiquette to greet the royal family." Yong casts Akari an apologetic glance.

She returns a weak smile before asking, "Why are they both in white if this is the Festival of Colors?"

"White is reserved for the royal family," he explains. "It represents peace..."

The rest of his reply is drowned out by the deafening bang of the gong, marking the start of the celebrations. Canorous music fills the courtyard as the first troupe of performers sway to the beat in perfect synchrony. One after another, Akari watches an endless series of sensational performances by singers, dancers, musicians, magicians, and acrobats—even gifteds in their midst— between mouthfuls of delicacies.

Once their appetites are sated, the guests spill onto the golden carpet, drawn by the infectious music. They clap their hands, stomp their feet, and spin with abandon, making merry with every fiber of their being as they rejoice in the season of spring.

Andelovia is truly a city that teems with vibrance. It is stunning by day and dazzling by night— especially accentuated by the Festival of Colors. Against the stark white canvas of the palace and the jet-black backdrop, the colors all around them are exceptionally vivid.

Akari has never seen any celebration of this magnitude. The unassuming Lantern Festival, with its simple charm, seems a far cry from such a spectacle. This would indisputably have been one of the most magical nights of Akari's life if she weren't waiting anxiously for the signal to assassinate King Alvaro.

"Welcome back to Andelovia!" Yong says with a smile, his voice recapturing her attention. "It's not as bad as you thought it would be, is it?"

"No, not at all..." Her lips curve upward perfunctorily, but her smile doesn't reach her eyes.

He doesn't seem to notice as he rises from his seat and extends his hand gingerly toward her. "May I have this dance?"

"I... I don't know how to dance," Akari objects, her toes curling.

"You don't need to," Yong assures her. "Besides, it's about to be the last dance of the Festival of Colors..."

And our last dance as well... she realizes when they lock gazes. Drawn in by his alluring crescent-moon eyes, she's soon rendered defenseless as her hesitation melts away.

"Alright," Akari says, taking his hand.

He leads her onto the gold carpet, where they take their places opposite one another. The world shrinks to just the two of them. Before hesitation can take hold, Yong pulls Akari toward him, his hands firm yet gentle as they find her waist. Then, with effortless strength, he lifts her into the air and twirls her, faster and faster...

She gasps as the wind kisses her cheeks. The world blurs at the edges, dissolving into a whirlwind of motion. The enthralling silks of the guests' garments and the glow of the incandescent lanterns swirl into a captivating maelstrom of ruby, gold, and sapphire. Yet, amidst the shifting chromatic tapestry, their lovestruck faces remain in sharp, unwavering focus. In this instant, they've become far more than childhood playmates.

"I've been waiting so long for this!" Yong exclaims, his voice tinged with joy, as they move to the music as one.

"I hope it was worth the wait," Akari says breathlessly, her heart racing—not just from the dance, but from him.

For the first time in what feels like forever, she surrenders to the moment. Akari allows music and movement to drown out her grief and burden, thoroughly reveling in Yong's presence. Her radiant laughter peals through the night as she gives herself to the Festival of Colors and dances her heart out with him.

Akari's reaction elicits a satisfied smile from Yong. "Every moment," he declares. "I want to draw a picture of us—right here, right now. I haven't seen you looking this happy in a while. You seemed so distracted all of today, despite having distracted me all of tonight."

Utterly flattered, Akari returns a shy smile. "I'm sorry... I didn't mean to..."

He lets out a chuckle. "I'm afraid the damage has already been done." With that, he leans in until the tips of their noses skim past one another.

Akari is about to close her eyes when she catches sight of a short, stocky drummer standing amidst a troupe of percussionists, looking directly at her from behind Yong. Despite being dressed in a ridiculously garish costume, complete with sequins and feathers, Akari recognizes him right away. *Hanwell*.

She freezes momentarily before snapping back to reality, her flustered eyes darting back to meet Yong's. *No! It's you who's distracting me!*

Just as he registers that something is amiss, a mysterious gust of wind extinguishes all the lanterns and candles—the signal for Akari to act.

As the Iris is swallowed by the night, the musicians falter and the dancers freeze. The following moment is a void—no light, no sound, no movement. Seizing the calm before the storm, Akari carefully backs away from Yong, casting one last wistful glance his way before slipping toward King Alvaro.

Behind her, Yong's worried voice cuts through the silence. "Akari! Where are you going?"

But she doesn't look back. Even in the darkness, Akari senses others weaving through the bewildered crowd, moving in the same direction. The rest of the Protectors must be making their move as well. She presses forward alongside them, her steps hasty as they advance down the gold carpet.

Fortunately—or perhaps unfortunately—the luminous white garbs of King Alvaro and Queen Jocelin render them especially conspicuous in the dark, even from afar. With her eyes fixed on the target, Akari draws the dagger Emeraude slipped beneath her clothes and starts up the marble stairs.

Around them, the palace maids scurry to restore light to the courtyard. Some emerge with more lanterns and candles, while others attempt to reignite those that were extinguished.

As a faint glow returns, Akari catches sight of two dozen Protectors—disguised as drummers—splitting apart their chunky drumsticks to reveal cleverly concealed blades. Hanwell, Prisci, and Aloy are among them, surging toward King Alvaro with deadly intent.

"Assassins! Protect the king and queen!" the chief guard of the Royal Regiment bellows, his voice thundering through the mayhem.

In an instant, the guards form a tight line of defense in front of King Alvaro and Queen Jocelin, both of whom have frantically risen from their seats, eyes wide with panic.

There's barely a split second before the sound of blades clashing ricochets around the Iris, accompanied by deafening battle cries. The People's Protector and the Royal Regiment are quickly entangled in a deadly fight. Bodies are strewn all over the courtyard, fresh blood staining the gold carpet red. The harrowing sight sends the frenzied, screaming guests scrambling to flee or hide.

Amidst the chaos, the People's Protector feigns a retreat, drawing the Royal Regiment down the stairs in what appears to be a desperate fallback. The guards, sensing an opportunity to press their advantage, push farther from their posts and pursue the Protectors, their formation unraveling as they give chase. When most of the guards are a good distance away from the king and queen, locked in fierce combat on the stairs, Akari knows her moment has come.

She stealthily maneuvers through the remaining handful of guards, her heart pounding in her ears as she climbs the final steps. Eventually, she reaches King Alvaro. At the sight of the assassin directly before him, he collapses back onto his throne, a silent acknowledgment of his impending fate.

Akari leaps up onto his seat, one foot perched on each armrest, trapping the king in his throne. She grabs him by the collar, digging her elbow into his chest to pin him down. With her other hand, she raises the dagger, ready to strike. But right before Akari deals the fatal blow, she takes in her target.

King Alvaro's pallid complexion, which betrays more than a hint of yellow, is closer to that of a dead body than a living human. His breathing is quick but strained. The king's eyes jut from his sunken eye sockets, his cheekbones protruding from his gaunt face. Beneath his jeweled crown, his wavy graying hair is styled smartly above his bony shoulders and shrinking frame.

It's clear as day to a healer's daughter that King Alvaro is dying. Akari realizes the yuriq brew is meant for *him*— and even this potent concoction can't prolong the king's life much longer.

Her hand trembles with hesitation, the dagger glinting in the faint light. *How can I kill a man already on the brink of death? Even though I would almost be doing him a favor by ending his life...*

But she knows she'll waver given even the smallest chance to contemplate—and for Ty's sake, she can't afford this.

As she observes King Alvaro, Akari notices he doesn't even have the slightest strength to resist. He writhes feebly in the minor discomfort she causes him simply from holding him in place, as though he'd give anything to end even the smallest suffering. It dawns on her that, despite drastic efforts to prolong his life, the king isn't too averse to death. Yet, this doesn't make it any easier for her to kill him.

For the first time, Akari doesn't view him as an enemy or the root of the outskies' misery. Despite being king, she realizes he's only human as well. *How can I bring myself to kill him—anyone at all?*

"I'm not afraid of death," King Alvaro whispers hoarsely as he senses her reluctance. He seems to have been stuck in his lonely, hopeless struggle for too long, growing much too weak to fight any longer.

Weariness—and perhaps guilt, too—have crept up on him all these years. The immense pain the yuriq brew has inflicted on him as it prolonged his life must also have been excruciating to bear. It wouldn't be surprising if the king entertained the thought that death could liberate him.

"Except tonight, there is someone I've been waiting a long time to see," he murmurs.

Akari forces herself to dismiss any excuses, brush away any second thoughts, and focus on the suffering of the gifteds—harvesting, insanity, death, even abandonment. *He deserves it...* she tries to convince herself, as though it'd make it any less unbearable to execute this mission. Akari shakes herself mentally, and Ty immediately comes to mind. *I can't abandon him. I must get him out. And I need the People's Protector to help me rescue him.*

Mustering all her determination, Akari thrusts the dagger toward King Alvaro's neck. Just as the blade breaks his skin, she sees a pair of honey-colored eyes—a mirror reflection of her own—staring back at her, distracting her from her mission.

Akari blinks as she gazes blankly at them. Their emotions are undecipherable, but their resemblance is undeniable. Her stomach sinks.

Doused in shock, Akari loosens her grip on the king's collar and lowers the dagger. *Could he... could King*

Alvaro be my father? She shakes her head in vehement disbelief, refusing to let herself consider this possibility.

But his familiar eyes widen with both joy and sadness at the same recognition. A single tear rolls down his crumpled cheek.

"Akari?" King Alvaro calls out, his voice raspy, quavering. "Is that you, my little princess? Don't you remember your papa?"

Princess? Papa? These words knock the wind out of Akari. Her body turns rigid, her mind grows numb. Yet, despite her inability to process the situation, she registers a few things.

The Royal Regiment guards charge at her, and their chief guard yells, "Take down the assassins!"

Somewhere behind her, Akari hears Hanwell's slimy voice. "Kill him, Miyahara! What are you waiting for?"

She wheels around and finds him dashing toward her. From his expression, Akari has no doubt Hanwell is aware she's recognized her father—and he hadn't intended for her to.

No longer trusting her to conclude the assassination, he raises his weapon, taking it upon himself to deal the killing blow. Akari cries out in desperation and attempts to intervene, but Hanwell knocks her aside ruthlessly and plunges his blade into King Alvaro's chest.

22. Kill or Be Killed

Akari blinks as she gradually regains consciousness. She sees neither the familiar aged wooden beams of her bedroom in the outskirts, nor the ivory ornamental plaster ceiling of the guestroom in the Lee Residence. Instead, a rough stone slab looms overhead, sealing her away from the world above.

She is in a grim underground prison cell, unable to tell day from night. The walls enclosing her—oppressive and unyielding—devour all light and sound, as if this place has been forsaken as thoroughly as the captives who had languished within it. As she sits up on a measly layer of straw that barely cushions her from the cold damp floor, Akari realizes her sore, stiff body has been dressed in some tattered, bloodied prison garb.

Despite her disorientation, the first thing that comes to her mind is the shocking revelation that leaves her reeling. *King Alvaro is... my father? How is this possible?* She shakes her head vigorously in a desperate but futile attempt to dispel this unimaginable truth.

Akari isn't sure how much time has passed since her attempt to assassinate the king, but the look of his wide, ambivalent, honey-colored eyes is still fresh in her mind.

✦

All Akari could see were King Alvaro's eyes staring straight into hers as he slouched on the throne in a state of minimal consciousness. He reached his hand feebly in her direction, opening and closing his mouth in an incoherent attempt to speak. Blood streamed from the wound where Hanwell had punctured his chest moments earlier, causing stark stains against the king's white robe—although they were deceptively well camouflaged on Akari's scarlet ensemble. Perhaps Emeraude had picked out the outfit for this exact reason.

"Papa!" Akari screamed horrifically as she lunged toward King Alvaro and Hanwell, touching them both simultaneously. *I can't lose my father when I've just found him!* A cosmic pulse of energy surged within her as the Jewel of Compassion emitted a warm red glow.

Hanwell clutched his chest, fresh blood spilling between his fingers from the wound Akari had intentionally deflected back onto him. He staggered backward, tumbling down the long flight of stairs until his body finally came to a stop at the bottom, sprawled across the gold carpet.

Witnessing the fall of their leader, the remaining Protectors frantically scrambled to flee. Some Royal Regiment guards immediately gave chase.

Akari swayed on the spot, willing herself to stay conscious. Deflecting a wound of such severity had drained her profoundly—more so than ever before—leaving her body feeling like lead, her senses clouded. Each heartbeat echoed in her ears, amplifying the crushing pressure in her head that threatened to pull her into oblivion.

Even as she struggled to hold herself together, Akari twisted back to face her father. Although the king was no longer wounded, his frail body remained slumped on the throne, his breath faint, his heavy eyelids barely open. As Queen Jocelin rushed to his side, she shot Akari a glare of fury.

But Akari barely noticed. In a daze, the world spun around her. Despite vaguely hearing Yong call her name in the distance, she couldn't peel her bleary gaze from King Alvaro as his honey-colored eyes closed shut.

"Papa?" she cried out, her voice raw, unrestrained.

A Royal Regiment guard grabbed Akari and flung her to the ground, while several others formed a protective barrier in front of the king.

"Don't come any closer! Surrender!" the chief guard of the Royal Regiment barked.

Teetering on the brink of collapse, Akari couldn't process the situation, her disoriented mind still grappling with her father's identity. Despite the guards blocking her path, she staggered toward King Alvaro with dogged determination.

"Kill any assassin who doesn't surrender!" the chief guard ordered. Instantly, the Royal Regiment guards surrounded Akari, leaving no route of escape. Before she could react, they charged at her.

The first guard to reach Akari slashed her left shoulder. Fighting to even remain upright, she couldn't muster any strength to retaliate. But in the blink of an eye, the guard stumbled backward as his left shoulder split open without warning. He cried out in pain, his eyes wide with horror.

Meanwhile, the wound on Akari had vanished. The Jewel of Compassion emanated a soft red glow once again.

Before the other guards could register what had happened, several more rushed in to subdue her. Their blades cut Akari's body everywhere—her arms, legs, chest, abdomen, back... But as soon as blood began flowing from her wounds, her attackers writhed in pain, bearing the exact same injuries they'd inflicted on her, while she seemed unscathed once again.

It dawned belatedly on the horrified Royal Regiment guards that every single wound they dealt Akari was being deflected back onto themselves. As a wave of startled cries about her gift rippled through them, they were thrown into a chaotic mess, torn between attacking and retreating.

Before they could reorganize themselves, Yong broke through the circle of guards. "Stop! Hold your attack!" he yelled as he rushed toward Akari. "This is an order!"

He stood protectively by her, wielding a sword he'd picked up from a fallen guard, poised to kill anyone—his fellow guards included—who might hurt her. Despite the questionable instruction from their vice commander, the Royal Regiment guards stopped in their tracks.

"Akari! What did you do? Are you alright?" Yong asked, horrified, his eyes seared with worry as they checked if she was hurt.

But before she could answer, she collapsed into his arms, as though she knew she would be safe there.

"Sir, this is an assassin..." the chief guard interjected.

Yong didn't deign to glance his way, his dark eyes refusing to veer from Akari. "This is someone you cannot afford to touch!" he warned, wrapping his arms tightly around her.

Even on the verge of unconsciousness, Akari saw the circle of guards part for a figure in white to come through. She met Queen Jocelin's piercing gray eyes, their sharpness cutting through her hazy vision. Just before Akari surrendered herself to oblivion, she dimly registered the queen's cold, unfeeling voice.

"If you're not already dead, I'll see to your end myself."

♦

As she sits in a daze inside the dreary prison cell, sparsely lit by a few sporadic torches along the murky corridor, Akari attempts to recollect how she has landed in this state.

I'm in the capital. King Alvaro is my... my father. I tried to assassinate him. Queen Jocelin is his wife. She hates me. Mari is my mother. She's dead. She was King Alvaro's lover—even before he met Queen Jocelin. Ty is my best friend. He's been captured by Zatori. Yong... Yong... Yong is my—

"Let me see her." A deep velvety voice seizes Akari's attention.

She hurries to the gate of her cell and peers down the corridor, spotting Yong with a prison guard at the far end.

"Queen Jocelin instructed that no one is to see her, sir." The guard sounds tentative as he tries to refuse him.

"I'll be quick," Yong insists. "No one will know I was here."

"But sir, she's dangerous..." The prison guard replies, clearly desperate to find another reason to turn him down. "When we tortured her—"

"You tortured her?" Yong erupts. "Who issued such a command?"

"Queen Jocelin ordered us to get information from her, but we couldn't. That assassin... she deflected her wounds back onto the guards who tortured her," the guard explains before dropping to a whisper. "She's dangerous... She's gifted..."

"I don't care about that!" Yong thunders, fuming. "Do you know who she is?" he demands, although he doesn't care for an answer. "You'll be dead if you lay another finger on her! Stop all the torture, do you hear me?"

"Yes, sir..." the prison guard answers meekly.

"Let me see her now. This is an order!" Yong's gritted teeth barely contain his roiling rage.

"I can't, sir... Queen Jocelin gave strict instructions that no one is to see her... especially not you..."

Yong doesn't appear surprised. "Open up," he commands with an uncharacteristic disregard for authority.

Put on the spot, the guard wavers as he weighs his options.

"Open up. I won't repeat myself," Yong asserts in a quiet voice, his tone final. "Please don't make me resort to force to get this done. You and I both know I'll get to her today, with or without a fight."

Well aware he's unlikely to beat the vice commander of the Royal Regiment in a fight, the prison guard eventually yields under pressure. "Yes, sir... Come this way..." He leads Yong down the corridor until they reach Akari's cell.

Yong's anxious face appears between the iron bars. Standing on the opposite side of the gate, Akari feels a strange mix of guilt, shame, relief, and eagerness. Tears well up in her eyes. Just days ago, she never could have imagined being in such a predicament—in a prison cell in the capital.

The prison guard hesitantly unlocks the gate and lets him into the cell, before locking it again behind him. Yong gives a nod of gratitude, and the guard steps away to give them a moment of privacy.

When their eyes meet, Akari and Yong seem momentarily lost in a world of their own. Although they're on opposing sides—and despite the many secrets they've kept from each other—nothing stands between them in this instant. Akari still finds solace in his presence.

Yong worriedly pulls up the sleeves of her bloodied prison garb to check if she's hurt. Fortunately, just as the guard had said, Akari appears unscathed. He heaves a sigh of relief.

"I'm fine," she says in a small voice. "You know my gift—"

"That's no excuse to constantly dive head-first into danger!" Yong exclaims heatedly. "The first time I lost sight of you in Andelovia, you ended up being trapped in Lord Vykroux's memory and traveling back in time. The next time, you tried to assassinate King Alvaro and landed yourself in the most heavily guarded and carefully hidden prison in all of Xylon. Didn't you promise me that you wouldn't put yourself in peril again?"

Even though there's anger in his words, Yong pulls Akari into his arms and hugs her too tightly.

When she squirms, he immediately loosens his iron grip, although his strong arms remain firmly wrapped around the small of her back. For the length of their embrace, the cell doesn't seem so cold or grim after all.

With her head on his chest, Akari takes a deep breath of Yong's crisp mountain air scent and wonders if she'll live to see daylight again. *But I deserve punishment, not freedom. I attempted to take a life.*

"Aren't you afraid of me? Of what I've done?" Her soft voice belies a profound fear.

Yong reluctantly releases Akari, gazing into her eyes with a simmering passion. "At this point, I'm more afraid of the magnitude of my love for you," he confesses, his tone almost quavering.

His answer catches her off guard. She'd braced herself for hostility, expecting him to hate her—to treat her like an enemy. Yet, she detects no trace of this.

"I... I don't... deserve any of it..." Akari barely manages a whisper.

"Even though you tried to kill King Alvaro, you also tried to save him," Yong reminds her.

"Is he still alive then?" she asks worriedly. "How is he?"

"No one knows for sure. The king has been at death's door since the assassination attempt and no one has seen him since. Queen Jocelin wants it this way. But no news is good news—it means King Alvaro should still be alive," Yong says. "It's the same with you. The queen wants you hidden from the world. It took me a while to locate you."

"How long has it been since the assassination?" Akari is unable to perceive time in this underground prison, especially after innumerable rounds of torture and interrogation, which she remembers only as a numbing blur.

"Three days."

Akari's breath hitches. "King Alvaro was dying even before the assassination, wasn't he? And he's been taking the yuriq brew to prolong his life, hasn't he?"

"Yes. I knew the king was ill for a long time, but I didn't realize he was *dying*—until I was buying those herbs from you," Yong says. "He must have been hoping to reunite with you before he breathed his last. You're the special guest he was expecting."

Akari gasps as the pieces fall into place. She finds comfort in the failed assassination, despite knowing it's a heinous crime to feel this way as a Protector. *But I don't want to be a monster who killed my—*

She shakes her head, as though to dispel the truth that King Alvaro is her father. "I can't make any sense of it."

"Of what?" Yong's tone is tentative, careful.

"That... that King Alvaro's my... he's my father..." Akari looks at Yong, scrutinizing his expression, half hoping he will tell her she's wrong.

But he remains silent, confirmation etched in his eyes.

"How's this possible? Did you know this whole time?" she demands, her voice uneven.

Yong's eyes dart around anxiously before meeting Akari's with a certain unease, as though he has been harboring this secret for too long. "Yes. Even when we were children."

A sense of betrayal creeps over her. "The last time I asked you about my father, you told me that... that you... you wished you could tell me... and that you never saw him around..." Akari realizes how cleverly his response had been worded.

"That wasn't a lie." Yong shifts around guiltily as he tries to justify himself.

"Why didn't you tell me? Why did you keep this a secret from me?" Her voice rises a notch.

"It wasn't my place, nor was I allowed to speak a word of it," he explains. "When King Alvaro sent Emeraude and me to the outskirts to look for the missing royal regalia, he separately entrusted me with a second and infinitely more important mission—one not even Emeraude knew about. I was tasked with looking for his long-lost daughter and her mother—you and Lady Mari. The king informed me that the Jewel of Compassion was in your possession. After searching your home to verify this, I intended to escort both of you and the royal regalia back to Andelovia on the first day of spring. But my plans were thwarted by Zatori."

So, the drawing in Yong's room was just a reminder of... "A mission... Was that all I was to you?" Akari asks quietly, hurt tainting her face. "Was I the *merchandise* you were tasked with bringing back to the capital?"

"No! Akari... how could you think that?" Yong asks incredulously. "I've never thought that way about you... You know that!"

"I don't know anything anymore!" she fires back.

"Ever since I joined the Royal Regiment five years ago, searching for you was the one mission I'd been waiting for. I knew King Alvaro would send me at some point, when he thought I was ready. After all, few have seen your face, and your mother's. The hope that I'd finally be put on this mission got me through the hardest of days, the toughest of trainings, and the deadliest of missions..." Yong seems immensely relieved to finally let it all out. To him, joining the Royal Regiment has never been for recognition or prestige, but for love—one that runs much deeper than Akari has ever realized.

Touched by his unwavering love, she looks up at him with a mix of gratitude and guilt, thoroughly lost for words.

"And now, my only mission is to get you out of here," Yong informs her.

His selflessness puts Akari to shame. "How are you going to do that?" she asks, her tone warming. "Wouldn't you be breaking all the rules? Won't you risk losing everything you've worked so hard for over the past five years?"

Yong shakes his head firmly. "If I don't get you out, I'll lose my everything," he says with a recklessness that's atypical of him. "I didn't work so hard the past five years just to lose you again. Akari, haven't you already figured out that you're my first love?"

She hadn't. But now, the things he mentioned during their first date begin clicking into place. *Eons ago, I fell in love with a princess... She was more beautiful than anyone could imagine... It was one-sided... She didn't even know about it...* Akari gasps. The hints had been there all along. She'd just failed to read them.

"Although you don't know much about capital-related matters, you were right about one thing—Xylon doesn't have another princess, or even another heir," Yong continues. "Akari, you're the princess I fell in love with eons ago. And even after all this time, my feelings haven't changed. You're always going to be my first, last, and only love," he declares.

Princess? The unfamiliar sound of this title is unsettling. *Who am I to be a princess when I almost assassinated the king?* Akari's muddled mind doesn't help her string words together effectively. "I couldn't— can't possibly be... We're enemies... Yong, you shouldn't have anything to do with me... You don't have to—"

"That's alright. It's my decision to make," Yong assures her. "Besides, I've come too far to turn back. I'm already breaking all the rules for you."

"I don't want you to do things for me that you'll regret," Akari says worriedly, but he gives a mirthless chuckle.

"I'll regret if I *don't* do these things."

She lets on a slight smile, but her voice is shaded with concern. "Yong..."

"So, will you try to understand me, for all the things I've had to hide, and all the things I've had to do... You've no idea how many times I've wanted to tell you that you were my childhood playmate, that I'm part of the Royal Regiment, that I've been tasked with finding you and the missing royal regalia, that King Alvaro's your father... And how it had hurt me when I injured you in the fight after I searched your home..."

Akari nods. "I'm sorry I got mad... I, of all people, should understand... I've had to do similar things too..."

Yong raises his eyebrows. "What else have you had to do, besides attempting to assassinate the king?"

"On the exact same day you searched my home, I... I—" She stumbles over her words.

"Were you the one who searched my room, and Emeraude's?" he asks, his eyes narrowing.

Akari gasps. "You knew all along that someone searched your room? How?"

"Yes, so did Emeraude," Yong informs her with a slight laugh. "All our things weren't as we'd left them."

"Maybe I should've been suspended from non-combat missions as well..." Akari sighs sheepishly, her face twisting into a grimace. "Ty and I searched the rooms as part of our mission for the People's Protector. They wanted to know what you two were doing in the outskirts, but we couldn't figure anything out. We didn't know what the zephanerix on your badges represented back then..." Apparently, there was much to be learned from the room search, but neither of them knew how to interpret the clues.

"A *mission*... Was that all I was to *you*?" Yong asks, shock plastered on his face.

"No! You know that's not true!" Akari says anxiously, but then she catches a playful twinkle in his eyes.

He chuckles and she purses her lips.

"I guess we're even now," Yong says light-heartedly, and his face flushes. "So, it was you who saw the picture then... The one I drew of you with the Jewel of Compassion..."

Akari nods guiltily. "I wasn't expecting that..."

"Well, that's what you get for snooping," he says with a nervous chuckle. "But now you've seen my drawing of us on our paper lantern, I don't suppose the one I did of you will surprise you much more."

"Wasn't that a reminder of your mission to look for me and the Jewel of Compassion?" she asks.

"No! That's the furthest thing from it!" Yong clarifies with a resolute shake of his head, before a shy smile appears on his face. "I meant to give you that drawing as a token of love when I confessed my feelings for you... at the right time, after you'd come to know about your father and the Jewel of Compassion. But I couldn't help blurting it all out the very day I hurt you," he shares, his expression turning serious. "That was the first time I was afraid I could be the one who put you in peril. I'd never be able to forgive myself if that happened."

Warmth pools inside Akari. Although Yong's confession wasn't as he had planned, it was raw and genuine—and it has touched her heart.

"You already made up for it when you had me deflect my wounds onto you," she points out, her thoughts drifting to Ty. *I also deflected my wounds onto Ty. I was the one who put him in peril. If he were to be hurt in any way, I'd never be able to forgive myself either.*

"Was Tyler Kane the reason you attempted to assassinate King Alvaro?" Yong asks, as though able to read her mind.

Akari nods, her eyes veering down to her bare feet. "The People's Protector promised to save him if I assassinated the king."

"Right... Even though you must do as you're told, I figured they must have had something on you to make you even contemplate killing..." There's a short pause before Yong adds, "But I told you I'd help you to save Tyler Kane!"

"I know. But when I found out you were part of the Royal Regiment, I thought that we would be enemies... that we would be standing on opposing sides..."

"Even if the Royal Regiment and the People's Protector were enemies," he says after taking a deep breath, his tone more certain than ever, "you and I—we could never be on opposing sides."

A smile tugs on Akari's lips, but it doesn't last long. "What's going to happen to Ty now I've failed my mission and I'm stuck here in prison?"

"Instead of thinking about rescuing Tyler Kane, maybe you should focus on getting yourself out alive!" Yong reminds her with exasperation. "Queen Jocelin seems determined to get rid of you, and you've conveniently given her a perfect excuse. Given King Alvaro's precarious condition, the queen—now acting on his behalf—holds absolute power that she can use to erase your existence forever."

Akari looks at him in horror. She's about to ask how long it'll be before the queen does so when he holds a hand up, his brow creasing as he thinks.

"But why you?" Yong wonders puzzledly. "Something feels off about it."

"What do you mean?" Akari asks.

"Logically, you shouldn't be the People's Protector's first choice to carry out the assassination, considering what happened with Philippe and Ethan. There were already enough Protectors on the mission. Yet, they still appointed you to make the killing blow... running a risk for themselves... But why?"

He's right! Akari's eyes widen in shock. She has never thought about the assassination mission from this perspective, and could kick herself for not asking more questions before trying to kill someone.

"How did you get your hands on the dagger?" Yong asks, suspicious. "You went through the body search and we were together the whole night..."

Emeraude! Yong doesn't know she's a double-crosser! Given how Emeraude had so easily allowed Ty to fall into Zatori's hands, it would be anyone else's first instinct to sell her out. But Akari holds her tongue, well aware that if anyone learns of her identity, there'll be only one outcome for her—death. And she doesn't want any more deaths on her hands—not even that of someone as unlikeable as Emeraude.

"A Protector gave it to me right before the assassination, when it was all dark," Akari lies as convincingly as she can.

Yong doesn't seem to notice. "Do you mean one of those disguised as the drummers?"

She nods quickly.

"There are too many things about this assassination mission that don't add up," he surmises, his brow furrowing again. "For instance, why are you the only one who's been captured?"

"I am?" Akari's eyes flare with surprise.

Yong nods. "The rest have either fled or died."

Some of the Protectors got out? Their retreat was organized and efficient, even when everything went wrong. But it suddenly dawns on Akari she'd never been informed of the escape route.

"How about Hanwell Weilcox? The one who stabbed King Alvaro... and the one I deflected his wounds onto... Is he dead as well?" Akari wonders as she recalls him lying motionless on the blood-stained gold carpet.

"I don't remember who he was," Yong says. "Why do you ask about him?"

"Hanwell's the one who delivered the mission to me, and he was the leader of the assassination mission," Akari replies, hesitating before she adds, "I think... I think he knew that King Alvaro's my father..."

"He couldn't possibly have known!" Yong interjects, his eyes darkening. "Only a few people are aware of your true identity, none of whom will ever tell. But if the People's Protector *did* know, it would explain why they chose you, a long-lost daughter seeking revenge—the perfect scapegoat..."

Akari doesn't know what to think, her chest contracting.

Yong sighs, shaking his head. "There's something else that doesn't seem quite right. When Lord Vykroux rebuilt the People's Protector, they swore that neither the happenings in Andelovia nor matters surrounding the throne would ever be any of their concern."

"I was surprised too. The People's Protector's purpose is to protect, not to rebel, and never to kill," Akari admits. "But we weren't trained to question our missions."

He gives his lopsided smile. "You don't look like someone who doesn't question her missions."

She purses her lips, although she has to admit he's hit the nail on the head.

Switching back to a serious tone, Yong advises, "There's more to this than meets the eye. When you get out of here, you need to be wary of the People's Protector."

"If I even make it out..." Akari says matter-of-factly, glancing at the bars.

"You will! I'm going to get you out no matter what it takes. You're King Alvaro's daughter. You're a princess. You aren't allowed to die just like that!" There's absolute conviction in Yong's voice. He reaches out and caresses Akari's cheek. "Trust me, will you?"

Her insides flutter. She's tempted to just accept his words, but instead, she manages to ask, "Won't you get into trouble with Queen Jocelin?"

"You don't have to worry. I'm the one person who can get away with it," he says with a sad smile that doesn't touch his crescent-moon eyes.

"Why?" Akari probes. *What else is he hiding?*

But before Yong can respond, the shuffling of footsteps in the corridor seizes their attention. When they turn to the gate, they find themselves looking at Queen Jocelin Ashgenov of Xylon.

With her sharp pale face, deep-set gray eyes, and strikingly tall stature, she is unquestionably statuesque, but in an unsettling, perturbing way. Her straight, silvery blonde hair, parted immaculately down the middle, is topped with a shiny tiara. A multitude of layers in varying shades of pale blue and vibrant silver constitutes her crystal-studded dress, enveloping her body and trailing the ground behind her. The queen, dripping with diamonds, looks ostentatiously out of place in the drab prison cell.

She says nothing, but her icy stare is command enough. The prison guard promptly unlocks the gate to

Akari's cell, letting her in, along with four Royal Regiment guards.

As if it's a reflexive reaction, Yong immediately places his right hand over his heart, drops his right knee onto the ground, and bows down. "Long live Queen Jocelin..."

Beside him, Akari, thoroughly intimidated by the sight of the queen, freezes in shock, her eyes veering down to stare at her own bare feet.

The queen doesn't glance Yong's way even once as he remains on his knee, unable to rise to his feet without her permission. Instead, she breaks into an airy laugh that reverberates hauntingly around them.

"Your mother didn't teach you even the most basic etiquette, did she?" she remarks, smirking. "Those uncouth ways of the outskirts made me recognize you right away during the Festival of Colors."

Akari looks up into those terrifying gray eyes, her fear replaced by anger. "Don't speak about my mother that way again—"

Queen Jocelin's guard grabs Akari's shoulder and kicks her behind her knees, causing her to drop to a kneel.

But the queen waves him away nonchalantly. "Why teach manners to the condemned?" she trills, and a peal of manic laughter follows. "It won't be long before she joins her mother."

Akari's temples throb in trepidation. She looks at Yong and sees fear in his dark eyes for the very first time.

"No, Queen Jocelin! You can't kill her!" he cries. "She's the only heir to the throne! She's King Alvaro's—"

Just a lift of the queen's hand instantly silences Yong, leaving him utterly subdued. Akari has never seen him this way before.

"There's no heir to the throne who isn't mine," Queen Jocelin declares disdainfully. "And certainly not this bastard child who was raised in the outskirts." She takes a moment to study Akari's face, scrutinizing her every feature. "You look just like your mother. Even though I never thought I'd have to see this face again, I reckoned that I should at least come to see you for the very last time."

When her words leave Akari at a complete loss, the queen twists to Yong, finally acknowledging his presence.

"Who are you to decide whether this bastard girl lives or dies?" Queen Jocelin seethes. "I raised you to be loyal to me, and only me. Instead, you helped King Alvaro find this girl and brought her back to Andelovia. Worse yet, you fell for her, just like he fell for her mother! Do you know nothing of gratitude or shame? As a Royal Regiment guard, you shouldn't have anything to do with this bastard girl! Not that she's real royalty anyway. But how dare you associate with her? I didn't raise you this way!"

Queen Jocelin was the one who took Yong in? Reeling in shock at this revelation, Akari turns to him. Shadows dim his face as he hangs his head low, deliberately avoiding her eyes.

"He didn't tell you, did he? That I am his mother's childhood friend—the one who raised him after his parents died?" the queen spits in Akari's direction, then cuts Yong a glare. "Why do you always act like you're ashamed of me when you'd be nothing today if not for me? The two of you wouldn't have even met if I hadn't taken you in!"

Yong's shoulders tense, but he remains silent. His dark eyes are fixated on the cold damp floor, determined to continue avoiding Akari's gaze.

"If you do anything that goes against my wishes, I will have you stripped of your position in the Royal Regiment!" Queen Jocelin belts out before commanding her Royal Regiment guards, "Now, take him away!"

Two of her guards seize him by the arms and haul him away. He doesn't resist, casting Akari one last glance. "Wait for me, Akari! I'll come for you. I promise!"

"Yong!" she calls out, lunging for him. But she's pinned down by the other two guards before coming anywhere close.

"King Alvaro once loved you and your mother deeply, though it was driven by folly and delusion." Queen Jocelin's voice is especially jarring as a chilling emptiness perfuses the cell. "But time has made him forget you both, and the assassination attempt has turned those feelings into hatred. Now, he wants you gone from his life, just as you've been the past ten years."

Although this doesn't come as a surprise, a sinking feeling drenches her insides. Akari tries to rearrange her pained expression, barely managing to keep her tone even as she asks, "How's King Alvaro? Is he alright?"

"Why worry when you were the one who put him in this state?" Queen Jocelin snaps back, waving away her questions.

"Let me see my father, please!" Akari begs.

"The king isn't someone you can see as you please," the queen reminds her, scoffing, "and we won't knowingly send an assassin to him. Besides, he doesn't want to see you. Your father wants nothing to do with you. He'll never forgive you for the attempt on his life."

"That can't be true," Akari says despite the kernel of doubt taking root. "Yong said he's been searching for me and my mother all this time..."

Queen Jocelin breaks into a snicker. "Did you really think King Alvaro was searching for you? He was really looking for the Jewel of Compassion. If the king wanted to see you, he'd be here by now." The queen shatters Akari's last shred of hope with a gloating smirk. "You know, I pity you. Even your father wants nothing to do with you. He instructed me to get rid of you—quickly and quietly. He wants you dead."

Akari's heart lurches, her eyes veering down. *Perhaps it's true... that the Papa I've dreamed of reuniting with doesn't feel the same way... After all, I'm a monster who almost murdered him. What father would want to reunite with a daughter who tried to kill him?*

When she looks up, Queen Jocelin is eyeing the Jewel of Compassion hanging before her chest. Without warning, she reaches out and rips it from her neck.

"Give it back! My father gave it to me!" Akari cries, lunging to retrieve it, but she's immediately intercepted by the queen's guards and forced to kneel again.

Queen Jocelin gives a crooked smile as she inspects the jewel. "Did you really think a bastard child can wield this? The Jewel of Compassion will find a new wielder— one worthy of reuniting the three royal regalia. And that chosen one won't be you."

"Why do you hate me so much?" Akari asks.

"I don't hate you," the queen claims. "Your only sin was being born. But you're still a sinner, and every sinner needs to atone."

"Is that why you want me dead? Because I'm my mother's daughter? Or because I'm my father's daughter?" Akari wonders.

Queen Jocelin's eyes flash with a malevolent gleam. "Because you're an illegitimate daughter," she says, her lips curling into a smirk, adding, "who has given me a legitimate reason to get rid of her without me having to look. How convenient."

Is this what it's like to be in power? Akari has never seen anyone so brazen, much less in such a warped, twisted way.

"When I saw your mother with you and King Alvaro, I'd always thought that she'd won against me. This whole time, even though she wasn't by his side, she's been the only one in his heart. But now she's dead and you're about to follow, it seems like I've ultimately won." Queen Jocelin's face breaks into a wicked, triumphant smile.

"Why is winning so important to you?" Akari asks. She hasn't been concerned about winning since her games of hide-and-seek during her early childhood. *What makes it worth so much suffering and death?*

The queen is stumped, and her smile vanishes. All along, she's been so obsessed with winning that Akari could bet she never stopped to ponder the reason, nor has anyone questioned her about it.

"Isn't it because you've never known what winning truly feels like?" Akari asks in a quiet voice. She knows her question has touched a raw nerve when Queen

Jocelin's eyes flicker with fury and deep creases carve into her forehead. But after a few moments, her face relaxes and a smile reappears, sending fresh chills down Akari's spine.

"Well, let me tell you a little secret that you can take to the grave," the queen croons, her tone mocking. "I was the one who urged King Alvaro to give in to Zatori's threat and surrender the *Register of the Gifteds* in exchange for your mother's safety."

"So, *that's* the real reason he handed it over?" Akari gasps breathlessly. "It wasn't to protect his own throne?"

"Of course not! Your foolish father didn't care for that," she says with a derisive laugh. "When Zatori threatened to depose the king from his throne unless he handed over the *Register of the Gifteds*, he refused to yield. But he wavered when threatened with your mother. With a little push from me, your father eventually made a pact with Zatori and gave him what he wanted."

Akari is stricken with shock and guilt, horrified by the thought that she—alongside the entire outskirts— has been wrongfully blaming King Alvaro for surrendering the *Register of the Gifteds* to keep himself on the throne.

"Why did you do that?" she asks breathlessly. "What good did it do you?"

"I was killing two birds with one stone," Queen Jocelin says, spreading her arms as though this is obvious. "Firstly, I earned your father's trust. I knew how much your mother mattered to him. By suggesting he give up the *Register of the Gifteds* to Zatori in exchange for her safety, I let him think I cared about protecting her, that I was on her side—and thus his."

"Didn't you consider all the other gifteds who were going to die?" Akari gasps, taken aback by such callousness.

"Collateral damage," Queen Jocelin says with a casual shrug. There's no trace of penitence—or any other emotion—on her face.

"And didn't you care that Xylon was going to be divided in half?" Akari presses.

"Well, the more chaos our kingdom was in, the more King Alvaro would be cornered into leaning on me for support, and the easier for me to earn his trust," Queen Jocelin explains flippantly. "After he surrendered the *Register of the Gifteds* to Zatori and the Three Greats ensued, your father placed more and more trust in me. He had no one else to turn to." The queen pauses, letting Akari feel the full effect of her words.

She is appalled by Queen Jocelin's devious schemes and antics—and above all, her cruelty.

"And secondly, I got rid of your mother," the queen continues, her eyes gleaming with sadistic delight. "With her around, I never felt that the position of queen was truly mine, even though *I* was the one who was married to King of Xylon. But I knew from the very start that Zatori wasn't one to uphold such a pact, and that he'd still help me get rid of your mother eventually. He'd never pass up harvesting a gift like hers!"

Fury, agony, and disgust churn inside Akari. "You're the reason my mother and I had to flee the capital for the outskirts! You're the reason my family's broken! And worst of all, you're the reason my mother's dead!" She springs at Queen Jocelin, only to be hurled against the rough stone wall by her guard, the breath knocked from her lungs. As Akari crumples onto the straw, she can't help but wonder, *Is the capital really a place where you kill or be killed?*

"And do you know what the best part of it all was?" Queen Jocelin chirps, the glint in her gray eyes similar to that of a hunter about to deal the killing blow to their prey.

Akari braces herself quietly, although she has no clue what to expect.

"I was the one who informed Zatori of your existence," the queen divulges with a hysterical laugh. "You used to be a secret your parents so carefully kept from the world. After Zatori learned of you, there was no doubt he'd use you to get to your mother—and King Alvaro would have no choice but to let the both of you go. Just as I had planned, you two were soon gone from Andelovia and the White Palace—out of sight and out of mind!"

Akari glares at Queen Jocelin, wondering if there's anything that could be worse. And the expression on the queen's steely face suggests there is.

"So, don't tell me I don't know what winning feels like," she says, her voice deathly quiet. "Especially now that you're going to follow your mother in death."

"No! I need to save my best friend, Ty! He's been captured by Zatori, and if I don't go to him, he'll die. If you let me out, I promise you'll never see me again," Akari pleads fervently.

A hollow laugh escapes Queen Jocelin. "There's only one way to make sure I'll never see you again."

With that, she turns to go, her guards following close behind, leaving Akari all alone.

As she sinks in despair, Akari hears the queen's discordant voice reverberating through the corridor. "Execute her first thing tomorrow. I want her gone by daybreak."

Kill... or be killed.

23. Repercussions

It's certainly not Akari's first time pondering her own death, especially of late. Although she has considered different ways of dying, it never crossed her mind that she could be *put* to death.

With every passing moment in the bleak prison cell, Akari finds herself more dejected, losing any reason to live. *Even Papa wants me dead.* A tear rolls down her cheek as she recalls her father's loving gaze when he gifted her the Jewel of Compassion. *Where has that Papa gone? What's become of him? Am I the one who pushed him over the edge, such that he now wants me dead? Is this the repercussion of my actions?* Even as regret eats at Akari, it doesn't undo the fact that she really did attempt to assassinate her father. *I'm sorry, Papa... Maybe only death can redeem me...*

However, there's still one thing Akari needs to do before she dies. *Ty risked his life to save me... Now I'm headed for my death, who will save him from Zatori? The assassination has failed and the People's Protector won't rescue him on my behalf... Will Yong still help me get Ty out even if I'm gone?* She worries incessantly, guilt festering in her gut. *I'm sorry, Ty... You would have been better off if you weren't my best friend...*

Akari doesn't catch a wink of sleep until the early hours of the morning, when she drifts off from sheer fatigue. But the reprieve doesn't last long. She's abruptly awakened by two prison guards binding her hands in front of her with a thick coarse rope. Akari struggles to break free, but the well-built guards easily overpower her and whip a blindfold over her eyes.

With darkness foisted upon her, she can only rely on other senses. Akari hears the gate of her cell being unlocked. "Let's get moving," one of the guards hollers. There's a tug on her bound hands, quickly followed by a shove from behind when she doesn't move promptly. With no other choice, she allows herself to be led out into the corridor. The gate slams shut, and the second guard's footsteps echo behind her.

"Where are we going?" Akari asks, her voice shaking.

Neither of the prison guards answers as they escort her in silence. They seem to walk endlessly—making several turns, going up numerous stairs, and passing through at least five more locked gates—until she's greeted by a fresh breath of spring breeze. *I'm finally back on ground level again. Just how deep underground have I been all this time?* Despite having emerged from the depths of the earth, not a shred of light peeks through her blindfold. *It must still be a while before daybreak...*

The neighing of nequilouses interrupts her thoughts. The guards prod her onto some sort of cart. Still exposed to the elements, Akari knows she hasn't been given the luxury of a carriage this time. She reaches out, and her bound hands brush some vertical metal bars, similar to those of her prison cell. Akari imagines being in a cage of sorts. Whatever it is, it jerks and shudders as the nequilouses take off into the sky.

The journey is neither long nor short, and certainly not the most comfortable. Akari is flung around the cage whenever the nequilouses lurch in the air. Bound and blindfolded, she's unable to cushion the impact of the rough ride. Without the sun to warm her up, the predawn chill penetrates her tattered prison garb, raising the hairs on her skin.

After the nequilouses make their landing, she is unceremoniously extracted from her cage and the walking resumes. This time, Akari's feet tread on an uneven, rocky surface that cuts into her soles with every step. But the pain is overshadowed by anxiety. *Where are we headed to? What are they going to do to me?* Her silent questions are met with a stench of carrion permeating the stale frosty air, unusually cold for the capital.

When one of the prison guards whisks away the blindfold, her surroundings are scarcely brighter than the darkness she's just been relieved of. Akari is in a cave of sorts, its surface marred by cracks and ridges, as if time itself has gnawed away at it. Mineral deposits glisten faintly in the dim torchlight, while patches of dampness cling to the crevices. Just a few feet ahead, the ground gives way to a deep, dark pit.

A figure in shimmering turquoise, flanked by four Royal Regiment guards, stands in a distant cave across the abyss. *Queen Jocelin. Is she going to have me thrown to my death?* Akari wonders in horror as the queen observes her.

"Let me see my father!" Akari begs. "Let me see him once more before I die!"

The queen's derisive laughter echoes throughout the countless caves that riddle the pit in every direction. "Didn't you hear me earlier? King Alvaro doesn't want to see you. Even your own father wants you gone. You're better off dead!"

Akari stares at her beaten-up bare feet, now covered with blood and dirt, and wonders if Queen Jocelin is right.

"Now, I can tell you this is what winning truly feels like," the queen says with a crooked smile. When she nods, the prison guards drag Akari toward the edge of the pit.

"Let me go! Let me go!" She struggles vehemently, her scream piercing the air.

On the opposite side, Queen Jocelin has a smirk dangling from her lips while she enjoys the spectacle, as though she's watching a performance at the Festival of Colors.

When Akari reaches the edge, she makes out something moving at the very bottom of the pit. A savage-looking, gray-blue dragon, his crown and back lined with serrated spikes, paces listlessly among the remnants of skeletons, some with rotting flesh still hanging from them. *I'm being fed to a dragon!*

Sensing Akari's presence, the beast unfurls his massive, wilted wings, revealing a jutting ribcage, before shooting toward her ferociously. The caves tremor with each strenuous flap and strained rumble, the air growing thick with the force of his ascent. He climbs and climbs, covering the immense depth with vicious urgency. His glazed eyes, the size of shields, with whites like cloudy opal and irises resembling dull onyx, lock onto her. Two rows of jagged yellowed fangs, each the length of a dagger, gnash wildly as he draws near.

Akari scrambles back in terror, another horrified scream tearing from her throat.

The dragon's monstrous head is inches from her when he jolts to an abrupt stop, unleashing a blood-curdling roar. Iron chains clank around his feet, tethering him to the bottom, interrupting his ascent. Like her, this dragon is a prisoner.

Furious, he beats his wings in a maddened rage, thrashing erratically as he attempts to lunge again. He yanks violently against the chains, but they don't give way.

"Patience, you filthy creature!" the queen barks.

As though he can understand her, the dragon releases another roar which has Akari cowering, unable to shield her ears with her bound hands. He reluctantly returns to the bottom of the pit, impatiently awaiting his meal. Akari wonders if she'll first fall to her death or be eaten alive, and which would be—*will* be—worse.

"Any last words?" Queen Jocelin asks mockingly.

Akari stays silent, refusing to give her the satisfaction of a response.

"No? Well then, I think my pet has waited long enough," the queen concludes, nodding again. The guards seize Akari by the arms, her feet scrabbling for the ground as they drag her to the edge once more and hurl her into the dragon pit.

The abyss plunges toward Akari, its darkness swallowing her whole. Although she's taken the Leap of Faith many times, nothing prepares her for this—perhaps except the very first fall, when she truly believed she was going to die. Even then, Ty was by her side, and it made all the difference.

Giving up any hope, Akari squeezes her eyes shut and embraces death. Her life—now a mere collection of memories—flashes before her. She sees herself playing hide-and-seek, receiving the Jewel of Compassion, fleeing the capital, standing against Zatori and the Harvesters, escaping from the White Blaze, settling in Cheyvelenia, befriending Ty, falling in love with Yong, finding Mari dead, escaping back to the capital, attempting to assassinate King Alvaro, realizing he's her father, and finally, him sending her to her death... All of these have inadvertently led Akari to her impending doom. So, this is the repercussion of having lived the life she has.

She takes one last breath and prepares to lose herself to nothingness. Just as Akari expects her world to cease existing, she hears a familiar, deep, velvety voice calling out to her.

"Akari!"

Never before has her name sounded so sweet. *Yong! He's come for me! He kept his promise!* Her eyes fly open, and she sees Zephy nosediving toward her, his anxious caw echoing throughout the pit. He accelerates faster than gravity pulls her, closing the gap between them. When the zephanerix catches up, Akari spots Yong perched on his back.

While skillfully clutching the reins with one hand, he extends his other hand toward her as she plummets. Their fingers brush a few times, but no matter how far Yong leans out, he can't seem to secure a firm grip on her bound hands.

Sensing things are going south, Zephy does something he's never done before. He acts of his own accord, swerving unexpectedly, almost throwing Yong off his back. But Yong clings on tightly, barely keeping himself from falling to his death.

Zephy slows slightly, positioning himself directly above Akari, before propelling toward her with his claws outstretched. With absolute precision, those mighty claws swoop in, clasping themselves firmly around her. As soon as she's secure, he swiftly adjusts his body, hovering parallel to the ground to let her climb onto his back.

"Take my hand!" Yong reacts just as quickly, helping Akari into the seat in front of him. Just as he cuts the rope binding her hands, they hear the savage roar of a dragon that's been deprived of breakfast.

Akari and Yong look down to see the beast hurtling toward them. Zephy caws in shock and instantly shoots up into the air, the dragon gnashing at his tail.

"Sit tight!" Yong commands.

"I'll get it!" Akari seizes the reins from his hands and kicks her legs urgently, deftly navigating Zephy in his flight, putting distance between them and their pursuer.

Yong wraps his hands tightly around her waist, glancing behind to assess the situation. But suddenly, she feels his grip loosen and turns back to find him locking eyes with the dragon, his nostrils flaring as he sniffs the air, perplexed.

"Watch it!" Akari shouts, her voice sharpening his focus. Yong hastily tightens his hold on her, but he and the dragon don't break their gaze, both still sharing an odd look in their eyes.

The beast stops gnashing, cocking his head in confusion. He gives up his pursuit, instead circling the pit before releasing a heart-wrenching roar so starkly different from the blood-curdling one earlier on.

"What are you doing?" Queen Jocelin shrieks angrily. "Chase them! Eat them, you useless creature!"

This time, the dragon lets out a hair-raising roar in blatant defiance before descending to the bottom of the pit.

When Akari ascertains that he's no longer hot on their heels, she guides Zephy to a stop, hovering in front of the queen.

"What are *you* doing here, on a *zephanerix*?" Queen Jocelin demands of Yong, her tone laced with surprise.

He instantly snaps back to his usual self. "Long live Queen Jocelin," Yong greets, placing his right hand over his heart and bowing deeply. "I apologize for startling you, but I've come with direct orders from King Alvaro. He has requested to see Princess Akari."

Doesn't the king want me dead? Akari thinks. *Why does he want to see me now? I don't even have the Jewel of Compassion anymore...*

The queen's gray eyes flicker with fury at Yong's untimely arrival. "Has he?" she seethes. If there is one person in the entire kingdom whose authority she can't blatantly defy—even in her ruthless pursuit of power—it is King Alvaro. Now, her hands are tied, her plan to get rid of Akari thoroughly thwarted. "Well, our friend waiting below still needs his breakfast."

Queen Jocelin nods nonchalantly. In the cave where Akari was tossed from, the two prison guards exchange worried glances. Without giving them time to do anything else, two of the queen's Royal Regiment guards appear from behind and shove them into the dragon pit.

Their screams echo hauntingly as they fall, until the dragon snaps one in half with his mighty jaws, while the other crashes to his death with a dull thud. Without lifting a finger, Queen Jocelin has taken two innocent lives.

Yong, not in the least surprised by the brutality, doesn't betray a hint of emotion. But Akari gapes in horror, unable to hide her disgust. *They died in my place as dragon feed! They died because of me! The capital really is a place where you kill or be killed.*

"You can't just do that!" she yells indignantly.

"Yes, I can," Queen Jocelin retorts, her voice cruel, haughty. "I'm Queen of Xylon."

The sound of crunching bones fills the pause that follows. Akari clamps her hands over her ears in revulsion, but she's unable to drown out any of it.

Well aware that she can't bear staying even a moment longer, Yong respectfully informs the queen, "We have to be on our way to King Alvaro."

He places his right hand over his heart and bows deeply, then casts one last glance at the dragon below. Taking the reins from Akari's hands, Yong kicks his legs. Zephy takes flight, while Queen Jocelin looks on in wrath.

As Akari and Yong fly among the clouds, the sun rises before them, gilding them with its dazzling brilliance. The journey to the White Palace has been relatively quiet so far, their minds both occupied, albeit with different matters.

Eventually, she turns to him, saying softly, "Thank you for coming, Yong."

From behind, Yong slides his arms around Akari's waist, squeezing her tightly in an embrace. With a sigh of relief, he rests his chin on her head. "I was so scared that I wasn't going to make it in time... that I was going to lose you..." he confesses, the timbre in his voice betraying a rare vulnerability. "I've never been so afraid before..."

Akari takes his hands in hers. "I thought it was all over for me," she says quietly. "When I was thrown into that pit, I thought I was going to die."

"I'd never allow that to happen..." Yong whispers, placing his hands over hers. "I can't bear the thought of losing you again."

"I'm sorry for putting you through this..." Akari sighs.

"Well, I'll just have to add this to the count," he informs her, giving the lopsided smile she never thought she'd get to see again.

Akari leans back against Yong, reveling in his embrace. But curiosity soon takes over.

"Why were you so distracted by the dragon back there?" she asks, doubting it's simply because dragons are unheard of this far south, typically preferring the cold.

"The dragon? Right, the dragon... I... I think I've seen this... this particular dragon before—when he was still wild... free..." he says, seemingly caught off guard by the question. "The exact shade of his gray-blue scales, the way his spikes curve... I'm positive he recognized me too. But now, there's something different about him... his eyes... He doesn't look fully conscious..." There's an uneasiness in Yong's voice.

"Why do you think he's this way? Do you think Queen Jocelin did something to him?" Akari wonders, horrified at the possibility.

"I'm not sure if she did... But what I'm sure of is that he's probably gone mad from starvation and captivity," Yong replies, a sad look hanging on his face. "Dragons don't typically feed on humans—even if they kill them—since they abstain from eating any living beings of similar intelligence. Unless they're no longer in their right minds..."

Akari breaks into shudders, although she's unclear if it's due to Queen Jocelin or the dragon.

"Why? Are you scared of them?" Yong asks, concern eddying in his dark eyes.

She nods. "Well, that wasn't a pleasant encounter by any means. I almost became dragon feed. But then again, it's hard to say that I wouldn't come to love another one who wasn't trying to eat me."

Akari's response has Yong chuckling.

But her mind no longer lingers on the dragon, instead spiraling into a whirlwind of thoughts about King Alvaro. *What do I say to someone I tried to kill? And what do I say to someone who also tried to kill me? Does that make us even? Or will we forever have something standing between us?* Despite all this, Akari knows she must face King Alvaro sooner or later—and the repercussions of her actions.

"We're headed for the White Palace, aren't we?" She's already jittery at the thought of it.

"Yes," Yong says.

"And we're going to see King Alvaro, aren't we?"

"Just you," he clarifies. "Are you worried about meeting the king? Didn't you want to?"

"I *do* want to see him... But still, I'm afraid of how it might go..." Akari admits. "Especially since I tried to kill him the last time we saw each other..." The assassination is still fresh in her mind, just as she knows it must be for her father.

There's also something she still can't wrap her head around. *Why does King Alvaro now want to see me rather than kill me?* But just as Akari is about to ask, the sight of the White Palace growing larger beneath them captures her attention. Zephy has already begun making his descent.

Yong takes a deep breath and straightens up, releasing her from his embrace. "I hate to break this to you, but I need to warn you that once we land—once we're back in the palace—you'll need to be prepared for a lot of changes," he informs Akari. "There'll be many rules you need to follow... The words you're allowed to speak, the people you're permitted to see, the etiquette you're supposed to abide by... Mostly you..." He pauses to let his words sink in, before finally laying it bare. "But also, us both..."

Akari marks the apprehension roiling in his dark eyes.

"Not that I'm going to give up on us—I never will," Yong proclaims. "It's just that things will be... different—"

As soon as Zephy makes his landing on the palace grounds, two dozen Royal Regiment guards and servants arrange themselves in an orderly fashion beside him. One of them takes hold of his reins to steady him while another offers his hand to help Akari dismount. Zephy caws loudly, overwhelmed by the crowd.

"Please forgive me, Akari," Yong whispers as he leaps off, then offers his hand as well. "I know you're going to hate this."

"What?" Akari asks as she takes his hand instead of the guard's and follows him down.

But she doesn't get a reply. Instead, Yong and the other men simultaneously place their right hands over their hearts, drop their right knees onto the ground, and bow down. "Long live Princess Akari..."

She stands awkwardly, looking cluelessly at the entourage that's come to receive her. With her tattered, bloodied prison garb, beaten-up bare feet, and disheveled hair, there's no part of Akari that looks like a princess.

24. Family

It takes a dozen palace maids to get Akari looking like a princess. They work quickly but—unlike Nana Eleanor—quietly to bathe her, dress her, and do her hair and makeup.

When the maids are done, she is in a lightly but elegantly embellished white satin dress—simple by Andelovian standards—and a pair of matching slippers, both of which she's been told once belonged to her mother. To complement the outfit, Akari's makeup is understated, and her ash-brown hair is knotted back neatly into a bun, adorned by the white ribbon she's just learned is made of the finest silk. Compared with her look for the Festival of Colors, this one is modest and innocent—the antithesis of an assassin.

When Akari is deemed presentable, the maids shepherd her to the inner palace, where most of the royal family's private wings are ensconced. She is directed into the grandest bedchamber she's ever seen—probably the grandest one in the entire kingdom.

The sight before Akari is nothing short of regal. Rich tapestries adorn the damask-patterned walls, each one alive with legendary scenes from Xylon's history. Beneath her feet, the polished marble floor is so smooth and flawless they mirror the opulence enveloping her. A plush rug stretches across one side of the chamber, its elaborate weaves of breathtaking landscapes and mythical beasts almost too beautiful to tread upon. Above, a gilded crystal chandelier droops from the high vaulted ceiling, casting a warm glow that complements the morning light streaming in through nine arched windows.

The monumental bedchamber is lined with exquisite furniture—a pair of intricately carved armchairs and a matching chaise longue, a wardrobe with doors of polished rosewood inlaid with gold leaf, and a writing desk where heavyweight parchments and fine quills lie in meticulous order. At the heart of the chamber stands a mammoth bed, draped in lustrous silk and velvet in royal hues of gold, silver, and white.

Akari shifts uncomfortably amidst this overwhelming lavishness, so impressive yet intimidating it makes her feel small within its grandeur.

King Alvaro sits propped up on the bed—his deathbed—his honey-colored eyes brimming with tears as they quietly observe Akari. His deathly countenance aside, he seems to radiate joy—rather than hatred—at the sight of her.

"Papa?" Akari blurts instinctively despite the surrealness of it all.

"Yes, it's me... Akari, my little princess... Come over here..." King Alvaro's voice is weak and hoarse, but palpably expectant. He raises his trembling hand, beckoning her over.

She hesitantly makes her way to him, stopping by his bedside. The king is almost all bones, with too little flesh and too much skin. His graying hair is sprawled messily above his hollow face. Even though it's only been days since Akari last saw him, he appears to have aged another decade. Without his crown to lend him an air of royalty, King Alvaro looks exactly as he is—a feeble, dying man.

Although Akari resents him for abandoning the gifted outskies, for driving her and her mother away, and for wanting her dead, her heart still aches when she sees him in this state—especially because she was partially responsible for it. But out of pride, she schools her expression and attempts to harden her heart.

The king pats the bed, gesturing for her to take a seat beside him. But she refuses to budge, the proximity unnerving her. After wanting each other dead, she's more comfortable with some distance between them. He lets Akari be and takes a long look at her, surveying her every feature.

"It was the eyes, wasn't it?" King Alvaro finally asks.

She nods. It was undoubtedly those honey-colored eyes—a source of both solace and perplexity—that helped Akari recognize her father and prevented her from assassinating him.

"That was how I recognized you too," he shares in a quavering voice, smiling weakly. As the king struggles to prop himself up so he can see better, his bony arms shake beneath the baggy silk pajamas he's grown too emaciated for. "I can't believe that after all this time, you stand before me, alive and well... You've grown so much from the tiny child I remember... And you look so much like your mother..." he reminisces. "And I heard that, like her, you're gifted too..." King Alvaro makes it sound tragic. To him, gifts are the reason for his divided kingdom and broken family.

"I can't believe any of this either..." Akari says, still struggling to register the reunion. "Growing up, I thought you were dead. That's what Mama told me..."

He lets out a resigned sigh. "Mari never let you know I was your father... that your father is King of Xylon, did she?"

"No..." *She left out that minor detail.*

"It seems Mari kept her word till the very end," King Alvaro breathes.

Akari isn't sure if she senses bitterness or admiration, or how *she* feels about it. Not quite knowing what to say, she remains quiet, letting her father talk instead.

"You know, that ribbon in your hair was a token of love from me to your mother when I professed my feelings for her," he reminisces. "Mari was my first, last, and only love..."

"She never told me any of this..." Akari murmurs.

"Initially, your mother didn't want anything to do with me," he recalls. "She knew with her being a commoner and me being king, our relationship would be forbidden. It took a long time for me to convince her to accept my love. I gave her this white ribbon because I wanted her to know, in my eyes, she was already part of the royal family—part of *my* family."

Akari touches the ribbon at the back of her head self-consciously, feeling the delicate weave of the silk. "Mama used to wear this every day—even in the outskirts."

King Alvaro's tears of joy quickly turn to those of sorrow. "So, is it true that Mari... that your mother is... gone?" he whispers fearfully.

Akari nods. "Just two weeks ago..." She clenches her fists, struggling desperately to fight back tears.

The king winces, as though he's been inflicted with immense physical pain. He releases a heart-wrenching howl and crumples into sobs. Tears spill from his honey-colored eyes, the sight sending a tremor through Akari's chest.

Her shoulders shudder and her vision blurs. Emotion swells within her, and before she can stop them, regretful tears streak down her cheeks. A strangled cry escapes her lips, and in that moment, the weight of their grief overtakes them both. They weep without restraint, their sorrow echoing through the chamber.

Very carefully, he reaches for her hand and holds it. Akari doesn't pull away. In this moment, the father and daughter share an intimate bond as they mourn the loss of Mari together. For the first time in a decade, they feel like family again.

After a long while, King Alvaro finally asks, his quivering voice teeming with devastation, "It was Zatori, wasn't it?"

Akari nods, almost choking on her tears.

"Zatori Valakhan!" Her father sits straighter, the pure rage roaring through his veins lending him strength. "That wretched monster made a pact with me that he would leave Mari alone if I handed the *Register of the Gifteds* to him. He's broken it yet again! The next time I see him, I'll have him torn apart!"

Anger boils within Akari as well, and she pulls her hand away from her father. The weight of his mistakes has crushed their moment of tenderness. "All of this started because you surrendered the *Register of the Gifteds* to Zatori! If you hadn't, the Great Harvest wouldn't have happened, so many more gifted outskies would still be alive, and so would Mama!"

She knows the accusation isn't entirely fair, given Queen Jocelin's devious schemes, but her father still made the choice. *He* allowed the queen to come between them to save his lover and daughter, and it caused her mother's death anyway. Akari shudders, struggling to contain the mix of anger, grief, and disappointment that's turned her heart into a drum.

The king hangs his head low. "I'm sorry, Akari. I've realized for a long time now that it was a grave mistake. For the past ten years, there isn't a day that has passed when I didn't regret what I did. I've let my people down... and I've let your mother down... but can you let me make it up to you?"

"No!" Akari exclaims, indignation flaring in her eyes. "Didn't you want me dead just this morning? Didn't you want me out of your life, just as I have been for the past decade?"

"No!" King Alvaro is wide-eyed in denial. "What do you mean? I've never wanted that!"

"You were dead to me all along anyway! You can continue being that way!" she cries. "You were the last person I wanted as my father anyway! You gave up your family and betrayed your people. I would rather have continued believing my father was dead!"

"Akari... You don't understand—"

"No! *You* don't understand!" Akari throws her arms up as she cuts the king off. "Mama and I had been doing just fine without you. And if not for you, she wouldn't have had to die! Now she's gone, there's even less reason for you to be in my life. I'm better off alone!"

A long silence follows before King Alvaro finally says, "Even though you and Mari weren't by my side, you were always in my heart. I refused to believe you were gone, no matter what anyone said. For the last ten years, I never stopped searching for the both of you. I've sent countless men across every corner of Xylon, but no one managed to find even the slightest trace— until Yong. All this time, he and I have been the only ones who truly believed you were still alive. Everyone else thought I was mad to hold on, but I knew your mother would protect you. That hope was all I had to keep going."

King Alvaro's steadfastness moves Akari, but she's too angry to forgive him just yet. "Weren't you looking for me because you wanted to find the Jewel of Compassion?"

"No! Akari, why would you think that—"

"Well, I don't have it anymore!" she lashes out, furious. "Queen Jocelin took it from me!"

"Jocelin retrieved it for me because she knew I was looking for it." The king pulls the Jewel of Compassion from his pocket.

"Retrieved?" Akari spits in disbelief. *She snatched it off my neck!* But she sees no point in mentioning it. *Who am I to do this, and what would change even if I did? After all, she is Queen of Xylon.*

"Akari, I understand you aren't fond of Jocelin," King Alvaro says, his shaky voice struggling to sound firm. "Although I don't love her the way I loved your mother, she's proven to be a great help to me in running the state affairs of Xylon when my poor health hasn't allowed me to. I hope you'll come to accept her as well."

Akari is rendered speechless, unable to wrap her head around her father's deluded perception. *Has his poor health gone to his head? Or does Queen Jocelin have him thoroughly wrapped around her little finger?*

"I knew that searching for the three royal regalia—the Jewel of Compassion, in particular—would lead me to you. Be it ten years ago or now, I've always wanted you to have it," King Alvaro continues, his tone raw, earnest. "Come here, let me put it on for you." He beckons his daughter to come closer.

Akari freezes, her heart wavering with indecision.

"Please, Akari Ashgenov. As King of Xylon, I've never had to beg in my entire life. So, can you please grant this dying man his last wish? I want you to keep it," he implores desperately.

Akari Ashgenov... This strange combination of words hits her unexpectedly, causing an aching twinge in her heart. *Was this my name from before? Is this still my name? How about Akari Miyahara? Are they two different people? Which one am I? Or are they both me?*

Reluctantly, Akari sits herself down at the edge of the bed, her back facing him. With trembling hands, King Alvaro fastens the necklace around her neck, just as he did on her sixth birthday.

When her father is done, he leans forward, whispering into her ear, "Just as I hoped, you've chosen compassion. And as it's turned out, the Jewel of Compassion has come to choose you as well."

The words resound in her head, and she remembers the first time he gave her the necklace. *Akari, this is the Jewel of Compassion. I hope you'll always choose compassion.* Childhood memories, hidden within her for so long, come scuttling back.

"What's compassion?" six-year-old Akari had asked shortly after.

"It's like light in the darkness," her mother replied with a smile as her father wrapped them both in his arms.

When present-day Akari looks into King Alvaro's honey-colored eyes, the way they glint tells her he's been reminiscing as well. It was a time their family was whole and happy.

The world pauses for her until King Alvaro eventually asks, "The Jewel of Compassion turned out to be your complement, didn't it?"

"Yes..." There's a faint tremor in her voice.

He gives a quavering, tearful smile. "Out of the three virtues, compassion has been the one I've always wished the most for you to embody. I've always seen it in you, Akari. But even then, never in the world did I expect you to become the wielder of the Jewel of Compassion. After all, it's been over three hundred years since the first king of the Ashgenov Empire wielded and reunited the three royal regalia."

"I know... This has to be a mistake. I'm not compassionate. I tried to kill you..." Akari shakes her head in denial.

"But you didn't. The royal regalia cannot be wrong. They make no mistake when choosing their rightful wielders," King Alvaro maintains. "You've always had compassion, Akari. You *are* the rightful wielder of the Jewel of Compassion—the future of Xylon."

Akari knows it's supposed to be an honor, but all she feels is horrified. "No, I'm not! I don't want to be the future of Xylon! You'll have to find yourself a new wielder," she says, fumbling to remove the Jewel of Compassion from her neck. But the king stops her with a shaky hand.

"It doesn't work that way. The connection between a wielder and their complement can only be broken in death," he informs her. "You'll share a bond with the Jewel of Compassion for the rest of your life."

For life... Akari stays silent as the full implication of his words hit her. It takes a surmountable effort to fight the urge to rip the royal regalia off her neck. *This responsibility is too huge for me to bear.*

"I still remember a time when the royal regalia were intact in the Albus Throne Room of the White Palace," King Alvaro continues in a feeble voice. "The throne room was heavily guarded at all times, making theft an impossible task. Even so, two of the three royal regalia still went missing—though we let the rest of the world believe it was all three.

"A few months after you turned five, the Sword of Courage was found missing at dawn one day. No one knows how it happened. It was impossible for anyone to enter or leave the throne room undetected. Nevertheless, I had the security tightened after this, doubling the guards on every shift. But shortly after, the Mirror of Wisdom went missing as well. Their disappearances have remained a mystery ever since.

"After that, I knew the Albus Throne Room was no longer the impenetrable fortress I'd thought it was. The Jewel of Compassion had to be moved to a safer place. I transferred it to a vault before giving it to you on your sixth birthday. After all, Akari, *you* were a secret from the rest of the world. No one knew Xylon had a princess, so no one could go after someone they didn't know existed."

A princess. Akari takes in the lavish bedchamber again. She wants nothing more than to forsake it all, to go back to a mother who loves her and a simple life at Moonstone Apothecary. *Stay safe, lie low, and keep out of trouble. Oh, Mama, why didn't I listen to you?*

"But little did I expect Zatori to uncover your existence," the king continues. "I soon lost the ability to protect you, your mother, and the last royal regalia. As the two of you fled from Andelovia, I sent Mari's bodyguard to do what I couldn't, but I never heard from her again."

"Mama had a bodyguard?" Akari's tone is incredulous. She almost laughs at the absurdity of the idea of having a bodyguard in the outskirts, but quickly catches herself. An ursine figure springs up in her mind, caring but powerful, someone who knew her mother and could look out for her.

"I remember her name was Salam," King Alvaro recalls.

"Do you mean Salam Esquenald? The bear lady?" Akari checks, more to give herself time for it to sink in than anything else.

"That's her," the king confirms with a nod.

Why did I take so long to realize? Finally, the pieces are falling into place. "I knew Salam used to be part of the Royal Regiment, but I never would have guessed she was Mama's bodyguard..."

"She's still alive, then?" he asks in surprise.

Akari nods.

"After Salam helped the two of you escape during the Great Harvest, I never heard from her again," the king recounts. "All this time, I've equated her silence with death. But seeing that she cut off all communication with the capital and stayed in the outskirts to watch over you and Mari, it seems her loyalty laid with your mother rather than me."

Once again, Akari isn't sure if she senses bitterness or admiration.

But before she can figure it out, her father adds, "Regardless, I'll have you assigned a new bodyguard from the Royal Regiment."

"I don't need one," she protests. The idea of any form of royal treatment appalls Akari, especially when her best friend is out there, suffering—*dying*—at the hands of Zatori.

However, King Alvaro stands his ground with all the strength his dying body can muster. "This is an order, Akari," he insists. "Just as you tried to kill me, there'll be people trying to kill you. I can't allow anything to happen to you—especially now we've lost your mother."

Akari releases a sigh, quietly relenting. After all, she has played a crucial role in proving his point. *A bodyguard didn't stop Mama from helping people. Why should I be any different? I'm still going to rescue Ty.* The king narrows his eyes, and she wonders if her penchant for peril is written across her face in ink.

"You need to stay away from the People's Protector. They're not who you think they are. They participated in the Great Rebellion ten years ago, and now they've tried to assassinate me again. Even though they claimed to be neutral after the Three Greats and have since solely sought to protect the outskirts, they're nothing but a rebel army waiting to seize the throne! The People's Protector is Andelovia's enemy—Xylon's enemy!" King Alvaro's weak but furious voice reverberates all around the chamber.

"Salam would never allow that! She's the second-in-command of the People's Protector..."

"Salam is part of the People's Protector?" King Alvaro furrows his brow, struggling to gather his thoughts. "Even if she is, she's probably as powerless as you are. Don't you see? You were their puppet—one to be used and discarded! Even Salam and the first-in-command of the People's Protector—whatever his name is—are nothing but puppets."

Akari crosses her arms, unwilling to believe what she realizes should have been obvious. "And who's pulling the strings?"

For a moment, she manages to dismiss the argument between Maximus and Salam, Ethan's execution, even her own role as an assassin.

"Xavier Vykroux is the true puppet master—he sent you to kill your own father!" the king roars before breaking into a cough.

The shaky foundations of her argument crumble, and Akari's entire being is gripped with shock and horror. *For such a long time, I'd mistaken Lord Vykroux for my father, when he is really my enemy...*

"When I found out that Vykroux funded the rebuilding of the People's Protector, I should have known he wanted to build up his military strength so he could stand up against me!" King Alvaro rages. "To think I once thought of him as a brother... But now, by sending you to assassinate me, he's hoping that you and I both end up dead so he can seize the throne. He's doing all of this out of vengeance for losing Miriam and Sage during the Great Harvest! That might have been my fault, but I got my punishment. I lost you and Mari too!"

Beneath the anger, Akari sees the sadness in the king's eyes. Her heart twinges just the slightest for him. *I know what regret feels like.*

"To make matters worse, Vykroux hid the fact from me that you and your mother were alive and well in the outskirts this whole time, even when he was aware that I was searching high and low for you... and that my not knowing whether you were dead or alive was killing me... As if these weren't enough, he now wants me dead as well! I'm going to make him pay for all of this. I'm going to have him arrested and executed!" King Alvaro thunders, his frail body shaking violently.

"Don't you blame me at all?" Akari whispers. "For trying to kill you?" She is riddled with guilt, deeming herself undeserving of being forgiven this easily.

"You're still a child, and you're just their puppet," her father maintains. "Even though you tried to kill me once, you saved me twice."

"Twice?" Akari is confused.

"Yes," he confirms. "The first was the deflection of my otherwise fatal wound. And the second was the tanrine brew that helped me regain consciousness. Yong said you were the one who told him about it. For days following the attempted assassination, I was unconscious and on the brink of death until he had the royal physician concoct it in a desperate attempt to rouse me."

Akari's insides lurch. "The tanrine brew? It could have gone terribly, terribly wrong. You... you could have died!"

"I see you still care about me," the king says with a shaky smile. "I could have died either way. But I'm not afraid of death, Akari. I was more afraid of not being able to see you again before I die..." He pauses before continuing, "I want you to stay in Andelovia as my daughter, and in the White Palace as a princess. In the short time I have left, I want to make up for lost time with you."

She shakes her head vehemently. "No! I belong in the outskirts! I'll never move back—"

"That's nonsense! You belong in Andelovia! You are from the capital!" he interjects. "With your mother gone, I am your only family. There's no reason for you to return to the outskirts."

"My whole life is there. Everything I've ever known is there," Akari counters. "Besides, I'm an assassin. Everyone here knows that."

"Rest assured... I've already gotten rid of all the guards and servants who saw your face during the assassination. You can start your life afresh here in Andelovia and no one will be able to say a bad word about you," King Alvaro informs her.

"Gotten rid?" Akari gasps. "Did you have them... killed?" *Is this what the capital does to people?*

"Yes, I did," King Alvaro confirms without emotion.

Dread pools in Akari's stomach. "Weren't you talking about compassion just moments ago?" she asks in a strained voice. "How can you just murder innocents— *your own* servants—without remorse?"

"I do wish for you to have compassion, Akari. But even more, I wish for you never to be put in a position where you have to forgo it," King Alvaro explains tightly. "But this time, I had to—for you."

She shudders and takes a step back from him. "You're exactly the same as Queen Jocelin!" The king and queen's nonchalance about killing revolts Akari. "I can't stay here! I can't stay in the capital where I have to kill or be—"

Queen Jocelin's entrance stops her short. She grasps a tray with a bowl of spuming, walnut brown yuriq brew as she struts over.

"Long live King Alvaro." The queen greets him with a curtsy before announcing, "My king, it's time for your medicine." Her voice is saccharine but squawky, a combination especially hard on the ears.

She turns to Akari, mockery flickering in her eyes. "Did you just mention me? Well, both your father and I would like you to stay here with us... especially now your mother's gone... and you have no other family left..." She sheds crocodile tears and offers a disingenuous smile. "Your father has been waiting so long for this day."

Although she already thinks the worst of Queen Jocelin, Akari is lost for words. Never has she seen anyone so blatantly and shamelessly hypocritical.

"Yes, Akari," King Alvaro chimes in. "Both of us welcome you to Andelovia and the White Palace with open arms. This was and will always be your home."

"No!" she yells, rage sluicing through her veins. "This isn't my home! And it'll never be!"

When Queen Jocelin flashes a smirk, Akari realizes this is the outcome she's wishing for. *Just like before, she*

*wants me gone from Andelovia and the White Palace—
out of sight and out of mind!*

Playing the saint, the queen brings the yuriq brew to the king's bedside. "Shall I feed you your medicine?" she asks with a coyness steeped in histrionics, making Akari want to gag.

"Yes, Jocelin. But one moment please," King Alvaro replies, his voice brimming with gratitude, before turning back to his daughter. "Since your mother was the royal physician, you must know what this brew is and what it does. It's been the hope of seeing you again that's helped me endure all the pain. Seeing you today has made it all worthwhile. Anything for my little princess..."

Once full of vigor, the king now seems sapped of life, leaving him with only death to look forward to. She wonders if the suffering is punishment enough for his misdeeds.

"Akari, you should go. I don't want you to see me taking the yuriq brew," he instructs, his seemingly noble attempt at dignity and consideration twisting her stomach in knots. "Meanwhile, give some thought about what I've said. Now, go."

Unsure what to think, Akari gives a reluctant bow and turns away from him.

When she is by the door, her father calls after her, "Remember what I said... No matter what happens, Papa will always love you, Akari. We'll always be family."

The last time he'd said these exact words to her, six-year-old Akari had, without even the slightest hesitation, told him she loved him back. But this time, she struggles to even part her lips.

Family... Do I still have one? Is Papa still family? Even after all this time? Even after all that has happened? Akari looks down at her white satin slippers, hiding her teary eyes, before slipping out of his bedchamber.

But not long after she closes the door behind her, a heart-wrenching scream ricochets around the entire wing—one so pained it can only be brought about by the yuriq brew.

Despite everything, Akari's heart still bleeds for her father. *I'm the reason he's putting up with the excruciating pain.* She can't help the guilt that arrives unbidden.

Unable to bear the screaming, Akari runs with no particular direction or destination in mind, so long as she gets far enough from it.

25. Destiny

Akari keeps running, past innumerable gardens with giant trees and cascading flowers, courtyards with spectacular fountains and magnificent sculptures, and hallways with exquisite paintings and intricate trimmings until, breathless, she eventually comes to a stop.

Without knowing how she's gotten there, she finds herself at the bottom of the familiar stair turret. Akari ascends the seemingly endless spiral stairs, eventually reaching the same wooden door and opening it. But the circular room isn't empty this time.

The voile curtains have been pulled up and affixed to the edges of the room, revealing the partitioned segment that was once hidden. Half a dozen guards stand at attention by the windows, donning the slate gray uniforms of the Royal Regiment. And a familiar figure is poised behind the desk, as if she's been waiting for her.

The blind old lady—the one from the maze of alleys— beams at Akari, her smile touching her opalescent eyes. Although she's still clad in purple, the vibrant amethyst dress with elegant gold detailing contrasts starkly with the dull unassuming robe she had on in the alleys. Beneath it, delicate velvet slippers of a complementary shade and pattern complete the ensemble. Although she clutches the same sandalwood walking stick, the old lady looks even more regal than she did previously, with a gold crown sitting atop her snow white hair.

Akari walks into the room hesitantly, asking, "What are you doing here, madam?"

But before she can get any closer, the guards immediately form a line of protection between them.

One of them steps toward Akari, demanding, "How dare you lack the proper etiquette and not address—"

Before he finishes speaking, the old lady has made her way around the desk, her walking stick in one hand, the other idly waving him and the rest of the guards away. "That's enough."

They promptly back down.

Turning to Akari, she says, "That should be my question to ask. This room belongs to me, my child. As does this wing of the palace. Welcome—or should I say, welcome back—to the Velum Room." She lets out a bright laugh as a look of amusement settles on her face.

Something clicks into place in Akari's mind. Her voice grows stiff with shock as she asks, "Are you... are you the queen dowager?"

The old lady nods before Akari finishes speaking. "Yes, my child. I am Arinya Ashgenov, Alvaro's mother and your grandmother. I'm your grandmama." She reaches for Akari's supple hands with her crinkled ones, remarking, "Your hands were half this size when I held them ten years ago..."

Akari looks into her opalescent eyes as she attempts to register the existence of another family member. But before she can recall any memories with her grandmother from her early childhood, the queen dowager pulls her into a warm embrace.

When Queen Dowager Arinya releases Akari, she says, "Are you lost again, my child? You seem even more lost now that you know who you are..."

Akari gasps. "Did you know who I was... even when we met in the alley?"

The queen dowager gives a firm nod.

"Why didn't you tell me?"

"You weren't ready then," she states simply.

"But I'm still not ready... I don't think I ever could be ready... for all of this..." Akari gazes round the room before meeting the opalescent eyes of her blind grandmother. "How is it possible? You couldn't have recognized me..."

Queen Dowager Arinya lets out a knowing laugh. "I can recognize you anywhere, my child, because I don't see with my eyes. I see clearer this way—I'm not blinded by other distractions," she says, as though this is explanation enough.

Akari glances at the guards, wondering how many cryptic answers they've heard while in her grandmother's service, until the implications of her words finally dawn on her. "Are you... gifted, too?"

"Yes," the queen dowager confirms with a wide smile. "Mine is the gift of perception. Even though your intentions were dark and dangerous when we bumped into each other in that alley, I saw light and kindness beneath. That hasn't changed after all these years."

Akari inhales sharply. "You knew that I... that I had plans to assassinate my own father?"

Queen Dowager Arinya gives a slow nod, and holds up a hand as one of her guards shifts at the mention of the attempt on King Alvaro's life.

"Why didn't you stop me? Or expose me?" Akari can't imagine how the queen dowager could stand by, knowing her son was in such danger.

"It would only have come from your heart if you figured it out yourself, wouldn't it?" she quips blithely.

"I could have killed him!" Akari exclaims in bewilderment. "I nearly did!"

"But I knew you wouldn't." Queen Dowager Arinya speaks with a calmness unbefitting of the subject.

"Even if I hadn't found out in time that he's my father?" Akari's tone is incredulous.

"Yes, even then," the queen dowager assures her confidently. "Because you absolutely abhor the idea of taking innocent lives."

"Have you ever been wrong before? With your gift of perception..." Akari wonders.

She quickly realizes the extended silence that follows implies her grandmother has. When the queen dowager finally speaks again, there's dread in her voice. "Yes... just once... and it was the worst mistake I could ever have made..."

As Queen Dowager Arinya's eyes shift uneasily, Akari immediately knows she has already been unknowingly and inextricably entangled in the debacle.

"What was it?" she asks, her heart pumping in trepidation.

"I never approved of your mother," her grandmother confesses. "Mari was kind and caring, but she was too mild and too soft to be queen—or so I perceived. And

469

naively, I believed the worst thing of all was her being a commoner. Since romance between royals and commoners is forbidden, I turned a deaf ear to Alvaro's pleas for my blessing for their marriage, even after they had you..."

Akari feels like she's been winded.

"To make matters worse, I pushed for your father's marriage to Jocelin. She came from aristocracy and was part of Andelovian society. Besides, I perceived her drive and ambition with this wretched gift of mine and thought she was right for your father—right for queen." Queen Dowager Arinya leans heavily on her walking stick and sighs. "This caused the first cracks in your parents' relationship."

"You're the one who tore my parents apart? You... you're the reason my mother's gone?" Akari exclaims, shaking her head in disbelief. "It wasn't just King Alvaro, or even Queen Jocelin... You're as much to blame as they are!"

The Velum Room suddenly becomes eerily hushed, except for the ringing that has started in Akari's ears. Her gaze sweeps over the guards, still standing at attention, silent sentinels witnessing her world falling apart anew. Akari glares at her grandmother. *You could have stopped it all.* She hopes the queen dowager is perceiving every ounce of her rage.

"I'm sorry, my child. I'm sorry for your loss. I'm sorry you had to suffer for my mistake," Queen Dowager Arinya says quietly, solemnly accepting the blame.

Akari balls her fists, but offers no other response.

Eventually, the queen dowager continues, "When Zatori came for your mother, Alvaro risked his own life and personally fended off the Harvesters to buy time for you and Mari to escape. Like you, your mother was furious at your father's actions, and she became determined to leave him, taking you along with her."

"Why didn't he explain himself? Why didn't he say something?" Akari demands, indignant for her father.

"Alvaro tried to, but he still ended up losing you and your mother," Queen Dowager Arinya recounts. "I'm not just telling you this to stand up for my son, but because I know how he's become. Alvaro would never explain this to you himself. He knows you'd never have listened. You'd have written his words off as excuses, just as your mother did out of anger—not that I blame her. Alvaro has become too afraid of rejection—he'd rather remain misunderstood."

The queen dowager pauses and takes a breath. When she continues, there's fresh passion in her voice. "Your father never wanted Jocelin as queen. Even now, even after all this time, his heart still only has space for your mother. And for you."

"But he trusts Queen Jocelin!" Akari spits bitterly.

"She now has Alvaro wrapped tightly around her little finger. It took Jocelin ten whole years to weave her way into the gap your mother left behind, but she eventually managed it. To think he didn't deign to look her way before..." There's more than a trace of regret in Queen Dowager Arinya's words.

"And you were the cause of it!" Akari exclaims heatedly.

"Despite Jocelin's questionable qualities, she has helped your father run the state affairs of Xylon rather competently. It's been to your father's advantage that she's stayed by his side all this time. The power of Jocelin's aristocratic family has also had a stabilizing effect on the throne despite all the underlying chaos in Xylon," Queen Dowager Arinya says.

Akari scoffs at her rationalization. "Was it all for power? Was that why my commoner mother was sacrificed?" She exhales in disgust and backs up, putting distance between herself and her grandmother. "Queen Jocelin planned for Zatori to harvest my mother's gift. She wanted my mother dead!"

"I was the one responsible for driving a wedge between your parents," the queen dowager claims. "If you must blame someone for all of this, it shouldn't be your father or even Jocelin... It should be me..."

As the last of Queen Dowager Arinya's words hit Akari, she whirls around. *They're all as bad as each other. Every one of them in the capital!* When she tries to make her escape down the spiral staircase which had led her to this Andelovian mayhem, Akari finds herself facing the queen dowager's guards, who've deftly formed a line to block her escape route.

"Let me go! Your mistake cost me my childhood and my mother! I don't want anything to do with you or King Alvaro or the Ashgenov Empire!" Akari cries as she attempts to tear her way past the guards. But they don't budge.

Queen Dowager Arinya looks on in silence, waiting for her to calm down. It doesn't take long for Akari, who's long been worn out from everything she's been through, to give up.

"That's enough." The queen dowager idly waves away the guards when she perceives Akari's sense of defeat, and the assemblage disperses as quickly as it formed.

Akari turns around slowly, staring at her grandmother in helpless resentment.

"I admit my mistake, Akari. And believe me, I'm trying to make amends. But in order to do that, I need your help. Your father may indulge you, but I can't do the same. You have a destiny to fulfill."

"And what might that be?" Akari asks quietly.

"Princess Akari..." Queen Dowager Arinya lets the unfamiliar sound sink in. "You're the heir to the Ashgenov Empire. Your father's days are numbered—"

"I don't want any of that," Akari insists, adamant. "I've already told you, I don't want anything to do with the capital. Besides, since my parents were never married, I can't be the heir to the throne."

"Ashgenov blood flows through your veins and the Jewel of Compassion hangs from your neck. It's a destiny you can't escape..." Queen Dowager Arinya reminds her. "I can see you clearer than you see yourself. Despite everything, I still see compassion beneath it all..."

Akari eyes her grandmother cautiously as she tries to decide how much truth lies in this perception.

"And curiosity... I see that you're curious about something in this very room... Is it the *Prophecy of a New Realm*?" The queen dowager smiles, and Akari doubts her grandmother needs her gift to know she's been caught off guard.

"How... how do you know about that?" she asks.

"I'm the one who perceived that prophecy," Queen Dowager Arinya divulges. "Not only am I able to perceive people with my gift, but I can also, on occasion, perceive prophecies."

Akari's face morphs from surprise to shock.

"The *Prophecy of a New Realm* was the last prophecy I perceived," her grandmother continues. "It happened to be on the day you were born, when my eyes were still working fine... which feels like a lifetime ago now..." Queen Dowager Arinya raises a hand to her face, and her opalescent eyes dart around anxiously.

"What's wrong with it?" Akari asks, sensing something amiss.

"It's not about what's wrong, but rather what's right." The queen dowager takes a deep breath before dropping to a fearful whisper. "All of the prophecies I've perceived have come true thus far, and this one will be no different. The *Prophecy of a New Realm* is already beginning to materialize..."

Silence falls, giving Akari a moment to recall the prophecy. But those words she'd received and recited elude her.

Eventually, Queen Dowager Arinya continues, "The first line of the prophecy goes, '*Compassion rises from the north.*' You returned from Cheyvelenia, the northernmost town of the outskirts, with the Jewel of Compassion."

It's just as I thought, Akari thinks as Queen Dowager Arinya gingerly touches the royal regalia hanging from her neck. When the queen dowager's cold, wrinkly hand brushes against her collarbone, she can feel it trembling. Akari isn't sure if it's due to old age or fear.

"And how about the rest of the prophecy? Aren't the Mirror of Wisdom and Sword of Courage still missing?" she asks.

"Yes, they are. Since '*Wisdom hails from across the Great Divide*,' my guess is that the Mirror of Wisdom is still right here in the capital," Queen Dowager Arinya surmises.

Akari lets out a small gasp. "And how about the Sword of Courage?" she presses.

"This one is the most baffling of all. '*And from beyond the end of land comes courage—forgotten but not lost.*' I have no clue where the Sword of Courage could be. We'll have to see how the prophecy unfolds," the queen dowager says with a shake of her head.

"As for the very last part, '*Only their treacherous reunion shall bring peace of a new realm*' suggests that reuniting the three royal regalia, a journey fraught with difficulties, is the only way to restore peace." Queen Dowager Arinya releases a sigh, and when she continues, she almost sounds defeated. "However, the prophecy also implies that peace is only possible in a new realm, which would mark the end of the Ashgenov Empire... And that means the end of your father, the end of me, and the end of you..."

Akari freezes in horror, then lets out a frightened whisper. "Is there any way around it?"

"Since the prophecy was created by me and delivered to you—*by* you, we'll need to find out how to overturn it."

"You knew that... I... I was the one who delivered the prophecy? That I traveled back in time?" Akari asks, perplexed. "How was that even possible? How did I even do that?"

"It was an intervention," Queen Dowager Arinya says, as if that means anything to Akari.

She eyes her grandmother curiously. *That's what Sage called it too. But what does it do, exactly?* It doesn't take a gifted to perceive Akari's confusion.

"It's the act of intervening with someone else's gift—interrupting, redirecting, or even changing the nature of it," the queen dowager explains. "Interventions are so rare that they've been unheard of for a long time. While all complements enhance the gifts of their wielders and protect their lives, only the royal regalia allow their wielders to intervene with another person's gift."

"Does this mean that... that I'd intervened with Lord Vykroux's gift of visiting his memory such that I was able to travel back in time?" Akari is incredulous, even though she can't think of another explanation.

"Yes." And as though she's able to read Akari's mind, Queen Dowager Arinya adds, "But you weren't able to reverse the death of your mother. What was going to happen still happened."

"Why didn't my mother do anything to prevent her death when she knew this whole time when, and how, she was going to die?" Akari asks.

"Because you are safe, Akari. And this future was enough for her." These were the same words Mari said during Akari's time travel.

"Couldn't both of us be safe?" she wonders.

"It mustn't have been possible. I'm sure your mother must have tried all ways and means, Akari. You have to trust that she did," the queen dowager assures her.

"Why didn't she tell me about it? I could have saved her! She didn't have to die!" Akari cries.

"This was precisely why she didn't tell you," Queen Dowager Arinya points out. "Your mother wanted to protect you. She wanted to keep you safe."

Yes, this is what Mama would have wanted. Akari sighs despondently.

"But I can't coddle you like your parents," the queen dowager maintains. "It's no coincidence that the prophecy was delivered to you, by you. Fate has placed a responsibility of utmost importance on your shoulders, Akari. You must ensure your mother's death wasn't in vain."

"What do I have to do?" she asks nervously.

"Our only chance at preventing the end of the Ashgenov Empire is by reuniting the three royal regalia and reigning over the kingdom—and you're the only one who can do that. You're the heir to the throne and the future of Xylon. This has always been your destiny, Princess Akari." Despite her blindness, Queen Dowager Arinya still manages to fix her granddaughter with her unseeing gaze.

"I'm not capable of reigning over Xylon!" Akari shakes her head vehemently. "I've only been in the capital for a few days. How can I rule over this kingdom?"

"The alternative is the downfall of the Ashgenov Empire. This *will* happen if the royal regalia fall into the hands of Zatori or the People's Protector. Besides, the trouble you've been getting yourself into during your stint in Andelovia shows you're capable of much, my child." The queen dowager spreads one arm out, the knuckles of her other hand white as she tightens her grip on her walking stick. "Despite the prophecy and everything else, you're still in control of your destiny—even ours."

"And what of the new realm?" Akari breathes, her voice barely a whisper scraping the back of her throat. "The inevitable new realm..."

"This is the part I've yet to unravel," Queen Dowager Arinya admits. "But what I can perceive, Akari, is that you possess something extraordinary inside of you—something I've never seen in anyone else. You are our only hope—our final chance."

Akari inhales sharply, then tries to protest, "How am I supposed to find the two remaining royal regalia when they've been missing for years? How can I forge our future when the prophecy has already predicted the end of the Ashgenov Empire?"

"Those are indeed difficult questions with no easy answers. You seem lost again, my child," the queen dowager remarks, pausing briefly before adding, "But that's alright... There are still times I feel the same..."

Before Akari can form a response, she is abruptly interrupted by her grandmother's bright laughter. Queen Dowager Arinya's opalescent eyes are trained on something—someone—behind her. Akari wheels around to find Yong emerging from the spiral stairwell.

"I see that this time, your seeker has found you hiding in this room," the queen dowager announces gleefully before breaking into a giggle. "And it seems he has plans for both of you..."

So, this is how else Grandmama's gift can be used... An unamused Akari cringes at her grandmother's teasing.

After Yong passes through the doorway, he places his right hand over his heart, drops his right knee onto the ground, and bows down. "Long live Queen Dowager Arinya and Princess Akari..."

Akari stares at him incredulously, still unused to this treatment.

"Please rise," the queen dowager commands, a cheeky smile spreading across her face.

Yong gets to his feet. "Queen Dowager Arinya, I... I'm here on King Alvaro's orders to escort Princess Akari—"

"Yes, I know!" she interrupts him excitedly. "I know Alvaro sent you here to take Akari to get some rest. And I also know you secretly want her to yourself for the rest of the day..."

"Grandmama!" Akari bursts out, her cheeks flushing as red as the Jewel of Compassion. "We don't have any secrets..." she lies blatantly to the very person who has the gift to see through her.

"Akari, you're not speaking from your heart. Surely, you didn't think you could hide the romance between the two of you from me, of all people..." Queen Dowager Arinya laughs as she continues her relentless teasing.

Yong drops to his knees instantly. "Queen Dowager Arinya, punish me if you have to! The fault is mine, not Princess Akari's—"

"Get back up on your feet, Yong. I'm not going to punish anyone. I no longer think the way I did back then about romance between royals and commoners," she reassures them light-heartedly. "Well, it seems to me that the two of you have intentions that are quite... aligned. Off you go, both of you, before I expose your little secret."

"Thank you, Queen Dowager Arinya. We'll take our leave," Yong says embarrassedly, placing his right hand over his heart and bowing deeply.

In a fluid motion, he takes Akari by her hand and leads her out of the circular room. Without looking back, they start down the spiral staircase into a world of their own.

♦

Ten years ago...

Six-year-old Akari hopped out of the Velum Room and closed the door behind her. As she waited for her mother to speak to the fortune teller, she heard eight-year-old Yong hollering from the bottom of the stair turret.

"Akari! Is that you all the way up there? It's dangerous!"

Oh no... How could he have known it's me? Akari immediately softened her footsteps, but it was still too late.

"I know it's you, Akari... Stay there! I'm coming up to get you!"

"It's not fair! You didn't find me! Mama already did!" she protested, no longer bothering to remain quiet. "She said our game is over, so this can't be counted—"

Akari heard Yong starting up the spiral stairs with swift, sure-footed steps. Even as a child, his strides were poised and dexterous.

"Alright, alright... You win at hide-and-seek! Alright?" Yong pacified her as he quickened his pace.

"Whoop! Alright, I'm here. I'm up here!" Akari yelped triumphantly as she began hopping down the stairs as fast as her little legs could carry her, her bright voice and unsteady footsteps reverberating throughout the turret.

"Slow down, Akari! Don't fall!" Yong warned as he flew up anxiously.

With the disparity in their paces, the two children met somewhere around three-quarters of the way up. Even though Yong stood a step below Akari, his eyes were still level with hers.

Steadying her in his arms, he complained, "You could've fallen all the way down if you weren't careful! How many times do you need me to save your life? Do you want me to start keeping count?"

"No." Akari looked at her shoes guiltily.

"Then promise me that you won't put yourself in peril again," Yong said, softening his tone.

She nodded profusely. "I promise I'll try my best..."

His lips curved into a tiny lopsided smile, his crescent-moon eyes twinkling. "There's one more thing..." he said. "Happy birthday, Akari. I wish you many happy returns."

"Thank you." Akari answered with a radiant smile.

"I have something for you," Yong said nervously.

"What is it?" Her eyes lit up expectantly.

He led her down some more steps, coming to stop inside a small alcove. A narrow window had let in a shard of sunlight that landed on a weathered stone wall with a vivid chalk drawing of two children looking fondly at each other. The little girl had bright almond eyes and long straight hair, while the little boy had crescent-moon eyes and wavy hair.

"Wow... It's beautiful..." While being careful not to smudge it, Akari touched the drawing with her tiny fingers as gently as she could. Although it was nothing like Yong's current drawings, it was undoubtedly a fine piece of work for an eight-year-old.

"Well, thank you," Yong said, a mix of pride and shyness tinging his voice.

"Did you draw this?" Akari continued, finally shifting her gaze to Yong. "Of us?"

He nodded. "I hope you like it."

"I do! I love it! It's wonderful, Yong! Thank you!" Akari reached forward to hug him.

He returned a warm embrace that was too tight and too long, as though he didn't want to let go.

"So, what do you wish for this year?" Yong asked.

"I wish for us never to be apart," Akari declared as she attempted to squeeze him even tighter and longer.

"I'll try my best to make your wish come true—"

"Akari, my baby... where are you?" They heard Mari call out from the top of the stairs.

"I'm here, Mama! I'm coming!" Akari hollered back and squirmed to release herself from his arms. "I need to go. I'll see you during our next hide-and-seek."

Yong was unusually quiet, his dark eyes darting furtively in every direction except hers. "No matter where you are, I promise I'll find you," he swore.

"We'll see! I'm quite good at hiding," Akari claimed, smiling proudly.

"And I'm quite good at seeking," he countered, his half-smile betraying a hint of melancholy.

"But today, I won!" she reminded him.

"Yes, you did," Yong conceded.

"Alright then, goodbye, Yong!" Akari chirped as she made her way back up. Once again, her bright voice and unsteady footsteps reverberated throughout the stair turret, the last time for a long while.

"Goodbye, Akari..." he replied softly, his crescent-moon eyes wistfully following her until she disappeared around the turn.

Although they wound up being separated for a decade, the destinies of the two children became more intertwined than either could have ever imagined.

26. Reminders

Somewhere more than a quarter of the way down the spiral staircase, Yong comes to an abrupt halt. Akari, trailing his footsteps, bumps into him.

"Sorry..." she says sheepishly.

Even though Yong stands a step below Akari, he's now half a head taller than her. Without saying a word, he takes in all of her.

For the first time in a decade, she's dressed in keeping with her royal status—a look that's both strangely foreign and comfortingly familiar all at once. He gazes at her flowy white dress, which catches the sparing light in the dim stair turret to give off an almost luminous glow against her smooth, light bronze skin. Yong can't help but notice how her ash-brown hair has been tied back to accentuate her charming features, save the few wisps which delicately frame her beautiful face. Now that Akari looks the part, she appears more alluring—but even more untouchable than ever.

The reality of forbidden romance between royals and commoners has Yong's lips parting to release a sigh. He deliberates long and hard before gingerly reaching toward Akari's shoulders, only to hastily retract his hand before he touches her.

All his life, Yong has been a stickler for rules—and it's served him well thus far. But in this very moment, he feels the urge to throw caution to the wind. Without giving himself another chance for second thoughts, he musters the courage befitting one of the best fighters in the kingdom and swoops up Akari tightly in his arms.

"Akari..." Yong breathes, letting out another sigh. He has a hand around her waist and another at the back of her head, gently caressing her hair.

After an exhausting day of reuniting with her family, all Akari yearns for is the solace of Yong's company, and wonders if her grandmother already knew this before she did. She lets her guard down completely and snuggles up against him. He smiles wearily, pressing his lips gently on the top of her head. They stay locked in an embrace for a while.

After what feels like an eternity, Yong releases Akari and leads her into the small alcove—now even smaller than she recalls. "Do you remember this place? This was where I last saw you ten years ago after our final hide-and-seek game. I bade you farewell right here."

She nods, glancing around.

"Do you also remember this?" he asks, pointing at the chalk drawing.

Akari's gaze lands on the same little girl and boy looking fondly into each other's eyes. To her surprise, the chalk on the stone wall of the stair turret still seems fresh, looking unlike anything that's been there for the past decade.

She nods again. "But how is it still here?" A mix of awe and disbelief washes over her.

"For the last ten years, I could only see you in my dreams, and I was so afraid I'd forget how you looked. So, every time the rain ruined the chalk drawing, I'd come here to draw it back, as close as I could recall. That helped me remember your face, and later helped me recognize you in the outskirts," Yong shares. "But now I've found you, I don't have to do it anymore. I can just look at you."

A tingling warmth surges through Akari. While being careful not to smudge it, she grazes the drawing with her fingertips, as though she's touching the faces of the children in the flesh.

"I guess there's a part of me that really did belong in the capital after all..." she whispers. The chalk drawing isn't only a reminder of Akari's existence in Andelovia, but also of someone in the capital holding on to her, missing her, loving her... *Can first love actually last?*

"Yes, of course," Yong declares. "Back then, I was right there with you from the very beginning... And now you've returned to Andelovia, I'll be right here with you as well, till the very end..."

Akari's lips curve into a small smile. "I'm glad you found me." She reaches around his neck, and he returns a reassuring squeeze, planting a kiss on her forehead.

"Follow me, there's somewhere I want to take you." Yong smiles as he releases her. Taking her hand in his, he carefully leads the way down the spiral staircase.

"Where to?" she asks.

"Somewhere I know you'll want to go," he replies cryptically.

Yong leads Akari through an endless series of gardens, courtyards, and hallways, before finally stopping in front of a pair of elaborate double doors. She finds herself in an unusually quiet but particularly beautiful wing, still on the periphery of the palace.

"This is it, isn't it?" she asks breathlessly. The familiarity amidst the unfamiliarity awakens something inside her.

"Yes, this is the Amoris Wing of the White Palace. It used to be your mother's," Yong answers. "It's coming back to you, slowly but surely, isn't it?"

Akari nods as fragments of memories from her early childhood flash through her mind. A decade ago, she used to toddle along this arched hallway leading to her and Mari's bedchambers. But all of it now seems like a lifetime ago.

She studies the white oak doors before her apprehensively.

"Go on, Akari..." Yong offers an encouraging nod, giving her strength to push open the doors to Mari's bedchamber.

As soon as a crack appears between them, she is ambushed by a furry creature. It shoots straight into her arms, licking her face as she tries to regain her footing.

"Kami! I wasn't expecting to see you here..." Akari tears an overexcited Kami away before drawing her close once more in a tight embrace. They snuggle their faces into each other's.

"Thank you for bringing her here," she says gratefully.

"My pleasure. I knew you'd be missing her and that it would help to see something or someone familiar," Yong replies, beaming. "Though it's funny how she started acting all territorial once she got here, like she owned the place..."

Akari giggles, until the sight before her takes her breath away. She beholds a palatial bedchamber, its grandeur emphasized by a soaring double-volume ceiling and seven imposing arched windows that flood the space with golden sunlight. Though nearly as opulent as King Alvaro's, this chamber exudes a softer elegance, with pastel accents gracing the ecru walls adorned with gold trimmings and swirling floral motifs.

Against one of them stands a plush four-poster bed, its silken curtains cascading gracefully from the top, framing the cloistered enclave within. On each side, an ornate nightstand holds a vase of fresh telmezias, their delicate petals perfuming the air. Although Akari's memories of this place are hazy, Mari's bedchamber still seems as she remembers, stirring a bittersweet ache deep within her chest.

"King Alvaro kept the Amoris Wing in the exact state your mother left it," Yong informs her as she takes everything in. "Under his instructions, the palace maids have been maintaining this place, even replacing the flowers every single day for the past ten years."

Akari's eyes widen in awe as she looks around, noting there isn't a sign that the bedchamber has been unoccupied for a decade. The condition of the furniture is exactly as it was when she and her mother left, without a speck of dust or a hint of mustiness around it. She wonders if this is proof that first love can actually last—that this is King Alvaro's way of showing his unwavering devotion.

A small red robe hanging from the clothes rack catches her eye. *This used to be mine.* Although it once fit her, it now looks tiny. *Have I really grown this much in the last ten years?* Akari raises her hand and lightly grazes the fur trimmings on the garment—another reminder of her existence in the capital. *My past in Andelovia had indeed been real.*

Beside it hangs a soft pink robe with intricate beaded patterns—the one she saw Mari wearing in Lord Vykroux's memory—as though her mother had worn it only yesterday. Akari clasps it in her hands and buries her face in it, before closing her eyes and taking a deep breath. The robe smells of a unique blend of fresh flowers and herbs, just as Mari did. In this moment, Akari feels so close to—yet so far from—her mother.

It dawns on Akari that the scariest thing about death isn't how it puts an end to something, but rather how everything else moves on. Yet, this time capsule of Mari's bedchamber offers her solace that there's at least one place in this entire kingdom that has stopped to remember her mother.

For the first time since Mari's passing, Akari finally has a quiet, uninterrupted moment to process and grieve. Her mother had given her best years—and more—to bring her up. Had Mari stayed in Andelovia, she could have had it much easier, enjoying a cushy life with servants at her disposal, without ever having to lift a finger. Instead, she chose the hard path, earning a living with her bare hands and raising her daughter alone—without a man by her side—until her untimely demise. Akari wonders if she's come to appreciate the extent of her mother's hardship and sacrifice too late. The finality of Mari's death eventually overcomes her, unleashing a flood of pent-up sorrow as tears spill down her cheeks.

Unsure how else to comfort her, Yong gently strokes Akari's shoulders before wrapping her in his arms. She seeks solace in his crisp mountain air scent and his warm, protective embrace. Knowing this might be one of the only places she's safe, Akari buries her head in his chest in a feeble attempt to hide from the world.

"Are you wiping your tears on my uniform?" Yong's tone is tender but incredulous.

She lets out a soft, indiscernible sound and snuggles her damp face deeper into his chest.

"Alright... Hush, Akari..." he murmurs, gently caressing her hair. "I know you miss your mother very badly."

"It feels like there's this gaping hole inside me—a huge void... Whatever was there went missing or died alongside my mother..." Akari whispers, sorrow tinging her words.

Yong nods in understanding. "I feel the same way with my parents. Although I can't say I miss them because I never really knew them, their passing has left an emptiness within me." Despite the pain in his voice, he wants to be brave for Akari. "It may be a long time—perhaps an unimaginably long time—before things get better, but take all the time you need. I'll be by your side the whole way—from the very beginning to the very end."

A warm sensation courses through Akari, soothing her until the weeping subsides. Yong releases her, wiping the tears from her face before leading her to the expansive balcony that spans the entire length of the bedchamber.

It overlooks a garden where labyrinths wind between bushes teeming with Andelovian flowers—a sight indisputably and enigmatically beautiful, yet far too manicured—too capital-esque—for Akari's liking. She briefly hesitates before stepping gingerly onto the balcony, taking a pensive walk down memory lane.

♦

Ten years ago...

"How could you?" Although Mari didn't raise her voice, it was evident that she could barely contain her anger. She was rarely anything but graceful and gentle. However, her usual serenity had been replaced with a quiet fury as she looked coldly into the eyes of the man she was once so in love with. "How could you hand over the *Register of the Gifteds* to Zatori?"

King Alvaro was silent. He, too, now knew he'd made a grave mistake.

Sitting on the bed in her mother's bedchamber, little Akari quickly caught on that something was wrong, although she didn't know what, exactly. Her eyes were wide with fear, never having seen her loving parents at odds with one another, much less this angry and disappointed. They'd tried not to let the cracks in their relationship show—especially not in front of her. But now, barely weeks after her sixth birthday, it had reached breaking point.

"You didn't just abandon your people, but also your family!" Mari seethed. "Or does marrying the queen mean Akari and I are no longer your family?" She couldn't even bring herself to say Queen Jocelin's name, as if it would leave a bitter taste in her mouth.

"No! Mari, listen to me. You know I never wanted to marry Jocelin. It was just a political move—one I thought you understood," the king explained tirelessly. "You have and will always be the only one for me."

"Isn't giving up the *Register of the Gifteds* to Zatori yet another political move? Wasn't it because you decided to sacrifice the gifteds so Zatori would back off from eyeing up your throne?" Mari challenged. "You've changed, King Alvaro. I don't know who you are anymore."

The king stayed quiet, deliberating telling Mari the true reason he'd surrendered the *Register of the Gifteds* to Zatori. While he didn't want her to carry the burden of his actions, King Alvaro desperately wanted the mother of his child to look at him with the admiring gaze she once had—for them to be as loving as they once were.

"No... The pact Zatori and I made was that he'd spare you from harvesting if I handed him the *Register of the Gifteds*!" he eventually revealed. "I'd never, ever give you or Akari up for anything in this world. But I *am* willing to give up this kingdom—even my people—for you. I just didn't know... I didn't expect Zatori to break the pact and come for you!"

Mari's eyes flickered with warmth, her heart softening for just a moment. But her pent-up resentment since Queen Jocelin's intrusion into their lives had already hardened her. "How could you be so selfish to have sacrificed your people for me? So many lives have been lost—Miriam's and Sage's included—and many more will follow! How could you be so foolish as to believe Zatori? His depravity knows no bounds. He won't stop here. I warned you that he's after your throne!" She spoke with a chilling iciness, her eyes frosting once again.

"I know, Mari. I realize I was wrong. I thought by appeasing Zatori, I could... I might have the chance to keep you by my side. But now, it has driven you away from me instead." King Alvaro was confessing a mistake that was only partially his, not once pushing the blame to Queen Jocelin.

"Now Zatori's used me against you, Akari will be the next one he'll threaten you with. I can't let that happen," Mari declared, her fists clenched in resolution. "Even if it means leaving Andelovia." She started picking out some of her and Akari's belongings and tossed them into a satchel.

"No! Mari, please don't go! You've never been outside Andelovia! It isn't safe in the outskirts. It's not a place to raise a child." The king reached for Mari as he tried desperately to convince her. "You and Akari won't last a day there!"

"Yes, we will," Mari maintained, her tone steeped in determination.

King Alvaro hurried to Mari's side, reaching for her again, almost piteously. "You know I'll never let Zatori hurt Akari. She means just as much to me as she does to you. She'll be safe here. The Royal Regiment will protect both of you."

Mari retracted her arm brusquely, sweeping across the bedchamber to gather more belongings. "No, we won't be safe while we're in Andelovia with you. We won't last a day *here*!"

"I can hide you and Akari in places Zatori will never be able to reach," the king begged weakly.

"We can't hide forever. Look at what happened to Miriam and Sage!" Mari continued packing without so much as glancing his way. "Akari has already spent her whole life hiding from the world because we were never officially man and wife. It only got worse after you married the queen last year."

"Mari, even before Jocelin and I got married, I offered to take you as my queen, but you refused. You said you didn't want a marriage without my mother's blessing." King Alvaro's voice is doused with hopelessness. "I might have been a bad king, but I haven't been a bad father. Give me one more chance, Mari..."

When she finally turned to look at him, she said, very quietly, "If you want to be a good father, let us leave—and let Akari forget you."

The king fell silent as he registered Mari's words. They seemed to consume him. When he spoke again, it sounded as though he was in pain. "Are you leaving because of Zatori... or Jocelin?"

"I'm leaving for Akari," Mari said, casting him a sorrowful glance. "I want her to grow up somewhere where she doesn't need to be hidden—where she can be safe."

With the satchel slung over her shoulder, she took Akari by her hand and headed toward the balcony, telling a Royal Regiment guard, "Prepare a nequilous—"

Salam burst into the bedchamber, prowling toward them urgently. Before she finished performing the customary bow, she reported, "King Alvaro, Lady Mari, the Harvesters are fighting their way up here as we speak. You need to leave now!"

There was an unsettling moment of stillness as they took in the news.

"Prepare a zephanerix," King Alvaro commanded the guard with a wave of his hand. "The fastest one."

"No," Mari objected. "If we take a zephanerix, we'll forever be linked to the royal family."

"Please, let me do this for you, if not Akari. Zephanerixes are much faster. You'll be much safer this way. Besides, no matter what, you and Akari will always be part of the royal family—part of my family." The king spoke with irrefutable authority as he took Mari's hand in his. "Salam and I will hold them off. Mari, take Akari. Go now, and stay safe." His demeanor was completely different this time. Gone was the pleading voice and self-absorbed manner, replaced by a sudden resolve—a man stepping up to his responsibilities.

"King Alvaro, staying behind is dangerous for you—" Salam pointed out with a growl. But a single glance from the king instantly silenced her.

"My word is final. This is a command. Salam, if Zatori and the Harvesters go after Mari and Akari, I want you to protect them at all costs."

"Yes, King Alvaro." Salam accepted the order with a sharp nod.

"Mari, I trust you to protect our little princess." King Alvaro put his hand on Mari's arm, their eyes locking as he said, "Once this mayhem dies down, I'll join you both. This time, I'll give up everything to be with you. Although I couldn't make you my queen, I'd renounce my position as king for you."

"No! You can't give up the throne! Akari will be safe with me. But the Xylonians... your people need you," Mari insisted, but the king had already turned his attention to Akari.

Kneeling, he reached his other hand toward her, and she clasped his sturdy index finger with her tiny hand.

"Akari, my little princess... Papa will be with you very soon. I promise." King Alvaro's honey-colored filled with tears, his attempt to hold them back in front of his daughter futile.

Six-year-old Akari nodded cluelessly. "Papa, I'll miss you. Come to us soon—"

A resounding caw filled the air as the Royal Regiment guard arrived on the balcony with Zephy. Mari hurriedly led Akari toward them and King Alvaro quickly followed.

He and Mari shared a quick embrace before he helped her onto the zephanerix. Then, he hugged Akari tightly and lifted her up, placing her in front of her mother. With no time to lose, the king tapped Zephy's rear, commanding, "Go! Go now!"

Zephy flapped his wings powerfully, taking off from the balcony. As he soared toward the sky, Mari and Akari turned to see that Salam and the other Royal Regiment guards had begun fending off the Harvesters, some of whom were already giving chase on their nequilouses. King Alvaro, while protected by his guards, fought valiantly to prevent the Harvesters from pursuing his family. Even amidst the turmoil, he kept Mari and Akari in his peripheral vision until they vanished into the horizon.

That was the last King Alvaro and Mari saw of each other.

♦

"After the Great Harvest, King Alvaro wanted to give up the throne in search of you and your mother, but Queen Dowager Arinya wouldn't hear of it. There was too much chaos and instability in Xylon and the kingdom couldn't afford to lose its king." Yong's voice draws Akari back to the present. "Knowing it was what Lady Mari wanted him to do as well, King Alvaro stayed on the throne and devoted himself to Xylon, but it wasn't long before he began ailing."

Akari pictures her father withering under the weight of his choices, along with his health and morality. She can't help but feel a sliver of pity for the king, although it's nothing compared to what she feels for those who've suffered and died because of his mistakes.

"King Alvaro used to visit the Amoris Wing when he missed you and your mother," Yong continues. "But each time he set foot here, it was like ripping open an old wound. Eventually, it got too painful, and he stopped coming. But even then, he never stopped searching for both of you."

"Are you sure the king wasn't just looking for us because he wanted to find the Jewel of Compassion?" Akari looks at Yong, her eyes searching for an answer.

"Of course not!" He seems taken aback by the idea.

"Queen Jocelin said—"

"You can't believe a word she says." Yong's voice is flat, devoid of emotion.

Akari remains silent, wondering if she shouldn't have mentioned her. As much as she detests the queen, she was still the one who took Yong in after his parents passed away.

A sharp exhale escapes him. "What you need to know is that King Alvaro was even willing to give up the throne to be with you and your mother. He loved—loves—both of you very much," Yong continues with absolute conviction. "I know it isn't easy, but have some faith in your own father, will you?"

Akari nods, apprehensive. "I'll try..." she whispers weakly. "It's just that a lot has changed overnight. There's too much to take in."

"Sleep." Yong's voice is gentle but firm. "What you need now is sleep." He takes Akari by the hand, leads her to the bed, and sets her down. "You should take a nap. I don't remember the last time you had a good night's rest."

"Now? Here?" she asks in surprise as she looks at the four-poster bed she used to share with her mother.

"Yes," Yong confirms before casually adding, "Didn't I mention that the Amoris Wing is now yours?"

Akari gapes at him. "You might have left out that minor detail."

"I guess I didn't..." Yong mutters to himself.

She eyes the bedchamber nervously, unused to all the flagrant extravagance Andelovia has to offer. "You can't be serious..."

"Like it or not, I am," He chuckles, lays down a pillow, and motions for her to get into bed. "Now, make yourself comfortable. I'll tuck you in." After Yong wraps the quilt around Akari, Kami slinks over and curls up beside her.

"You know, I'm not planning to stay in the capital," Akari reminds him. "I'm going to save Ty and go back to the outskirts."

"You're not going anywhere. You need to rest up," he replies.

She shakes her head. "Have you found out where Ty is yet?"

"No, but I've already had Emeraude looking into it."

"Emeraude?" Akari raises her eyebrows skeptically, but reminds herself that he still doesn't know she's a double-crosser.

"Yes," he confirms, reading Akari's skepticism as dislike. "I know you aren't fond of her, but Emeraude is good at her job. I'm sure she'll find out where Zatori is holding Tyler Kane very soon."

Akari barely stops herself from rolling her eyes. *She sure is good at her job. If only you knew what Emeraude really does.*

"And once I find out where Tyler Kane is, *I* will get him out," Yong continues, casting her a warning look. "*You* will have no part in it."

"No! *I* have to save Ty! *I'm* the reason he was caught by Zatori and the Harvesters," Akari protests, her voice raised.

"Do you know how hard it's been for me to keep you alive so far?" he asks, a mix of desperation and exasperation tinging his words. "I can't have you risking your life like that. I promise you that I'll save—"

"No! I can't have anyone else losing their lives for me again!" Akari fires back, shaking her head stubbornly. "Much less you..."

But Yong crosses his arms and stares down at her. "I won't lose my life, or allow you to risk yours! King Alvaro will agree with me on this."

"You're a Royal Regiment guard through and through, aren't you?" Akari remarks scathingly, refusing to back down.

"I know Tyler Kane has been an important part of your life, but you are to me too! Even before him..." Yong inhales deeply, taking a moment to compose himself. "We were childhood playmates first, but a twist of fate took you away from me—and with it, any reason for me to smile again. For you, I was quickly replaced by Tyler Kane, but there wasn't such a person for me, Akari. I bore the pain alone, burying myself in training and work as I waited, biding my time until the day I could finally reunite with you. Now you're back in my life, I can't lose you again!"

Akari sighs, remembering what Nana Eleanor said about Yong being withdrawn as a child. After finally emerging from his shell under the refuge of her and Sage's friendships, he quickly relapsed back into it after the two of them were gone. *We could've had an entire childhood together.* Perhaps, if she'd stayed in Andelovia, they'd have been inseparable—and they'd have fallen in love with each other, time and again.

She reaches from under the quilt and takes his hand. Yong's competence has served as a front, hiding his pain from the world, and had her naively assuming he was above it all. But now, she knows she was wrong. *Perhaps he's only human after all.*

Akari looks into his dark unsmiling eyes, recognizing his loss and sadness for the first time. "I'm sorry, Yong... I never knew... I never thought... that you—"

"That I was susceptible to hurt?" he asks, his eyes betraying a shadow of the pain he's suppressed for too long. "Akari, you're too precious to me. I need you to be well. So, for now, will you please get some sleep? We can figure out what to do about Tyler Kane when we find out where he is."

This time she nods, finally relenting, before letting go and sinking her head into the plush pillow, eliciting a lopsided smile from Yong.

Akari stares up at the pastel curtains that hang from the four-poster bed, reliving memories. She clamps her eyes shut in an attempt to get some rest, but finds herself recalling how she and Mari had shared this very bed, their hands linked as they fell asleep.

Despite having had her own bedchamber right down the hallway, Akari often preferred cuddling up with her mother as she'd been too afraid to sleep alone. She continued to do this at times, even after they moved to the outskirts. But now, even with Kami by her side, the bed feels painfully empty.

Yong is about to leave when he catches on. "What's wrong?"

"I can't fall asleep... All I can think of is my mother... Being back here, it's hard not to..." Akari tries to steady her quivering voice.

He kneels by the bed, hesitating slightly before reaching his hand out to caress her cheek. "I know it's hard, Akari... But try to clear your mind and rest your body. You need it..."

She turns to her side to face him, narrowing her eyes attentively. "Are you trying to stay away from me?"

Yong's eyes dart away. "It's not that... It's just that I can't stay here with you. It's not that I don't want to... I'm not allowed to... I'm a commoner while you're a royal, Akari."

"But you've always known who I was! Nothing has changed!" she protests, sitting herself up.

He sighs and shakes his head. "No, everything has changed. Being back here in Andelovia and the White Palace changes everything," he reminds her. "I did warn you that things between us will be different from now on."

"But you also said you wouldn't give up on us," Akari retorts.

"I'm not giving up on us. I'm just following the rules... to protect you. I've always been protecting you and I still am, Princess Akari."

Hearing Yong, of all people, directly address her by title winds her. She forces herself not to flinch, never realizing before just how much it would sting.

"In Andelovia—the White Palace, especially—there's a rule for everything," he continues, his voice strained. "A princess and a guard don't go well together—it's not the way things are done here. The capital isn't very forgiving, and going against the rules could mean death for me and dishonor for you. Look what happened to your parents..."

Akari inhales sharply, quietly contemplating his words and their implications. *Being a princess is the worst thing that could happen to me... I never wanted any of this...*

"I know you hate any form of rules or restrictions— especially if they're capital-related—but this isn't something either of us can do anything about," Yong adds in a softer tone. "Despite working my way up to be the vice commander of the Royal Regiment—and despite being taken in by Queen Jocelin—I'll always be a commoner by birth. And you, Princess Akari, despite having grown up in the outskirts, will always be royalty by birth."

Akari shakes her head in denial. *Is this my future in the capital? Even more reason to not stay here...*

"Do you remember how, in the outskirts, you once told me that I'm up here, and you're down here?" Yong says, placing his left hand before his eyes and his right hand in front of his chest. "Well, now your status has been reinstated, you're up *there*, and I'm down here..." He shoots his right hand into the air, lamenting the cruel joke destiny has played on them.

"And then you told me that you'd bring me to you," Akari reminds him. "I'd do the same for you too." She takes his left hand and raises it all the way up.

Yong drops both his arms, giving a smile that doesn't touch his eyes.

"Not that I care," she reassures him. "I don't care about any title or status. It's never mattered before, and it won't matter in the future either."

"I know... I know *you* don't care. But the rest of the world does," he says resignedly. "I don't care how they see me—I'm nobody. But I care how they see you. Now the world knows you're a princess, all eyes will be on you. And if they knew about us, I'm afraid they'd see you differently—and for worse."

"I don't care what the rest of the world thinks of me either," Akari insists.

"Alright, alright..." Yong half smiles at her stubbornness. "I want to give us—you especially—time to get adjusted to everything. Let's just take everything slowly—a step at a time—shall we? And the first step for you is bedtime. Now, lie back down, will you?"

Akari nods, nestling back under the quilt as he tucks her in again. After a slight deliberation, Yong bends over and presses his lips gently on her forehead. A warm tingling sensation spreads through her.

"Will you stay for a little bit?" Akari whispers, her voice tentative, vulnerable. It's the first time she has ever made such a request.

"Alright... Go on, close your eyes. I'll stay with you until you fall asleep, but I'll have to leave before anyone sees me." Yong takes her hand and perches at the edge of her bed. "Sleep tight, Akari."

In the dim moonlight, she feels every inch of his hand, from his long fingers between her delicate ones to his rough palm against her supple one. Akari tightens her grip, hardly believing he is still by her side after all that's happened. Yong returns a reassuring squeeze, as if telling her that he'll always be there for her.

Not long after Kami has wriggled her way between them, Akari finds her body easing, exhaustion setting in. As her eyelids grow heavy, the last thing she remembers before drifting into a long dreamless slumber is Yong's slate gray Royal Regiment uniform.

27. Double-Crosser

Akari blinks drowsily as she awakens. She barely takes in the ecru double-volume ceiling, as well as the drapes of pastel silken curtains extending across it, framed by the gold rails of her four-poster bed. Her vision is still hazy when the slate gray Royal Regiment uniform edges into her peripheral view.

"Yong?" she calls out expectantly, a subconscious tenderness to her voice.

A Royal Regiment guard performs the customary bow. "Long live Princess Akari." Their tone is courteous but cold.

A whiff of a familiar cloying Andelovian floral scent has Akari bolting upright in embarrassment. "Emeraude? It's you?"

A pale elfin face, framed by a cascade of fiery red hair, snaps into focus. As the greeting resounds in her mind, Akari recalls their previous interactions. Emeraude has always been rude and condescending, glaringly so. Now, even as she addresses Akari in accordance with the etiquette of the royal court, the contempt in her emerald eyes is still evident.

"What are you doing here?" Akari asks, narrowing her eyes.

"King Alvaro assigned me to be your bodyguard, Princess Akari," Emeraude replies.

Dread grips Akari. *Clearly, she isn't here out of free will... But how can I have Emeraude Eleaconde, of all people, as my bodyguard? She hates me. And worse, she's a double-crosser!* She kicks herself for remaining quiet. *Although I don't want her dead, it doesn't mean I want her trailing me all around the capital, even if I'm not staying for long. Why couldn't Yong be my bodyguard instead?* This time, Akari doesn't forget to school her expression, careful not to let the disappointment show. She doesn't want to be embarrassed again.

"Yong is the vice commander of the Royal Regiment," Emeraude explains, still seeing through Akari, whose face flushes. "If not for that, King Alvaro would have assigned him to you, given his skill, and that he found and brought you back to Andelovia." She's still down on one knee.

"Right..." Akari realizes Emeraude isn't allowed to move an inch without a word from her. "Get up, please," she says with a trace of exasperation.

Emeraude rises to her feet and stands at attention. Without her clunky armor or flamboyant Andelovian clothes, her petite frame makes her appear somewhat fragile for the first time.

The two look at each other in silence. Akari fidgets self-consciously as her bodyguard takes in her white Andelovian-style dress, knowing full well that Emeraude wouldn't be passing up the chance to make a snarky remark if not for her status as a princess.

However, anger rises up and quells her embarrassment. *You were a key part of the assassination attempt, and you knew plenty more than you let on.* Akari strides off to the balcony to get some space, but Emeraude follows unfailingly, remaining uncomfortably close.

Akari twists around. "How could you! How could you help me kill my own father? How could you hide it from me?"

"I... I didn't know—"

"Don't lie! I don't believe you even for a second!" she spits, furious. "How could you not have known King Alvaro's my father? Even if Yong didn't tell you, Hanwell must have!"

"No! I wasn't aware! Never in a thousand years would I ever have guessed that..." Emeraude insists. "And who's Hanwell?" Her pointy features rearrange to form a puzzled expression.

"You don't have to put on an act in front of me. I saw you together at the Cavalier Restaurant in the Colossal Inn," Akari informs her.

"Oh, him..." Emeraude tries not to appear surprised at her knowledge of their meeting. "None of us use our real names for these things," she explains coolly, as though this is general knowledge.

Akari deliberates her words. *You may be telling the truth, but still, you're fortunate I take after my mother. My father would've had you thrown off the balcony by now.*

"Did Hanwell really know that King Alvaro's your father? I know you don't believe me, but he never told me any of this..." Emeraude's tone seems sincere. "My role has solely been to supply the People's Protector with intelligence about the capital and to carry out the orders they give me. I've never been provided with any information that isn't necessary to fulfil my obligations."

Akari still isn't sure whether to believe her.

"Do you really think the People's Protector set you against your father on purpose?" Emeraude asks.

Akari nods.

"Believe me, Princess Akari. I didn't know King Alvaro was your father until the assassination attempt was over," she maintains. "I wasn't even aware of the separate mission Yong was given to search for you and your mother. I only found out about your true identity after the king regained consciousness and sent him to rescue you from the execution."

A rare earnestness flickers in her emerald eyes. Despite the dislike and distrust Akari harbors, she decides to believe Emeraude this time.

"I wouldn't have helped you kill him, had I known the truth. That would have been acting against the little conscience I have left..." The unfamiliar rawness—perhaps even guilt—in her voice catches Akari's attention. "I know how much it hurts to be deprived of a father's love."

The words take Akari by surprise. Emeraude has never mentioned anything about her family—or even herself. Despite the acrimony between them, Akari barely knows anything about her. For the first time since they met, Emeraude has shed her icy, impenetrable armor, unveiling a vulnerable side that's usually deliberately concealed.

"What happened to your father?" Akari asks cautiously.

"Oh, he's alive and well," Emeraude informs her with a bitter smile and an unconvincingly nonchalant shrug. "He was never around much when I was growing up. And when he was, he was never much of a father. Not once did he think I was good enough for him."

More accustomed to her snobbishness, Akari becomes uneasy in the presence of this foreign, wounded person. Her anger dissipates, and she finds herself wanting to console her. "Well, for the most part, I grew up without my father too—"

"It's not the same." Emeraude's face is glacial again. "Your father loves you, Princess Akari. That's something I've never had and never will."

Akari wonders what Emeraude's father must have been like to make her so rancorous and aloof, and how devastatingly lonely her childhood must have been. Although Akari lacked her father's love growing up, her mother more than made up for it.

She glances at Emeraude, whose emerald eyes dart away to avoid her gaze. *I guess I'm not the only one feeling uncomfortable at the display of vulnerability.*

"Don't you dare pity me," Emeraude warns, finally meeting Akari's eyes. "I'm not bothered by it anymore." There's an edge to her voice, a sharpness that's been whetted by her upbringing.

"I don't pity you," Akari is quick to clarify.

"That's good." Emeraude's tone closes the subject of her father.

After a long pause, Akari asks, "Do you know what happened to Hanwell?" She recalls him lying motionless at the bottom of the stairs—another victim of her gift.

"He's dead," Emeraude answers without a shred of emotion. "I saw his body among all the others on the carts that were wheeled out of the Iris."

A gasp of horror escapes Akari. *Is that what he deserved, or is it my fault?* As much as she dislikes him, it feels wrong. After all, he was once her comrade. This leaves her all the more certain she can't have anyone else dying for her.

She leans on the balcony, gazing into the distance for a while before she continues with her questions.

"What did you tell Hanwell during your meeting at the Cavalier Restaurant?"

"I told him that many believed the Ashgenov Empire was doomed because King Alvaro was dying and there wasn't an heir to the throne—or so I thought..." Emeraude says.

"Is this the reason you decided to betray the Ashgenov Empire? Because you thought it would fall?"

"You could say so," Emeraude replies curtly.

"And does the People's Protector know your identity as a double-crosser has been compromised?" Akari presses.

"Obviously not. If they did, I'd be dead by now." Emeraude's casual tone is unbefitting of the gravity of her words. Unlike Akari, she seems to view death with an uncustomary indifference. *How can she be so desensitized to it?*

For the first time, Akari wonders if Emeraude, like her, is also a puppet of the People's Protector—one to be used and discarded. It scares her to think how she'd trusted them so wholeheartedly, and how they'd so easily cast her aside after the failed assassination mission. *Will Emeraude suffer the same fate?*

"So where does your true allegiance lie?" she asks. "Is it with the Ashgenov Empire or the People's Protector?"

Caught off guard by the question, Emeraude hesitates before saying, "The side from which I stand to gain the most. The Ashgenov Empire gives me a roof over my head, but the People's Protector puts food in my stomach. So, I give them both what they need and watch their fight unfold. Truth is, it doesn't matter to me whether King Alvaro or Sir Maximus is on the throne, so long as I continue to benefit."

Emeraude's ability to utter such distastefully honest words without any shame never fails to surprise Akari.

"Don't you have a side you actually feel you belong to?" she presses, casting an incredulous look.

Emeraude gives a nonchalant shrug. "I don't belong anywhere."

There's a sadness to her answer, one Akari wasn't expecting. She squashes the sympathy welling up inside her, knowing full well it's the last thing Emeraude wants. "And if not for yourself, shouldn't you stand on the side that would benefit the people?"

"There isn't such a side," Emeraude claims indifferently. "When I was younger, I thought it didn't matter to me who is king, so long as the people are content. But when I grew older, I realized that, no matter who is king, there'll always be people who are suffering."

With every passing comment, her bleak incisiveness has Akari questioning her reality. "But even then, don't you care if people die because of what you do?" she demands.

Emeraude shrugs again. "Why ask when you already know I don't? Besides, people die every day, Princess Akari. It's just a matter of who." There's a slight pause before she adds, "If you'd seen the things I had to see, you wouldn't care too much about whose head is rolling as long as it isn't your own."

Utterly stumped, Akari is left without words to rebut with. Although she might not have grown up as a princess, Mari had always ensured she was protected—sheltered, even. She struggles to imagine the life Emeraude has led, forgetting to school her expression for a moment.

"Don't look at me like that, as though you're a much better person than I am, *princess*," Emeraude seethes. "You're just luckier to be born to a better father. Besides, weren't you so willing to kill him before you found out you were related?" she challenges, her scathing voice rising a notch. "Ultimately, both of us have ties to the People's Protector and the Ashgenov Empire. You're no less of a double-crosser than me. Being a princess doesn't take any of that away—it just draws attention from it."

Akari detests the comparison, but she can't deny there's some truth to Emeraude's perspective. *Maybe I'm not so different from her after all...*

"But I have to say, I was surprised when they called for the assassination of King Alvaro," Emeraude continues. "As a part of the People's Protector, you know their purpose is to protect, not to rebel, and never to kill."

Akari nods in agreement.

"I was even more surprised when I was told that you, of all people, were appointed as the main assassin. I didn't think you'd succeed—for a different reason. But still, I was right." The tinge of smugness in Emeraude's voice eases as she adds, "But I had to do as I was told."

"I had to do as I was told too... so they would help save Ty..." Akari tries to explain, knowing she only has herself to count on now.

Emeraude looks at her quizzically. "Why would you do that? You're a princess from the capital, and you're gifted. He's a nobody from the outskirts, and he's a nullus. What's Tyler Kane to you?"

"Why does any of that matter?" she challenges. "Isn't there anyone at all besides yourself that you actually care about?"

Emeraude's sharp features twist with perplexity, as though she's never been prompted to think about this before. But a flicker in her emerald eyes suggests she's managed to think of someone.

Just as Akari wonders who they are, and how warm-hearted they must be to melt such icy armor, Emeraude looks her in the eye, asking, "Why didn't you tell on me? Why didn't you tell Yong or King Alvaro that I'm a traitor? I mean, you obviously hate me..."

"I may not be fond of you, but I don't hate you. And most of all, I don't want another death on my hands— not even yours," Akari explains, her thoughts drifting from Mari to Hanwell. She knows Emeraude will undoubtedly be executed if her secret is let out of the bag.

"If you turn me over, you'll get a brand-new bodyguard. Surely, I won't be missed." Emeraude's words belie the truth that Akari has moved her. She shifts from foot to foot, visibly uncomfortable at being the recipient of something as strange to her as kindness.

Is it that difficult for her to understand me not wanting to have her killed? Akari wonders. "But neither will I have a hold over the new bodyguard," she maintains, flashing a small smile. "Now that I know your secret, you have no choice but to pledge your allegiance to me—without acting as a double-crosser this time. You won't be able to help me if you're dead."

Emeraude's delicate lips return a rare smile as she finally accepts that Akari genuinely means to protect her. "Well, you already know I can pledge my allegiance to you, just as I've done to the Royal Regiment and the People's Protector. I've done it too many times and I can always do it again," she says, perhaps a friendly warning that she isn't serving with all her heart.

Akari deliberates. *I'd much rather trust someone than have them killed just in case.* It feels surreal—and wrong—that she even has the power to make that choice. *As if I needed another reason to get away from here.*

"So, is there something you need from me?" Emeraude asks, eyeing Akari carefully.

"I'm allowed to give you orders, right?" she checks, clearly not used to possessing authority.

Emeraude sighs, her exasperation at being stuck as Akari's bodyguard, of all the royals, evident. "Yes, Princess Akari. And even if you aren't, you have a hold over me now, like you said. I'll have to do what you wish or face death," she reminds her impatiently.

Akari nods along. "Hopefully, one day, your service will be on your own terms."

Emeraude casts her a hard, somber look, then lowers the pitch of her voice to give it a condescending edge. "This is how you should speak if you want people to know you're giving a command. It establishes your authority." Although she seems unusually good at this, Emeraude is forced to soften her tone and gaze. "Now, please give me your orders, Princess Akari."

Akari takes a deep breath before giving her best shot at mimicking her. "Emeraude, I want you to inform me of Ty's whereabouts once you know them."

"That's not too bad for a first attempt," Emeraude acknowledges, although Akari is certain she has seen better. Surely, Queen Jocelin must excel at this.

"Yong already had me looking into this. And I've just managed to find out where Tyler Kane is."

Akari's heart races. "Where is he?"

"Zatori has him held captive in the Hollow."

She lets out a gasp. "The Hollow?" Her voice trembles as she says those words.

"Yes, Princess Akari," Emeraude confirms.

"But... no one who's entered the Hollow has returned alive."

"I'm well aware."

"And how's Ty? Is he alright? Is he alive?" Akari leans back against the balustrade, her knuckles turning white as she grips it tightly with both hands.

"Yes, you don't have to worry about that. Tyler Kane is a nullus—he's of no use to Zatori," Emeraude answers matter-of-factly.

Akari heaves a sigh of relief. *We can still get him out alive. He doesn't have to pay for my mistakes with his life.*

"There's also a message... that... that I... was asked to relay..." Emeraude stutters, uncharacteristic of her usual poise.

"What is it?" Akari eyes her with a mix of curiosity and suspicion.

"Zatori wants you to take the Jewel of Compassion to the Hollow—*alone*—in exchange for Tyler Kane. If you bring anyone else, you'll never get to see him alive again," Emeraude says, her tone strained.

Akari's eyes are stricken with fear. *Of course, that's what he's after! Zatori wants to reunite the three royal regalia!* While she so badly wants to stop him from achieving this, Akari knows trading the Jewel of Compassion for Ty is the only way to save her best friend.

"I'll do as he says," Akari pronounces with incommensurate certainty. "I was already planning to go alone anyway. I don't want anyone else risking their lives for me." She pauses briefly before asking, "Emeraude, have you told Yong that you've found Ty's location yet?"

"No, I haven't."

Akari nods in approval. "That's good. Let it stay that way. Keep it from Yong as long as you can." She attempts to speak with authority once again before emphasizing, in case it isn't clear enough, "This is a command."

"Yes, Princess Akari." Emeraude's trained response is accompanied by raised eyebrows, perplexed by her apparent willingness to walk straight into danger despite being so afraid of death. But she quickly shakes off any unnecessary budding concern for Akari, adding, "Surely it won't come as a surprise to you that King Alvaro not only sent me to protect you, but also to keep an eye on you in case you flee the White Palace and Andelovia. As your bodyguard, I have the responsibility to stop you from going." However, they both know nothing is going to stand in Akari's way.

"Emeraude, you have to help me. You're the only one who can," she says earnestly—desperately.

516

"That's not true. There are people in better positions to help you," Emeraude points out, evidently reluctant to comply.

"I can't run the slightest risk of Ty getting hurt for me... and King Alvaro and Yong will never let me go, especially not alone..." Akari can't bring herself to imagine the disappointment and worry on their faces when they realize she's gone. "Besides, in the event something doesn't go as planned, it won't hurt you, unlike them. You already hate being my bodyguard anyway."

Emeraude doesn't refute this.

At least there's one redeeming quality about her, Akari thinks. *Emeraude's honest about her disdain for me.* "Besides, you also have to repay me for not selling you out," she reminds her.

Emeraude sighs sharply. "So, what exactly do you need me to do?"

"I need you to bring Zephy to me tonight," Akari says. "Kulning will attract too much attention and he isn't exactly wild anymore."

"Yes, Princess Akari. I'll bring him here after sundown," Emeraude replies.

"I'll also need you to make sure the coast is clear as I leave the White Palace," she adds.

"You don't have to worry. Zephanerixes won't get shot down when they fly across the White Palace or the Great Divide. You'll be safe in Andelovian skies," Emeraude informs Akari, casting her an odd glance.

"Why are you looking at me like that?" Akari asks.

"Aren't you afraid of death? Don't you care about your own life at all?"

"Yes, I am—terribly afraid, in fact. And this is why, even more so after my mother's death, I can't let my best friend die." Akari tries to sound braver than she feels. "Besides, I have the Jewel of Compassion. If Zatori wants it, he'll have to do as I say and let Ty go. I'll be able to save him this way."

"Don't you want to see Yong again before you leave?" Emeraude asks, but Akari shakes her head.

"No. Seeing him again will make it harder for me to leave. Besides, if Yong gets even a whiff of my plan to rescue Ty, I won't be able to act on it."

Emeraude gives a hesitant nod.

As the girls look out at the enigmatic palace garden bathed in the golden afternoon sun, they realize that, perhaps, they dislike each other a little less than they'd thought. After a long while, their peace is interrupted by a knock on the door.

A Royal Regiment guard enters the bedchamber and greets Akari. "Princess Akari, Madam Salam is here to seek an audience with you."

28. Secrets

"Let her in, please!" Akari whips around expectantly, hopping back into the bedchamber from the balcony as Emeraude trails her. She's never been this excited to see Salam. However, someone else seems even more eager.

As soon as Salam appears between the double doors, Kami darts toward her with a wagging tail and pinned-back ears, jumping into her arms and licking her face.

"This dog is a funny one!" Salam exclaims, holding Kami at arm's length to prevent her face from getting any wetter. "Dogs don't usually like me. They're usually scared of bears. And I think it might be better that way," she concludes with a rambunctious laugh.

"Kami seems to like you," Akari says as she approaches, laughing as well. "She usually barks at strangers."

Kami's playfulness is suddenly replaced by a rare solemnity as she casts Salam a steady gaze. Both of them seem unable to peel their eyes away from each other.

"Surely, this can't be..." Salam murmurs under her breath, the rest of her words lost as she takes Kami in her huge furry arms and nuzzles her snout.

"Madam Salam!" Akari salutes in true military style when she reaches her, then leaps forward for a hug, only to find her arms wrapped around Salam's neck instead of her waist.

Salam has her right hand over her heart, her right knee on the ground, and her body bowed down. "Long live Princess Akari," she greets, abiding by the etiquette of the royal court.

Akari immediately helps Salam to her feet and gives her a warm embrace. "Just Akari, please. You can drop the formalities when it's just us."

"It's been a while since I've been able to greet you properly," Salam remarks somberly as she wraps Akari in her arms. "I can't believe it's been ten years since we were last in this chamber..."

Akari nods. "I can't get used to being a princess again... I barely even remember being one..." she admits, taking in the grandeur all around her before returning her attention to Salam. "King Alvaro said that you used to be my mother's bodyguard, and that you've been protecting us this whole time, both in the capital and the outskirts. I never would have thought that—"

"That the moment you left my watch, you almost assassinated King Alvaro Ashgenov of Xylon, for goodness gracious sake!" Salam lets out a reverberating growl.

"It was a mission ordered by the People's Protector. I thought you—"

"The assassination was ordered separately and entirely by Maximus Fontan!" she quickly clarifies. "I was completely unaware of it."

"And I was completely unaware that I could be royalty, or that my father's king! No one told me—neither my mother, nor you!" Akari's voice rises a notch.

"You've always been Princess Akari Ashgenov, and you always will be. Forgive me for hiding it from you all this time, but it was just too dangerous for you to know this before," Salam says with a deep bow.

Akari nods along. She has heard different versions of these familiar words too many times now.

Salam's attention shifts to Emeraude, her gaze simmering with suspicion. "Isn't she the Andelovian girl who was in the outskirts?"

"Yes, this is Emeraude and she's been assigned to be my bodyguard," Akari explains. "It turns out that she and Yong are part of the Royal Regiment—"

"And they were in the outskirts looking for you, your mother, and the missing royal regalia?" Salam finishes for her. "I should have known what they were up to when we found out they were part of the Royal Regiment."

"You knew *that*?"

"Princess Akari, you were the one who told me about the zephanerix badges in their rooms," she reminds her.

"Back then, I didn't know what zephanerixes stood for—" Akari tries to explain, but quickly finds herself interrupted.

"*You* were the one who searched our rooms?" Emeraude exclaims.

"Yes. I already told Yong—"

"*I* commanded her to." Salam speaks with a mix of authority and finality, drawing the subject to a close.

A breeze blows into the bedchamber and her black bear nose twitches, catching a scent. She follows it, inching toward Emeraude.

"You smell like a bit of everything," she growls menacingly. "The Royal Regiment... the People's Protector... and... and what's this smell?"

Akari turns her head in Emeraude's direction and takes a whiff, but only smells her usual cloying Andelovian floral scent.

Meanwhile, Salam gives herself completely to her ursine side, sniffing Emeraude up and down with closed eyes. Emeraude stands her ground with an uncomfortable stiffness during the thorough olfactory inspection, until she staggers backward when Salam breaks out into a deafening roar.

"This is the smell of a traitor!" Salam thunders, her eyes meeting Emeraude's in a deadly stare. "This girl is one of the eyes and ears Maximus Fontan planted in the capital. She's an insider for the People's Protector!"

Akari and Emeraude momentarily freeze in shock before locking eyes, jointly deliberating their next move. Salam tracks their exchange, immediately catching on.

"Princess Akari! You knew?" she bellows frustratedly. "And despite that, you still have the audacity to keep her around?"

Akari's eyes veer downward guiltily to find her satin slippers, silently accepting Salam's accusations. When she finally looks up to meet her deadly gaze, she meekly asks, "How did you find out?"

"It's the same smell as the note you took from her room. It smells a little of her and a little of Hanwell... My nose never betrays me!" Salam explains.

Emeraude cuts Akari an accusing glare, but there's no fear in her eyes.

In fact, Akari seems more flustered as she hastily springs to her defense. "Emeraude is my bodyguard now! She's already pledged her allegiance solely to me," she lies without blinking.

Emeraude's expression softens slightly, even if she still doesn't understand kindness.

"And you believe her?" Salam challenges, coiling her gargantuan body into a crouch, as though preparing to pounce on prey. "She betrayed the Royal Regiment and the Ashgenov Empire! Let me take her to King Alvaro!"

"No! Stop!" Akari yells, worried that the massive Salam will easily take down the petite Emeraude in a single swoop. She steps forward, strategically placing herself between them. "You can't send Emeraude to her death!"

"Princess Akari, are you out of your mind? You can't keep someone like that around you. It's too dangerous!" Salam warns. "She assisted Hanwell with the assassination of King Alvaro, and she could well be plotting yours next! Look where Hanwell is now... Dead!"

"No!" Akari says, hoping her voice carries more conviction and authority than she feels. "Besides, we all have ties to the People's Protector and the Ashgenov Empire. This makes the three of us the same. Each of us is no less of a double-crosser than her."

"Our circumstances are incomparable!" Salam unleashes an infuriated roar. "I served both sides openly and wholeheartedly. And more importantly, during my time in the People's Protector, I only sought to protect, not to rebel, and never to kill! This girl is neither loyal to the People's Protector nor the Ashgenov Empire, and she helped in the assassination attempt of King Alvaro—your father!"

"So did I, Salam..." Akari reminds her as she pleads on Emeraude's behalf. "Let's give her a second chance."

"This is just trouble waiting to happen," Salam warns.

"I'll be careful, I promise."

"I'm afraid you may come to regret this, Princess Akari..."

"Even so, it's my decision to make." Akari gives Salam a hard, somber look and lowers the pitch of her voice to give it a condescending edge, putting her commanding presence into practice. "This secret will stay between the three of us. This is an order."

Salam lets out an exasperated growl, ruffling her fur defeatedly. "Yes, Princess Akari," she answers before remarking begrudgingly, "It seems to me that you're getting used to being a princess again quite quickly."

Emeraude's eyes brim with newfound gratitude, and she gives Akari a nod of approval. It seems, in just a matter of minutes, Akari has moved up her rankings of authoritative royals.

Salam takes one last sniff of Emeraude, commenting pointedly, "I still don't like the smell of her. She smells all wrong. I smell something more—"

"Salam, please stop that!" Akari orders.

Salam freezes mid-whiff, casts Akari a sheepish look, and slaps her furry paws over her nose. "Yes, Princess Akari." But when she continues, there's urgency lacing her tone. "There's something else that brought me here today. I would like to speak with you—in private." She glances at Emeraude pointedly.

Akari nods at her new bodyguard, who promptly performs the customary bow before leaving the bedchamber.

"What is it?" she asks as soon as the double doors close.

"Are you alright?" Salam asks, deeply concerned. "I heard you were the only one who was caught after the assassination attempt. The rest of the Protectors had either fled or died."

"I'm fine," Akari replies. "But what's going on with the People's Protector? How is it possible that you were unaware of the mission to assassinate King Alvaro?"

"I came here today to warn you that there's been some... reorganization in the People's Protector..." Salam discloses in a somber voice. "And that I've been... expelled."

Akari gapes at her. "How could you be expelled? You rebuilt the People's Protector!" she exclaims indignantly. To her, Salam is synonymous with them.

"Or you could also say I left of my own accord," she clarifies. "The purpose of the People's Protector has always been to protect the outskirts when King Alvaro has been unable to. But Maximus believes in replacing what he thinks is an incapable king. When he learned of your true identity the night Zatori came to Cheyvelenia for you and your mother, Maximus wanted to use you to get the throne for himself.

"Given my ties to the royal family, there was no way I could agree with him. After a huge, ugly argument, Maximus expelled me from the People's Protector. By then, I could no longer find any reason to stay. Just as he wanted me out, I wanted myself out as well."

More guilt hits Akari squarely in the gut. "It's my fault again, isn't it? First my mother's death, then Ty's capture, and now your expulsion..."

"No, not at all. I don't want to stay in a place that's no longer aligned to my beliefs," Salam insists. "After I left, Maximus ordered the mission to assassinate King Alvaro under the New People's Protector and intentionally appointed you to make the killing blow. Guessing his plan, I came to Andelovia to stop it.

"But no longer being part of the Royal Regiment meant I couldn't cross the Great Divide easily, and no longer being part of the People's Protector meant I had no access to the gateways. By the time I got to the capital, it was too late. Thankfully, you didn't succeed in the assassination. I may have taken Lady Mari's side when I cut off all communication with Andelovia, but I'd never do anything to hurt King Alvaro—nor will I let you hurt yourself."

Salam's still trying to protect me after all this time, Akari thinks, finding solace in this.

"Furthermore, we both know from our last People's Protector mission—the decoy—that there's still a spy for Zatori within our... their ranks," Salam continues. "The late Ethan couldn't have been the traitor who leaked false intelligence. Just as we thought, he was merely a scapegoat."

"Ethan died a wrongful death," Akari laments. "I knew he wouldn't have betrayed us."

"His execution was Maximus's warning to me," Salam says sadly, "and to everyone else who belonged to my school of thought. By now, it's no secret that he won't hesitate to kill. The New People's Protector is headed for darker, more dangerous times—and you should keep your distance from them."

"The New People's Protector... Have they grown so different from the original People's Protector overnight? Did Sir Maximus really set me up to kill my own father?" She knows these are pointless questions with answers she dreads.

"Yes, Princess Akari. I'm afraid you were a convenient tool. And the truth is, even if you were successful, they'd never have saved Tyler for you," Salam tells her. "Maximus would still be after the Jewel of Compassion hanging from your neck."

Akari's stomach sinks. *My father is right... I was only a puppet of the New People's Protector—one to be used and discarded. And now, I can't let Ty be discarded in my stead... I can't let him pay the price for me.*

"In that case, I'll save Ty by myself," she declares, her voice quiet but determined.

"No! You cannot risk your life like this again! Especially now you've been reinstated as a princess!" Salam bellows in disapproval.

"I can't just leave him there to wait for his death either," Akari retorts. "Ty's my best friend."

"The only reason Zatori is keeping Tyler is to use him to get to you. If you go to his aid, you will only die alongside him! And if you send the Royal Regiment to rescue him, Zatori and the Harvesters will kill him before they even get close." Salam's tone is almost quavering, but she speaks with certainty. "You should forget about him. Tyler's as good as gone!"

"No! That can't be!" Akari exclaims. "There has to be a way to save Ty."

Salam shakes her head firmly. "There's no other way besides walking to your death. It may be hard now, but with time, you'll realize that forgetting Tyler is better for you." There's no anger in her voice, and somehow that's worse. "Remember our conversation before your first mission? When I asked you to be hard-hearted? I know this isn't your forte, but you'll have to try your best this time."

And where would I begin with that? For a moment, Akari is back with Ty, hurling snowballs at the Verge. She's teasing him for his insatiable appetite, and he's making some suggestions that will get them into trouble. And it's all dust that won't change Salam's mind. While it was difficult to persuade her to give Emeraude a second chance, Akari knows it'll be impossible to convince Salam to allow her to risk her own life.

"You should accept that Tyler's gone and focus on your new responsibilities as Princess Akari, the most basic of which is self-preservation," Salam tells her gently. "Don't forget, you're the future of Xylon."

Akari's fingers graze the Jewel of Compassion. "If I give this to Zatori in exchange for Ty, neither of us will be hurt..." she says, more to convince herself than anything else.

"Princess Akari! I risked my life not only to protect you and Lady Mari, but also to safeguard this royal regalia. You cannot simply hand it over to Zatori!" Salam snarls. "This would mean handing over to him the legitimate claim to rule over Xylon! When that happens, hell will reign. Many lives will be lost—even more than during the Great Harvest!"

Akari's eyes veer downward. Deep down, she knows Salam is right. Handing over the Jewel of Compassion to save her best friend is a selfish move—as selfish as King Alvaro surrendering the *Register of the Gifteds* to keep her mother safe. But now Akari finds herself driven into a corner, she can't help but empathize with his actions a decade ago. This is when Akari knows she is, without a doubt, her father's daughter. *Perhaps we aren't so different after all.*

When Akari lifts her head, she finds Salam studying her. "Princess Akari, giving up the Jewel of Compassion is almost as bad as giving up your life, for goodness gracious sake," she says more softly this time. "Lady Mari tried so hard to keep both you and the royal regalia safe. Now that she's gone, I need to do that on her behalf..."

I know it'll be dangerous, but I still have to try. Although nothing can change her mind about rescuing Ty, Akari pretends to relent. "Alright..." she says, as reassuringly as she can manage. "I'll stay in the White Palace for now."

"That is a wise decision, Princess Akari," Salam replies, a relieved smile appearing on her ursine face. "I've just paid King Alvaro a visit before coming here. He wants me back in the White Palace, and I've agreed to stay. As much as I love the fresh air and freedom of the outskirts, there's no reason to be there if not for you and Lady Mari."

"Are you going to rejoin the Royal Regiment?" Akari asks. "Are you going to serve King Alvaro again?"

"Yes, I am," Salam confirms. "Even though the king has already assigned you a bodyguard, he has offered me the position if you will agree to having your current one replaced—which I do very much think is a good idea. I don't trust that double-crosser around you. I can take her place right away—"

"No!" Akari yelps, knowing full well that if Salam is by her side, she'll never be able to leave the White Palace to save Ty.

Realizing her perceived bluntness has probably left Salam a little hurt, she quickly tries to salvage the situation.

"It's not like that... I'd love you by my side, but Emeraude isn't all bad. In fact, I'm starting to like her," Akari lies through her teeth. "Besides, you've already done more than enough for both me and my mother." This time, the words are from the bottom of her heart.

"It was my duty to," Salam says with a sad shake of her head. "I'm so sorry about your mother. I miss her so much, and I know you miss her even more."

Akari nods slowly. "I miss her more than I even thought was possible..." Her voice quavers. At the sound of this, Kami leaps into her arms, as if to comfort her.

"Lady Mari will always have a special place in our hearts. I hope she's in a better place now, and I'm sure she's still watching over you," Salam says, stroking Kami. "Princess Akari, I buried your mother in Havenswill. It was one of Lady Mari's favorite places in the outskirts—and one of the few places where she, like you, could feel completely herself."

Akari looks at her with grateful eyes. "Thank you for everything, Salam."

"Well, I should thank Lady Mari. Do you remember this?" Salam holds apart her fur, revealing the long scar

Celestine left. "This happened during the Great Harvest, when I was fighting the Harvesters who were chasing both of you as you escaped Andelovia. I was on the brink of death in the then-unfamiliar Cheyvelenia when your mother found and healed me, saving my life with her gift. After the White Blaze, I decided to repay her by cutting off all communication with Andelovia and staying in the outskirts to protect the both of you."

"But I don't remember seeing you around until I joined the People's Protector..." Akari recalls.

"I knew it would be better for you and Lady Mari to have a quiet and fresh start in the outskirts, and I was afraid my bear hybreed self would attract too much unwanted attention, so I watched over the two of you from a distance. Even though I couldn't be right beside you, it still warmed my heart to have been able to see you grow up."

Akari gives a heartfelt smile. "My mother always kept to herself so much, but I'm glad she had a friend in you. You must have been her best and only friend in Cheyvelenia." *Just like Ty was to me.* She tears up at the thought, and in moments she's weeping softly.

Salam takes Akari in her arms, embracing her and Kami in a bear hug. "Your mother is very proud of you," she reassures her, her voice rough but soothing. Gradually the sobs subside, and Akari takes a deep, shuddering breath.

"You've always had compassion, Princess Akari," Salam continues. "A complement never chooses the wrong wielder."

"You knew? This whole time?" Akari's eyes grow wide in surprise.

Salam nods. "I could always see why you're the wielder of the Jewel of Compassion—even as a child."

"What do you mean by that?"

She releases Akari from the hug, answering, "Lady Mari knew the Jewel of Compassion was your complement since the premature first-sighting of your gift when you were six. Your first-sighting happened when you were so unusually young because you were already in possession of your complement—a royal regalia at that. It enhanced your gift and unleashed the true potential of your power."

Akari's jaw drops. "Are you saying I've been the wielder of the Jewel of Compassion since then? And my mother knew too? This whole time?" *Yet another secret I can never ask Mama about.*

"Yes. Lady Mari knew she had to hide this truth from the world," Salam explains, reading her thoughts. "That was why she hid the Jewel of Compassion from you as well. She was too afraid it would give Zatori one more reason to come after you."

And now, I am the one going to him, Akari thinks regretfully.

"Even if she didn't want to admit it, Lady Mari always knew you'd wield it well, and that it's always been your destiny." There's a slight pause before Salam adds, "This is why your mother kept the Jewel of Compassion and sold her complement after moving to the outskirts. Lady Mari always put you before herself."

Akari gasps, clutching the Jewel of Compassion in her hand. "My mother had a complement too?" She's never had the slightest inkling of its existence.

"Yes. How else do you think she created the White Blaze and saved both of your lives during the Great Harvest?"

Akari gasps again, finally understanding how her mother was able to achieve that feat. But there's still one thing she can't wrap her head around. "Why did my mother sell her complement?"

"So you could keep yours," Salam informs her. "When the two of you went to Cheyvelenia empty-handed, save for the two complements, she knew one of them would have to go to start your lives anew in the outskirts. When making the decision, she didn't hesitate for one moment. After Lady Mari started earning a living, she tried searching for it to buy it back, but she never managed to find it again."

Akari feels a pang of guilt. *Mama really made endless sacrifices for me.*

"Don't hold it against yourself," Salam urges. "Lady Mari kept this from you because she didn't want you to blame yourself. Besides, you did bring it back to her— twice, in fact. And I believe each time held a special meaning."

"I did? What was it?" Shock and curiosity simultaneously grip Akari.

"It's the silver moonstone ring you traveled back in time to give her, just in time for her to use it to conjure the White Blaze," Salam reveals. "And it's also the very ring you got for her after you joined the People's Protector."

Akari reels as she tracks the ring's journey—from Tinkler's to her, then to her mother. Mari had left it around Kami's neck when she died, and it had come back to Akari, only for her to drop it when she went back in time, presumably for her mother to find.

Akari doesn't need to ask how Salam knows all this. *I was best friends with Ty, and we didn't keep secrets from each other. It must have been the same for Mama and Salam. They just hid endless secrets from me instead. What else have I yet to uncover?*

♦

Ten years ago...

Zephy hurtled through the sky to escape from Zatori and the Harvesters. Just once, very early on in the flight, Mari and Akari looked down far behind them and saw a ring of blinding white light—the White Blaze—puncturing Moira Island with a deep dark hollow before it dilated and combusted, wiping out everything in its way.

"Mama, did you make that?" six-year-old Akari asked, her honey-colored eyes wide with awe.

As Mari shielded her gaze from the White Blaze, Akari noticed the silver moonstone ring on her mother's finger emitting a soft white glow. She was about to ask about it when Mari said, her voice firm, "There's nothing to see, Akari, my baby. I want you to forget everything that happened tonight."

Little Akari nodded obediently.

The rest of the flight from Moira Island back to the mainland was particularly quiet. Mari steered Zephy carefully while Akari nodded off, thoroughly worn out from the night's events.

Although Mari knew nothing of the outskirts, she was well aware that Zephy, a rare precious creature—not to mention a royal emblem—mustn't be seen here. She had him land in a meadow outside town before taking Akari into Cheyvelenia.

It was the early hours of the morning. All of Cheyvelenia, a town Mari didn't even know existed when they first arrived, was still sound asleep under a blanket of darkness. With Akari on her back, she wandered down a few streets before finally crumpling on the cobbled sidewalk. With trembling hands, Mari held her daughter close.

Their reality finally hit, and she wept silently. For the first time in Akari's life, she saw her mother shed tears. But six-year-old Akari was unable to grasp the severity of their circumstances.

Mari wasn't sure how long they'd stayed huddled up in the cold and dark, when she finally made up her mind to start a new life with her daughter in Cheyvelenia—the farthest place she knew from the capital—and never return.

But she quickly realized they had arrived with nothing to their names. Even the satchel she'd packed had fallen from Zephy during their escape, plunging from the sky. Mari glanced at the ring on her finger, then at the necklace around Akari's neck. One of them would have to go to feed and house them. Without the slightest hesitation, she decided which would be sold.

Even then, Mari knew that they would not have a grand home to live in, fine cuisines to feast upon, lavish clothing to put on, not to mention dutiful servants to cater to their every need. *But at least Akari will be safe here.* And this, to Mari, was more important than anything else in the world.

"Akari, my baby, it'll be just us from now on," she whispered.

"We'll be together forever, Mama." Akari's words were laced with innocence.

Mari nodded, wanting to believe this and determined to protect her. "I'll do everything I can to keep you safe."

"I'll protect you too, Mama. With my own hands, with my gift, with my everything..." a drowsy Akari replied with pure naivety.

Mari squeezed her tightly in her arms.

"I heart you with all my love, Mama," Akari declared before falling asleep in her mother's lap.

"I heart you with all my love too, Akari, my baby," Mari replied as she gazed lovingly at her daughter, gently caressing her hair.

At daybreak, Mari woke Akari. With her sleepy daughter in tow, she stepped into Tinkler's Oddities and Antiquities, which happened to be right across the street.

After casting the silver moonstone ring one last look, Mari slid it off her finger and held it out to the storekeeper. "How much will this fetch? Can you give me a good price for it?"

She wasn't sure if it was because it was so early in the morning, but Mr. Tinkler seemed to have barely woken from his slumber. He took the ring clumsily, inspecting it with squinting eyes. "This ring is special, but it's not worth a lot—"

Something else caught his eye, immediately rousing him from his sleep. "But *that* would get you a very good price," he said, pointing to the Jewel of Compassion hanging from little Akari's neck.

A flustered Mari hastily tucked it back under Akari's clothes. "We're not selling that. It's a birthday present she received from her father just weeks ago."

"Of course. Your little girl should keep it," Mr. Tinkler assented. "What's her name?"

"Akari... Miyahara..." It was from this moment that Akari began taking her mother's last name.

"Akari Miyahara... She's special. I like her. I'll give you a good price for your ring. How does twenty-two sound?" he offered.

"Yes, we'll take twenty-two silvers," Mari said, feeling thankful that the storekeeper had given her a fair price despite her obvious desperation.

"I meant twenty-two golds," Mr. Tinkler corrected.

Mari hesitated, knowing full well this was an unusually good price. But she also knew she was no longer in the position to refuse any generosity, especially for Akari's sake. "Yes, we'll take it! Thank you so much. We'll forever be grateful."

Mr. Tinkler put the gold nuggets in Mari's hand before casually waving her away. She looked down at the money, still doused in a state of surrealness. When she finally glanced back up, the storekeeper had already drifted back into a deep slumber.

29. Sacrifice

As soon as Salam leaves the bedchamber, Akari begins preparing for her solo rescue mission. She gathers some essentials, sharpens her kris, puts on her armor, and then heads out to the balcony. Tension coils within Akari as she paces about, anxiously awaiting Zephy's arrival.

The zephanerix flies in shortly after the sun sets, with Emeraude perched atop his back. They make a smooth landing on the balcony, and she nimbly dismounts.

"We don't have time for formalities," Akari says, stopping her bodyguard from dropping to one knee. She urgently strokes Zephy's beak to reassure him, knowing full well that he can feel her urgency.

"Princess Akari, are you sure about this?" Emeraude asks, her hesitation a stark contrast from her usual nonchalance.

"Yes, I have to go. Ty's my best friend," she maintains without so much as glancing her way, immediately proceeding to check that the bridle and saddle are secure.

Emeraude lets out a muted sigh. "I know you and Tyler Kane are best friends who'd risk your lives for each other. But I don't understand why both of you did the same for me. I mean nothing to either of you. Why did he save me from the Harvesters? And why did you defend me from Salam?"

Akari looks up and shrugs. "I guess neither of us can bear seeing anyone around us get hurt."

"Now I can see why the two of you are best friends. You're both kind-hearted fools," Emeraude remarks exasperatedly. "I'm only going to say this once, so will you please listen to me? Princess Akari, don't go to Tyler Kane. It's too dangerous." Her typical cold hard glance is replaced by a vulnerable gaze.

Akari's heart softens, but she refuses to let herself be won over. "Why say this when you already know you can't change my mind?"

Emeraude shakes her head in resignation and pulls out an archivian milk fang hanging from a silver chain. "In that case, take this."

Akari instantly recognizes it as the one she saw while searching Emeraude's room. It catches the moonlight beautifully, reflecting a delicate sheen.

"Isn't this for King Alvaro? Or Queen Jocelin? Or Queen Dowager Arinya?" she asks, puzzled.

"No, it's mine. I see you know what it is. Take it for good luck," Emeraude says with a small, cryptic smile.

"Why are you giving this to me?" Such a thoughtful, extravagant gesture leaves her suspicious.

"I'm not giving it to you. I'm *lending* it to you," Emeraude clarifies. "You'll have to return it to me when you get back."

"No, it's fine," Akari declines, not wanting to owe any favors. "I don't need—"

"Please, I insist." Emeraude pushes it at her, her tone firm.

"Alright, thank you. I'll bring it back to you." Akari gratefully accepts the archivian milk fang, fastening its chain around her neck. "Please send my regards to Yong. Tell him this is entirely my idea and not to be mad at you for covering up for me."

"Don't worry, Princess Akari. I'll do that. But I have no doubt he'll still be furious. And he should be... since I'm your bodyguard, and I'm still letting—even helping—you go..."

"Thank you, Emeraude," Akari says in a soft voice.

"Good luck, Princess Akari," Emeraude replies with a bow.

Just as Akari is about to turn to Zephy, Kami darts up to her. She whines incessantly, tugging on her clothes with her teeth, as though she can sense the forthcoming danger.

Akari scoops Kami in her arms and strokes her, then plants a quick kiss on her forehead. "I'll be back as soon as I can. Be safe while I'm gone, alright?"

Kami quietens and gazes into her eyes with newfound calmness, as though she's able to understand her. Akari hands her to Emeraude, saying, "Please look after Kami for me while I'm gone."

"Yes, Princess Akari. She'll be safe with me," her bodyguard reassures her.

With no time to waste, Akari leaps onto Zephy's back, reins clutched tightly in her hands. With a kick of her legs, they take off into the inky night sky.

The full moon shines ominously above the Kingdom of Xylon. As they fly northward, Akari glances down at the magnificent White Palace and the sprawling, bustling city of Andelovia. Her flight reminds her of the one a decade ago, when she and her mother fled the capital for the outskirts—except this time, she is alone.

Previously, Akari's stubborn determination to rescue Ty had overshadowed her fear of the immense danger. But now, as she heads for the Hollow, the gravity of the situation finally begins to sink in.

Akari strokes Zephy's champagne-gold feathers, their lustrous sheen gleaming brilliantly under the moonlight. He caws softly, but it's her own unease she seeks to quell. Then, with the same shaky hand, she grips the Jewel of Compassion to steady herself as they soar into the unknown.

♦

With little rest, Akari flies for seven grueling days from Andelovia, over the Great Divide, and across the outskirts. After what feels like an impossibly long journey, she finally leaves the mainland of Xylon behind, soaring over the vast Telos Ocean, its once-frozen waters now churned into restless gray-green waves that stretch endlessly toward the horizon. At last, she catches sight of the Hollow, a gaping abyss where the ocean seems to have collapsed into itself, the only lingering trace of Moira Island.

Although Akari has glimpsed it from afar countless times while growing up in Cheyvelenia, she has never seen the Hollow up close. Now, as Zephy hovers directly above, the sheer enormity of the desolate void strikes her.

Although spring has arrived, the colossal icicles of the perpetually frozen Hollow Falls remain unmelted. The mid-afternoon sun slants across the Hollow's icy rim, casting light and shadow about its rugged edges, while the rest of the pit remains doused in darkness. As Akari peers into the black nothingness below, she is overwhelmed by a crippling fear that the Hollow will devour her and never let her emerge again.

She steels herself with a measured breath before steering Zephy into a descent. The bottom is too deep—too dark—to be visible. As they drop a hundred feet or so, her eyes slowly adjust, revealing vague glimpses of the Hollow's interior.

The sheer walls of ice plunge downward for what feels like an eternity, their immense depth rivaling the towering heights of the Great Divide. Caves riddle the frozen expanse in every direction, yawning maws carved into the frostbitten stone, eerily reminiscent of the dragon pit where she once faced death at Queen Jocelin's command. The same putrid stench of carrion clings to the dank air. The deeper they dive, the more pungent the odor, and the more the cold gnaws at her skin. Eventually, they hit the bottom.

Akari hops off Zephy's back, kicking something on the ground as she lands. She squints in the dim light—and recoils. A dismembered body sprawls before her, chunks of decaying flesh dangling from its bones. Her breath catches as she sweeps a frantic glance around the pit. Scattered across the ground are countless skeletons, most of them mangled and mutilated. A chill slithers down her spine. *Who did they belong to? What happened here—*

Zephy lets out a sharp warning caw, and Akari's head snaps up. The caves around her stir with movement. Over a hundred Harvesters, with their signature iron archivian masks and sweeping black cloaks, stream to the edges of the caves, lingering on the shadowy periphery of the pit.

Among them are two glaringly distinctive figures—Celestine, with her metallic talons and spiky hair, and Philippe, with his dwarfish stature and bald head.

Zatori is the last to appear, emerging with an unhurried gait from a cave above all the Harvesters. Then, from a height which would kill any normal human, he leaps lithely to the bottom of the pit, landing deftly before Akari. For a moment, the shifting sunlight illuminates his pale gaunt face, accentuating his haunting angular features.

"All hail Sire Zatori!" An eerie wave of salutations echoes throughout the Hollow.

Akari's pulse pounds in her ears. She turns a full circle, taking in her enemies, until she meets Zatori's sinister, sunken black left eye and white right eye. Even after a decade, they never fail to unnerve her. She wrenches her gaze away, scanning fervently for Ty. But he's nowhere to be seen.

Akari wheels back around toward Zatori. "Where is Ty?" she demands, trying not to let her fear show. *Did something happen to him? Is he still alive?*

A cold, lifeless laugh escapes Zatori. "What's the rush, little deflector?" he asks with a monotonous drawl. "It's been ten years since we met here. You remember Moira Island, don't you? It once laid right above us before your mother destroyed it with the White Blaze, along with so many of us on it. Besides me, not many Harvesters managed to make it out alive.

"Weak and low in numbers, we were forced into hiding. Who would have expected us to lie low and regroup at the very place we disappeared? For the next ten years, we made a hideout of the Hollow and rebuilt our strength and numbers—with the exception of Celestine, who kept an eye on you and your mother in Cheyvelenia."

Akari peers around once more, still reeling in disbelief that the Hollow is where they've been hiding this whole time.

"Who were all these people?" she asks nervously of the skeletons around them.

"Curious explorers who should never have ventured here," Zatori answers casually.

"Did you kill them?" Akari's eyes are stricken with horror.

"Yes, we did. Every single one," Zatori admits blithely, his thin lips curving into a smirk. "A pity they never lived to tell the tale of what became of the Hollow. You'd be amazed by what they saw in their final moments."

She shoots him a disgusted look, although it's no longer new to her how easily he and the Harvesters take innocent lives.

"Your expression suggests you disapprove," Zatori remarks. "But you, too, have learned to take lives, haven't you? Or at least tried to?"

Akari hangs her head in silent admission. *At least I feel guilty about it... But does this make us so different?*

"So much has changed during this time, hasn't it, little deflector? Or should I observe proper etiquette and say, Princess Akari?" Zatori taunts her with an unsettling smile, placing his right hand over his heart and bowing histrionically.

The hairs on her body stand on end as she wonders how he has learned of this. But she maintains her composure, making sure to keep a neutral expression as she says, "Let's not waste time. I've brought the Jewel of Compassion. I'll give it to you, and in return, you'll have to let Ty go."

"Princess Akari, the deflector and the wielder of the Jewel of Compassion..." Zatori muses, intentionally ignoring her request. "Since we met a decade ago, I've always wondered why your first-sighting was so premature. It's only of late I've finally come to realize that it was because you wield a royal regalia."

"I said, where is Ty?" Akari presses, paying no attention to his ramblings.

Zatori glances up at a cave that's as high as the one he leaped from, raising his hand as though to beckon something from within. At first, Akari sees only a swirling mist, until Ty emerges head-first.

Paralyzed in a flurry of frost, he floats out of the cave and into the center of the Hollow, hovering about a hundred feet above the ground. His frozen body hangs suspended in the air, his limbs stiff at his sides, head tilted backward, eyes squeezed shut. The frost enveloping him reflects the scant sunlight that barely reaches the pit, lending him an eerie, ethereal glow. There's no telling if he's dead or alive.

"Ty!" Akari gasps, breath catching in her throat. Horror shadows her eyes, and she's seized with a chilling dread that he could already be gone.

After a while, Zatori lowers Ty to the bottom of the pit, where he hovers a few feet above the ground.

"Ty! Are you alright?" Akari rushes forward impetuously. But before she can reach him, a brutish Harvester knocks her over, sending her crashing face-first onto a jagged shard of ice.

Warm blood spills from her lip, staining her cheek red. She picks herself up, wipes the blood away, and deflects the wound back onto the same Harvester. Beneath his iron mask, fresh blood flows from his jaw, trickling down his neck.

Zatori dismisses the Harvester with a wave, then claps his hands patronizingly. "You *have* become quite a fighter, haven't you?"

"What have you done to Ty?" Akari demands furiously.

"Don't you worry about your little friend. He's just resting," Zatori informs her. "He was making such a ruckus, refusing to shut up about how I harvested his father's gift and made his mother go mad. So, we made him comfortable—and quiet—while waiting for you. But before that, Celestine had some fun with him. It seems the two of them had some old scores to settle."

Horror flashes through Akari as she bounds toward Ty again. She stops before him, observing the frost with caution. *One wrong move and I'll be frozen in an interminable slumber, just like he is.*

Akari deliberates, then takes the archivian milk fang and presses it against her heart—a move she read about in one of her mother's books on mythical medicine—and gingerly reaches for Ty with her other hand. When she touches the frost, the frigid cold eating into her bones is immediately neutralized by the surging warmth from the fang that radiates through her body.

Much to the shock and chagrin of the Harvesters, the frost engulfing him begins to dissipate. They exchange anxious glances, their baffled whispers rippling through the Hollow. "This is impossible! How did she do that? She should have been frozen!"

When the frost has disappeared entirely, Ty's limp, lanky body drops to the ground, still unconscious. Akari crouches worriedly by his side. The wounds on his neck and below his left collarbone from their previous fight have only healed partially, and more have since been added. Every inch of visible skin on both his forearms, exposed by his rolled-up sleeves, is covered with red splotchy burns. Her stomach rolls as Celestine's scorched cookies spring to mind.

Akari winces. She shakes Ty, only to find his body still colder than ice. "Ty... wake up! It's me, Akari... Can you hear me?" But he doesn't give even the slightest response, remaining soundly in paralysis.

Fear grips Akari at the thought that she's arrived too late. "Ty... wake up... Please wake up! You can't leave me behind!" She removes the necklace from her neck and places it around his, tucking the archivian milk fang under his clothes so it rests directly over his faintly beating heart. *Please let it warm him like it did me...*

More whispers break out around her. "Where did she get that? How does she know about it?"

But Akari's attention is trained solely on Ty. After what seems like an eternity, he begins to stir. "Ty!" she yelps anxiously, releasing a small sigh of relief.

Only his ocean blue eyes, now adorned with frosty lashes, seem vaguely capable of movement. He opens and closes them languidly, as if he's just been roused from a long, deep hibernation. Finally, they focus, first locking onto Akari's worried face before drifting to the Harvesters surrounding them. When his gaze finally lands on Zatori's expressionless face, Ty's eyes widen in horror.

"A... Aka... Akari..." He struggles to speak, white plumes billowing from his mouth as he expends every ounce of energy to muster a hoarse, urgent whisper. "Run!"

Akari stares blankly at him, frozen by his sheer desperation.

"It's a little too late for that, isn't it?" Zatori muses in a quiet voice.

Ty's eyes dart fearfully between them. "You shouldn't have come! It's a trap! You need to get out of here!" he sputters, his teeth still chattering. "Zatori isn't just after your royal regalia—he wants *you*!"

Akari shakes her head in stubborn denial despite the fresh wave of panic rippling through her. "No! I've brought the Jewel of Compassion in exchange for you. I'm going to get us both out of here."

"I can't move... I can't feel a thing..." Ty's strained voice is drowned out by Zatori's smug words.

"Unfortunately, your nullus friend is right. Surely you didn't think that the interpretation of the *Prophecy of a New Realm* is as simple as reuniting the three royal regalia, did you? That might have kept a king on the throne, but it's certainly not even close to being adequate for establishing a new realm—much less any sort of peace," he informs her.

How does he know about the prophecy? Akari grips the Jewel of Compassion for strength, but it doesn't do much. *Everyone else knows more about the bigger picture than I do*, she thinks. *I really am just a puppet...*

"What good is a complement without its wielder? What good is the Jewel of Compassion without you, my little deflector? It's you I really want—even more than before! It's the three wielders of the royal regalia I seek to reunite." Zatori lays his intention bare, his black left eye and white right eye gleaming with delight. "And *this* is the true interpretation of the *Prophecy of a New Realm*!"

Akari trembles at the revelation. *Compassion, wisdom, and courage—it's the three wielders, aside from their royal regalia, who need to be reunited for the peace of a new realm!* When she finally finds her voice again, she whispers, "Is this why you got me to come to the Hollow today? So you can begin fulfilling the prophecy?"

"Yes, my little deflector. And you've so kindly delivered yourself to me! Did you really think I had you come personally just to hand me your royal regalia?" Zatori laughs mockingly. "If I hadn't passed along that message, there's no other way you would be here today, with the Jewel of Compassion. But think about it, little deflector. You should be thanking me for giving you what you so desperately wanted—some hope of rescuing your little friend."

Akari's fear morphs into fury—not at Zatori, but at herself—for being so naive as to believe him, for letting him use her hope against her. She draws her kris and steps in front of Ty protectively. "Stay away from us, you monster!"

"Monster or otherwise, I believe I was bestowed my gift of harvesting for a reason. I'm the only one in this entire kingdom who can harvest and reunite the gifts of the three wielders of the royal regalia," Zatori declares, his eyes glinting. "And when I've done that, I'll gain unimaginable powers and seize the throne from your father. After all, he isn't a very good king. You thought the same too, didn't you, Princess Akari?"

"I thought those Harvesters were lying when they told me you're a princess..." Ty breathes in disbelief. "Is it really true... that you're King Alvaro's daughter?" He seems repelled by the fact—possibly, even her.

"I don't lie unless I absolutely have to, unlike your friends in the People's Protector," Zatori says, clearly enjoying taking his time. "Or have they now become your enemy as well?"

"You won't get anywhere near my father or the throne. The Royal Regiment will destroy you and your Harvesters before you get close," Akari warns shakily.

"I see you've swapped your friends in the People's Protector for those in the Royal Regiment..." Zatori reveals a knowing smile. "Regardless, you did manage to get very close, didn't you, Princess Akari? Now, don't you see, I'm really doing you and your father a favor. Neither of you truly desires the throne."

Akari continues glaring at him, but she's at a loss for words.

"After all, weren't you so willing to trade the Jewel of Compassion for your little friend's safety?" he adds. "Just as your father was so willing to trade the *Register of the Gifteds* for your mother's safety?"

"You treacherous monster! You broke your pact and still went after my mother!" Akari is boiling with anger. She welcomes it as it burns away her panic, even if only temporarily.

Zatori doesn't say a word, his thin lips still curled into a half-smirk.

"I'll never let you harvest my gift. I'll never see it turned against innocents," she declares stubbornly.

He laughs. "You know, Princess Akari, your mother said this a decade ago somewhere right around here. And look where she ended up."

"You murderer!" Akari feels like she's about to split apart from the intensity of the rage that's now fired up inside her. *I'll avenge you, Mama! I'm not sure how, but I'll find a way.*

"I may be a murderer, but as I told you the last time we met—I didn't kill your mother," Zatori claims with an incendiary earnestness, relishing the opportunity to toy with her. "*You* did."

Akari isn't sure if it's the calmness or pity on Zatori's face, but something tells her he's speaking the truth. But she still shakes her head in denial, far too afraid of entertaining this alternative. "That's not true! You're lying!" Even with her teeth clenched, she can barely keep her voice even.

"I've already told you. I don't lie unless I absolutely have to. And there's no need for that now," Zatori drawls as a chilling smile spreads across his face. "Did you even know your mother? The secrets she kept? Her life besides you?" he questions, goading her.

His words hit a raw nerve, rendering her silent. *Mama, I know you wanted to protect me, but I was ready to know these things... And I wish I got to learn them from you instead...*

"Did you even know her true gift? And her gift to you?" Zatori presses, his tone taunting.

"The gift of healing?" Akari asks, although she has a hunch there's more to the questions.

"That's only a part of it. Lady Mari's gift wasn't just the ability to heal, but also to manipulate energy—the energy of life itself," Zatori divulges. "By choosing to use her gift only for healing, your mother was severely underutilizing it. Her gift was so much more useful than it seemed, and I could've done so much more with it. This is why gifts are so fascinating. The part that can be perceived is only a scratch on the surface. No one else ever really knows how much potential lies beneath, until a complement unearths it—or I harvest it."

"So, what was my mother's gift to me?" Akari dreads the answer, but she can't stand being kept in the dark any longer.

"When I almost harvested your mother's gift ten years ago, she thought she was faced with death and made the ultimate decision to transfer her remaining life to you," Zatori informs her with a crooked smirk, pausing to let the full effect of his words sink in. "However, it was her complement—which I knew nothing of back then—that caused an interruption and saved her from death. This produced a huge burst of energy—the White Blaze—that destroyed the very island that once lay above us and gave you both a chance to escape.

"Even so, a good portion of your mother's life was transferred to you. Over the next ten years, Lady Mari lived on the remaining energy of life left in her until it ran out. She breathed her last just as I arrived. I didn't harvest her gift, nor did I kill her. She died because of you, Princess Akari. The rest of her life now lives within you. And when I harvest your gift, all of that will become mine as well."

Mari's voice resounds in Akari's mind. *I don't feel well... I don't have much time left...* The words hit

Akari, making her stagger. She sways, thoroughly debilitated by shock and devastation. Akari takes heaving gasps as her chest constricts, her mind crumbling into pandemonium. *Was I really the one who caused Mama's death? Was it my fault her life ended prematurely? And now, Zatori is going to harvest what she gave me...*

"This is the truth you have been denied the past decade," Zatori confirms. "I'm sure your mother's bear bodyguard knows of all this too."

"Salam... she knew?" Akari whispers, barely able to stand.

"Of course she did. She knows more about Lady Mari than you do—the parts your mother hid from the world, even the parts she hid from you," he replies. "Your dear mother would never allow her precious daughter to know the truth or blame herself. Lady Mari was always protecting you, shielding you, and coddling you, until she couldn't anymore. How noble! A mother's love truly knows no bounds! Especially seeing that she willingly made the ultimate sacrifice of life itself... But don't you feel repulsed by yourself? By the fact that you caused the death of the life that sustains you? *You* are your mother's murderer."

Akari hangs her head in despondent silence, looking down at herself in utter disgust. *This is all my fault... I should be the one dead... Mama... she didn't have to die...* As the words she spoke while kneeling by Mari's body come to mind, Akari realizes there is more truth to them than she realized. *Is Mama's life really flowing through me this very moment? Now that I know, how can I stand living with myself?*

"Don't listen to him, Akari!" Ty cries shakily. The truth he's pieced together while listening to their exchange leaves him in utter disbelief.

But Akari twists around, casting him a sad look, and he falls silent.

"Don't worry, Princess Akari. I'll relieve you from all of this very soon," Zatori continues with a drawl. "After I have harvested your gift, I'll lay you to rest for eternity. You do know how the connection between a wielder and their complement is severed, right? For me to possess your gift and complement, you'll have to die."

Akari knows her prospects of making it out alive are dwindling before her eyes. *But even if I can't save myself, I have to get Ty out.* She pushes back against her despair, hoping she can stave it off for just long enough.

By now, the archivian milk fang appears to have warmed Ty and dissipated some of the frost within him. The feeble wiggle of his fingers jolts Akari back to reality.

She rushes back to his side, taking his freezing hands in hers to warm them. "Ty, are you feeling better? Are you any warmer?"

"Yes, yes, I'm fine..." he says, retracting his hands from Akari's. He attempts to prop himself up, but his elbows slip from under him, and the base of his skull hits the ground with a dull thud.

"Ty!" she yelps, quickly supporting him as he tries to sit up again, this time successfully.

"I told you I was fine," Ty insists, brushing her away brusquely.

Akari's chest tightens when her concern is met with coldness, never having seen him act this way with her before. *Does being King Alvaro's daughter really change who I am?* A sigh escapes her lips. While keeping her distance, Akari watches on quietly as Ty gradually regains his mobility.

"It's astounding how much such a tiny fang can do, isn't it? It brought your little friend back from the brink of death," Zatori muses. "I'm impressed that you know of its existence and uses. Your healer mother must have taught you well. Not many even know archivians exist, or that they used to rule this kingdom. Being blessed with the abundance of gifts, they are, without a doubt, the greatest beings to have graced the earth."

Akari looks from Zatori to the masked Harvesters, confused by his obsession with archivians.

"Well, I digress," he continues as he turns to Ty. "You've regained consciousness at the right time, nullus boy. Now, you can watch your little deflector friend have her gift harvested and forever live with the guilt of her sacrifice. Unless you'd prefer to join her in death as well..."

"Don't you dare touch her!" Ty yells. Despite his steeliness toward Akari, he scrambles to his feet to defend her. But his knees shake beneath him.

Akari steps in front of him, kris raised, shielding him from Zatori and the Harvesters.

"Get her!" Zatori's command shudders the Hollow. "Capture the deflector!"

Scores of Harvesters spring from the edges of the caves to the bottom of the pit as effortlessly and inhumanly as Zatori did. They draw their weapons and charge, but Akari fends them off, deflecting any newly inflicted wounds right back onto them.

Celestine lunges with her ten outstretched metallic talons. But before she can come close, Akari deflects all of Ty's wounds—both old and new—back onto her.

Celestine staggers backward, but quickly steadies herself. Even as blood and pus ooze from the blistering burns on her forearms, she points to the partially healed wound below her left collarbone. "Do you know I missed his heart on purpose, to keep him alive so Sire Zatori could get to you? I could easily have killed him back then." She unleashes a grating laugh. "And look, here you are now!"

"Now, I see Ty has always been right about you. You are a nasty one," Akari fires back, bounding toward Celestine, her kris angled for attack. "I'll have to make sure not to miss your heart this time!"

Celestine blocks blow after blow, but Akari continues striking relentlessly, slicing off two talons before aiming her kris directly at Celestine's heart. She's about to go for the kill when a quiet voice says from behind her, "Make another move, and your best friend dies."

Akari wheels around to meet a morbid smile peeking through Philippe's mask. He has Ty's arms twisted into submission, his spear pressed against his throat.

"Destroy Celestine! And Zatori!" Ty hollers. "Don't listen—" Philippe deals him a vicious kick to the back of his knees, forcing him to drop to a kneel, bringing them to similar heights.

"The deflector is the one who's going to be destroyed today!" Celestine chimes, shooting a bolt of violet lightning at Akari's kris. It conducts electricity down its wavy blade, through its hilt, to her hand.

Akari's muscles seize, her lips drawing a sharp gasp. Celestine pounces, digging her metallic talons into her shoulders, sending rapid waves of electric shock coursing through her body. Akari flails uncontrollably, her limbs jerking in spasms as her kris slips from her grip.

"This is going to be the end of you!" Celestine declares in her usual high-pitched voice, cracking a malicious laugh as she drags Akari before Zatori. "I've got the deflector for you, my sire." She gives a submissive bow.

Zatori waves Celestine to release her. With a monotonous drawl, he says, "Let's make a pact, shall we? Everything will be smoother if you let me harvest your gift. So, give me what I want, and I'll let the nullus boy go."

"What if you're lying? What if you break the pact again?" Akari spits as the tremors in her limbs ebb. "Like how you tried to harvest my mother's gift despite promising my father you wouldn't?"

"I broke that pact because your mother possessed a gift I wanted dearly, whereas your nullus friend has nothing to offer me," Zatori says. "I've no need to lie now, and I've no reason to break this pact with you."

Akari quietly contemplates his words, her resolve to save Ty unwavering—even at the expense of her own life. And making a pact with Zatori seems like the only way out. *Ty sacrificed himself for me. It's time to return the favor.*

"Alright," she says, an unexpected lightness filling her heart. "I'll let you have what you want, and in return, you'll have to promise to let Ty go."

Zatori gives a triumphant smirk followed by a curt nod. "I promise." He steps in front of Akari, bending down such that his face is just inches from hers, coming uncomfortably close. His black left eye and white right eye bore into her, leaving her frozen in desolate silence.

Zatori's peculiar ancient scent—a musky mix of frost and dust—hits Akari, and her nose wrinkles. In turn, he takes a whiff of her, like a predator would its prey before devouring it. "I've been waiting a decade too long for this moment. After all this time, I'm finally a step closer to the throne." He flashes a chilling smile before placing an icy hand on her face.

The frigid cold sears Akari's skin, and she unleashes a delirious scream. She'd wanted to hold it in, to deny Zatori the satisfaction of seeing her suffer, but she can't seem to help herself. But, as time seems to slow, the cold numbs Akari's mind and body, relieving her of pain. She stops screaming. An unnatural calmness washes over her, as though she's come to accept her end.

"No! Stop that! Let her go!" Ty's fervent pleading in the background grows distant. She wants to comfort him, to tell him not to worry, but she's lost all ability to do so.

With every passing moment, Akari feels more of her gift—alongside her soul and life—being sucked out of her. Eventually, she loses the last ounce of strength, succumbing completely. Akari begins hovering off the ground, arching backward. The Jewel of Compassion dangles from one side of her neck, emanating a warm red glow that Zatori basks in.

The last things she sees are the shifting sun and passing clouds, framed by the glistening, rugged rim of the Hollow. Her senses begin slipping away, until she finds herself plunged into a realm of darkness.

As death nears, her mother appears before her, alive and well. *Mama!*

Mari looks rejuvenated and well rested, as though she hasn't had to worry in a very long time. Her dark, almond eyes gaze fondly at Akari as she reaches toward her daughter for an embrace. Akari is overwhelmed with an intense, instinctual urge to run into her mother's arms, but finds herself incapable of movement. Longing and grief overcome her as she watches Mari from afar. *Mama, I miss you so, so much...*

Akari feels the weight of the Jewel of Compassion, a reminder of the price her mother had to pay for it to be in her possession—and for her to be alive. Guilt eats at her for handing herself over so easily. But just as Mari had given up her complement—and her life—Akari is now doing the same for Ty. Even as her heart twinges wistfully, she takes solace in the thought that she is, without a doubt, her mother's daughter as well.

Dying in place of Ty has to be a death of some worth at least. And hopefully, it might redeem me from the fact that I'm the cause of your death, Mama. After all, when I die, I'll get to be with you again. I know you wouldn't approve, but I think you'd understand. Without questioning or reproving, Mari simply offers an empathetic smile.

This is when Akari sees him, standing casually with his arms crossed in front of him. *Yong!*

Yong's dark, crescent-moon eyes beam at her, laden with affection. She has no idea how long he's been there for, and why she hasn't noticed him earlier. *Will you remember me when I'm gone? Will you miss me?* In the face of death, Akari asks questions she has never dared to before. *I know I'll always remember you and I'll always miss you.*

But from the start, we were never meant to be... I'm the daughter of King Alvaro and Lady Mari; you were taken in by Queen Jocelin. I grew up in the outskirts; you in the capital. I'm a princess; you're a guard. Although we crossed paths as children, we were too quickly pulled apart. Fate has never been on our side.

This time, I must finally let you go. Goodbye, Yong. I'm thankful for everything you've done for me. I'm sorry I couldn't keep my promise of not putting myself in peril again. I'm sorry I never finished repaying you for all the times you saved me. And most of all, I'm sorry I didn't have the courage to tell you that I love you—

"Akari!" Amidst her visions, she hears a familiar, deep, velvety voice calling out to her.

Akari jolts to a start. She looks at Yong, puzzled. But his smiling lips haven't moved.

She suddenly realizes it isn't the Yong from her vision calling out to her. It's the *real* one—the one she once played hide-and-seek with, parted ways with, reunited with, and fell in love with...

30. Intervention

Yong and Emeraude, alongside eighty other Royal Regiment guards, briefly stop their nequilouses on the jagged, icy edge of the Hollow. The turbulent Telos Ocean rages behind them. During the entire journey from the capital to the Hollow, Yong has been exceptionally withdrawn, not speaking any more than he needs to.

"You can be honest with me, Yong," Emeraude finally plucks up the courage to say. "You wouldn't be this mad at me for failing my duty as a bodyguard if the royal I was guarding wasn't Princess Akari." After all, there's no telling if any of them will still be alive after the rescue mission.

"Akari didn't just slip out from under your watch, Emeraude. You let her—*helped* her—go!" Yong seethes, his voice quavering despite his effort to steady it. "Didn't you know you could be sending Akari to her death? And that her death would have meant yours as well? King Alvaro was so mad at you, and he didn't even know you helped her escape!"

"I could have sworn you were even madder at me than he was..." Emeraude mutters under her breath.

Yong shoots her an icy stare.

"You know Princess Akari well... *too* well..." Emeraude continues. "You know she'd have found a way to go, even without me. Besides, you don't have to pretend you care about me as well."

He takes a sharp inhale. "I do care about you..." Yong treads carefully, well aware of the feelings she's been harboring for him. "We've been friends since the first day you joined the Royal Regiment. Of course I care about you."

But not the way I want you to... Although Emeraude has always known she'll only ever be a friend to Yong, his words still feel like daggers stabbing at her heart.

But she doesn't let it show. She's long been good at hiding her pain. "You know, you've changed since our mission to the outskirts," she remarks. "You never used to let your emotions get to you."

Yong glances at Emeraude, pondering her words. "I know... Of late, I've even come to surprise myself at times..." he admits quietly. He has no doubt about what—or who—caused this change. "But, you know, you've changed since our mission to the outskirts as well."

Without so much as a pause for consideration, she shakes her head vehemently. "No, I haven't. I have no reason to."

He shrugs. "Maybe you just haven't realized it yet."

"No one can change me like that," Emeraude says dismissively. "No one ever will."

"Someone will, Emeraude, as soon as you open your heart," Yong replies.

She remains silent, not for a moment believing his words.

"Also, we're on a mission now," he continues. "You know you can't address me by name."

"You call Princess Akari by name all the time," Emeraude points out with a tiny smirk.

Between embarrassment and exasperation, Yong struggles to find words. "Are you... are you trying to be the death of me?"

"I'm just stating the truth," she says matter-of-factly. "I know what Princess Akari means to you—and you to her. And I also know what it means for you both in the White Palace. Haven't you already seen how it ended with her parents?"

He releases a long sigh. "I won't let that happen to us."

"I hope you're right..." Emeraude's tone is earnest.

A short-lived silence lingers between them before Yong turns his attention back to the mission. "Emeraude, when we're in the Hollow, get Tyler Kane."

"Why bother?" she asks, perplexed. "King Alvaro sent us here solely to save Princess Akari."

"She won't leave the Hollow without him. And I know she'd want me to," Yong says plainly. "Don't ditch Tyler Kane this time. This is an order."

"*He* was the one who told me to go!" Emeraude explains, indignant, but adds, "Yes, *sir*," when he casts her a warning look.

"Emeraude..."

"Yes, sir?"

"Be careful." There's a softness in Yong's voice.

Emeraude feels a tug on her heartstrings as a strange mix of consolation and desolation overcomes her. But just as she always has, she shrugs it off. "Yes, sir."

"Let's make our way in!" Yong commands the rest of the Royal Regiment guards with a wave of his sword.

"Kill Zatori or any of the Harvesters if they stand in your way. But remember, our main purpose is to rescue Princess Akari."

"Yes, sir!" they reply in unison, and follow his lead into the Hollow.

♦

"What are *you* doing here?" Ty eyes Emeraude suspiciously, marking her Royal Regiment uniform, as she dismounts from her ginger-brown nequilous at the bottom of the Hollow, not far from him.

"I'm saving your ass, you fool!" Emeraude gives a quick snort before shooting him a patronizing smile. "But I wouldn't have bothered if I had a choice. Yong made me."

"That much I know," Ty snipes back. "You ran for your life during the last fight, which is precisely why I'm here now."

"I escaped then so I could save you now," she claims brazenly.

Ty rolls his eyes. "You escaped to save your own ass."

"*You* were the one who told me to go!" Emeraude reminds him, infuriated that she has to justify herself yet again.

"And you can go now if you want to!"

"I can't ditch you again! This time, I'm under strict orders not to!" she informs him. "Besides, it'll make me look bad..."

But Ty no longer pays her any attention. Emeraude tracks his eyes, which have shifted frantically to Akari.

Zatori still has her suspended midair as he harvests her gift. Emeraude then glances toward Yong, whose gaze barely veers from Akari, even as he battles the Harvesters alongside other Royal Regiment guards. All her life, she's never had her love reciprocated—not even by her own father. Disheartened, Emeraude forces herself to peel her eyes away.

Ty scampers in Akari's direction, but she steps in his way. "Princess Akari will be fine. Yong's got her," Emeraude insists. "Look, I brought you something." She whips out Ty's battle-ax from behind her, tossing it toward him. "I found it in the meadow after your last fight."

He stares at her in disbelief, clumsily catching the battle-ax right before it hits his face. "I never thought I'd see this again," he says, flexing his fingers on the haft. With fervent excitement, he swings it in the air, feeling its grip and weight. Although it's been a while since he last wielded it, Ty has no doubt this really is his beloved battle-ax.

"You didn't just run away then..." he realizes. This time, he gazes at Emeraude with newfound gratitude.

"You can thank me later—if you get out of here alive," she informs him with a snarky smirk. "And the archivian milk fang hanging from your neck—yes, it's expensive and it's mine. It's also the reason you're alive. You're welcome."

"Although your baby tooth is of some use, it's not like it can be eaten!" As an unexplained warmth permeates Ty, he wonders if it's the fang or something else entirely. Emeraude's cockiness, once repulsive, now amuses him, lifting the corners of his lips.

But his smile is wiped away when Philippe, accompanied by a herd of Harvesters, closes in on them. Ty and Emeraude quickly find themselves cornered and outnumbered.

Seeing no other way out, he steps forward to battle the Harvesters with every remaining ounce of strength in his semi-frozen body. But she grabs his hand and pulls him into an obscured cave behind them, leaving a trailing blaze of fiery red hair as they disappear into the darkness.

Ty catches a whiff of Emeraude's sweet Andelovian floral scent, now beguiling rather than revolting. He smiles faintly, his large, callused hand firmly clasping her small, callused one.

Even in darkness, Emeraude skillfully leads them through the maze of caves, navigating a series of narrow shafts he can barely make out, as though she knows them like the back of her hand. Her razor-sharp senses seem second only to Yong's.

Although they don't look behind, they know from the menacing footsteps and threatening yells on their tails that Philippe and the Harvesters are giving chase. Emeraude doesn't slow her pace even the least as they weave through endless tunnels. Soon, Ty is huffing and puffing, his stamina markedly compromised after being engulfed in frost.

"I can't keep up. You should go!" he pants dispiritedly, knowing full well he's holding Emeraude back.

"I won't allow you to die just yet. I still want my milk fang back," she insists, tightening her grip on his sweaty hand, refusing to let it slip out of hers. "Unless you hand it over now," she quips.

"No way," Ty replies breathlessly as he fights to keep pace. "I love expensive things."

In the dark, Emeraude's lips curl into a half-smile.

After what feels like an eternity, they finally appear to have lost the Harvesters. Their surroundings are quiet, and they seem to be alone. Emeraude eventually comes to a stop, allowing Ty some respite while she figures out their next step.

Before he can catch his breath, a big hairy Harvester with a spiked club emerges from a nearby shaft and barrels toward them. Ty and Emeraude immediately turn in the opposite direction, hoping to flee, only to find Philippe quietly waiting. This time, with both possible escape routes blocked, there's no way out besides a fight. Standing back to back, Ty and Emeraude raise their weapons and face their enemies.

"Who do you want to take?" he asks. "The small bald one, or the big hairy one?"

Emeraude snickers. "I'll take the small bald one." She fluidly shifts into a stance for battle.

"You always want the easy way out, don't you?" Ty remarks.

As Emeraude flashes a smirk, she makes the first move, lunging with her spear. Philippe fends off the attack with ease before returning a blow, which she just as effortlessly parries. Predisposed with small builds, both of them are incredibly nimble. They swiftly alternate between attacking and defending, their moves so quick they're barely discernible to the naked eye. The clashing of spears reverberates through the caves.

"You foolish girl! You never should have come here!" Philippe spits, fuming.

"Where should I be then? At home in my mother's arms?" Emeraude shoots back, rendering him speechless.

The other Harvester charges at Ty, taking heavy-handed swings at his head with a spiked club, each one aimed to kill. Traces of sparks fly with every move—a result of his gift. Ty struggles to defend himself, barely dodging the blows, his reflexes significantly slowed after the paralysis.

Despite this, he steals glances in Emeraude's direction, only to see that neither side has made any progress. But his brief lapse of attention allows his attacker in. A spike on the Harvester's club narrowly misses his eye, slashing his cheek instead. Ty howls in pain, the wound burning from the searing sparks, only to be promptly neutralized by the frost lingering in his body. Rebounding as rapidly as he can manage, he returns a strike, slicing the Harvester's arm.

"Mind your own fight!" Emeraude yells, tracking Ty's moves after a sweep that's forced Philippe to retreat momentarily. "You're in no position to worry about me!"

"I wasn't worrying," he denies vehemently. "If anything, it seems Philippe's giving you an easy time."

Emeraude rolls her eyes and snorts. "*You* won't stand a chance against him! You're a block of ice and you're much slower than your *usual* slow. Philippe would kill you in three moves—five on a good day! Besides, the frostbite helps soothe the burn, doesn't it?"

Ty realizes there's truth to her words. Whatever brute force the Harvester possesses, he lacks in speed and accuracy. His relatively weak gift of igniting sparks is of no threat to Ty in his semi-frozen state. *I guess I do have*

*a better chance against this Harvester than Philippe...
The Andelovian girl* is *saving my ass...*

As the four of them battle it out, their fights edge closer to each other's, almost entangling. Amidst the chaos, the big hairy Harvester seizes the opportunity to make a lunge for Emeraude. Thoroughly focused on the fight with Philippe, she doesn't realize the impending danger behind her.

The Harvester swings his spiked club at her head, but Ty hurls his battle-ax, striking him squarely from behind when he's inches from smashing her skull. The weapon cleaves through his back and severs his spine. He collapses instantly, dead.

Emeraude twists toward the muffled crash to see the fallen Harvester behind her. She casts Ty a grateful look, some other emotion flickering in her emerald eyes, before turning her focus back to Philippe. Without a word, Ty leaps to retrieve his battle-ax and launches at the remaining Harvester, assisting Emeraude in her fight.

As if luck is on their side for once, half a dozen Royal Regiment guards appear. Seeing that the situation isn't in his favor, Philippe briskly slips into a narrow shaft. The guards immediately give chase.

Ty is about to follow when Emeraude grabs his elbow, stopping him. "Once you go in there with Philippe, you'll end up dead," she warns. "We need to get back to Yong and Princess Akari."

He nods, wiping his sweating forehead with his arm.

With her impossibly acute senses, Emeraude leads them back to the center pit of the Hollow, where Zatori is still harvesting Akari's gift.

Not far away, Yong tracks her as he fights with desperate fury, but there are still hordes of Harvesters between them.

"Akari!" he yells. "Hang in there, please!"

♦

This time, Yong's cries—now louder, clearer, closer—stir Akari in her trance. At first, she wonders if his voice is a figment of her imagination, like her visions were. But from the raw mix of worry and fear in his words, she has no doubt he's come for her.

A single tear escapes her tightly shut eyes. Barely seconds before, she was on the verge of accepting her end. But now, Yong's presence rekindles a burning desire and compelling reason to continue living. Yet, with every passing moment of harvesting, Akari's life bleeds out of her, leaving her precariously close to death.

"Akari!" She makes out Ty calling her name as well, amidst the deafening clashes of weapons. "Is she still alive?" he asks anxiously.

"Barely," Yong breathes, his tone steeped in fear. "And she won't last much longer..."

"We have to stop Zatori!" Ty cries.

"You know we can't stop him—none of us can." Yong's answer is also laced with desperation. "I'd have done something already if I could!"

"If we interrupt Zatori's harvesting, Princess Akari will lose her sanity and forever be stuck in limbo..." Emeraude explains, but Ty already knows this.

A moment of silence follows. Even in her semi-conscious state, Akari knows he's thinking about his mother.

"What can we do?" Ty asks helplessly.

"Nothing," Emeraude says as a matter of fact, her voice exuding its usual coldness.

"This is a battle Akari has to fight alone," Yong concludes tightly.

Can I really reverse my fate by myself? Despite her doubts, Akari tries to summon her energy, attempting even the smallest movement. But she remains completely immobile, unable to assert any control over her body.

Akari struggles to rouse herself, again and again. But the harder she tries, the more exhausted she becomes, until every last ounce of energy is depleted. A wave of frustration, apprehension, and hopelessness washes over her. Finally, fear takes hold—the fear of never waking up, or worse, never seeing Yong again.

Still engulfed in a realm of darkness, Akari's senses fade as she drifts through the void. It's as though death itself has finally descended upon her. *So, this is the end... my end...*

"Akari!" Yong's voice wrenches her back from the brink of unconsciousness once more. But it's the Yong from her vision calling out to her. This time, his lips are moving.

"Yong?" She looks at him, perplexed. "Is it really you?"

"Yes, it's me." He smiles, uncrosses his arms, and walks toward her.

"Are you really here? Or do I have to do this alone?" Akari asks nervously.

"Although this is a battle you have to fight yourself, I have been, and will always be, by your side—from the very beginning till the very end. With me, you'll never truly be alone," Yong assures her as he reaches out. "Here, take my hand."

With monumental effort, Akari wrestles for any semblance of movement, eventually managing to grasp it. His touch sends a warm, tingling sensation through her entire being. Yet, she can't seem to escape the realm.

"I still only see darkness..." she says defeatedly.

"I've told you before, *you* are light in the darkness," Yong reminds her.

Akari gives an apprehensive smile that doesn't reach her eyes. Not only is she frightened of her own gift, but she's also terrified of failing to live up to her role as the wielder of the Jewel of Compassion.

"Are you afraid?" he asks, his tone gentle.

"Yes," Akari answers meekly.

"Close your eyes. I'll count to three with you," he offers, his soothing voice instantly calming her.

He releases Akari's hand, walks behind her, and places both his hands over her eyes, just as he did when they were on the frozen Telos Ocean.

"Are you ready?" he checks.

"Yes." She squeezes her eyes shut, feeling the comforting warmth of his hands on her eyelids.

"Here we go."

Their voices blend as they count in unison, "One..." *Forget the world*. For a moment, Akari forgets she is in a vision, that Zatori is harvesting her gift. She gives herself to the realm of darkness, ensconcing herself in complete oblivion.

"Two..." *Forget your fears*. Akari relinquishes her crippling fear of Zatori and the harvesting, of death and insanity—and most of all, of her own gift. Instead, she seeks peace within herself, letting what comes come. For the first time, she fully embraces her gift—even the parts that scare her.

"Three..." *Never forget yourself.* Akari has always questioned her legitimacy—and worthiness—to have a royal regalia as a complement. But this time, she finally accepts herself as the wielder of the Jewel of Compassion. It chose her, just as she has chosen compassion. And now, she'll have to draw upon its strength to save herself.

When Yong removes his hands from Akari's eyes, calm lingers within her. She feels light and powerful, as though liberated from the fears that have been weighing her down. No longer afraid, she feels ready to face the world—and her own destiny.

"Remember, Akari, you're infinitely more powerful than you imagine," he says from behind her.

She wheels around expectantly to face him. But no one is there. Yong has vanished into thin air. Yet, although she's all by herself in the realm of darkness, Akari now knows she isn't truly alone.

Drawing comfort from the thought to fuel her, Akari summons the energy from the Jewel of Compassion to complement her gift. It emanates a soft red glow that rapidly intensifies until it seems to burn red-hot. The jewel teems with so much energy that it quivers violently, jolting Akari to a start.

"Stop! Stop the deflector! She's creating an intervention!" Philippe's warning reverberates through the Hollow. But it's too late.

When her eyes fly open, the deep glow of the Jewel of Compassion erupts into a blinding Red Blaze, with Akari at its center. *I am light in the darkness*. Reminiscent of the White Blaze ten years before, the dilating Red Blaze douses the entire Hollow with a red sheen, accentuating the bloodbath that's already unfolded.

For a moment, there's an unexpected reversal. As a surge of energy flows from Zatori back to her, not only does Akari break out of his harvesting, but she also intervenes with his gift, thereby regaining possession of her own.

Nothing like this has happened to Zatori before. No one has ever upended the most powerful and dangerous gifted in all of Xylon. Horror and panic flashes across his face—the first display of fear Akari has seen from him—before the Red Blaze hurls him backward, slamming him against the icy walls.

Tremors ripple through the Hollow, throwing the Harvesters and Royal Regiment guards off their feet. Icicles crash down, impaling those too slow to flee. Water floods in, steadily rising and threatening to drown anyone in its course. Pandemonium erupts as they scramble frantically for refuge.

Ty, utterly dumbstruck, finds himself fumbling for words. "Holy... Akari!" He turns to Yong for an explanation. "How did she do this? How's this even possible?"

But Yong is thoroughly occupied with his own thoughts. "Akari... Light in the darkness..." he mutters under his breath. He's always been aware of her incredible power—far beyond what she herself realizes—but witnessing Akari unleash the boundless potential of her gift still feels surreal.

Behind them, Emeraude gazes at the Red Blaze, seemingly devoid of emotion. She observes the chaos with a distinct detachment, recognizing that regardless of their allegiances, both the Harvesters and Royal Regiment guards share the same fear of death. With her customary aloofness, she calmly sidesteps a plummeting icicle that nearly pierces her skull.

When the deep red glow of the Jewel of Compassion fades, Akari's body drops from its hover. With lightning speed, Yong catches her before she hits the ground. As though sensing she's safe in his arms, her eyes close once more. Akari lies completely still, showing no signs of life. Water pelts her body relentlessly and a few icicles crash mere inches away.

Ty scurries to her side, and Emeraude watches over them, alert. Yong wraps his trembling arms around Akari's shoulders as Ty clasps her hand. Both of them study her for signs of life. Although Akari burns with feverish heat, her breathing is faint and her face is drained of color. None of them have ever seen her so dangerously close to death.

"I can't lose you again, Akari... I barely just got you back..." Yong speaks shakily, stricken with fear that she may not pull through. He rocks her gently, begging her to wake.

After what seems like an eternity, Akari gasps for breath, her eyes fluttering open. The first thing she sees is the familiar slate gray uniform of the Royal Regiment.

"Yong?" Akari calls out instinctively. As she blinks, his hazy face gradually comes into focus.

"Akari!" Both Yong and Ty simultaneously heave a sigh of relief, flashing a quick smile at each other before turning back to her. Beside them, a rare smile also creeps onto Emeraude's face.

"You made it!" Ty cheers, although his heart twinges that it wasn't his name Akari called first.

"You did it!" Yong exclaims, locking her in a protective embrace. "You fought this battle yourself and broke out of Zatori's harvesting!"

Still in a daze, Akari shakes her head feebly. "No, I was never truly alone... You were there with me the whole time..."

Ty stares at her, concern whorling in his eyes. "Has she... has she gone..."

"Akari, what are you talking about?" Yong furrows his brow in confusion, releasing her. The boys anxiously assess her sanity, fearing it may have been lost during the harvesting.

"You came for me, just like you promised..." Akari continues, her grateful eyes still fixed on Yong.

"And you came for me too, just like *you* promised..." Ty interjects in a small voice, wondering if their promises still matter to her. "I could never live if you gave your life to save mine..."

"It's the same for me too..." Akari says, finally turning to her best friend.

Ty shakes his head wordlessly, simply taking comfort that she hasn't been driven to madness.

Yong, having arrived at the same conclusion, doesn't fail to inform her, "I'm going to add this to the count."

Akari breaks into a tired smile.

As he takes a long hard look at her, a single tear rolls down his cheek. Akari is at a loss, never having seen Yong so emotional. Noting the crease in his brow, she's uncertain if he's more overwhelmed with worry or anger.

He hastily wipes the tear from his face, chiding her, "Are you out of your mind? How could you come here alone? You just never stop putting yourself in peril!"

Akari hangs her head guiltily. "I knew you wouldn't let me come if I told you..."

"And with good reason!" Yong's voice is raised despite his attempt to contain his anger. "You shouldn't have come at all!"

"Are you mad at me?" she asks meekly.

"No!"

"But you seem to be..."

"I'll get mad later, after we make it out safely," he breathes, lifting Akari back up on her feet before whipping around to survey their surroundings.

Akari's eyes flicker in shock as they trace Yong's around the Hollow, finally taking in the devastating aftermath of the Red Blaze.

"What have I done?" she gasps, horrified.

"Something much like the White Blaze your mother conjured," he replies. "I told you, Akari, you're infinitely more powerful than you imagine. This merely scratches the surface of your full potential—"

"An intervention by the little deflector!" Zatori, assisted by Celestine and Philippe on either side, croaks. He appears pathetically battered as he crawls back to his feet—a sight unbefitting of his usual untouchable self. But Zatori quickly regains his composure, offering a half-smirk and a patronizing round of applause. "Princess Akari, you're truly the wielder of a royal regalia. You have no idea how useful you are. Your gift of deflection has made you a perfect shield... and a perfect weapon!"

Akari's past disagreement with her mother about being useful resurfaces in her mind. Back then, Mari had feared others would try to use her, in one way or another. Although her mother had always sought to protect her, Akari now knows she has to protect herself—and that she's strong enough to. She stares into Zatori's eyes, no longer terrified.

"From now on, my usefulness will only be determined by myself!" Akari declares with unprecedented resolve. "And I'll do everything within my power to stop you from harvesting gifts and taking lives!"

Crackles tear through the air as several icicles overhead dislodge, hurtling toward them. Yong swiftly yanks Akari out of harm's way, mere moments before Celestine unleashes bolts of violet lightning, shattering the icicles into a thousand fragments. The pieces drift atop the rising water, now reaching their waists, creating a stark divide—Akari, Yong, Ty, and Emeraude on one side, while Zatori, Celestine, and Philippe stand on the other.

As they eye each other warily, Yong notices cracks beginning to form in the ice at the Hollow's mouth. "We have to get out of here before it's too late!" he yells, commanding the Royal Regiment with a wave of his sword. "Retreat! The Hollow is doomed!"

Yong dives into the water to retrieve Akari's kris, before ordering, "Emeraude, take Ty. I'll take Akari." With a firm grip around the princess, he wades toward Zephy.

"Yes, sir." Emeraude nods, jumping into action.

"*I'll* take Akari. I don't need anyone to take me—" Ty tries to protest. But with an immense strength disproportionate to her dainty body, Emeraude has already begun dragging him through the choppy waters, toward her nequilous.

"Why am I always stuck with you?" he complains but doesn't resist.

"Don't you see? It's because the two of us are the unwanted ones," she spells out with mock nonchalance. As Emeraude glances at Yong, Ty finds his gaze landing on Akari.

Yong lifts Akari onto Zephy before climbing on behind. His arms flank her as he seizes the reins and kicks his legs, steering them to an ascent.

Watching them, Ty feels his gut wrench but struggles to hide it. Emeraude's face betrays nothing of her emotions. They mount her nequilous and take off in silence, trailing behind Zephy. The surviving Royal Regiment guards swiftly follow, leaving Zatori and the Harvesters behind.

As soon as they emerge from the Hollow, the cracks at its mouth splinter deeper. Chunks of ice cave inward, swallowed by the rushing waters that gush in. It won't be long before the Hollow is completely filled, entombing everything—and everyone—left inside.

"Is this it? Is this the end? Do you think Zatori's really gone forever this time?" Akari asks, daring to be hopeful. She can't imagine how else Zatori and the Harvesters can possibly survive the Red Blaze and the destruction it wreaked.

But her voice is drowned out by Zephy's caws of distress as he begins circling the Hollow. Yong tugs repeatedly at the reins, but the zephanerix doesn't obey his cues, refusing to head back toward the mainland of Xylon.

"Come on, Zephy! Let's go!" Yong coaxes urgently.

Never having seen him behave this way, Akari asks, worried, "What's wrong—"

She is cut off by a barrage of chilling roars. A pack of dragons shoots out from the Hollow, spiraling through the late afternoon sky before hovering in front of the Royal Regiment.

The terrifyingly magnificent beasts, some flying unsteadily because of their injuries, are plated with tough scales of varying sheens. Despite their massive size, their wingspans vary dramatically, ranging from twenty to seventy feet. Jagged spikes frame their faces, crown the tips of their wings, and run in ridged lines along their spines, tapering down to the ends of their whipping tails. Their fangs resemble curved scimitars, lethally sharp and unnervingly adapted to perforate armor with ease. Then, as they unleash a rumble of blood-curdling roars, they begin breathing... frost.

Akari's nose wrinkles. "Archivians?" she gasps, turning to Yong in disbelief.

"Archivians..." he confirms with a mix of shock and awe, unable to tear his eyes from them.

Ty, Emeraude, and the rest of the Royal Regiment guards seem just as horrified by their appearance.

"But they're meant to be extinct!" Akari cries.

Yong shakes his head, still transfixed. "It seems they've been hiding themselves instead..."

"I didn't see them when we were in the Hollow. Were they hiding in the caves?"

"No. They were right there with us," he explains tightly. "In their human forms..."

A chill runs down Akari's spine. At second glance, she realizes the three archivians in the center are frighteningly familiar.

The rust-colored one on the left resembles the runt of the pack, the lack of spikes on his face and head lending him a bare, awkward appearance. *Philippe Sulech!*

Although the mousy brown one on the right stands out from most of the brawny, masculine archivians with her lean, feminine lines, it's the lethal talons shooting bolts of violet lightning that are most telling of her identity. *Celestine Lithezyne!*

In the very middle, the ivory archivian, the palest of the pack, has gigantic white spikes covering his entire body, peppered sparsely with tiny black ones. But the most perturbing of all are his black left eye and white right eye. *Zatori Valakhan!*

The hairs on the back of Akari's neck stand on end as she gazes at these creatures from myth. She realizes the iron archivian masks worn by the Harvesters are an exact replica of their faces in dragon form. Except now, they show their true faces.

Zatori's survival during the White Blaze is suddenly obvious. He and the surviving Harvesters forged into their dragon forms and escaped by flight, the dark night sky serving as perfect camouflage. However, the bright daylight provides no such cover this time as they escape the Red Blaze.

"Princess Akari!" Zatori's voice booms all around them, his dragon form deepening the drawl. "Your ancestors seized the White Palace, your mother obliterated Moira Island, and you annihilated the Hollow! You and your family have destroyed all our homes. Now we've been forced to show our true selves, war is upon us!

"How naive of your ancestors to think they could exterminate us. Instead, we've hidden from the world, waiting patiently to reunite the three royal regalia and their wielders. Now, the time has finally come for us to reclaim our rightful place. We will return for you, Princess Akari. And when we do, you won't remain princess for much longer—and neither your father king. The end of the Ashgenov Empire is near!"

With that, the archivians make a sharp turn, flying northward into the horizon and the nothingness beyond, leaving only a trail of frost in their wake.

Akari watches them recede into the distance. She is utterly paralyzed by the declaration, as though frozen by the lingering frost.

"Let's chase the archivians down!" Ty cries fervidly.

"No!" Yong and Emeraude exclaim in unison. They turn to each other, their eyes meeting briefly, flickering, before he concludes, "We've accomplished our mission today. We'll save the fight with the archivians for another day, after we have rested and regrouped."

When the archivians disappear, Akari casts the Hollow one last glance. The Red Blaze erupts in an astronomical explosion, obliterating everything in its path. Monstrous slabs of ice from the perpetually frozen Hollow Falls— once sustained by the archivians' frost—crash down in a cataclysmic collapse. Torrents of water from the surrounding Telos Ocean surge in, drowning the last vestiges of the White Blaze Mari conjured a decade ago.

The Hollow is no more.

31. Home

Akari wakes to the familiar aged wooden beams of her home in Cheyvelenia. Under the quilt, her fatigued body has been recharged somewhat by a long, dreamless sleep.

For the past three nights, she has been resting in Mari's bed, where she'd fallen soundly asleep on her mother's shoulder countless times, their hands in each other's. Now, even in Mari's absence, this stiff mattress with coarse sheets, faintly scented with a unique blend of fresh flowers and herbs from her mother, still offers Akari a measure of comfort. It reminds her of home—at least of what it used to be. She closes her eyes and takes a deep breath, letting Mari's fragrance envelop her. Tears begin to well up.

Akari insisted on stopping in Cheyvelenia before returning to the capital. Although Yong and Emeraude were given strict instructions by King Alvaro to rescue and escort her back to Andelovia, they have little reason to deny her this brief respite. After all, Cheyvelenia, the town closest to the Hollow, offers them a much-needed rest before their week-long journey. More importantly, they understand the significance of this last visit as Akari bids farewell to her home, her mother, and her childhood.

Since arriving, Yong and Emeraude have been tirelessly trailing Akari to ensure her utmost safety, especially since

Zatori and the Harvesters—the archivians—have declared war on the Ashgenov Empire.

Emeraude has been occupying Akari's bedroom to keep a close watch on the princess, knowing better than to let Akari out of her sight this time—or help her disappear.

Before the rescue mission, King Alvaro made it clear that she couldn't afford to lose Akari again. As punishment for her "negligence of duty," Emeraude's head will roll if she doesn't redeem herself by returning the princess to the White Palace unscathed.

Yong has stationed himself in the consultation room downstairs—still near enough to protect Akari while giving her the space she needs. But whenever she's cried in her mother's bed, he's been with her within seconds, holding her until she's finally fallen asleep.

The two of them have had many long conversations about her future. Although he's been tasked with returning her to the White Palace, Yong knows better than anyone else that she won't comply unless her heart is truly convinced as well.

Just days ago, Akari had been so sure she wouldn't stay in Andelovia any longer than she had to, wanting more than anything to return to Cheyvelenia as soon as possible. But now, she realizes there are too many reasons to go and too few reasons to stay. The re-emergence of the archivians and the impending war, the responsibility of reuniting the three royal regalia and their wielders, and the urge to rebuild ties with her father and grandmother all draw her back to the capital.

On the contrary, her being here—where every nook and cranny, every turn and corner, constantly remind her of her late mother—hurts even more than not being here at all. It doesn't take Akari long to realize that while lingering in Mari's shadows might offer her some solace, it also leaves her trapped in grief. She decides, after grave and careful consideration, that she will head back to Andelovia.

For the first time in three days, the house is completely quiet. Yong and Emeraude have already left for Havenswill, where they'd be waiting for her. Akari has specifically asked to be left alone on her last day in Cheyvelenia. She wants to relive her time at home as she once knew it—as much as circumstances permit.

Without any urge to sleep in, she gets up and makes the bed as her mother would have liked it. Then, she prepares some powder-pink telmezia tea and sips on it, relishing its mild sweetness before the bitter aftertaste sets in.

Just as Akari thinks it isn't so bad this time, Mari's voice resounds in her mind. *Are you really tasting if you only taste sweetness? Are you really living if you only feel happiness?* She finally understands what her mother meant. *There's been no lack of bitterness and sadness lately...*

Akari's eyes drift toward the very spot her mother's body last lay. *Mama only died because she'd given her life to me...* An unbearable pain wrenches her heart. She had always believed that Mari, with her gift for healing—or wielding the energy of life—was invincible, not once realizing she was her mother's greatest weakness.

Although Akari thought she'd appreciate a moment alone to remember Mari in private, she quickly realizes the loneliness is too overwhelming to bear. She pours the remaining telmezia tea into a flask, gathers a few of their remaining belongings, and takes a final glance at the two empty bedrooms before heading downstairs.

She is greeted by a musty smell that Moonstone Apothecary never used to have. Perhaps some of the herbs have gone bad, or the air hasn't been circulating for a while, or both. Akari heads over to the counter, randomly opening and closing a few drawers on the way. Sure enough, some of the herbs inside have gone limp, and others give off an odd smell. The ones hanging from the twines have long since dried but have yet to be taken down. None of this would have been allowed to happen under Mari's meticulous care.

A thin layer of dust coats every surface of the shop. With her bare hand, Akari sweeps one of the stools clean and sits down, the empty seat beside her a poignant reminder of her mother's passing. She hesitates before dusting the vacant stool as well, fully aware that her action serves no real purpose. In contrast to Mari's bedchamber in the White Palace, which has shown no signs of being unoccupied for the past decade, Moonstone Apothecary has been quick to show signs of neglect.

But Akari knows it isn't the dusty surfaces or the rotting herbs that really bother her. It's the revelation that her home doesn't feel quite like it now her mother's gone. The truth hits Akari hard—she no longer *has* a home.

A dull ache eats away at her chest and her nose tingles. Determined not to shed tears on her last day in Cheyvelenia, Akari shoots up from the stool, jaw tensed and fists clenched, and heads outside, closing the front door gently behind her.

It's a glorious day, a reminder that life goes on regardless, rhythmically undeterred. Under the brilliant morning sun, spring brings warmth to even the coldest, northernmost town of the outskirts. Ty, entrusted by Yong with the task of escorting Akari to Havenswill, waits outside the apothecary, a bunch of white flowers clutched in his hands.

He has struggled to keep up with the whirlwind of changes, from the *Prophecy of a New Realm* to the New People's Protector. The sheer volume to take in has Ty wondering how Akari has managed to cope. The hardest part has been accepting that his best friend is King Alvaro's daughter and Princess of Xylon. Torn painfully between kinship and friendship, Ty finds it nearly unbearable to meet her gaze.

All his life, he hasn't been shy about his hatred for King Alvaro, blaming him for his family's predicament and his arduous childhood. Yet, in a cruel twist of fate, his best friend turned out to be the daughter of his enemy. Things had already taken a painful turn when she didn't reciprocate his deepening feelings. The most heart-rending blow, however, has been Yong's reappearance in Akari's life as her childhood playmate turned lover. All of these have created an insurmountable distance between the best friends.

Yet, Ty clings to the hope of forgetting it all. Deep down, he still wishes that Akari will stay in Cheyvelenia, that they can revert to their former selves—innocent, carefree, and happy.

Seeing her fight back tears as she emerges, Ty knows she's resolutely determined to leave. For some time now, as much as he hates to admit it, Akari has been gradually slipping away from him. There's a tightness in his chest as hope flickers and dwindles. He feels broken, crushed.

But as they make their way through the town, Ty still tries to hold on to her. "Akari, you don't have to go... You don't have to leave..."

When she turns toward him, she notices his eyes are dull and somber. Her heart sinks, but she maintains, albeit wearily, "You know I have to, Ty... My father's in the capital and he's dying. I have to be with him."

"King Alvaro isn't fit to be your father!" Ty states disgruntledly. "He was never family to you!"

"I know what he is," she says. "And what he's done... But despite everything, he's still family. I can't give up on him."

"He was the one who first gave up on you and your mother!" Ty points out, exasperated. "That's why you ended up in Cheyvelenia!"

Akari shakes her head adamantly, a mix of anger and sadness searing her eyes. "My father never wanted to! And he never truly did! Even after a decade, he was still looking for us!" She finds herself jumping to King Alvaro's defense. Even though she can't excuse all his mistakes, she understands them more now. *I offered Zatori the Jewel of Compassion to save someone I love. I made the same choice my father did.*

Although Akari has yet to accept the king, it hurts her to hear anyone else speak ill of him. "King Alvaro was misled into giving up the *Register of the Gifteds*!" she continues. "He was tricked into it! He's suffered losses too, just as we all have..."

"And the *Register of the Gifteds* contained both my parents' names!" Ty fires back heatedly. "Haven't you seen what happened to them? And the rest of my family?"

"I'm sorry, Ty. My father regretted it too," Akari admits. "But that aside, the *Prophecy of a New Realm* calls for me. It's a responsibility that's fallen on my shoulders... something I have to do... something only I can do... It's a destiny I have to fulfill."

"You don't have to do anything!" Ty cries, his voice cracking. "You don't have to fulfill any destiny or realize any prophecy just because you're King Alvaro's daughter! You don't have any obligation to save the Ashgenov Empire!"

"I'm not trying to save any empire," Akari clarifies. "I know you've always joked that you joined the People's Protector for the food and money but, deep down, we both know our real reason was to protect the people— the people we love and the people who couldn't protect themselves."

Akari tries to touch his arm, but he pulls away. After a moment, she drops her hand sadly and continues, "This is one thing that hasn't changed for me. And this is precisely why I have to find the other missing royal regalia and their wielders before they fall into the hands of Zatori Valakhan and the Harvesters, or Maximus Fontan and the New People's Protector. If that happens, many more people will end up losing their lives. And I can't afford to lose anyone else."

Ty quietly mulls over Akari's words, and she's fully aware he shares the same deep-seated desire to protect those he cares about.

"Will you come with me to search for the rest of the royal regalia and their wielders?" Akari asks, knowing it's a long shot—her last shot. But the words are out of her mouth before she can stop herself. "I know you hate the capital, but will you consider coming with me? I can settle your parents in—your sisters, even—just as we promised to look out for each other's families. Being in Andelovia will be much safer, especially since Celestine knows you. Besides, the New People's Protector is no longer as it once was, and you have no reason to stay."

"I'll never leave the outskirts and move to the capital!" Ty declares stubbornly, too proud to accept her offer. "And no matter how dire my circumstances are, I'll feed and protect my family with my own hands. Receiving charity from King Alvaro is the last thing I want!"

His reaction isn't beyond Akari's expectations. Even so, watching him harden his heart still leaves an aching pain inside her.

"I'd help you if it didn't mean helping King Alvaro," he says through gritted teeth. "But what happens when we find the rest of the royal regalia and their wielders? What then? Do I have to help King Alvaro strengthen his rule, defend the Ashgenov Empire from the archivians and the New People's Protector, or watch you ascend the throne? I'm sorry, Akari, but I refuse to be part of this. You know I hate the Ashgenov Empire and I can't pretend not to."

Defeated but unsurprised, Akari stays silent. She knows that, not long ago, she'd have felt the same.

"Besides... you won't need me by your side now you have Yong," Ty adds bitterly.

"Is this it? Is this because of Yong?" she asks tightly.

"I'm sure you already know by now how I've always felt about you... I like you, Akari... more than just a friend. I know you don't feel the same way, but I still wanted to tell you, so I won't live with regrets," he confesses. He looks relieved to have finally said it out loud, even though it's too late. "I've been such an idiot, taking this long to realize how I feel, only after you've already fallen for someone else."

Her heart grows heavy. But Akari doesn't show it, fearing—and knowing—that Ty would read it as pity and only feel worse. "I like you too, Ty... as friends... as the very best of friends..." She struggles to find the right words to soften the blow.

He waves away the hurt as nonchalantly as he can—a skill he must have picked up from Emeraude—but Akari can see her words have shattered him. "You've always been so much more than a best friend to me. You're a gifted, you're my savior, and you're family... You're everything to me—everything I've never had and everything I've ever wanted. So, will you please stay in Cheyvelenia for me... even if you have every reason to go to Andelovia... and even if I can't compare with any riches of the capital..."

A long sigh escapes Akari. "Even if I do stay for you, I won't make you happy..." she says, her tone strained. "You deserve someone who can give you that..."

Ty shakes his head obstinately. "I'd rather be with you than be happy! I don't want anyone else to make me happy!"

"You will, Ty, as soon as you open your heart," she maintains.

"You know, I've always wished that you'd take the leap of faith with me..." he says wistfully. "We'd been doing everything together for such a long time that I'd foolishly thought we would always stay that way. I never imagined that things between us would change."

"Our friendship is never going to change, Ty," Akari reassures him. "Not for me at least."

"Don't you see? It's already changing. Everything's already changing," Ty claims, his voice tight. "You're leaving Cheyvelenia for the capital. You've found your father—King Alvaro, of all people. You're a princess and the wielder of the Jewel of Compassion. You have Yong by your side now. Nothing's ever going to be the same again."

Akari looks into Ty's ocean blue eyes and finds herself lost in the depths of their melancholy, before she eventually drops her gaze to her capital-made boots.

He notices them and eyes her simple crimson robe. Even though she wears the most understated of pieces, there's something about their sheen and drape that echoes the refinement of Andelovia—and starkly dissonant to his raggedy garb from the outskirts.

Ty sighs in resignation. "You've changed too, Akari..."

She shrugs, perhaps accepting there's some truth in his statement. After all, so much has changed for Akari that it would be surprising if she hasn't as well. "I may have..." she concedes. "But perhaps what's changed more drastically is your perception of me..."

"Perhaps... But what I'm sure of, is that I miss the old times..." Ty remarks poignantly. *And the old you...*

She returns a sad smile before they continue through the town, an unspoken tension lingering between them. In the nine long years that Akari and Ty have been friends, they've never felt more distant. The chasm between them has run so deep that she doesn't know how—or if—it can ever be bridged.

But perhaps time can heal all wounds—even those that can't be deflected. After all, time spares none. It stops for nothing, and nothing can stop it. While Akari's life has changed since she left the outskirts, so has what she knows of Cheyvelenia. After some time away, she finds these changes even more conspicuous.

As Akari walks down the streets, she notices that a neighbor's boy has grown at least two inches taller, almost reaching her nose. A little girl playing in the streets has cut her right elbow, a wound Mari would undoubtedly have been able to heal, but Akari finds herself playing the passive observer instead, with no desire to deflect it onto anyone else. One of the homeless boys has had the first-sighting of his gift—the ability to control wind—and has since spared no efforts in using it to prank the other boys, blowing flower petals in their ears and closing doors in their faces.

And, most glaringly, the fallen sign and broken windows of Heavenly Bakery suggest that the store has been abandoned since Madam Celine—Celestine—emerged from hiding and rejoined Zatori. To Akari, each sliver of unfamiliarity further reinforces the thought that Cheyvelenia and the outskirts no longer feel like home.

As Akari and Ty start to walk out of town, he asks, "Won't you miss home when you move to the capital?"

"The home I miss so desperately... the home as I know it... it doesn't exist anymore..." She struggles to fully articulate her feelings, wondering if he'll ever come to understand her. "Home isn't home anymore. Not without my mother around. And being back here, surrounded by constant reminders of her, is too painful."

"We've spent our last nine years running through every alley in Cheyvelenia together. Don't you realize that when you leave, I'll be surrounded by constant reminders of you too? It'll be just as painful for me!" Ty yells.

Akari casts him a sad look, realizing how she's never truly considered things from his perspective. But she can't change her plans. There's too much at stake.

"And now, you're leaving me and escaping to the capital—for your new family, and for money, power, love..." Ty continues scathingly. "Doesn't our friendship mean anything to you?"

Hurt shadows Akari's eyes. "You know it does..." she starts, looking for any words that can explain how hard everything is. "It's not that I want to leave you. I just can't stay in a home where I saw my mother... lying there..."

Realizing he might have been too harsh, Ty quickly softens his tone. "I'm sorry, Akari. I'm so sorry about Madam Mari too. It must be terribly hard for you, but I know you're strong."

"Sometimes, not as strong as you think..." she says resignedly.

Just as they've done countless times together, Akari and Ty head toward the forested foothills. However, they walk in silence this time as they disappear into the forest, embarking on a windy, overgrown dirt path with jutting branches, which he quietly holds to allow her to pass. Soon, the boughs thin out and Havenswill comes into sight.

The lush meadow teems with life. In the comforting breeze, birds and crickets alike chirp in harmony, while flowers of every hue blossom in celebration of spring. At the far end, Yong, Emeraude, and the rest of the Royal Regiment guards wait, showing no haste to greet the princess. Behind them, the snow-capped mountains rise majestically, composing a breathtaking backdrop. From high above, the splendid sun breathes life into all below it—except for a solitary tombstone erected at the very center of Havenswill.

With a heavy heart, Akari walks toward her mother's grave, Ty following close behind. They stop before the fresh patch of dirt where Mari has been laid to rest.

Akari takes a long, hard look at the tombstone—a tall slab of raw white quartz with its jagged surfaces catching and reflecting the scintillating sunlight. Engraved by Salam's bear claws, the words on the tombstone are rounded and uneven, yet unmistakably clear—*In loving memory of Mari Miyahara, mother of Akari Miyahara Ashgenov.*

Akari's chest tightens, a hollow ache winding through her. *Mari Miyahara...* Each letter stands as a testament to a life lived, lost... and transferred... *Mama, if only I'd known our time together was so ephemeral, slipping by before I even realized...*

Her eyes drift down to her own name, and an unexpected numbness washes over her. *Akari Miyahara Ashgenov... Akari Ashgenov... Is this who I am now? Is this who I've always been? Is this who I'm supposed to be?*

Ty tracks this but chooses not to comment. He knows that, apart from Zatori, King Alvaro is possibly the last person Akari would have wanted as a father. Life has played a mean, cruel joke on her. Even so, he can't forgive her for leaving—for *accepting* it.

The duo stands in somber stillness before Mari's grave, observing a moment of silence in honor of her. In stark contrast, the slender blades of grass around them sway gracefully in the whispering wind.

After a while, Akari pulls out her flask and pours the telmezia tea onto the earth where Mari rests, certain her mother will be missing its bittersweet taste. As the liquid seeps into the soil, she scatters the remaining telmezias over the grave. Their petals are swept up by the wind before gently drifting to the ground, creating an achingly beautiful pink floral flurry.

When it settles, Ty steps forward, bowing slightly as he offers the white flowers he has brought. "Madam Mari, I can never thank you enough for all the kindness you've shown me. I only wish I had expressed my gratitude and repaid your generosity sooner. May you rest in peace."

He pauses, staring at the tombstone for a moment longer as the weight of his words lingers in the air.

Eventually, he turns to face Akari, any remaining light in his eyes dimming. "Akari, I've always been indebted to you and your mother. You saved me from Hanwell's bullying and from Zatori's capture. Through it all, your mother helped feed me and my family. If it weren't for both of you, I wouldn't be alive today. You and Madam Mari were family to me."

Were. Is Ty beginning to draw the line between us? Akari wonders, yet unable to blame him for it. After bidding farewell to Mari, perhaps he's also bidding farewell to her... and his unrequited feelings...

After a brief hesitation, Ty pulls Akari into a long embrace. Knowing that it may be their last for a while, his eyes start to prickle. He brushes the tears away, embarrassed, not wanting her to remember him this way. "I know the path you've chosen will be fraught with difficulties, and you'll have to face yourself—your past, present, and future. Although I won't be there with you, I wish you luck, Akari. I mean it, from the bottom of my heart."

"I wish you luck too," she breathes from between his arms.

His gaze sweeps over her as they break apart. "If you ever need anything..." His glance cuts to Yong before he concludes, "Actually, I don't think you will... Well, thank you for saving me. Time and again."

Ty repeats the words he'd said to Akari when they first met, as if to close the chapter.

Things have come full circle. But for better or for worse? she ponders. There's no easy answer.

"Only because you first gave yourself up this time... Thank you for saving me too, and for everything else..." Akari says softly. "Even if I'm not with you in the outskirts, you'll always be my best friend."

Ty smiles wistfully, wishing things could be different between them. But he knows they aren't. "I have to go now. Goodbye, my best friend."

"Goodbye, my only friend," Akari murmurs, her voice tinged with reluctance.

With that, he turns and retraces his steps without once looking back. Her tear-filled eyes remain fixed on him until he disappears into the forest. Perhaps the duo isn't as inseparable as they'd thought...

In this moment, Akari feels profoundly alone. Although there's so much she's longed to say to Mari, her mind becomes a massive void when she turns back toward the grave. Eventually, the emptiness gives way to grief.

Memories swirl through Akari's mind—her mother searching for her after games of hide-and-seek, embracing her and her father when they were a whole, happy family, shielding her from Zatori and the Harvesters by creating the White Blaze, kulning with her in this very meadow, picking herbs together in the glade, laughing as she spat out the bitter telmezia tea, gifting her Kami after her incessant pestering for a dog, fuming when she discovered Akari had joined the People's Protector... Now, these fleeting moments feel all the more precious, crystallized by the weight of her mother's passing.

Akari melts to her knees, her trembling fingers tracing the letters of her mother's name on the tombstone in a futile attempt to steady herself. Yet, the tears she's been holding back begin streaming down, unstoppable.

"Mama, I'm so sorry..." she whispers, her face moist and her shoulders shaking. "I'm sorry you gave up your life for me... I'm sorry for joining the People's Protector behind your back... I'm sorry for choosing to go to the capital to be with Papa... Please don't hold it against me. Will you forgive me? Understand me? Support me?" But her woeful pleas echo into silence, destined to receive no answer.

"I know you've always wanted me to stay safe, lie low, and keep out of trouble. I promise that I'll try my best," Akari vows earnestly. Even when they disagreed, she always understood her mother's intentions, knowing they stemmed from a place of love. Until her last breath, Mari remained true to her convictions, ultimately giving up her life for her daughter—a burden Akari will forever carry. More than ever, she resolves to make her mother's sacrifice meaningful.

"But Mama," Akari continues, dwelling on the gravity of her words. "I'm going to look for the rest of the royal regalia and their wielders. It'll be a long, tough journey. I know you'd rather I didn't embark on this mission, but people's lives will be saved, and Xylon will be a better place for it. Now I've learned to control my gift, it can help me be safe. You'll be watching over me too, won't you, Mama? This time, I want to do it with your blessing." When she closes her eyes, Akari sees her mother smiling empathetically and wonders if this is a sign that she's finally at peace.

"Mama, I heart you with all my love—now and forever," Akari professes between sobs as she pays her final respects. When her cries eventually subside, she rises to her feet.

After wiping away her tears and dusting off her robe, Akari cups her hands around her mouth, letting the 'Summoning Song' escape her lips. As the lyrical melody of her kulning wafts skyward, she's both surprised and consoled to hear a subtle yet unmistakable hint of maturity in her voice that echoes Mari's. For the first time in a long while, a slight smile graces Akari's face as she seeks solace in the realization that her mother will always be with her—in some form or other. After all, Mari's life now flows within her.

In the distance, Zephy caws in response and glides toward Akari. He quickly descends through the clouds, making a smooth landing in front of her. She presses her forehead against his beak, drawing comfort from the gesture, knowing her mother had done the same before.

As Zephy turns toward Mari's tombstone, he releases a mournful coo, as if sensing she's been laid to rest here. With a solemn dip of his head, he pays his respects.

Yong eventually approaches. He places his right hand over his heart, drops his right knee onto the ground, and bows down before her grave. After a moment, he rises, taking Akari's hand firmly in his.

"Lady Mari, on my life I promise to care for Akari in your stead," he swears. "Even though I'll never come close to what you've done for your daughter, I assure you I'll give nothing less than my best. May you rest in peace."

Akari meets Yong's gaze, her honey-colored, almond eyes imbued with gratitude and admiration, her expression softening into an affectionate smile. Yong returns a warm smile, his dark, crescent-moon eyes beaming with adoration.

After a long while, he reluctantly releases her hand and waves his sword at the rest of the Royal Regiment guards. At his signal, Emeraude and the entourage of guards march toward them, coming to a stop before Mari's tombstone. They simultaneously place their right hands over their hearts, drop their right knees onto the ground, and bow down. "Rest in peace Lady Mari... Long live Princess Akari..."

Akari gives the Royal Regiment guards a nod, allowing them to rise. For the first time, she stands as princess with a natural grace, finally embracing her birthright.

"Shall we?" Yong asks.

She nods, taking one last look at her mother's grave before mounting Zephy. As soon as Yong climbs up behind her, she reaches for the reins and kicks her legs. "Come on, Zephy. Let's go!"

The zephanerix gives his majestic wings a powerful flap and takes a graceful leap into the sky. Behind them, Emeraude and the rest of the Royal Regiment guards follow on their nequilouses.

"Let's go home," Yong breathes, his arms encircling Akari's waist as he pulls her closer to his chest, tucking her head under his chin.

From the air, she glances down at Cheyvelenia. It isn't entirely unfamiliar, yet no longer the home she once knew. "Home? Cheyvelenia doesn't feel like it now, but the capital isn't either..." she whispers, her words steeped in sorrow. "Yong, I don't have a home. Not anymore..."

From behind her, he gently caresses her hair, planting a soft kiss on the back of her head. "That's not true, Akari," he murmurs, his tone disarmingly gentle.

She turns to challenge him, but before she does, Yong states the undeniable truth. "Home is wherever we both are."

A warmth sings through Akari's entire being, planting a seed of hope deep within her chest. She realizes that while darkness lurks, light shines—and while hatred condemns, love prevails.

"I have something for you," Yong says nervously, reaching into his indigo robe.

"What is it?" she asks, curious.

As soon as Yong pulls out the drawing of Akari—the very one she'd seen when she searched his room in the Colossal Inn—his voice begins to resound in her head.

I meant to give you that drawing as a token of love when I confessed my feelings for you...

"I know moving to the capital and living in the White Palace will be very difficult for us, but nothing will change my love for you," he professes, holding out the drawing to her. "I love you, Akari. I always have and I always will—from the very beginning till the very end."

She smiles and takes the drawing, studying it closely. Just as she remembers, every detail—from the depth of her eyes to the arch of her eyebrows, and from the silkiness of her hair to the glow of the Jewel of Compassion hanging from her neck—has been impeccably portrayed. As she admires Yong's work, Akari notices something she hadn't seen before. The piece of parchment is folded in half.

She unfolds it to reveal a drawing of Yong on the other side. His wavy raven hair is elegantly braided on both sides, with a few loose strands caught mid-wind, imparting a sense of life to the portrait. His delicate nose sits between gently protruding cheekbones, his full lips framed by an angular jawline, the light and shadow capturing every contour of his face. And from the way he gazes at Akari, his inexorable love for her is beautifully conveyed with every stroke.

Put together, the entire picture mirrors the chalk drawing on the wall of the stair turret Yong sketched ten years ago. However, instead of two children looking fondly at each other, it depicts two adolescents gazing at one another with profound affection. Compared to the earlier piece created by a talented eight-year-old, this drawing is a stunning work of art rendered by a brilliant artist with more than a decade of practice in his craft.

For quite a while, Akari has tried to convince herself to let Yong go. But now the image has been etched in her mind, she releases her worries instead. Summoning her courage, she finally says the words she has long felt but was too afraid to admit.

"I love you too, Yong."

His radiant laughter chimes through the sky. "I've always known that, Akari! I was just wondering how long it would take you to say it!"

She offers a shy smile, nestling deeper into Yong's chest as he envelops her within a warm embrace. *Yes, perhaps first love can actually last...* Feeling hopeful for the first time in a while, Akari tightens her grip on the reins, deftly navigating their journey back to the capital.

Somewhere out there, Zatori Valakhan and the Harvesters—the archivians—as well as Maximus Fontan and the New People's Protector, are poised to end the Ashgenov Empire and seize the throne. There are also two other royal regalia—the Mirror of Wisdom and the Sword of Courage—as well as their wielders, waiting to be reunited. Yet, as Akari and Yong cruise through the sky on Zephy's back, they are unsullied by the rest of the world.

Far into the distance—beyond the forest, the town, the cliffs, and the shore—the sun rises further above the ocean, casting a shimmering golden glow on their backs. With a touch so light it's barely perceivable, Yong's hand finds its way from Akari's waist to the back of her neck, gently turning her face toward his. This time, with all the pieces falling into place, there's nothing left holding her back.

Throwing caution to the wind, she leans in until their lips meet, the kiss setting off fireworks through every inch of her body. In this speck of time and space, as they become momentarily lost in each other, Akari has no doubt she's found home again.

- The End -

About the Author

Nicole Liang has lived in four countries across three continents. Born and bred in Singapore, she completed her BA at Cornell University in upstate New York, served a stint as a trader in Hong Kong, and earned her MBA from London Business School. Nicole's multicultural background, diverse life experience, and penchant for romantic fantasy have led to the birth of *The Deflector*, her debut novel and the first book of the *Gifted* trilogy. Besides writing, Nicole enjoys traveling, skiing, golfing, horse riding, practicing yoga, playing the piano, dabbling in fashion, and walking—or getting walked by—Tiara, her Shiba Inu.